For Richard 'Tony' Reece and Dei 'Nilig' Hughes:
together in forestry for the best part of forty years.
They taught each other.

'You are savage . . .' said Michelis, making up his mind to speak.

'I'm just,' retorted Yannakos. 'If Christ came down on earth today, on an earth like this one, what do you think he'd have on his shoulders? A cross? No, a can of petrol'

— Nikos Kazantzakis, *Christ Recrucified*

The superfluous property which you hold you have stolen

— St Ambrose

Prologue

Tŷ Gwydr, 2016

Geth feels the light through the sheet of glass before he really opens his eyes and sees it. When Tŷ Gwydr was built in '57, people in town said it was an eyesore, something between a greenhouse and a factory, squat cubes of wood and glass. When you're inside, though, you feel as if you're suspended in the trees, untethered and floating above the lake. At night, the water is the same ripe indigo as a fresh bruise – silver, if the sky is clear – until around dawn, when a sliding panel of iridescent grey shifts across the ridge of pines. He feels the light pass over his closed eyes and warm his skin, and for a moment before he wakes properly, he feels good. He feels real and substantial. The shadows of the tree branches flit as pencil etchings on the wall panels and across the old wooden floorboards. The parquet is gritted with dust.

It's around five and the dawn chorus is so loud it's deafening. His mind starts to surface against the wishes of his body, which longs for more sleep, so he keeps his eyes shut. It's futile: he can make out the light webbing in patterns through his closed eyelids. This is when he starts to feel very bad. His mouth tastes like stale fags and Stella, and his body feels as if it's rocking gently, as if he can't get a purchase on stillness. He thinks the same thought that he always thinks when he wakes up like this; he sees his science teacher in Year Nine – the one with the Nescafé breath and the short-sleeved, polyester shirts, gridded like the pages of a maths book. The smell of sulphur and Bunsen burners and the scarred lab tables, mutilated with generations of compass points and biros. He hears the precise cadences of Mr Jones's accent – Merthyr, Chapel – telling the disgusted fourteen-year-olds that when you're hungover, your brain shrinks away from your skull. The idea of it makes him recoil and, without thinking, he pushes down on his head to keep it all in. His eyes open involuntarily, and he now knows for sure that he's here, at the house. The sunrise here belongs to him.

He reaches for the bottle of water on the floor next to him, and he swallows its contents whole, deforming the old plastic in his palm as he drains it. It tastes rancid. Everything tastes rancid after however many pints and a pack of Pall Mall, but water especially – because it's so pure, especially the water around here. He's been conditioned to be proud of Welsh water. The English flood villages for it, for Christ's sake. It's like gold.

Scousers. It was for Scousers that they flooded that village: water for Liverpool or something. But Scousers are all right. They're a laugh, even though you better watch your stuff when you're with a bunch of Scousers. Geth thinks about the girl from last night. She was from Cheshire, so she thought she was posh, they're up themselves, Cheshire people. When Geth thinks about the girl he realises how hard he is. He remembers the ersatz fruit of her lip balm and his hands all over her in the pub toilet, pushing his fingers into her soft mouth, rolling up the hem of her dress with his free hand. The way the elasticated fabric stretched over the curves of her body. Back out again and another pint and a shot of tequila. She was all sparkling with mischief, the shine of it playing across her cheeks. He remembers the noises she made as he touches himself, and the way the small, soft swell of her belly felt as he grabbed her and pushed himself further inside her. When he comes, for a minute or so the pressure on his head is released. He lies on his back, and he feels the thoughts course through his body, one by one like falling dominoes – some of them illuminated briefly but mostly just rushing through him and making him feel alive. He wipes his hand on an old T-shirt and he breathes in the morning deeply. Even inside, Tŷ Gwydr smells like the woods.

Geth always takes his boots off at the door, no matter how drunk he is. He's no slob – he cares about the house. He cares about the house more than anything else in the world. He pulls on the ratty old jumper that his *nain* knitted him sometime before the millennium, feels the acrylic raise the hair on his arms. Boxers. Jeans. Socks. Work boots. Coat – even in June it's sharp outside at this time. He checks for his keys in his pocket but he doesn't bother to lock the door behind him. It's just to be safe – the wind up here's a law unto itself, even on a still, summer day like this one. Outside on the veranda, the new air of the morning settles on his stale skin. He makes his way to the end of the little wooden jetty, which the veranda gives on to. The sunlight glints off the water.

It had started yesterday evening at the rugby club in town. He was just going to have the one drink after doing the job up at Bryn Glas, but he'd run into some of the lads from school – Meg's cousin Ste Edwards and some of his lot. Honestly, when he'd seen them come in out of the corner of his eye, his first thought was to neck what remained of his pint and to get the fuck out of there, but Ste had already seen him trying to skulk off round the back.

3

'Oi!' he shouted. 'Where d'you think you're going, Gethin? Think I didn't see you?'

Geth had very little desire to have a pint with Ste Edwards. Steven Edwards was a moron.

'Ite, Ste? I didn't see you there,' he said, grazing the other man's hand.

'Bullshit, you miserable old prick. Come on, come and have a drink. On me.'

Geth momentarily bristled at the idea that he needed someone to pay for his drink, but Ste wasn't like that. He was all right, all things considered.

He makes his way to the edge and slips out of his boots, feeling the cool damp of the wooden boards beneath the soles of his feet. He picks out the *pew pew pew* of a greenfinch and thinks he sees a flash of it – a contrail of chartreuse glinting off the surface of the lake – as he bends down to pull off his clothes. He's dying for a piss. Straightens up, stretches, and watches the jet of liquid arc and catch the light as it lands in the lake. The noise of it, of water slamming into water, is violent. 'Piss like racehorses, you lads do,' his mother used to say to him and his brother, as if it were something of which they should be proud, something that signalled youth and vitality. He sheds the coat and the jumper, shakes out his limbs to prepare himself for the shock of it, and before he can let himself hesitate, he hurls his body – agile, strong, taut despite the drinking – into the freezing water.

'*Iesu mawr.*' His voice is grizzled, pushed through the bars of his gritted teeth. 'Fuck, fuck!' he gasps to no one in particular – to the greenfinch, to God – muscles tensing in the glacial shock of the water.

*

The problem with drinking with Ste and his mates was that you had to drink a lot to put up with them. Right bunch of chauvinist bigots, but all right after four pints. Four pints was the golden hour. About halfway through the third, you started to feel that glittery release of the endorphins prick your skin, like sequins under electric lights. Then the first sip of the fourth. On the fourth pint Geth finds himself animated and enthusiastic all of a sudden, and he forgets how fucking miserable he is the rest of the time. Everything means more. Jokes are funnier. Perceived slights grow claws. Music is so moving he feels like he has to breathe deeper to accommodate it – like he has to inhale it and let it fill his lungs. Last night there was a band playing. Four lads – must have been about sixteen, which means they were born so recently that Geth can barely comprehend it. They probably went to his old school. They started playing songs from when he was their age – Oasis, Pulp, Catatonia, the Manics – when they started playing Manic Street Preachers he felt as if his blood was heating up and reacting with the oxygen as it made its way up to his brain. He felt fantastic all of a sudden.

Once he's got used to the cold he kicks his legs out, rippling the water with his movements. It feels like an act of creation, this displacement of light and shadow and liquid, as he darts out to the middle of the lake. He turns through the water on to his back, feels the almost-warmth of the first rays of sun. Greenfinches, God – this all belongs to him. He floats along like driftwood, and closes his eyes again.

★

Of course what he'd really wanted – once he'd stopped counting drinks and had let his body sag happily into blind feeling – was a girl. Distinct shortage of those in town, mind. The ones that were his age were either wives or exes, or else the kind you wouldn't touch with a bargepole: tramp stamps. Architectural haircuts. Suspected chlamydia. The younger ones were dangerous now too though. There was no shortage of nubile teenage girls making eyes at the band, but Geth wasn't a creep. He didn't want to fuck someone born after the bloody millennium, did he? As he feels the shadows of the larch trees graze his face, he remembers going to the toilet and pulling out his phone. He remembers flicking through the app as he took a piss – adjusting the settings to expand the geographical radius of potential. Two miles. Five miles. Ten. Sometimes, when Geth just wants an easy lay, he drives out to Chester, or to another big town nearby, and he sits in a pub there and opens one of the apps on his phone. Potential suitors double, triple, multiply endlessly, and concertina out beneath his thumbs. You don't get that in town, and if he tried here, at Tŷ Gwydr, there'd probably be no one. *No matches within this distance.* The chances were bleak as fuck up here. When he stumbled back out of the gents though last night, he was in luck. Ioz Griffiths and Rich Jones had turned up and were trying to get people to come out to Liverpool. If they split a taxi, it wouldn't be that bad. Geth had felt the weight of his phone in the pocket of his jeans and he imagined a world of possibility.

By the time he gets out of the lake, it's morning proper. His body still thrills with the exhilaration of the cold water as he pulls on his boots again and makes his way around the back of the house to his pick-up. It's a single-cab Hilux MK3, 1996. Old ones like this are rare as rocking horse shit these days, but Geth picked it up second-hand for a song before they had gained *cult status*. Red, but not clean, like – with welts of rust right across the paintwork and filler under the wheel arches. This is a truck that was made to work, not one of those poncy 4x4s that rich guys buy their wives to ferry the kids back and forth from school in: Range Rovers with approximations of forced nicknames as number plates; Discoveries in silver and '*Bordeaux*', polished so much that the sun comes off the bonnet like burning magnesium, blinding you at a T-junction. That kind of car makes Geth sick. People have too much money. This morning, the sight of his own pick-up turns his stomach, because the idea that he'd decided to drive last night gives him the momentary sensation that someone's scooped out his insides. He remembers all at once how he'd crawled along the Old Bwlch at twenty to be on the safe side, the mist thickening into something solid over the moor.

He needs coffee. He climbs into the cab and roots around for the old camping stove and the jar of instant that he knows are stashed somewhere in amongst all the other crap in the footwell. Crisp newspapers turned the colour of bad teeth. An old Sonic Youth T-shirt that smells like sap, sweat and sawdust. His mouth is furry. Too sweet. There's the pressure at his skull again.

Time's barely grazing six and Coed-y-Grug is a private woodland anyway, but if someone were to walk past, if someone were to spot Geth through the trees from the ridge up behind the house, they might think that he was meditating. Back down by the water, he sits on the beach with crossed legs and he closes his eyes waiting for the rattle of the kettle. Geth thinks that any kind of religion – Western,

Eastern, otherwise – is bollocks, but as he digs his palms into the damp earth what he feels, although he'd never deign to articulate it as such – is something like communion. When he was a kid there were still a fair few number of hippies in town – middle class, English *bohemians* who had fled to Wales in the seventies to become potters, or weavers or bad landscape painters. He used to take drugs with their kids before he got too old for that crap – before the kids all left anyway to move to places where things apparently *happened*. Names like Taliesin. The parents had given them Welsh names but had lifted them straight out of the *Mabinogion*; they may as well have called them Lancelot or Galahad. Tal sometimes talked about 'communion with the earth'. Geth thought it was a pile of wank, but this morning, he can almost feel the soil hum beneath his fingertips. The movement of the water as the breeze unstills it may as well be the movement of blood through his own body. He finds himself concentrating on inhaling and exhaling despite himself. He doesn't have a lot, but he has this.

The girl was called Chloe. He matched with her on the walk from the car park to the first pub. She was at the lower end of his age bracket; probably about the same age as his truck, he thinks. The first photo was the obligatory bikini shot. Cracking body. Fit but not too skinny – something to hold on to. After that, one in nice, tight leggings and a sports bra, her hair piled up in a messy bun on the top of her head. You couldn't really make out her face; she was doing some sort of yoga thing. 'Watch out, mate,' Rich had said, leaning over his shoulder to get a look at the screen. 'Body of *Baywatch*, face of *Crimewatch*.'

Chloë. 22. Student at Liverpool John Moores. Yoga. Travelling. Feminism. Getting Aperol spritzed with my girls! Hablo español ;)

In the next photo she was clutching a glass of lurid orange liquid that Geth took to be the spritz to which she was apparently so devoted. Her face wasn't half bad either, she was obviously just aware of her main selling points. He matched with two other girls before he'd even ordered his first pint, but Chloe was the one he chose.

After the coffee, he decides that since he's up and about he may as well split the load of firewood that he'd logged yesterday for Dr Prys-Jones. His felling trousers aren't in the truck but he's got a splitting maul and his gloves in the cab. Jeans will suffice. Prys-Jones is a good customer and he likes him, so he's felled him a nice ash – about thirty feet tall with an eight-inch trunk. A year or two older than Chloe. The whole process takes about half an hour. He's slow today and the ash has a twisted grain, so he has to get his chainsaw out to quarter some of the logs. He manages to get splinters in his bloody jeans, and although the air is still cool, inside his gloves his hands are slick with sweat. Pearls of it bead at his forehead and run down his face. The flies start to buzz around him and the nerves in his brain crunch unbearably each time he slams the axe down on the log, like the bones of an animal crushed in a plough. He can feel the alcohol ease out of his body as he works. By the time he finishes, his T-shirt is soaked through and he feels a tangible sense of accomplishment. Last night Chloe was visibly impressed when he told her about what he did for a living. He showed her a scar he'd got from a chainsaw kicking back when he'd first started the job. She trailed a perfectly manicured finger along the length of it and her mouth formed a pouty little 'O'. People always are impressed. It's romantic, like – noble, virile. He loads the wood into the back of the truck, and before he leaves, he does a final sweep of the woodland. There's a couple of hanging branches that could do with sorting out and some dead sycamore that needs to go, but he can do that over the weekend – it's not like he's got anything better to do. When he goes up to the house again, to grab some stuff and lock up, he loiters for a while at the big window. Vague, brindled versions of the trees are rendered in pools of shadow on the surface of the water. He touches the glass with his fingers.

Down in the truck, when he turns the key in the ignition, the CD player jerks into life and music tears through the cab at full volume, the heart-breaking scream of the harmonica eviscerating the peace of the morning. Townes Van Zandt. He must have been feeling pretty drunk and gloomy when he drove home last night if he was listening to Townes Van Zandt at full volume. Geth likes country music because he identifies with it. He feels as if country music validates his way of life, but more than that, as if it blows it up to heroic proportions. It makes him feel part of something colossal. It makes him feel relevant. He likes to listen to the greats: Hank Williams, Merle Haggard, Waylon Jennings, Willie Nelson. He likes songs about down-and-outs, long, dusty highways, gas stations, booze and dangerous women. He thinks that the oozy, heartache sound of a pedal steel guitar is the most exquisitely painful one available to mankind. He feels torn about Americana. On the one hand, it speaks to him, it values people like him; but on the other, he can't help but suspect that they're a bunch of fucking racist morons. He ejects the CD and rummages through the glove compartment for another. He wants to listen to something that swaggers and soars. As he pulls out down the track, the first chords of the opening song thud down defiantly on the keys; then her surly, *up yours* growl: Patti Smith. His girl. Patti fucking Smith. The song climbs and climbs, and peaks as he tears along the S-bends down by Tan-y-Graig. He hammers the steering wheel with his fingers as proxy drumsticks, and he momentarily wonders if he's still over the limit. When 'Gloria' finishes he turns down the volume and he reminds himself sternly to get a grip. The last thing he needs is any more points on his licence.

The semi-detached bungalow is one of four at the end of Ffordd yr Orsaf, or Station Road, so-called because when there was still a railway running through town, the squat Victorian terraces that they built for the workers looked down over it. The bungalows were a later addition. Ex-council. Built just after the whole line was closed at the beginning of the sixties. Down where the tracks used to be, there's just a squalid little footpath. The council had tried to make it appealing, laying down gravel and installing a couple of benches. They'd planted raised beds of simpering primroses and daffodils. Now the gravel is picked through with old Carlsberg cans, empty cigarette packets, Dairy Milk wrappers and the odd used condom. When Geth was in school, Cae Gorsaf, the park, was synonymous with the kind of girl that lost her virginity to a much older man in the bushes and was thereafter contaminated. As he approaches the house, he feels that dull, sinking feeling that he always gets when he looks at it. The state of it. The hallway's a shit-pit. The lads who live next door are borderline rancid, and inside, their stale air seems to seep through the damp, paper-thin walls. The curtains are drawn, and he's just about go and open them when the landline starts to ring. The stark, alien sound of it fills the dark room and feels like a threat. There's something about a phone ringing the moment that you walk into a room that feels theatrical and preordained. He lets it ring for a moment, watching it as if it might spontaneously combust. The longer he avoids it, the longer he gets the faintest, unnerving impression that he's being watched. At last, he grabs the receiver.

'Hello.' His voice is gruff.

'Hi there,' says the soft, feminine one on the other end, a polished, professional, telephone voice. 'Am I speaking to Mr Thomas, please? Gethin Thomas?'

He fingers the seam of the curtains. 'Yeah.'

'Mr Thomas. Great. Brilliant,' she says affirmatively, as if she's been sincerely looking forward to speaking to him all morning. 'This is Stephanie Leray here. I'm calling from the Dalton Estate. It's concerning Tŷ Gwydr.'

She pronounces 'Tŷ Gwydr' hesitantly and with a clumsy English accent: *Tea Gwidder.* Geth feels his head tingle. 'Go on.'

'Well. We've got some quite exciting news with regards to the property. As you know, it's been a while now since the family have been using Tŷ Gwydr and Aubrey Dalton passed away, sadly, last December.'

Aubrey Dalton was in his nineties. The home had been his second one – or more like his fifth or sixth – since the 1970s. Geth couldn't quite find it in him to pass on his sincere condolences.

'Well, it's been six months now, and Mr Dalton's children have decided that the best way to proceed is to sell.'

Geth knows that somewhere, in an office space in London, Stephanie Leray is still speaking, and that thanks to the miracle of telephone lines and hundreds of miles of wires and cables, her sweet, enthusiastic voice is spilling out of the plastic receiver into his miserable little bungalow on Ffordd yr Orsaf. Although he can even hear himself grunt an occasional noise of acknowledgement, he can no longer make out the words that either of them is saying. He gives in to an automatic, muscular impulse and he lets his legs fold underneath him. The words swell into hazy, indecipherable noises. When he hangs up the phone, he goes into the bathroom and throws up.

Part One

GREEN FUSE

SOMEWHERE, in a box in Margot Yates's attic, or in a squalid symphony of greasy plastic resisting rot in a landfill, there's a video of Gethin by the lake at Tŷ Gwydr. He's young – nineteen, maybe twenty. It's late spring and dusk, and a low sun leaks white light into the horizon behind the dark fringe of trees. Olwen is filming. Her parents bought her the Hi8 video camera for her birthday. The year is 1999, and a significant number of people are scared that a glitch in computerised timepieces is going to bring about the annihilation of mankind in less than a year's time. Gethin narrows his eyes at the camera. Her bodiless voice says to him, I love it here. He says, good. This place is ours.

2016

ABOUT A MONTH after the phone call, a photographer was dispatched to Tŷ Gwydr to take photos of the house. The secretary explained to Gethin that they were being sent by the estate agents, who weren't just 'normal estate agents', but 'purveyors of exquisite, heritage design'. The Modernist published a quarterly architectural digest and had 600,000 followers on Instagram. Geth knew about the last part because the secretary helpfully sent him a gushing email with links attached, and he lost twenty minutes of his life scrolling through images of 'striking, three-bedroom maisonettes' with 'bright, terrazzo-tiled kitchen extensions, combining original Victorian character with elegant, modernist innovation'. He clicked through the floor plans in disbelief. One point five mill for seventy-five square metres and a shared lease in south London. Most of them just about had a patio. He wondered how much they'd ask for Tŷ Gwydr, for the woods, for the lake.

He got there early the day that the photographer was supposed to arrive. He sat on the jetty with his boots off and watched the lake. It was about the size of two big swimming pools, and at the far end, where the tall, blond bulrushes cracked the surface of the water, he saw the silhouette of the heron. An engine rumbled at the top of the track. The bird opened up like a flower in bloom, and took flight.

1987

HE WAS SEVEN years old the first time he saw Tŷ Gwydr. He knew that because one of his formative memories was putting the experience into written language the following day at school. He wasn't sure now if he really remembered it, or if his mind, over the next three decades, had created the memory, having spent much of his childhood staring at the piece of paper that his mother had proudly pinned on the notice-board above the kitchen worktop. In Welsh, and then in English, underneath the date, which was in March 1987, Gethin had written: 'Yesterday Me and Danny and Mam went to Tŷ Gwydr it is a glass house in the woods and my mam is going to work there sometimes.' In English he had added a rogue 'H' to 'went'. None of the other children in his class were learning to write in both languages yet, but Gethin, despite a pathological lack of effort, was what Mrs Price, his teacher, suspiciously referred to as 'very able'.

By the time his mother died in 2013, Geth had forgotten entirely about the written record of that afternoon. He found the piece of paper in one of the drawers in Ffion's dressing table, with a matchbox full of baby teeth and a strip of photos that he had taken in a photobooth when he was a teenager, with centre-parted, shaggy hair framing his newly angular face. He was with Megan. She'd just got her nose pierced. He was wearing a plaid shirt and trying to look as disenfranchised as possible. He remembered that day too, when he saw the photos. That was the problem with Geth. His memory was too good. It made him sentimental. The slip of paper upon which he'd apparently constructed some of his first sentences was thin to the point of translucence. The pencil was so faded that it took him a second to realise what it was, but when he did, he remembered the yellow walls and the big windows in Mrs Price's classroom. He remembered the smell of crayons and poster paint and the sweetness of new grass stains on his school shirts. The thwack of a football being kicked across the field. The sour tang of orange squash.

The three of them went up to Tŷ Gwydr for the first time one day after school. Outside, the rain had deepened the light of the afternoon, shifting it closer to evening. The air smelt more intensely of the earth. The pigment of the landscape was denser somehow – the greens of the hedgerows bluish and glossy. In the car on the way up to Coed-y-Grug, Ffion told them that they were going to meet Nerys Williams to get the keys, because she would be looking after the house from now on, as one of her jobs. Nerys was getting too old to get up and down the track.

'Is it a mansion?' Geth said.

'It's posh.'

'Posher than Haf and Iestyn?'

Danny pulled a face. 'Iestyn and Haf aren't posh, stupid.'

'They're rich.' Gethin pushed his small feet into the balding fabric of his brother's seat. 'And Haf thinks she's posh.' He watched Ffion's reflection in the rear-view mirror, and felt pleased with himself because she was trying not to smile. Iestyn was her older brother and lived at Bryn Hendre, the farm where she'd grown up on the outskirts of the village. Now, she and the boys lived on the estate in town, and Gethin was too young to understand why that was a source of tension.

'We'll go up to Bryn Hendre after this, to see Nainy,' Ffion said. Ffion only ever went to the farm to see her mother. The boys trailed Iestyn. Danny worshipped him because he'd taught him to drive the tractor. Iestyn had hoped that both of his daughters were going to be sons, and had been disappointed both times. There were a lot of things that Iestyn was disappointed about.

The rain was coming down in sheets when they pulled up in the lay-by at the top of the track. The windows of the old Renault 5 were opaque with steam. The windscreen had dissolved, was something fluid.

'We're going to have to walk from here, boys. The car'll never make it.'

'Mam, it's pissing it down.'

'Danny. Language.'

Gethin didn't mind walking through the woods. 'Don't be a big girl, Dan.'

'You little shit.'

'*Danny.*'

Geth fled the car, scaled the closed gate and began to sprint down the track through the woods. The air was cool, damp, fragrant. The ground underneath his trainers was slick. He ran until he couldn't any more, towards the clearing at the crest of the hill where the canopy of trees thinned. He was laughing still, doubled over. He'd left his coat in the car and his dark, curly hair was plastered to his head. His bare legs were flecked with mud. He wiped his hands on them, straightened up, and saw Tŷ Gwydr for the first time.

He didn't speak for the hour or so that they were there. He was aware of his mother and Danny approaching; of the breath of air shifting as Ffion dropped his waterproof on to his shoulders; of Danny grumbling some kind of threat when she'd gone on ahead – a 'don't think you got away with that, stupid', another forbidden swearword. Danny's voice ricocheted off him much in the same way that the bullets of rain snapped back from the surface of the lake. When Nerys greeted the three of them on the veranda, she asked if he was shy.

'Normally you can't shut him up,' Ffion said.

In Nain's sitting room, Geth and Danny sat on the floor by the electric heater and listened to the women speak. They ate the top layers of their bourbon biscuits and scraped off the cream in the middle with their teeth. The heater smelt of damp metal.

'It's pocket money really,' Ffion told her mother, 'but there's hardly anything to do there. Bit with the garden. Keeping an eye on the place. It's all cash in hand.'

'They never come, do they, the family? You remember them, from when you were little?'

'Hardly. They had a son my age, didn't they? But I think he went away to school when they lived here.'

Nain raised her eyebrows. 'Obviously.' Swallowed a mouthful of tea. 'What are they called again?'

'The Daltons, Nerys said.'

'*Ynde.* That's it. The Daltons. I remember. They've owned land in the village for donkey's years. Not just Coed-y-Grug, but those lovely old Victorian houses too, out towards Cerrig. I remember when they built Tŷ Gwydr. Just before you were born. I've not been there but your dad went, just after they moved in. Said it was an eyesore.'

'What's an eyesore?' Gethin said.

His grandmother crossed her hands on her lap. 'Ugly.'

When they left Bryn Hendre, Iestyn was in the yard. It was about half six so he must have just finished the milking.

He was leaning on the door of the Renault in his faded blue boiler suit, oilskin hooked over his right shoulder. He narrowed his eyes at them as they crossed over from Nain's cottage. Took his flat cap off and started to fidget with it. He had hair like Gethin, dense, with the same lustrous sheen as new film reel. It was universally agreed in town that Iestyn Thomas was handsome. That he had been a 'catch' before all that unfortunate business with the police. Danny ran ahead to greet him. Iestyn ruffled his nephew's hair without taking his eyes off Ffion.

'Iestyn,' she said.

'Heard you were up at Tŷ Gwydr.'

'How on earth did you hear about that?'

'Haf saw Nerys in the shop on Sunday.'

Ffion sighed.

'You really gonna start working for those *Sais* bastards?'

'*Iesu mawr*, Iestyn. Give me a break. It's piss easy work and I need the money.'

He sneered. 'Maybe you should be trying a bit harder to get that pikey to pay you child support?'

'Get in the car, boys. It's home time.'

Iestyn took a pack of Rothmans from the poacher's pocket of his oilskin and shook a couple out. 'Want one?'

'No.'

'Come on. Look, I'm sorry about that. It wasn't a nice thing to say about John.'

'Not really, no. Especially not when the boys are right there.'

He sighed, bowed his head, pinched the cigarette between his forefinger and thumb and rooted in the pocket again for his lighter. 'I'm just a bit surprised, that's all. That you're going to start working for those people.'

'It's hardly a proper job, Iestyn. It's cash on the side. We didn't all inherit a nice big farm to raise our kids on, did we?'

Iestyn smirked.

'I'm leaving now. Goodbye.'

He stepped aside.

'Come on, boys, *brysiwch*.'

'See you soon, lads. You gonna come help out on the farm this weekend, Dan?'

Gethin thought his brother was pathetic, sucking up to Iestyn like that. He got in the car without saying goodbye. The rain started up again as Ffion reversed. Gethin watched his uncle slowly become something abstract – a pillar of dark blue cotton – and then disappear altogether as they turned on to the track.

In the summer term of that year, Geth's teacher set the class the task of making Father's Day cards. 'What if you don't have a dad? Like Gethin,' one of the other boys asked. Geth felt the pink, dizzying creep of shame crawl up his neck from the collar of his polo shirt like something with legs. It burnt around his ears. He felt his eyes swim. Mrs Price winced with sympathy. 'Gethin can make one for his uncle, or his big brother.' Her voice was laced with sweetness, but Gethin felt indignant with humiliation.

'I do have a dad.'

'Of course you do, Gethin. Everyone has a dad. Even I have a dad, and I'm a grown-up!'

'No, but I mean I have a *real* dad. He's even here. He lives in Llanelgan.'

Gethin knew that it was wrong to lie but he felt good watching all of the other children hang on this new revelation.

'Oh,' said Mrs Price. 'Well, that's nice.'

'It's true,' he insisted, urged on now by a brilliant idea. 'He lives in that glass house in Coed-y-Grug. It's really posh. It's like a mansion. There's a lake and everything. I can go swimming there when I go and see him.'

Geth had been up to Tŷ Gwydr a few times now with his mother, and the strange beauty of the house, with its panels of glass and reddish wood, had caught him like the barbed wire that snagged on his jeans climbing over the fences at Bryn Hendre. It had become a fully cemented tenet of the landscape of his imagination. Now, he could picture his father there – or the man that his mind had created in lieu of one, at least. A composite of Jon Bon Jovi and Han Solo based on the shaggy-haired, white-toothed man that he'd seen in the odd photo, holding Danny up over his shoulders on the beach near Abersoch, pale Levi's rolled up around his ankles and the water eddying at his feet. *Top Gun* sunglasses. He gripped his pencil so hard that his knuckles blanched. He drew the round of the lake, ringed with Christmas trees. He drew the façade of the house that gave on to it, with the raised veranda and the little jetty, and a squat square of glass behind it. He drew his mother and father standing inside, shoulders touching, Danny and himself next to them, their heads barely scraping the level of their dad's knees. In the right-hand corner of the page, he drew a huge, spiky orb for the sun: grinning and in aviators. When he finished the card at the end of the week, it had gained such talismanic properties that he was scared of spoiling it before he could take it home. He had the panicked impression that it might spontaneously dissolve in his hands, or under the light-bulb glare of the other children's gaze. As soon as the glue underneath the trails of glitter on the lake had dried, he hid it in his school drawer and waited for the end of the day. When he gave it to his mother, he watched her look at it. Her smile stayed fixed on her face but something flickered across her eyes.

'It's us with Dad. We're at Tŷ Gwydr 'cause that's where he lives.'

Ffion blinked. 'It's beautiful. He'd love it.'

When Danny came home from school, he saw the card tacked to the fridge and tore it off. The magnet skimmed across the laminate kitchen floor. Gethin was round the back, kicking a football against the fence.

'What's this?' Danny demanded.

'It's us.' The ball ricocheted across the tiny lawn. 'It's us with Dad.'

Danny glared at his brother and then at the card with a look of fury so acute that Geth felt it sting his own cheeks.

'Give it here,' he said.

Danny ignored him.

'Danny, give it here. I made it.'

When Danny had torn the card in four he let the pieces fall on the floor.

'Dad's dead,' he grunted, and let the patio door slam behind him.

On Monday at school, Daf from the year above came up to Geth in the yard at playtime.

'You're a liar, Gethin. Your dad doesn't live in that house. I asked my mam. She said that your dad's a druggie and that he's probably in prison.'

It was a moment of shame so exquisitely concentrated that, decades later, if Gethin thought of it, his mind couldn't actually focus on the memory at all. He turned his head and spat on the floor, like he had seen Iestyn do when the idea of something had disgusted or offended him beyond articulation.

'He's not in prison. He's dead.'

26

2016

THEY MUST HAVE been about halfway down the track when they gave up and the engine cut. By then the heron was long gone. Geth heard the slam of car doors and then a pair of voices. So there were two of them then, not just the photographer. At some point, he started to catch snatches of what they were saying. A disembodied man's voice said, 'Fuck me . . . beautiful and everything, but you couldn't actually live here, could you?'

'Well, *you* could. Didn't you grow up in, like, the Cotswolds?'

Their words became obscure again in a tangle of mock indignation, and then he made out the bloke's voice more clearly. 'I mean, it's the sticks . . . nearest civilisation is . . . and even that's pushing it.'

The woman laughed, and just before the two voices appeared as people approaching his truck, she said, 'Some rich fucker will buy it as a second home, though, I guess, right?'

Geth watched the man run his left hand along the bed of the pick-up. He started to nod appreciatively. 'Nice. Could see myself getting one of these.'

The woman, who Geth guessed was in her late twenties, and presumably the photographer, judging by the equipment that she was carrying, scoffed. 'What, and cruise around Clapton in it?'

'Shut up! At least I can drive.'

Neither of them had seen Geth, watching them from the edge of the jetty. They looked like chimeric visions from another reality. She was south Asian, tall and attractive, and wearing a long black leather coat and a Liam Gallagher bucket hat. So those were in again. He was about the same age – white, chinless, but tall, and stylish enough to pass as good looking as well. He was in a pair of enormous scuffed work boots and, most improbably of all, the kind of blue boiler suit that Iestyn wore for the milking.

'This must be the caretaker's then.' He slapped the bonnet of the truck. Geth winced. 'He's supposed to meet us here with the keys.' He took a pouch of American Spirit out of one of his pockets and started to roll a cigarette. He asked the photographer how much she was getting paid.

'Not too bad. They pay pretty well. I mean, I guess they're raking it in, right? Better than the real work I do. Plus travel expenses.'

'Yeah, I was well chuffed to come to Wales. We used to come here all the time when I was a kid. My grandma owned a little cottage in Pembrokeshire. I love Wales. *The Valleys.*'

'Was that supposed to be a Welsh accent or were you micro-aggressing me?'

'Stop it. I can't tell if you're joking or not. You got a light?'

Geth stood up. Better to get this over and done with.

1994

TALIESIN YATES and his sister, Olwen, were the first posh people that Gethin ever knew. They lived at the nicer end of Llanelgan, in a dusty, Victorian red brick called Tawelfan, with huge sash windows, a sloping slate roof and a driveway hedged with copper beech. They had gone to private school originally, so for years they'd existed in the imaginations of the village kids as purely spectral entities, glimpsed through the back window of an old Land Rover pulled up at the village shop, where their parents had a standing order for the *Observer*.

Geth met Olwen first. It was early September, and he'd just started secondary school in town. He was on the swings outside the shop with his friend Shane, and Olwen – a skinny nine-year-old with long, white-blonde hair and the kind of tan you picked up abroad – had emerged from the 4×4 to come to talk to them. When they heard her small, BBC voice, they creased up. Shane said something to Gethin in Welsh that had set them off even more, until eventually, softened by her patent mortification, Geth decided to be kind.

'Listen, we're not laughing at you. You've just got a funny voice, y'know? Posh, like.'

Olwen jutted out her jaw defiantly. 'I'm not posh. My parents are artists. We're actually very poor.'

For a long time after that, the Yateses' existence barely so much as registered with Geth. When he'd first come across Tal in secondary school, he'd dismissed him as an irredeemable weirdo. He'd had long hair but was at that unfortunate age where it had just made him look like a girl, or like one of those freaky god botherers from America who weren't allowed to go to hospital, or that lived in the desert with wagons or whatever. He used to lurk around the music department mostly, skinny and dwarfed by a variety of comically large instruments. There'd been a rumour in Year Seven that he was some kind of child prodigy – that his brain was so abnormally large that a specialist in some hospital in Liverpool had measured it. Geth didn't take much notice of him really. Tal was considerably beneath him on the social ladder. Geth was the kind of kid who knew everyone. He knew everyone in the Welsh form because he'd gone to primary school in Llanelgan, but growing up on the estate in town and playing football had given him an in with the English-speaking kids as well. Because of Meg, he even knew the girls, right from the beginning, when they were still an alien species. Megan Edwards was a kind of extra sibling to Geth. She lived two doors down, her brother was Danny's age, and their mothers were best friends. When they were little, Ffion used to look after them both in the afternoons whilst Jackie Edwards worked at the post office. At that time, Ffion was working as a dinner lady, and after she'd finished her shift at quarter to two, she took in work at home making curtains for a local seamstress. When Geth thought of that time, he remembered fabric spread across the entire length of the floor, the smell of cotton. He thought of his mother (young then, her hair hennaed and falling across her forehead, pins clasped between her teeth) kneeling over metres of 'Provençale' sunflowers, or scarlet poppies, or meagre, chintzy forget-me-nots. He remembered velvet, and braided fringing, and the plaited tiebacks that he and Meg were allowed to help her make, rolling out fat sausages of fabric in threes.

It was Megan who first took an interest in Taliesin. At the beginning of Year Ten, he had come back from the holiday and had somehow shifted from a consumptive Jesus freak into town's very own answer to Kurt Cobain. He'd painted his nails black and had taken to wearing eyeliner. The lads stopped taking the piss once they clocked the girls that had started to flit around him.

The first time Meg had taken Geth up to Tawelfan, Taliesin's mother, Margot, had answered the door. She was, as Olwen had claimed, an artist. She was in her late forties – older than either Ffion or Jackie – but she looked good. Geth didn't know then that it was easier to look good if you had money because he didn't know anyone who did. He didn't know that it was easier to look younger (regardless of all the Senior Service cigarettes that you'd started smoking at art school) if you'd never lost nights of sleep wondering how you were going to make the rent or the next utilities bill. Margot Yates had thick black hair, smooth, alabaster skin and cool, grey eyes. Seeing her around the village, Geth had never realised that she was beautiful, because of the stupid clothes that she wore: baggy, men's trousers in tartan or corduroy, polo necks, work boots.

'I suppose you're here for Tal?' she'd said in her deep, smoky voice. 'Come in then – we don't bite.'

He let Meg go in first, and as Taliesin's mother stepped aside, the enormous painting hanging on the wall behind her was revealed in full. It took him a second to register what the picture was and when he did, he dropped his eyes furtively to the floor, to his damp trainers, and hoped that no one had caught him looking at it. He crouched down to take off his shoes but the image of the pair of sinewy bodies, clutching at each other – of the woman's mass of dark hair behind her and then repeated between her legs, of the raw,

31

vivid red of her toes, of his knees, of their cuticles, of the intense, repellent exaggeration of tendons and muscles – reappeared in his mind.

'Oh, sweetheart, don't worry about your shoes. The house is a tip,' Margot said.

He coughed. 'Right. OK then.' He straightened up and tried not to look at the painting. He made himself make eye contact with Margot instead, and then his head was full of the idea of the image again, and of Margot lying supine on a towel like that, underneath a man with painful, anxious shoulder blades, and he thought, Oh God, not now, please don't let me think about that right now. But then how could he not, when they basically had porn up on the wall in the hallway?

'Geth.' Meg's voice was sharp. She smiled faux-brightly and jerked her head towards the corridor that Margot was – thankfully – now disappearing down. 'Why are you being so weird?'

'Did you see that painting?'

'It's *art*, Geth. It's Egon Schiele.'

'What the fuck is Igor Sheila?'

Margot, oblivious, called them from the room at the far end of the corridor. 'I think Tal's still with his dad in the studio, guys. But come in here, if you want. You want a cup of tea or something?'

In the bright yellow kitchen, an antique-looking radio was diffusing classical music. There was an enormous dining table, covered in paper, books and unwashed plates left over from lunch, which would have been hours ago by now, surely. The smell of cooking lingered in the air. A massive vat of stock was simmering on the Rayburn. From the armchair next to it, Taliesin's sister surveyed the newest arrivals.

'Olwen, get off your arse and make a pot of tea,' her mother said.

'I'm not your servant.'

'You're twelve years old. You're my chattel.'

'I should so ring Childline.'

'Good. Go ahead. Let them take you off my hands!' Margot shared exasperated eye contact with Gethin and Megan, and for a moment they felt tantalisingly older than their fifteen years. 'Take a seat, kids. Tal won't be long.'

'What's he doing in the studio?' Meg asked. The sucking up was dead annoying, but Geth was grateful to her for doing the legwork, allowing him to take everything in and above all to keep his head down. There were more nudes hanging above the Rayburn. No wonder Tal was such a weirdo, fair play. These ones were originals in charcoal. Big. Rough-looking. He wondered if this was some of Margot's work.

'Oh, he's just been sitting for Dave, for a new series he's working on.'

'And they're not even paying him,' Olwen interjected. 'It's basically slave labour.'

Margot shook her head. 'Olwen's been reading a book all about Jessica Mitford and is apparently *political* now.'

Meg smiled tepidly as if she understood what that meant and – gratitude aside – Gethin hated her for it. He focused harder on examining the papers on the table to avoid having to engage in any kind of intimidating exchange with Margot, or even with Olwen. He didn't want to be shown up by a kid. He could feel a scratch at his throat and he concentrated on not letting it manifest itself as a cough. He didn't want to make any sound at all. He didn't want anyone to notice him. He picked up a postcard and turned it over and flinched. It was another charcoal sketch, this one of a man's face pulled into a scream.

'Did you do this?' he accidentally said out loud.

Margot, who had been mid-sentence, paused and smiled. 'No. It's from a museum. It's a self-portrait by Max Beckmann.'

'Oh, right. Yeah.' He could feel heat collect on his face and the itching at his throat intensified. Of course he knew it was a reproduction, he wasn't stupid. He'd just thought maybe it was a reproduction of something Margot had made. He could feel Olwen watching him, and although he made an active decision not to meet her gaze, he just knew that she was laughing at him.

'Do you like it?' Margot asked.

'It's creepy. But, yeah. It's cool.'

'Have it.'

His face felt hotter again. 'I – no – don't worry. It's fine. Thank you.'

'Go on. Take it. Help me declutter.'

He was saved by the noisy eruption of the whistling kettle on the stove.

'Do you want milk with your tea?' Olwen asked resent-fully.

'Yes, please,' Meg said in her annoying, smooth new voice.

'And two sugars for me. Cheers.'

Olwen raised her eyebrows at him. 'You want sugar?'

'Oh, Olwen,' Margot groaned, 'don't be such a snob. Give the poor lad the sugar bowl.'

Olwen smirked as she placed the bowl down next to Gethin's cup of tea. He hadn't even known, before, that taking sugar was something to get snooty about. He felt

34

his embarrassment evaporate as indignation took its place. Stuck-up brat. He looked her dead in the eye as he stirred two, and then three heaped teaspoons of crunchy brown sugar into his mug. Tasted like crap, but worth it.

'Ta,' he said.

Taliesin didn't appear for a good hour, but once Geth had decided to not give a fuck – once his overriding indignation at Olwen had burnt away the unpleasant sensation of inferiority – he started to enjoy himself. Margot was warm. She was funny. She laughed like a drain – she laughed at his jokes. She smoked and she swore. Meg stopped talking like a *Blue Peter* presenter, and when they'd finished the tea, Margot asked them both if they'd like a beer from the fridge. It was October half term. The season was on the turn. Outside, the evening was starless and grim – the rain was coming down sideways – but here, next to the Rayburn, Geth could feel himself loosening up, could feel his charm turning on. Margot turned off the classical music and put on a Lou Reed CD. Even the bratty little sister was enjoying herself, and he was starting to think that she was cute, underneath the uppity veneer.

When Tal finally did join them, Geth was about to tell a story about Iestyn; he knew how well his impression of his cantankerous uncle would go down and he was enjoying anticipating their appreciation.

'Iestyn Thomas?' Margot squawked. 'From Bryn Hendre?'

'Uh-huh.'

'He's your uncle?'

'Unfortunately for me.'

'Huh!' She narrowed her eyes at him. 'Christ. Iestyn Thomas, there's a name from the past. You know, now you've said it, you do look like him.'

'Fucking hell, no.' Geth was still enjoying the novelty of swearing in front of somebody's mother. He took what he judged to be a manly swig of his beer.

'Iestyn was a good-looking lad back in the day.'

'Oh God, Mum, you can't help yourself, can you?' Tal had appeared in the doorway. He was standing there, in a Jesus and Mary Chain T-shirt and a knackered old pair of Wranglers, and Geth couldn't believe that he'd never realised that he was cool before.

The next morning, after Margot had given them a lift back to town, he stood in his rugby socks on the electric-blue carpet and looked around his bedroom with new eyes. The woodchip walls painted the same putty colour as Blu Tack. The Liverpool FC bedspread. The mould on the windowsill and the white skirting boards that his mother had told him to not be a princess about. He took the postcard out of his pocket and he propped it on the radiator, and he felt like something significant had happened in his life as he admired Max Beckmann, screaming.

Sometimes when Geth looked back on his friendship with Tal, he felt as if he had entered into a contract with the whole family. The Yateses dazzled him because they were glamorous and permissive, like exotic creatures off TV. They seemed to want to have Gethin and Megan in the house. The Yateses weren't like posh people were supposed to be. David smoked joints in his studio and Margot spoke enthusiastically about the Labour Party. If pressed, they referred to themselves as 'middle class', but even that epithet was accompanied with much self-deprecating eye rolling.

Until well into his twenties, Geth would believe that although Taliesin had taught him a lot about the abstract *world*, he was responsible for bringing Tal into the actual, immediate one, where he thrived. By the end of that school year, Tal was in two bands, had got rid of his virginity, and was no longer a non-entity in school. It was only when Geth was a bit older that he realised that Taliesin's social ascent had nothing to do with him; that people like Taliesin were already taught to thrive in whichever world they happened to land in.

When Geth used to get pissed with the other kids from the estate – when they would hotbox someone's Fiesta, or buy pills off Fred Skid in the Kwik Save car park – Ffion would go spare and remind him that it was a small town, that everyone knew who he was. She would tell him again that such-and-such a family were druggies, that so-and-so's dad was inside for glassing his cousin outside The Boars, or that that lad had already had three kids by two different girls, and was, incidentally, a shit to them all. He knew who was hard and he knew which people you didn't cross. When he dropped acid with Tal the summer after he'd finished Lower Sixth, and when Margot asked them at dinner if they'd enjoyed their trip, he realised that some people just got to move through the world in a different way. Some people got to glide.

2016

BOILER SUIT was apparently a journalist.

'Tie Gwidder's just such an incredible property that they've decided to commission a full-on feature on it for the magazine. Hence me,' he said cheerfully, having introduced himself as Robbie.

'Oh, yeah?' Geth's hand tightened around the keys in his pocket. Priya had taken her camera out and was wandering around the lake getting the photos. It wouldn't be hard to make it look beautiful in this light.

'Do you know much? About Tie Gwidder's history, I mean?'

Geth shrugged and decided not to correct Robbie's pronunciation, because then it would look like he cared.

'One of Aubrey Dalton's first properties.'

'What. The guy that owned it? The dead one?'

'He was an architect. Studied in California just after the war. His family were big landowners, and when he came back to the UK in the late fifties he built this place for fun. It was sort of an experiment, I guess, like a modernist folly. A prototype for the stuff he'd go on to do. He was quite obscure, to be fair. You not heard of him?'

Geth turned away from Robbie and pretended to be investigating something in one of the kitchen cabinets. He took his Leatherman out of the pouch on his belt loop and flicked it open to try to look more convincing.

'Nice bit of kit,' Robbie enthused. When Geth ignored him he added, 'Yeah, I reckon in the end that's why they just left the place sitting here empty all these years. Some kind of family history. Sentimental stuff.'

'Right.'

'Sadly, the good people at Dwell aren't paying me to go into detail researching the human-interest element. They just want me to go on about Aubrey Dalton, the Welsh Richard Neutra.'

Gethin straightened up, narrowed his eyes at him. 'He wasn't Welsh,' he said.

1996

THE HEAT WAVE that summer began around the last week of June, about a fortnight after they had finished their GCSEs, and it dragged on languorously right up until the end of August. Once study leave began, Geth went up to four days a week at the supermarket, stacking shelves and checking stock rotation. The job wasn't entirely bad. Closing shifts were the worst, because of the ominously named 'Job 23', a task performed daily and involving date checking every single item and meticulously recording all products due to expire the following day. At seven o'clock, the witching hour before closing, he would begin reducing everything on the turn to wild levels of cheapness. 'Reductions' at least afforded the opportunity of entertainment. Around quarter past, a pair of middle-aged women who lived for crates of 5p Royal Galas would arrive. There was Max Factor, widely known in town to be 'a hooker', and named for her devotion to thick layers of creamy, ivory foundation, and then there was Mrs Rees-Tomos, whose husband was the richest man in the county, a scion of agricultural irrigation. Mrs RT would saunter in and install herself by the magazines, pretending to flip through the pages, as she stalked Geth with hungry eyes. Geth knew it was wrong, but the very sight of her prim immobile perm and her lilac-tinged stockings aroused profound hatred in him, and he took pleasure in routinely hiding the best sell-by-date spoils from her until he was sure she was already at the checkout. The joy of seeing Max Factor parade a basket of yellow-edged broccoli and wilting carnations past Mrs Rees-Tomos as she headed to the car park was one of the greatest offered by the tedium of the evening shift. In general, he tried to get earlies as much as possible; the clutch of hours before the shop opened to the public were one of that summer's pleasures. Looser and brighter.

It was an idling, golden summer. When Geth looked back on it now, he thought of lying in the grass under the horse chestnut tree in Tal's garden, lurid green leaves fanning out from the heavy branches. Tal would play songs by the Velvet Underground and The Modern Lovers on his guitar, Megan would sing, and sometimes he'd deign to play what he scathingly called the 'soft-rock radio songs' that Geth liked, like 'Stairway' or 'Wish You Were Here'. At house parties and in The Vaults, where no one cared that they were underage, they'd neck pints and smoke packets of cigarettes, and the girls would scream when 'Common People' came on, because it was a song about them – united against rich people in London with dads who paid their rent. Megan taped 'A Girl Like You' by Edwyn Collins off the radio, and Geth remembered how the DJ's voice used to trail off into another pirated song as the cassette zipped forwards. She played it at full volume in her bedroom and sashayed across the puce carpet as if she were a girl in a music video. Taliesin's mother grew violet poppies and blurred, honey-sweet cornflowers around the edge of the lawn. The sky was always blue. Geth was always a little bit drunk or high, or sobering up or coming down. He remembered drunk-driving Danny's Fiesta around the rugby club car park at three in the morning, and then the perfume of damp, fresh fruit in the big fridge at work three hours later.

On the last day of July, Scott Roberts' parents went on a coach tour of the Yorkshire Dales. They left just after three, and by four o'clock the garden was heaving with hungry, limby teenagers. Sometime after dusk, nectarine stained across the sky, Geth and a few of the others went on an expedition to the supermarket to stock up on booze and frozen pizzas. The lads were talking about a girl in the year below called Amy.

'No la, Amy's rough as toast. I fingered her at Tom Williams' party. She's fucking gross.'

Geth walked ahead a bit, because he hated these conversations.

'She was begging to give me head, though. Gagging for it, that one. Body's not too bad, even though one of her tits is like tiny compared to the other.'

His distaste was doubled by superiority. Girls loved him. He didn't need to show off to the others about how many he could get to undress.

'Apparently her dad's a gyppo. It was probably him who gave her crabs.' Grunts and gusts of laughter. Geth rolled his eyes.

'Or Shane.' Their conversation sharpened into focus. 'Shane Gruff? In the Welsh form? He fucked Amy? I thought he was a gay.'

'He pretends not to be, but he's queer as fuck. Can't admit it, though, 'cause he's a hick. There's a bunch of them in town, you know. Do all sorts on the sly. Ask Geth, he'll know. He's a sheepshagger.'

'Oh, fuck off, you knobhead.' It was the sort of comment that would have provoked a sincere reaction a year ago, but that barely registered any more. He was as used to the 'English' lads calling the Welsh speakers hicks, as he was to the 'Welsh' ones calling the 'English' ones *Saeson*. They all came from town in the end. Some of them were even related. He carried on ignoring them.

'It's not just the Welshies,' Ste Edwards said. His chest

42

puffed with the glee of gossip. Ste had always been a right old woman. He lowered his voice for dramatic effect. 'Tal Yates.'

'Taliesin Yates?' one of them said. 'Tal's not a bender. He did Gemma and Siân last year.'

'Mate, that doesn't mean anything. Some of them get married, like. And look – I don't want to stir shit but I know this lad from Dinas Brân who knows Tal from all that North Wales band camp shit he does.'

'This is getting a bit tenuous, Ste,' Geth sighed.

'Yeah, whatever the fuck that means. Anyway, apparently he uses these like . . . *internet forums.*'

'You lot are talking out your arses,' Geth groaned. 'Tal's not gay.'

Ste grinned. 'I bet he'd like to see us talking out our arses.'

The other boys collapsed into hysterical laughter.

By the time they got back to the party, coherence had disintegrated. The evening was cool and blue, and people had shifted inside. Cigarette smoke snagged on Mrs Roberts' flesh-coloured curtains and the matching three-piece suite. A sprawling, sloppy card game that involved a communal jug of shit mix and impossible amounts of hand-eye coordination had taken over half of the living room, and the other had become a hot, sweaty dancefloor. Geth grabbed a beer from the fridge, rolled a joint. He had the impression that they were slowly spiralling out from the singular concentric point of the shit mix jug in the centre – that the brownish, sticky liquid was the beating heart of the party and something shared between them all. He wandered happily through the splintering sequences of scenes and he felt good. Clusters of people that he'd known all his life called him over, shared his spliff, dragged him towards a speaker to dance. One of the girls had put on D'Angelo and wanted to press herself against him. He was more than happy to oblige.

'Eleri, y'seen Megan?' Then his hand was cupping Eleri's arse in her cut-off denim shorts and the idea of Megan dimmed down into nothing again.

Later, in the garden, he found Tal, sitting on the tiled floor of the patio with Gaz Riley and crushing up crystals of MDMA on a copy of *The Guinness Book of World Records*.

'Want some?'

'Has anyone seen Megan, though? We should ask her if she wants any.'

'Afterwards, look at the Chinese woman with the fucking long nails. It's mental.'

When Gethin next went into the kitchen to get another drink, Eleri was leaning against the kitchen counter. 'Have you heard?' she said, 'Apparently Scott's next-door neighbour just came round threatening to call the police.'

'Huh. Really. They never do, though, in the end, do they?'

'I dunno. Scott's freaking out. The old woman was going insane, apparently.'

'Huh.' Geth shrugged off this information and reached for a Becks at the back of the fridge, where they were the coldest. 'You not seen Megan, though, have you?'

Eleri detached herself from the counter and smirked. 'Yeah, I have. She went off round the front with Jamie. Honestly, I know she's your mate but I feel bad for her. She got with Ryan, like two nights ago. You should really say something.'

Gethin flipped the cap off his beer with a lighter. 'How about you mind your own fucking business, Ler?'

'Jesus, Geth, I'm just saying. She's going to get a reputation. I'm trying to be nice.'

44

In the front room, a current of potential scandal pulsed through the throng of people. 'Fair play, maybe we should turn the music down.' 'Scott's just asked that people get rid of any weed, or pills, you know?' 'Pretty reasonable, to be honest.' Geth made his way across to the front door, acknowledging people with a nod of the head or a, 'Yeah, I'll be back in a sec.' He thought he at least ought to go and check that Meg was OK. She'd already been pretty drunk the last time he'd seen her. Through the frosted glass of the porch, the front garden looked empty, and when he stepped out on to the drive, all he could hear was the indistinct hum of the voices inside. The dull thud of the bass. A ripple of laughter. It took him a moment to pick out the noise just beyond the front gate: the ragged breath. A loud sniff.

'Megan?' he called.

'I'm fine,' she insisted when he came out on to the street.

'You don't seem fine.'

She peeled away from the neighbour's gate and rubbed her eyes.

'Where's Jamie?'

'Why should I know?'

'Eleri said she'd seen you come out here with him.'

'Oh. Of course she did.' She shut her eyes and her shoulders began to shake.

'Hey. What's wrong? Megan?'

As he went to hold her he felt her bones lose their rigidity in his arms. She started to cry.

'Meg. What happened? What's going on?'

'Oh, Geth, it was so bad,' she whispered. 'I feel like such an idiot.'

'What happened?' He held her tighter. He felt a premonition of anger flicker at his temples. In his jaw and his throat.

'Me and Jamie were kind of flirting. I feel so stupid. And

45

then we came out here because we were going to smoke a spliff together. He was trying to convince me to leave the party and go down to red rocks with him but I didn't really feel like it. I started to get this bad feeling, you know? Then we started to kiss, and he wanted to go in the garage. And I said we shouldn't and he started being really pushy.'

Geth exhaled through his nostrils. 'Go on.'

'I didn't want him to get annoyed so I told him I'd walk down to the Texaco with him – just to get some air – that's what he kept saying.'

'OK.'

'It's so stupid. I'm fine, I'm just really hammered.'

'Megan.'

She sighed. 'So we were walking down the bottom of the road and then at the turning to Tyn-y-Parc, he just like . . .' She stopped speaking and pursed her lips.

Geth held up his palm to his forehead and pressed down hard. 'Did he do something to you?'

She closed her eyes and shook her head. 'No. I mean, he tried a bit – he was kind of rough. But you know, eventually he got the message. But then he just started saying all sorts of stuff. Just being a right dickhead. It's stupid. I'm really drunk.'

'Right.' His pulse felt more vivid than it usually did. 'And where is he now, do you know?'

'No. Geth, just leave it, yeah? I just want to go home, I think.'

The flexed rod of the single streetlight shimmered like heat rising off tarmac. He heard himself spit an expletive.

'Can you just walk me home?'

'Just stay here, OK? I'm gonna come right back.'

'*Gethin.*'

When he found Jamie out on the patio, he felt violence

gleam at the tips of his fingers – like he wanted to kill him. He registered, perversely, that that impulse felt good. He crossed towards him in three long strides. Jamie scowled at him.

'Fuck do you want?'

Geth ran his tongue along his teeth. Shook his head.

'What, you starting on me?'

He grinned. 'Yeah. I fucking am.'

Neither the boys nor the exhilarated crowd that had gathered to watch them saw the blue light graze the lawn, or registered the music inside stop with a snap after that. There was a second's delay before collective realisation caused the spectators to disperse. Gethin didn't register what was happening until the policeman had both of his arms pinned behind his back. Pain glinted off his jawbone. His knuckles were hot and tingling.

'Think we need to cool down here, lads. Come on,' the policeman wheezed.

Jamie was writhing on the patio tiles, whimpering, despite the fact that seconds before his hands had been around Gethin's throat. Geth spat on the grass. It tasted like a mouthful of rust.

'Oi. I said *calm down*, all right?'

'Yeah, you can fuck off.'

'You what? What did you just say to me?'

'I said—'

He felt the policeman's fingers press harder into his arm.

'Search him,' said his colleague over Gethin's head. 'If he's got anything on him we'll take him in. Give him a good scare.'

At two o'clock in the morning, a policewoman came and woke Gethin up.

'Your uncle's here for you. Come on.'

'My uncle?'

The officer led him down the corridor and out to the front desk. Iestyn was standing apart from it, hands thrust in his pockets, eyes fixed on the door.

'You stupid git,' he hummed, in lieu of greeting.

'What are you doing here? I called Danny at the Glan Llyn.'

'It's Friday night. Your brother's in no fit state. You're lucky he called me and not your mam.'

'We're sorry to have brought you out so late, Mr Thomas,' the policewoman said.

Iestyn cleared his throat. 'No skin off my nose. If we could make this quick, though?'

Gethin watched his uncle fail to make eye contact with the officer. There was something wrong with his voice; something brittle in his posture. When they left the station, Geth could feel the nervous energy come off him like steam rising off boiling water.

'I'm not giving you a lift home,' Iestyn grunted when they got to the Land Rover. 'Walk'll do you good.'

'Yeah. Right. Fair enough.' He picked at a flake of dried blood just below his bottom lip. Ran his hands through his hair. 'Sorry about this,' he muttered, 'and, you know. Thanks.'

The cold, chalky streetlight bleached Iestyn's face. His skin was tinged greenish. He looked as though he might throw up. 'And, Gethin,' he said quietly.

'Yeah?'

He touched Gethin's forearm and for the first time, Geth noticed that his hands were trembling. Slowly, he dug his fingers in hard. Gethin winced.

'Don't you ever – *ever* – get me involved with the police again. Do you hear me? *Ever.*'

Palm Sunday, 1980

IESTYN HAD BEEN kicking around in the cell for about an hour or two when the hinges of the door winced. It was the woman officer again. Roberts? Smith? He couldn't remember her name. She was speaking to him in Welsh – that was a start – telling him he was to follow her. He felt nauseous and stale. She led him down a long corridor, ugly police-issue shoes squeaking on the laminate flooring. They didn't half give them a hideous uniform, these police*women*. Could barely tell she was a bird under the stiff, synthetic skirt. At the bottom of the corridor, she pushed open a door, knocking on the small panel of gridded glass. She gestured at the empty plastic seat and left.

'Iestyn Thomas?'

A plain-clothes bugger on the other side of the desk. Crew cut. Attractive, in a macho sort of way – shoulders upholstered by hours of training – but with piggy eyes the colour of dishwater. Iestyn dragged the chair out aggressively from under the table.

'I'm not gonna talk to you without a translator,' Iestyn said in perfect English. He'd detected a northern lilt when Plain Clothes had spoken. Manchester, maybe? Yorkshire?

Plain Clothes smirked. 'It's not in your interest for anyone else to be privy to what we're about to discuss, Mr Thomas.'

Iestyn tilted back on the hind legs of the chair. He was twenty-one years old. Good looking. Cocky. Still just about drunk enough to be flushed with confidence despite his situation. Plain Clothes cracked his knuckles like an actor in a bad cop film. 'They brought you in at, what? One? Two, this morning? First time in a cell?'

He shrugged.

'Affray. Damage to property. Attempted assault on an officer—'

'Oh, come on. I didn't even hit him.'

'Because you were so drunk that you managed to miss him. But you bloody well tried. Not to mention the verbal abuse.'

Iestyn felt the same spike of hot anger that he'd felt on the kerb outside The Vaults. 'Verbal abuse?' he exclaimed incredulously. 'Verbal abuse from *me*? That *Sais* pig called me a hick. I was clearly provoked.'

Plain Clothes smiled. 'It's funny, none of the other officers heard PC Taylor using such language – and you were very much under the influence, after all. I believe my colleagues breathalysed you when you were brought to the station. You can certainly tie one on, can't you?'

Iestyn pushed his tongue into the hollow of his cheek.

'Either way it's not looking good, mate. These are some serious breaches of the law of the land.'

'*Ddim fy nghyfraith i. A ddim dy dir di,*' he spat: Not my law. And not *your* land.

Plain Clothes ignored him. 'You're looking at a hefty fine. Maybe even some time, depending on whether Mr Owen decides to press charges.'

Dewi fucking Owen. That's where this had all started. The Vaults. The landlord had called a lock-in. Iestyn had gone for a slash and when he'd come out Dewi fucking Owen had started on Hywel. Or maybe Hywel had started on Dewi. Either way, you don't just leave your mate to get beaten up, do you? You do something about it, and Hywel

50

was only small, like. Dewi Owen was a right bruiser. Built like a brick shithouse.

'Not got anything to say for once?'

'I don't even know who you are. I'm not just going to shoot my mouth off, am I?'

Plain Clothes smiled with the bottom half of his face. 'Look,' he said, 'I think we've got off to a bad start, you and me.' He rolled his head around on his neck. 'You like jokes?'

'Jokes?'

'You hear the one about the bloke who turns up to a fancy-dress party with a condom on his nose?'

Iestyn deigned to raise his eyebrows.

'Host hands him a drink. Says, "Evening, Pete. What are you dressed up as, then?"' Plain Clothes grinned. 'Pete says . . . "Fuck nose!"'

His mouth twitched. It took him a second, but it wasn't bad.

Plain Clothes, once he'd stopped wheezing, said, 'Thought you'd enjoy a little off-colour gag, Mr Thomas, what with your interest in nefarious counter-cultural activities.'

'My what?'

The policeman ignored him. 'How about I introduce myself? You can call me Clive, OK? And I'm not trying to antagonise you. In fact, I'm very interested in a lot of things you might have to say.'

Iestyn tipped back on the chair again. 'Right.'

Plain Clothes Clive stood up. Crossed the room to the door. Glanced out of the window. 'I was wondering, for example, how well you were acquainted with an Eifion Williams, from Port Madoc way?'

'*Porth Madog*, it's called. Not Port Madoc.'

Clive smirked. 'And Mr Williams?'

In all the time that Iestyn had known Eifion, he'd never called himself Williams. Like a lot of the lads in that crowd, he'd dropped his English surname entirely in favour of his middle name, Wyn. Eifion Wyn – like he would have been called before the English had come along and had started to fuck with everything. Not untruthfully then, Iestyn said, 'I don't know any Eifion Williamses. Sorry.'

Plain Clothes raised his eyebrows. 'All right then. Let's try again. What about Williams' girlfriend? Good-looking bird. Redhead. Angharad Jones. Suppose you don't know her either, do you?'

It was Angharad, of course, who'd introduced him to Eifion – just the once, when they'd run into each other on the Maes last summer, having not seen each other for donkey's years. She was from Y Fro Gymraeg, Angharad – they both were, Eifion too – Pen Llŷn. She was a harpist who Iestyn had known from doing the rounds at Eisteddfodau when he was a kid. He'd had a lovely voice, Iestyn, before it had broken and lost its sheen.

'It's not ringing a bell, no.'

Plain Clothes chuckled. 'Funny that. You never run into them in any of the WSRM meetings you've been going to?'

Iestyn held his gaze. Fuck this. 'I didn't realise that Mrs Thatcher had made it illegal to have political affiliations now?'

Just saying the words made him feel a bit like Eifion. *Political affiliations.* Iestyn had in fact only ever been to two Welsh Socialist Republican Movement meetings and had zero intention of attending any more. He wanted to make things burn. He wanted action. He wanted to fuck things up, not hand out bloody pamphlets and talk about fucking Trotsky or 'overseas capital'. He'd gone to those meetings imagining Molotov cocktails and nail bombs. That's what they were saying on HTV News. Not all that chat about 'English imperialist oppression' and the 'international social- ist brotherhood'. He didn't give a flying fuck about Chile or South Africa. 'Have I seen you round town before?' he asked.

'I'm not from here.'

'Huh. And how do you know I was at those meetings then?'

Clive smiled. 'My job is to keep this country safe from subversives who threaten it. There's not a lot we don't know, Mr Thomas.'

'Well, you obviously don't know everything, otherwise you'd know I haven't been to any of those Che Guevara shit shows for months.'

When he laughed, Plain Clothes Clive's pinkish skin stretched across his skull and shone in the caustic glare of the strip light above them. It was almost sinister. When he recovered he said, 'Well. It is a shame you're not involved with Eifion Williams, because we're very interested in find- ing out a little bit more about him. Very interested indeed.'

'What's that supposed to mean?'

'What do you think?' Clive was making his way back to the desk. He sat down.

Iestyn felt the nausea anew. 'Are you even allowed to do that?'

'It's a question of public safety, Mr Thomas. I'm pretty much allowed to do whatever I want.'

Iestyn sucked the air through his teeth. Leant forward on his elbows. 'Yeah, well. Nice try, mate, but even if I think all that socialist republican stuff is a load of bollocks, I'm not gonna snitch to the English, am I?'

Clive nodded slowly, as if he were really chewing over what Iestyn had said.

'You got a lot of money kicking around back on the farm, then, yeah? Been saving your wages? Because you don't even want to know how much your fine's going to be for assaulting PC Taylor.'

'*Attempted* assault, you said before!'

'Did I? I really can't remember. These things aren't always black and white, you know . . . Which is how, if you're willing to cooperate, we could make them disappear altogether.' Clive paused. 'If you're interested, that is. Obviously you're not under any *obligation* to do anything.'

Iestyn closed his eyes. Pain thudded across his left cheekbone where Dewi had hooked him one.

'Of course, there is one other thing.' Clive sighed. 'Seeing as maybe money's not actually an issue for you at all.'

Iestyn opened his eyes. The policeman gave him a pained little look, as if he wasn't enjoying himself as much as he quite patently was. 'Well, I was just thinking you actually might be all right on that front, seeing as I've heard from my colleagues that you're quite the young entrepreneur.'

'You what?'

'I just can't believe you thought you'd get away with it. In a small town like this! I'm sure you know how these things get around.'

Iestyn knew what he was talking about immediately. He felt sick. It couldn't be that, though, surely? How could the policeman possibly know about that?

'You might have thought you were being clever, but my colleagues know all about your little business, Mr Thomas. We've just been waiting for the right moment, and now I'm wondering if maybe that moment isn't right now?'

'I've not done anything illegal. They're not against the law,' he said before he could help himself.

Clive eyed him smugly. 'They're not against the law' was tantamount to admission of guilt, as far as he was concerned. 'I think you'll find that selling magic mushrooms as they come from God's earth is, indeed, within the law. It's selling them prepared that's not. And as for the marijuana . . .'

Iestyn could feel the combative self-righteousness drain from his body. It had to be her. He felt sick. She was the one who'd put him on to it all in the first place.

'I'm not a druggy,' he insisted. 'I've never even taken anything.'

Clive nodded slowly. 'You are aware that you're not just looking at a *fine* for this?' He did something with his expression – softened his face. He handed Iestyn the glass of water at his elbow. 'Drink this. You're looking a bit peaky.'

Iestyn obeyed and put in the effort of swallowing the water. Clive nodded encouragingly, and then, with a paternal laugh, as if none of their previous exchange had taken place, said, 'You'll be wanting a lot of water today, the amount you tucked away last night.' He gave another one of his artificial smiles. Iestyn drained the glass and wanted to throw it all back up.

One by one he examined the events of the evening like a child inspecting toy soldiers. Dusk. Sitting in the GTI, pulled up in a lay-by out near Bont. Doing up his flies. Turning down the radio. Haf pulling on her jeans in the passenger seat and telling him, just like that, that she was a fortnight late. Dropping her back at her parents' house in Clawdd, the vague impression that the immaculate white sunset sinking into the hills was creating some kind of vacuum of visibility – like he couldn't see anything in front of him at all. The Boars with some of the lads, followed by The Feathers, and finally The Vaults. Enough pints in for

55

it all to feel like a joke. His hands clasping Dewi Owen's meaty neck. The police arriving. Leery, ratboy's face as he called him a 'Welshie hick'. Two weeks late. They'd only done it once without protection. She'd said it was OK, that she'd just had the curse. His mind – momentarily then, entirely against his will – briefly conjured the face of the artist from Tawelfan. Fucking bitch.

He exhaled slowly. 'What exactly do you want me to do?'

2016

AFTER PRIYA AND ROBBIE finally left, Gethin went and sat back out on the jetty. Time was grazing midday and the heat swelled the still air. He thought maybe if he sat down by the water he'd get a little respite, but waves of heat seemed to be rolling up off the lake. It felt unnaturally hot. Sweat trickled down his back and his palms were greasy with it. He lowered himself on to the wooden boards but he couldn't get comfortable. Every position he tried to sit in seemed to numb his limbs or make something twitch or ache or twist. He realised then that he was aware of his breathing to an abnormal degree, and once that had registered, the action itself became almost impossible. He consciously inhaled and exhaled as he stood up. It couldn't possibly be this hot, surely? His hands were throbbing and, just then, as he raised them to his face, he felt a debilitating pain in his head, like something inside him was expanding against his skull. The light was too bright. He needed to get into the shade.

Inside, he managed to make it into the cool bathroom. He lay down in the empty bath. The surface was cold and smooth. He made himself breathe, and when he'd finally got hold of himself, he took his phone and called Meg.

'DON'T GET ME WRONG, I'm glad he's doing it. Froze my fucking arse off last year on the top of town.'

Danny, who had condescended to give them a lift up to the village, grimaced in agreement with Meg. 'Yeah, fair dos. Don't miss that.' Since getting with Nia and moving up to the farm, Gethin's older brother had embraced being boring with religious enthusiasm. Gethin imagined the two of them, curled up on the sofa they'd inherited from Nain, wishing in the New Year with a TV dinner. This time last year Danny was throwing up in the rugby club car park. Part of it was that he was whipped; part of it, Gethin couldn't help but suspect, came from being in such close proximity to Iestyn all the time. Would put anyone off drinking, that.

Megan carried on, 'So, like, selfishly, I'm grateful. But Tal's mental. You haven't seen their house, Dan. They've got a lot of nice stuff. He's asking for it.'

Gethin leant forward from the back seat. It was so cold he could see his breath between the headrests as he spoke. 'Megan, *bach*. Chill out, love. It's a party. It's gonna be nice. Rather Tal's than the top of town, snogging some random when the clock goes and then trying to get into the club.'

'I just feel bad on David and Margot, you know. I felt so guilty when we saw her on Christmas Eve.'

David and Margot Yates were spending the period between Christmas and the New Year with old friends in London. Taliesin and Olwen had assumed that they would be invited and had been planning some kind of illicit, urban new year with their cousins (older, glamorous, worldly).

When Margot had told them that they weren't, they'd planned the party in revenge.

'Geth just wants to pull some princess, don't you, Gethin?'

He smirked. 'I like meeting new people. I'm a friendly guy.'

The party, already unimaginably exciting, given that it was being held indoors, came with the tantalising bonus of having strangers in attendance. In September, Olwen had left their school to go and board at some place in Cheshire where they wore blazers and did Latin. 'On a full scholarship,' Taliesin caveated defensively, unasked. Sometimes, Gethin had the impression that he had pulled everyone remotely interesting in town. He was looking forward to broadening his horizons.

Olwen had invited three female friends. One looked like a horse, one spent the entire duration of the night glued to a boy called Jeremy, and one had a shaved head, but was promising, given that he had overheard the horse, who was called Allegra, making fun of her for 'liking a bit of rough'.

Taliesin was already drunk when they arrived.

'I can't believe she talked me into this,' he said, swallowing a mouthful of Heineken. He was talking about his sister. 'She doesn't have to live with them. I'm fucked.'

Gethin took the rollie from behind his ear and put it into Tal's open mouth. 'Smoke this. Chill the fuck out. You're gonna be fine. Chris Eds is gonna bring some pills. That'll calm you down.'

'I cannot do any drugs, Gethin. Shit, the door. How many more people can there even be?'

The kitchen, where they were standing, was already full.

Olwen was holding court with her entourage of chinless wonders in the living room, and people were now drunk enough to be congregating in the garden – despite the sub-zero temperatures – and upstairs.

'How about to take your mind off things you give me the lowdown on Sinéad O'Connor?'

'Excuse me?'

'Your sister's mate. The bald one.'

'Phoebe? She's up herself. They all are. She shaved her head to try and get expelled from their school and called it a fucking *gesture of solidarity* . . . Allegra's quite nice, but I think she's a Tory.'

'No worries there, mate. She looks like she's about to chase a pack of foxes over a hedge, that one.'

'Gethin, you're a sexist knob.'

'Aren't Tories fair game?'

Tal leant back on the kitchen counter, which was grimy in a sticky, alcoholic way, rather than in the charming, artistic one that was customary in the Yateses' scruffy, *bohemian* domain. He inhaled deeply through his nostrils. From the living room, Gethin heard a group of lads (he suspected the rugby players) burst into the chorus of 'Come on Eileen' and drown out Taliesin's carefully curated mix tape. A feminine shriek. Someone turned up the music.

'What is your sister doing anyway? Haven't seen her since she left, little Olwen, striking out in the big bad world. She could be my in with Sinéad.'

'Phoebe.'

'What you need, la, is a drink. How about some of that expensive whisky that your dad keeps in his studio? That could be a classy start to the evening.'

'No one can find that whisky. Oh God. No one can go into the studio.' He polished off the Heineken and flinched.

Chucked the can into the sink. 'All right, maybe just us. Maybe that's actually just what I need.'

'Yes. That is the Christmas spirit I like to see, Taliesin!'

The living room was an inferno after the solid cold of the studio. Geth shed his coat and his jumper. Ran his hands through his hair. Felt his chin going to the opening bars of 'Beetlebum' that were grinding out of the speakers. He felt pleasantly buzzed. He'd left Tal in the garden with some of the lads from the year below; Meg was out there too, with some arty guy from Olwen's new school. The arty fuckers always fancied Megan. She had a cool Hope Sandoval thing going for her. Dressed like Buffy the Vampire Slayer in leather and knee-high boots. When she was singing with Tal's band in the pub, everyone fancied her. He'd watched old men – people's dads – staring at her through the smoke as if it was Pamela Anderson up on the makeshift stage, rather than a teenager in Docs and a crochet jumper singing 'Black Velvet'. Yeah. Fair play – *he* would. But he couldn't, though, not with Megan. Thinking about the relative attractiveness of Megan reminded him of the shaved-head girl again. There she was, by the fireplace, talking to Daf Parry. Pretty face and a cracking body, and there was something kind of cool and hard about the hairdo. She was giggling at Daf, touching his chest through the Everton shirt he was wearing. The horsey one was third wheeling and had a face like a bulldog licking piss off a nettle. He needed to get Sinéad alone.

He decided to go into the kitchen first to grab himself a beer, and there, pushing his way through the knot of people to get to the fridge, he finally saw Olwen. He stopped in the middle of the room. She had all of her dark blonde hair piled up on top of her head, and her neck and shoulders were bare. She was wearing some silky dress thing that looked like a nightie; had the kind of flimsy straps that you could nudge off with your thumb. Her collarbone. He'd never paid much attention to anyone's collarbone before, but now he was staring at hers and feeling how he used to feel when he smoked cigarettes before he'd got used to them – lightheaded, precarious. He swallowed. He opened his mouth to say her name, and as he did, some skinny guy he didn't know – some dickhead with curtains and a Levi's denim jacket – put his expensively clad arm around her neck and kissed the crown of her head. He was about to look away when she met his gaze. Held it for a second too long. She smirked and there was something in it, something reciprocal, some kind of complicity.

He decided against the beer. He needed to talk to Meg.

Megan was still outside with the *artist* from Olwen's new school, who was telling her that he'd love to paint her sometime. 'Oh, come *on*,' Geth muttered. 'Meg,' he said, putting his hands firmly on her shoulders, 'I need a word. Sorry, mate.'

'What are you doing?' she hissed as he steered her away.

'Rescuing you. I'm fucked.'

'Already? We've only been here for, like, an hour.'

'No, not fucked like that. Head-fucked. I'm in love with Olwen.'

Meg stopped allowing herself to be steered. '*Olwen?* Gethin, don't be daft.'

He ground his forehead into his palm. 'Meg, have you *seen* her?'

'Yes, I've seen her. She's still a complete knob.'

Megan had hated Taliesin's sister ever since she had corrected her pronunciation of the painter that she was doing her GCSE art project on – in front of Margot. Some dead

French guy who liked ballerinas and whose name, apparently, did not rhyme with Las Vegas.

She was laughing at him. 'Oh, Geth. Hun. Come on.'

'I'm fucked.'

'Geth, no offence, but Olwen Yates would never get with you. She thinks she's it. She thinks she's better than us. Forget about it.'

He pushed his knuckles into his eyes.

She sighed. 'You know who you need? Chris Eds.'

'What?'

'Come on, Gethin. It's New Year's Eve. Let's go find Chris.'

In the living room, a snatch of the Radio One jingle played between the songs that Taliesin had pirated for his CD. Once they'd established that Chris – and the pills – were no longer in there, Gethin wanted to get out as quickly as possible. He didn't need to see the girls dancing to Erykah Badu. He was in love with Olwen, he was fucked.

Meg followed him up the carpeted stairs and through the crowd of people queuing for the bathroom.

'Try Tal's room,' she said, and when that was empty, 'His mum and dad's?'

Margot and David's room was a place where neither of them had really ever spent any time, but they knew from the occasional forbidden glimpse that it was impressive – an attic conversion with an en-suite bathroom, like parents had on American TV shows. They made their way up the tiny staircase. The door was shut. Megan pushed it soundlessly, and both of them saw it at the same time. Directly across the room, in the doorway of the infamous en-suite, Chris Eds was leaning on the bathtub with his eyes closed in pleasure. His jeans were around his ankles, and Taliesin was kneeling on the floor in front of him.

'Oh my—'

Megan dug her nails into Gethin's arm and dragged him back down the stairs. On the bottom step, she pulled them both down to a seat. The two of them sat in silence for a handful of endless seconds.

'We haven't seen *anything*, Gethin,' she said, finally.

'Meg—'

'If he wants to talk about it, he'll talk about it. And for now, we're staying here till they come down.'

Gethin swore and leant his head against the banister.

'And for fuck's sake, act normal when they come.'

'Wish we had something to drink.'

Megan smiled. 'I thought you were already drunk on love after your little scene with Juliet in the kitchen.'

'You didn't see how she looked at me, Meg. There was something between us, I swear down.'

Geth thought about her eyes again. He wasn't an idiot; he wasn't soft; it wasn't like the rest of the room *melted away* or whatever – although it did, it definitely did. But there had been something implicit in the way she'd looked at him. He thought about it and shuddered, like an old car when the key turns in the ignition.

1998

'Savage Garden? No fucking chance.'

'It's a mixtape. There are other songs.'

It was June and they were free. They'd done their final exam the week before, and Gethin wasn't starting on the building site until the end of July. The summer – maybe because Meg kept insisting on framing it as such – felt significant. Taliesin was moving to London for university in September. Meg was going to do Art Foundation in Wrecsam, and Gethin was placating his newly ambitious mother, assuring her that he would apply to uni next year. He was starting to think he should never have gone to Sixth Form in the first place. It had given Ffion all sorts of ideas about what she'd started calling his 'future'.

He leant forward in the passenger seat to fast-forward the cassette. Megan slapped his hand away, 'You don't have to come with me, you know. You could always get the bus. You'd get there tomorrow.'

He put the hand in question on her thigh and gave it a squeeze.

'Don't get me started, Geth.'

He winked at her. 'Can I smoke?'

'No, you cannot smoke in my car.'

'It's not your car, it's your brother's.'

She pretended to glare at him.

'*Iesu mawr.* I never thought when you got your licence you'd be such a fascist about it.'

She shook her head at the extract of her reflection in the rear-view mirror – she'd been doing her make-up –

ridiculous, Geth thought, considering they were just going up to Coed-y-Grug for a bloody swim. She was smiling. 'You're pushing it, Geth,' she said, putting the car into gear and backing out of the estate.

Once they got out of town and on to the S-bends he couldn't help himself. 'You could be doing at least fifty here, Meg. Come on, girl, get your toe down.'

She pursed her lips. 'Last time I checked I was the one with the driver's licence and you were the one that failed.'

He flinched. 'Well harsh.' Geth was still smarting from his recent failure to acquire a licence. He had learnt to drive on the farm as soon as he could reach the pedals of the tractor. It was offensive to him that he'd even had to take a test. 'The guy was a racist.'

'A racist?' Meg repeated.

'I asked him if we could do the test in Cymraeg.'

'You didn't.'

'I did. I should write a letter to *Cymdeithas yr Iaith*.'

'Gethin, you speak English. We're speaking English to each other right now.'

'Ah *bechod*. A little *Saesnes* like you could never understand our plight.'

'Don't you dare call me English, Gethin.'

He smirked. It was painful to him to be driven around by Megan.

'Anyway. You failed because you're a cocky shit who wasn't using his mirrors and went straight from fourth to first at a junction.'

He put his foot up on the dashboard. 'Please tell me you're gonna have the balls to overtake that tractor that's just pulled out from McCarter's, at least?'

She squinted at the road ahead of them. 'Isn't that Iestyn?'

'Oh, fuck's sake. Well, he's never gonna pull over, so

66

you're gonna have to pass him at some point or we'll be doing twenty all the way.'

Megan frowned. She wound the window down and performed relaxation. The farmers were spreading muck, and the air stank. Iestyn didn't pull over. He didn't believe in taking mercy on nervous drivers – he'd be enjoying himself. Gethin sank into his seat when they finally made the turning for Tawelfan.

'Are you hiding from him?'

'No,' he lied.

'Oh. Great.' Megan muttered as they rounded the copper beeches and the house came into view. 'She's back, then.'

Gethin sat up. The gravel crunched under the wheels of the car. Olwen was lying in the hammock strung up between the two horse chestnuts in the driveway. She was reading a novel, with one arm slung over her face against the glare of the morning sun. She was in a bikini. He could barely make out her body, sunk as it was in the harness of thick, red cotton, but the implication of its existence, concealed in the folds of the hammock, disrupted the rhythms of his body – his breath, the thud of blood through his veins.

'Oh, stop perving on her.' Megan turned off the ignition. 'God, she's such an attention seeker. Imagine if the bin men saw her.'

'The bin men don't come on the weekend.'

'Of course you're making excuses for her. As if she hasn't seen us.'

When Megan got out of the car she made an effort to slam the door loudly. Olwen let her arm drop in a smooth, languid motion and she picked up the sarong that was trailing the grass underneath her. She didn't deign to raise her eyes. The morning felt newly charged.

'Hiya,' Megan sang as they approached the porch.

Olwen sat up. She pushed her plastic, tortoiseshell sunglasses up the maddeningly perfect slope of her nose and into her mass of dark blonde hair. She looked older again than she had done on New Year's Eve. Her tanned skin gleamed with sun cream and Gethin imagined the softness of it underneath his hands. He blinked to try to dispel the thought. This was Taliesin's sister and, as Meg liked to remind him, he didn't have a chance in hell.

'You not cold?' Megan said.

'Hardly. It's gonna be boiling by midday.' Her voice was a tone lower. Smoother.

Gethin said, 'You could come with us if you want. Up to Coed-y-Grug. We're gonna go swim in the lake.'

'Is Tal inside?' Megan said.

'What's Coed-y-Grug?'

'It's that private woods just outside the village with that weird house. My mam looks after it. There's a lake and stuff. We've been going up there all summer.'

'Private, as in you're not supposed to go there?'

This was too easy. He smirked. 'Why? You scared of getting in trouble?'

'Oh, please.'

'I'm gonna go find Tal,' Meg said.

'I'll get him. I need to go get my shoes,' Olwen said.

'You should probably get more than your shoes. It's not that private.'

She smiled. 'God, Megan, don't be such a prude. It's summer.' She said 'Megan' the English way; swallowed the 'a'.

When she'd disappeared into the house, Meg said, 'I can't believe you. Men are idiots.'

'What?'

68

'Oh, come on, Gethin, put your tongue back in your mouth.'

'I'm just being nice. She's probably lonely being back.'

'She's completely up herself.'

'Yeah, well. Who can blame her?'

Megan rolled her eyes. 'Can you still show us the surprise, though? If she comes?'

Geth felt the weight of the keys in the pocket of his jeans. 'Of course. It's Tal's sister. She's cool.'

He'd got the key to Tŷ Gwydr copied about a month before he'd decided to take the others there, and he'd been up to the house already, several times, on his own. He'd been fascinated by it since he was a child. Before he'd adopted default adolescent surliness, he used to beg Ffion to let him go up with her. The sheets of glass, and the boxiness of it, and the strange, sparse, wooden interior, and the way everything within was green-filtered, arboreal, became grafted on to his subconscious; would resurface in dreams. In May, his mother had gone on a package holiday to Turkey with a boyfriend who, at that time, had looked like he might become a permanent fixture. Mike: recently divorced, flashy, and new to the area from the Wirral. Did some non-job that Gethin didn't understand. Drove a soft-top BMW Z3 with a personalised number plate that was reaching. It was thanks to Mike and his glitzy holidays abroad that Geth had got his hands on the key and, without realising the significance of it at the time, had created a new layer of habit and meaning in his life.

Because she was there that day, and because her presence took on such significant proportions in his memory of the event, the idea of Olwen became associated with the house in the way that certain odours become associated with a place, or with a season – the way, for example, that the smell of the wild garlic on the forest road from town to Llanelgan was so fused to the feeling of that time of year, to the incandescent greenness of it.

Taliesin had called shotgun and Geth had happily obliged so that he could sit in the backseat with Olwen. Tŷ Gwydr was only a couple of miles out of the village. They didn't need to drive, but driving was still a novelty, so they did. Gethin sat there, the hot sun drilling down into the car from the cloudless sky, feeling excruciatingly, headily, aware of his body, of its proximity to Olwen's. He was sure she felt it too. Meg and Tal sat in the front, talking about the songs that came on the radio, about a geography teacher who had apparently got with a girl from the year below. 'He's always been dodgy,' Geth heard Megan say, as if through a film of glass. He felt like they were in a different car. He let his gaze slide down from the window, where he'd fixed it since they'd pulled out of the drive, to Olwen's bare, tanned thighs on the seat next to him. She had a pair of moles on each one, just below the hem of her shorts. He felt the pressure of her eyes on him and when he looked up and met them, she blinked and looked away, and he knew that she was embarrassed at having been caught. There we go then. He loved this part. He smirked, and looking straight in front of him, at a segment of Taliesin's neck through the gap in the headrest, he let his hand fall, the tips of his fingers grazing her skin. She started but she didn't move, and so he ran his thumb along the frayed, denim seam, increased the pressure of his fingertips. He became aware of the fact that her breathing had become audible, and of the heat collecting right through him. He risked looking directly at her; her lips were slightly parted, and her slender neck and shoulders were very straight, but trembling, so slightly it was barely perceptible, and he thought that it was probably more that he could feel it where his hand was touching her, rather than see it. She closed her eyes and let her head rest on the seat, and he watched the bow of her clavicle rise and fall as she breathed, and he knew he should stop, because he was hard, and they weren't far, but he also couldn't think straight, and he could see, when he looked down, that her own fingertips were pressing into the burred fabric of the car seat.

'*Gethin?*'

He snatched his hand away. Megan caught his eye in the rear-view mirror and he was relieved that she was still too nervous a driver to turn around.

'I *said*, did you ever tell Tal about what Mr Parton said to that girl in Danny's year? About his wife being a psycho?'

Olwen crossed her legs and cleared her throat, and Gethin took his rucksack from the footwell and placed it strategically on his lap. As they pulled into the lay-by he tried to think of Mr Parton, but given that Mr Parton was now associated with sex, that didn't really improve the situation. Geography. Oxbow lakes. Truncated spurs. Why did *truncated spurs* sound like something transgressive?

'So nobody lives here then?' Olwen asked as she climbed over the high fence, and he wished that she wasn't quite so capable so that he could gallantly offer to give her a hand. He followed her, passing the crate of Stella over first.

'Nah, not for donkey's years. It's some rich English family who lived here in like, the Victorian times.'

'The house is that old?'

'No, as in, in Llanelgan. They just own a shitload of the land around here still. House is dead modern, you'll see.' He landed on the other side of the fence. The ground was springy with damp bark and moss.

'Where do they live now?'

'Fuck knows. They must be minted to just have an empty house. They don't even use it for holidays. It's like they've forgotten about it.'

Olwen's nose wrinkled. 'I mean, who would? Want to live around here.'

'Fucking hell. It's not that bad, you know.'

'You couldn't pay me to stay here after school.'

The others were far enough ahead of them to have become inaudible other than the odd stray laugh carrying through the trees.

'God, you're a right drama queen, aren't you?' He smiled, to communicate that he was teasing her, even if he did actually mean what he was saying. He lingered by the fence, encouraging the distance between them and the others. He felt pleasantly tense with anticipation, with the possibility of humiliation.

'Are you coming then?' she asked.

He didn't break eye contact or say anything. He leant back on the fencepost.

'What?' she said.

'Come here.'

She tried to hide her embarrassment with indignation. She looked at the floor, her hand rose automatically to her forehead. 'What?'

'Come on, come here.'

'Why?'

'Why do you think?'

She performed an exhale of incredulity. From further down the track, Megan called his name, and then hers.

'They'll come back and find us in a minute,' he said. One of the other lads in his year had told him once that he was a right cocky shit with girls. The comment had stayed with him – he thought about it sometimes when he needed a boost. He jerked his head. 'Come on.'

She chanced a precautionary look behind her and then stepped towards him, her eyes still full of overstated defiance.

'That was nice before, in the car,' he said, as he reached out for her hand and pulled her towards him. He could feel the warmth of her body, the shape of it against his. Smell the sun cream, and the smell of sun on her skin, in her hair. He realised – he would have been embarrassed had he room for any other sensation – that he was shaking. He took her face in his hands, pressed his thumb into the blade of her cheekbone, and although it felt like a line, and probably sounded like one too, he told her that she was beautiful before he kissed her. She reciprocated, and he felt her body loosen in his, felt her palm on his chest as if to steady herself. He ran his hands through her thick hair, down the curve of her neck and along her spine. She pressed herself to him harder and he felt the pressure of her other hand at the nape of his neck. It had never been like this before, this degree of intensity was something new, and he tried to keep a hold of himself, to hold his nerve. He moved his fingers under the hem of her shorts, between her legs. The soft skin where her thighs joined her underwear was wet. He prised at the elastic with his fingertips, heard himself sigh, *fuck*, as he pushed them under the cotton, felt her respond, felt her body convulse as he touched her, heard her own sigh, and then, after a second, felt the hand that was touching his chest press harder and turn into a push.

'I shouldn't,' she said to the ground as she stepped away. 'I'm kind of involved with someone.'

He blinked. It was the sort of thing he'd usually take in his stride – it's not like they were married. But even he could hear how crushed he sounded when, despite himself, he said, 'You serious?'

The others were already waiting for them by the lake. 'You two took your time,' Megan smirked.

'*Iesu ffocen mawr.* Drop it, Meg, all right?'

A few weeks after that, he was sitting with Taliesin on the jetty at Tŷ Gwydr. It was too cold to swim; jumper weather again. Evening, and the air was bright with a fine-grain dampness, as if it might rain. Taliesin was rolling a joint. They'd got cocky by then. They were up at the house all the time. Neither of them spoke. Geth was thinking about Olwen again. He had spent so much time contemplating what hadn't happened with her that the memory of it had gained the substance of a recorded event. It was something he could return to like an old VCR, and each time, a new detail emerged with which he could torture himself.

'You know what your sister said to me?' he said. 'She said you couldn't pay her to stay around here.'

Taliesin inclined his head judiciously.

'What? Do you think that, too?'

Taliesin didn't reply. He concentrated harder on distributing the tangle of tobacco along the length of the Rizla. Gethin watched his pale, elegant fingers work, fingers that could prise music out of the indecipherable strings of a cello, but that didn't even know how to change the inner tube on his bike. He felt angry at him all of a sudden, personally slighted by the difference in their ambition.

'You two can be right fucking snobs when you want to be, can't you?'

Taliesin flinched. He sealed the joint and tapped the edge of it on the wooden boards of the jetty. Gethin pinched the bridge of his nose and felt ashamed.

'You know I can't stay around here, Geth. You know it's different for me, don't you?'

Gethin thought about the en-suite bathroom on New Year's Eve, Chris Eds leaning back on the tub. 'Yeah. I guess so. Sorry.'

1999

WHEN GETH announced to his mother that he was taking a chainsaw course at the local agricultural college, she squinted as if she hadn't quite caught what he had said.

'You're taking the piss, I hope?' She smoothed her hands down on her jeans, sat opposite him at the kitchen table and reached for the ashtray. 'Agricultural college.'

Geth shrugged, fixed his gaze on the lottery ticket tacked to the fridge and ran his tongue along his teeth.

'What was the point of all that school?'

He read Danny's birthday and then his own. Ffion had used the same numbers every week since John Major had licensed the lottery.

'Chainsaw course.' She swallowed. 'Right. I see. You wanna be like cousin Alun or something? Aiming really high there, Geth.'

'What's wrong with Alun?'

'Oh, come on, love. There's nothing wrong with Alun. I just thought . . .' She reached across the table and covered his hands with hers, 'I just thought you'd want to do something different, y'know? You're so bright.'

It had been a year now since Geth had finished school; twelve months almost that he'd been working on the building site, making vague noises about 'saving money to go travelling'. He'd read *The Beach* instead of revising for his English A level, and he had woolly ideas about going to Thailand, or somewhere like that. He imagined himself on a motorbike hightailing through streets teeming with people, a kaleidoscope of neon and smoke and straw and bodies. He imagined gurning his face off at an all-night beach party, chemical serotonin making his blood blaze. He imagined sun-glittered, lapis stretches of water and a sexy French girl with long, slim legs, tanned and trailed with henna. Or Olwen – he could wait for her; he had all the time in the world. He was nineteen – he wasn't in a hurry to do much of anything.

He hadn't applied for university like he'd told his mother he would. He couldn't really see the point of it. The impression that he'd got when he'd gone to visit Tal was that uni was undoubtedly an opportunity to doss, but one that was contingent on talking a lot of bullshit with a lot of pretentious wankers and regularly turning in pointless, arbitrary work. He liked reading, but Sixth Form had taught him that he didn't like it when it was prescribed. He didn't want to spend his days sitting at a desk in a single room in Manchester, Leeds or Cardiff. He wanted to make things and build things, or at least destroy things. He wanted to use his body. Someone like Margot Yates would say that he was *elementally physical*. He couldn't detach himself from his physicality. He had too much energy.

On Fridays, he drove out to Chester, where Olwen went to school. She boarded during the week, and when he'd finished work at half four he'd go straight there to pick her up. The first time he'd done it he'd felt guilty, like he was lurking, like he wasn't allowed to be there. Even though the girls were barely two years younger than him, he'd felt like a dirty old man, waiting for her at the school gates in his work boots and his cement-crusted jeans, smoking a fag, leaning against the car. It was something about their posh uniform. He watched the parade of girls, in their green kilts and knee socks as they filed out of the school gates, and he felt like a creep. He saw them eyeing him right back, though. He watched their shy eyes brush his shoulders and the arms that, after a year on the site, strained against his rolled-up T-shirt sleeves. He watched the more confident ones petition him with direct, challenging eye contact. It was the kind of thing that would have turned his head a year ago, but a lot had changed since everything had started with Olwen. The lads at work said he was whipped. He couldn't give a flying fuck what they thought.

It had begun just after Tal had left. He'd given Olwen a lift up to the village – he'd found her walking up from town on her own. She must have had a death wish, on that bit of road. He hadn't seen her since the summer, and honestly, he was still smarting. When it did happen, he wasn't surprised; there'd always been something between the two of them.

They'd kept it secret for the first few months. She was still with that lad, she'd said – and then she wasn't sure. He didn't want to push her, but all the same, it did feel pretty weird, dropping her off before the turning, meeting her at Tŷ Gwydr, where they knew that they wouldn't get caught. It felt good now to just be normal about it. All that sneaking around should have been exciting, but there was something wrong with it. It just didn't sit right.

Olwen's school didn't look like the one in town that he and Tal had gone to – the one that the new version of Tal had fictionalised to all his London friends as something that had been endured; something that had given him man-of-the-people credentials, a veritable, real life Jarvis Cocker. Olwen's school gates were folded arms of spindly iron, complete with Latin motto and crest. She moved through them gracefully, with ease, and when she spotted him, she flashed a row of beautiful white teeth, and peeled off from her group of friends. He didn't know any of them, and neither of them was particularly inclined to change that.

'You smell good,' she whispered in his ear, taking the lobe between her teeth, grazing it with her tongue. 'You smell like work.' She pushed her body against him and his into the car door. He walked his fingers up the back of her thigh and under her school skirt and she batted away his hand with a glint in her eye. She kissed him.

'Come on,' she said. 'Let's go. It's the weekend!'

She flopped down on to the passenger seat and glanced up to the rear-view mirror to check her reflection. 'Can we go the old way?' she asked. Olwen always wanted to go the old way, over the bracing ascent and plunge of the mountain pass. The dual carriageway was prim and dull and efficient. The pass was spine tingling. She rooted around for a cigarette in the glove compartment and watched her reflection light it and exhale languorously. Geth let his left-hand fall on to her bare thigh as he started the car. Her body hummed under his rough palm.

'Oh, no, not this tape again.' She wrinkled her nose and leant forward to eject the Led Zeppelin cassette. 'Let's listen to Neil Young.'

She liked sad songwriters with fragile voices on the cusp of disintegration. Years later, he would think that there was something parasitic about it, that it was as if she siphoned up all of her staggering robustness from the dwindling forces of others. It was a hot afternoon in May, the sky an opaque, uninterrupted blue. They drove with the windows down and Neil Young getting all electric; they crossed the border and climbed up off the main road to where it became a single-track lane orbiting the mountain. Light streamed down the valley and, higher up, the ground was bald, scorched with dry, yellow gorse on hot afternoons and then softened blue and lilac with the heather at night. Wind-stunned sheep milled about blindly on pin legs, and dry-stone walls grafted the land. A couple of the peaks around here were embroidered with the foundations of Celtic hill forts. It was a primal place; a place of vertiginous elevation and tangible magic.

'Go faster,' she said. He accelerated, tearing along the sweeping, horseshoe contour of the land, the wind in turn tearing through the open windows of the car, Neil Young's voice consumed by it, and then by the growl of the engine as Geth shifted into second. The tips of Olwen's long fingers blanched as she dug them into his leg. He laughed and gently pressed the pedal. 'Slow now,' she exhaled. Her chest rose and fell gently and Geth wanted to touch her heart through the thin cotton of her school shirt.

'Let's go to Tŷ Gwydr,' he said, suddenly.

The hoarse voice of the wind dropped with the speed, and the music swelled in the space it left behind. Olwen nodded. At the bottom of the old track, where the light was tempered and filtered through the trees, Geth took the hairpin bend that led to the winding road up to Llanelgan and, just before the village, he hung a left for Coed-y-Grug.

In what they pretended was their living room at Tŷ Gwydr, she unbuttoned her school shirt. Her ease with her own physicality had astonished him at first. The other girls that he'd slept with had all been such anxious inhabitants of their bodies. They did everything they could to manipulate them. Olwen didn't care if a few dark hairs trailed out of the seam of her knickers. She didn't care if she hadn't shaved her legs, or if that position made her stomach look anything other than flat. Her self-confidence was staggering.

Afterwards she lay on her back on the parquet, closing her eyes against the sun.

'Are we gonna try and go to that party tonight?'

A rumour had been circulating around town that a rave was being organised up in the woods a bit further along towards the coast.

'If you want. Why not?'

All he really wanted to do was to spend the night at Tŷ Gwydr. To swim a little until the evening made the water sting; to fuck Olwen, to press her into the woodland floor on the bank of the lake and feel her nails make crescents beneath his shoulder blades; to fall asleep in the house, and to be woken up by the first glisk of sunrise. To pretend that this was all his.

In the car on the way back to her parents' house, he told her about the chainsaw course.

'That's cool,' she said, and shrugged. 'You should do whatever makes you happy.'

Proximity to Olwen's boundless faith in both Freedom and Happiness made Geth feel the same way. He felt glad that he had told her; the conversation with his mother had made him question his decision and feel as if his future was a long, clinical, white corridor with a squeaky laminate floor and ugly, electric lights.

Olwen trailed a hand out of the window. 'You know, my English teacher told me today that I should apply for Oxford.'

He'd wanted to talk to her more about the agricultural college, but he let it slide and they talked about Oxford instead.

2016

ALTHOUGH GETH didn't have any work at that point, he still woke up early out of habit. The past year or two had been rough. Harvesters and processors were starting to take over all the contracts, and the skidder teams couldn't compete for tenders with machines. He'd finished his last job up at Bryn Glas and had been 'between jobs' now for just over a fortnight. It was before six o'clock when he opened his eyes. He thought about going back to sleep, but the glare of the rising sun was so insistent that he got out of bed, pulled on a pair of boxers, and went to put the kettle on. It was good to wake up early. The week after he'd found out they were selling Tŷ Gwydr he'd slept in until one o'clock every day, because he really had nothing to wake up for now.

The kettle boiled. He yawned and dropped a teabag into his favourite mug. He'd go for a run. When he finished his tea he'd put on his trainers and do a long run, up to Llanelgan maybe, a loop of the woods, a good 15k. Enough to obliterate everything he was thinking about. While the tea was steeping, he stuck the television on. Crappy little thing that he'd taken from his mam's when she died. An image appeared on the screen: Big Ben in the background, and the white-haired television presenter looking solemnly at the audience. He clasped his hands and eyed the camera earnestly. He said, '. . . that Britain has taken the decision to leave the European Union.'

A couple of days later when he was in the village, Gethin went to Eryl Lloyd's to buy some eggs. Eryl was out in the yard, changing a tyre on a trailer. His hands were black with oil and he wiped them on his boiler suit when he stood up to talk to Geth.

'Seen the news, then?' he said.

'Can't avoid it, can you? All they're blydi talking about.'

Eryl nodded. He grinned. 'That'll show David fucking Cameron, won't it? Wiped the grin off his blydi face. Smug git.'

Gethin wasn't particularly fussed either way. He was a political nihilist. It was a miracle he'd even gone to vote. Megan had made him do it, and once again it'd been proven that nothing he did made any difference to anything anyway. He shrugged. 'European Union. Westminster. Probably nothing'll change anyway.'

His next job wasn't until mid-way through July. He had other things to think about.

1998–2000

ABOUT A FORTNIGHT after they'd first got together, Geth and Olwen had gone and spent a Saturday on Ynys Môn. They were driving home late in the evening when they passed the turning to Traeth Llanddwyn and Olwen cried, 'I know this beach! Newborough Warren! We used to come here when Tal and I were little. Pull over!'

It was early October, cold out, and they had to walk right the way through the woods to get to the beach. 'You're fucking mental,' he said. 'It's freezing.'

'I'm impulsive,' she said, tossing her hair over her shoulder for effect. 'And we're going all the way out to St Dwynwen's church, by the way.'

'Are we fuck. And how do you know about Santes Dwynwen anyway?'

She was talking about the patron saint of love whose ruined church gave the beach its name. He'd learnt about her in primary school, where he'd read about most of the Welsh folktales he still remembered. He didn't think they would have known about that kind of thing in the type of school Olwen had gone to.

She shrugged. 'I was very into myths and legends when I was a kid. I pretty much thought I was a witch.'

The Irish Sea was a vast slab of onyx marbled with moon white. Under their bare feet, the sand was cool and lilac-grey and endless, the tide on its way out. The wind was viscid with salt and, up in the dunes, Geth wished he'd had the foresight to grab the old blanket he had stashed in the boot of his car. It had seemed only chivalrous that he should be the one to lie down on the ground (the marram grass jagging the powder-fine sand), and he'd wanted to see her, to look at the silver tint of her skin in the moonlight and see the network of stars, lucid in the sky behind her. He tried to keep his eyes open. He felt incandescent with sensation, with the audible drag of the tide, the novel texture of her hair as he held her head close to his, her skin.

Looking out beyond the ashy blur of the sea, she said, 'Imagine that under that sea there's a whole drowned island.'

'You what?'

'Cantre'r Gwaelod.'

'God, listen to Little Miss *Mabinogion*. Here I was, thinking you were English.'

Cantre'r Gwaelod was an island that had supposedly sunk into the Irish Sea at Cardigan Bay, so admittedly her geography was a little off. It had been low-lying and depended on a series of floodgates to stop the sea from reclaiming it. One night, the gatekeeper had got so drunk he'd forgotten to close the gates, and the island and everyone on it was drowned. When Geth was a kid, his muscle memory used to confuse it with Capel Celyn, the village that the English flooded in the sixties to make a reservoir for Liverpool.

'I love the part about how when there's danger the old church bells still ring,' she said.

Geth felt like his body was a belltower. A hollow steeple reverberating.

Sometimes he used to try to convince her to go and drink a half with him at the Glan Llyn. The pub was built a good decade before the chapel, making it the oldest building in Llanelgan. It was a rupture in the snake of grey pebble-dash that formed the architectural spine of the village – a squat block of thick stone with a Welsh slate roof, and tiny, warped windows, gridded with diamonds that swallowed the light before it could get inside. Usually, Olwen said something about having 'little desire to get drunk with a bunch of farmers,' and they'd end up going to Tŷ Gwydr or Tawelfan instead.

The one occasion that she did give in happened at the end of the following May, seven or eight months in. It was the beginning of Summer League season and the days were long. When the ref called full-time the sky above the pitch was rinsed out pink and stippled with the black ink-spots of the bats. Geth had scored against Llandyrnog in the eighty-seventh minute of the match and adrenaline had made him unusually defiant. He was surprised when she didn't even protest about going to the Glanny, just shrugged and said, 'Why not?' as if she hadn't spent every other week calling it 'the place where hope goes to die'. She insisted that he went in first. He pushed the heavy oak door, and immediately the air was so solid with the thick smog of cigarette smoke that it felt sticky. He saw Olwen touch her hair and he felt a sting of irritation, because she was an enthusiastic smoker in contexts where the habit was picturesque. She looked down at the cheap carpet rather than making eye contact with the old timers propped up at the bar, and it occurred to him then that maybe she was nervous. Maybe she could feel how much she didn't belong. He put his arm around her.

He saw his brother coming out of the gents, and raised his free hand to greet him. Danny nodded, gave Olwen the once-over, and then leant over the bar to order two more pints. Geth said, 'You've met Dan before, haven't you?' He didn't notice Iestyn at first, folded over the pool table like an opening hinge, about to take a shot. Olwen clocked him, though.

86

'Oh, good,' she said flatly, 'a family reunion.'

'Y'right, Danny?' Gethin said in English, to signal to his brother that Olwen couldn't speak Welsh.

'Ite la. You win against Dyrni?'

'Three-two, thanks to yours truly.'

Danny handed him a pint and for a second, a smile split his face. He recovered himself. 'Fair dos, though, Dyrni have always been pretty shit, like, haven't they?'

Since Danny had left home, he no longer had the power to wind Gethin up. He let the comment slide and passed the second pint to Olwen.

'Who's this, then?' Danny said.

'You know Olwen already.' He wasn't sure if Danny was being discreetly hostile or if he genuinely didn't recognise her. She'd lived in Llanelgan all her life, but had lived like a drop of oil skimming the surface of water.

'What happened to Megan?' Danny asked in Welsh.

Gethin watched Olwen's shoulders tense. 'Meg's not my girlfriend,' he replied in English.

'Yeah. Dunno why. She's fit. Always did think you two were weird. I don't think I've ever managed to be proper mates with a girl who I haven't—'

'Remember my friend Tal? Olwen's his sister.'

Danny scrutinised her with his mouth open and his eyes narrowed. Nodded his head. 'Oh, yeah? Got yourself a posh girl, have you?'

Olwen bristled, but, for once, she didn't come out with any lines about her apparent poverty. She glared at Gethin instead.

'Yeah, I know where you live,' said Danny. 'Your parents are all right, though, aren't they? Didn't your brother used to grow weed in the garden?'

87

Olwen shrugged condescendingly, as if it were deeply uncool to be concerned with such trivialities. 'My parents are fine with that kind of stuff.'

'The law's different for rich English people, Danny, *bach*, isn't it?' The voice, which was Iestyn's, came from behind Gethin's shoulder, along with a sweet fug of stale booze and tobacco.

Olwen stiffened. 'What's that supposed to mean?'

'Ignore him,' Danny said. 'He's shitfaced. He took the day off and went to Chester races with the lads this afternoon.' In Welsh, he told his uncle to be nice, as if he were talking to a three-year-old. Iestyn snorted. He leant harder into Geth, tipping the bar stool forward and only just avoiding pulling it over altogether as he rocked back on his heels.

'Blydi hell, Iestyn, how much you had?'

Iestyn had always been a monumental boozer – it was the stuff of legend. He'd famously got so drunk on his stag do that the other lads had driven him out to Holyhead and put him on the last ferry. He'd woken up in Dublin and had missed his own wedding. He detached himself from the stool and went and stood beside Olwen. His movements were loose and there was a glint of charming unpredictability in his eyes. He was wearing his good suit, with the tie swinging around his collar, open enough to see the dull silver chain underneath. His face was ruddy. He surged forward suddenly, making a grab for Gethin's glass, and when he'd taken a long swig, he said, 'Say what you want, lads, but I'll tell you something for nothing – I wouldn't have had all the trouble I had back in the day if I'd had a nice little Princess Diana accent like this one.'

'Oh, please,' Olwen said.

'You don't know the last thing about it, love.'

Danny shook his head indulgently and stood up to get his uncle a glass of water. 'Easy.'

'When they took me in, I was about, *duw*,' Iestyn squinted at Gethin, 'your age? Give or take? They got me for selling mushrooms, didn't they?'

Olwen rolled her eyes and opened her mouth to speak but Gethin put his hand on her knee to stop her. He tried not to look too encouraging in case Iestyn twigged that this information was new. 'Yeah,' he said, making his voice as cool as possible.

By now Iestyn had sat down on Danny's vacant stool. He was swaying gently from side to side, but his voice was calmer.

'Go on.'

He smiled wryly. 'I was quite the *entrepreneurial* type, me, and you've seen up at Bryn Hendre, they're all over the place, aren't they?'

Geth, who was rarely at the farm these days, registered this piece of information for future use.

'Didn't even take them myself. Hippy nonsense, all that. Not for me, thanks. Sold them to your parents once or twice mind, when they first got here.' He pointed at Olwen. 'For all I know, it might have been them who turned me in.'

'Sure.'

Iestyn pushed his tongue into his cheek like a grumpy teenager. 'Anyway, they had nothing on me. I'd barely sold any and it's not my fault they're on our land, is it? They're all over the place round here. Nature, isn't it? There was nothing they could do in the end, but they tried. And I had a very fucking nasty run-in with the police, didn't I?'

'What, and you think if I got caught selling drugs I'd get away with it because I say *baath*?' Olwen said.

89

'Yes – for starters. But more importantly, they wouldn't have tried to blackmail you like they tried with me.'

'You what?' Geth whispered. 'They tried to blackmail you?'

His uncle, who'd always liked an audience, visibly shimmered with pride. He lowered his voice. 'You know, Geth, when I was a kid, I got a little bit involved with Cymdeithas, went on a couple of protests . . .'

'What's Cymdeithas?' Olwen said.

'Hissht,' Iestyn pressed his index finger to his lips. 'Welsh Language Society. I was small fry. Went to a few meetings when I was a teenager. Hardly anything. Wasn't my cup of tea at all in the end. They were all proper radicals, like – dead left, talking about their *comrades in South America and Belfast*, or whatever, women's lib, anti-colonialism, all that nonsense.'

Olwen smirked.

'But the police didn't know that, did they? Tell you what, though, they must have had me on some kind of list somewhere, because when I was taken in for questioning some bloke turns up from *Special Branch* . . .'

Geth whistled.

'You know what it was like back then, with *llosgi tai haf* and everything. The arsons,' he said to Olwen. 'Special Branch type wanted me to fucking snitch for him, didn't he? Made all sort of threats. Said I could be in jail for seven years. Haf was pregnant with Sali, at the time.' He shook his head. 'It was a nightmare.'

'So what did you do?'

'Well,' he said, 'those WRSM and Cymdeithas types might have all been fucking communists, but I wasn't gonna snitch on them to the *Saeson,* was I?'

Danny appeared at that moment, with a pint glass full of water in his hand. 'Here,' he said, 'drink this. You'll thank me when your alarm goes off for milking tomorrow morning.'

Iestyn sat back and cleared his throat. He took the glass from his nephew and took a long gulp of water.

'Has he been behaving himself?' Danny said to Olwen.

She raised her eyebrows. 'He's quite the storyteller, isn't he?'

When they left the pub, the vivid apricot of the dusk had thinned out into pale, blue iridescence.

'How fucking mental was that?' Gethin said the moment they were out of the pub, speaking as if there were a full stop between each word.

'Oh, come on. You didn't really believe him, did you?'

'Well, yeah. Of course I believed him. Why wouldn't I?'

She squeezed his hand. 'Someone's been watching too many cop movies.'

He flinched.

'Geth, come on. You think your uncle had a run-in with Serpico at the police station in town? You saw him – he could hardly stand up straight, bless him. He was having you on. He was loving it – he was, like . . . *glowing* with the attention. It was almost sweet, I guess.'

Geth didn't say anything. The two of them walked on in the direction of her parents' house.

'I mean, come on. You really think my mum and dad bought 'shrooms off him? They could more than happily sort themselves out. And it's not even illegal to sell them fresh. Are you honestly telling me that he went round to my mum and dad's and brewed up some tea for them? Come on.' She stopped by a pull-in and gestured at a farm gate.

'Shall we cut through the field here?' Without waiting for an answer, she climbed over. She blew a strand of hair out her face. 'I'm sure Special Branch have bigger fish to fry than your uncle, no offence.'

At Christmas, when she dumped him for the boyfriend of her best friend – a boy from her school who was apparently 'a very talented artist' and who consequently 'got her' – Geth didn't see her for a few months. It turned out that he had been the only real thing that had rooted her to the place where she had grown up. Her school was a good hour away; her friends all came from there, and 'there' was exciting, with a cinema and bars and places to hang out. She didn't go out in town on Saturday nights, so he didn't see her in the pub or in the one nightclub, a dingy building on the edge of the industrial estate with palm trees painted around the bar and a corrugated iron roof. He ran into her once the next spring, at a party that someone had organised in the woods. She turned up with a bunch of her posh friends – dickheads, obviously. Geth made sure to get with the prettiest one, and he did his best to guarantee that Olwen would see them go off together. When they came back, she grinned at him, her eyes and her teeth glowing in the lilac light.

'Izzy's great, isn't she?' she beamed.

Geth had felt then like he'd wanted to hurt something. He'd clenched his fists and he'd shrugged, and he'd gone back to his car, where he had sat for a few hours until he had felt that he had enough self-possession to drive up to Tŷ Gwydr.

In the summer, he went travelling around South-East Asia. He slept with a lot of girls from all over the world, although none of them was French. He took wild amounts of drugs and he rode motorbikes and drank Chang and picked up a few tattoos. His skin tanned and he grew out his hair for a while. When he came back, he enrolled on the chainsaw course. He knew that the Yateses still lived in the village, and one afternoon, inevitably, he ran into Margot in the supermarket in town. He realised who it was when it was already too late to avoid eye contact and walk in the opposite direction, studying the ingredients of a cereal box with intensity.

'Gethin,' she purred, her voice softened with sincere affection. 'How lovely. Oh, I'm so glad – it's been forever.'

He smiled thinly. 'Hiya, Margot.'

'You look great!' she said, touching his arm. 'How are you? What are you doing these days? I wasn't sure if you were still in town.'

He nodded and sketched a vague, non-committal picture of his life. She was suitably enthusiastic. He managed to somehow enact the basic functions of polite conversation but his head felt as if he had balls of cotton wool stuffed behind his eyes, bulging against the sockets, against his temples, along the bridge of his nose. He managed to ask how her children were doing.

'Oh, they're good, they're good. Well, I mean I barely hear from them of course – they're far too busy to ring home – but I *believe* they're doing well,' she laughed. 'Tal's actually thinking of doing a PhD eventually. Ol's at Oxford . . .'

Margot rattled on about Olwen and about how thoroughly wonderful she was. Geth was good at revealing very little about how he actually felt about anything, and Margot Yates was oblivious to other people most of the time anyway.

93

'She still with that guy then? Will? James?' He hated himself for asking it. He winced inside at his own masochism.

Margot looked at him blankly. 'Will?'

He swallowed and looked at the rows of condiments. 'The artist.'

She wrinkled her nose, and then a visible wave of illumination passed over her features. 'Oh, *Will*. Will, yes of course, oh, poor Will.' She smirked. 'Hardly. Bless him, he really held a candle for her. Oh God, no, she got rid of him after a couple of weeks.' Margot chuckled and looked at him conspiratorially. 'I think frankly, Gethin, the only one who ever gave her a run for her money was you.'

The details of everything blurred and then sharpened for a second, as if he were focusing the lens of a camera. 'Me?' he repeated.

'Of course! She was mad about you – since she was little and you were her older brother's *handsome, broody friend.*'

Gethin felt his jaw clench.

Margot sighed serenely. 'I suppose in the end, though, the two of you just wanted very different things out of life, didn't you?'

2001

'THE REAL THING you've got to watch out for,' Jimmy said, with what Geth would soon discover was his habitual air of authority, 'is the townies. City folk in the woods? Total fucking nightmare. They should have to pass a national intelligence test before they're even allowed in.'

Jimmy was a fan of things like *national intelligence tests*. His politics were confusing and seemed to veer chaotically between total fascism, utopian socialism and then a sort of anarchic rebranding of rugged individualism. They were working Capel Curig way – a good pull from home – and they had started out early, at seven, when the roads were empty and the ground was still gleaming with dew. Dawn was whiting out across the hills. The air smelt of damp moss and sap. They didn't talk while they worked. When they'd arrived in the woodland, Hefin, who drove the skidder tractor and who had given Geth the job, had introduced him to Jimmy, the other chainsaw operator. It was his first real day of work out of college.

'You'll know Gethin Thomas,' Hefin had said, which is what Hefin said to Jimmy whenever he was talking about someone. Hefin presumed that everyone knew everyone. Jimmy, who was English and routinely cynical, would insist that he didn't. He always did.

'Every second bugger in Wales is called Thomas, why should I know this one?'

Hefin muttered an exasperated insult in Welsh under his breath. 'You know Alun Bod? And Iestyn Bryn Hendre? There we go then. Nephew.'

95

Jimmy raised his eyebrows. 'Iestyn?'

Geth detected a glint of judgement, but his new colleague was tactful enough to keep his mouth shut, and after that they didn't talk again, other than the bare minimum required, until they sat down at around half nine for *paned*, their first morning break. It was a cool morning in September. The mist was just starting to thin out and dissipate, and despite the chill, sweat poured down Geth's back and trickled along the edge of his helmet. He put it on the floor at his feet. Jimmy unscrewed the cap of his Thermos and filled it with tea.

'You've always got to keep an eye out for townies. They're like moths to a flame. Flies to horseshit. They're *drawn* to the sound of a chainsaw. You look up and there they are! There's always some moron who has decided that your warning signs don't apply to them, and they come strolling into your area of operation, all *oh what a fabulous job you have . . .*'

Hefin snorted. 'Yeah, right. Too hot in summer and you're covered in blydi flies—'

'Horseflies, midges . . .'

'Freezing in the winter. Then you get soaked when it rains—'

'Or lose a day's work.'

'*Fabulous* my arse. Nothing romantic about this line of work.'

'Then there's the suicides.'

Hefin grimaced in agreement.

'Suicides?'

'Mark my words, lad. You work here as long as us, don't be surprised if you come across some poor bugger who's topped himself.'

'You see some things in the woods.'

'And weirdos too. Remember the army guy, Hef?'

'*Duw anwyl*, he was a fucking creep.'

'Yeah. Right nutter. Some weedy lad in camouflage – setting up tracks and wires, hiding in the undergrowth . . . Basket case.'

'He was *twp*.'

'He was more than blydi *twp*!'

Hefin leant in. 'When the police eventually got on to him they found out he was making weapons in his mam's house. Had a bedroom wall covered with pictures of some girl from his school.' He shuddered. 'There's only one thing to be done to lads like that.' He made scissors with his first two fingers and cut a line through the air in front of Gethin's nose.

'The pervs love the woods,' said Jimmy. 'Watch out.'

As they were going back to work, Jimmy collared him. 'Here, pal,' he said. 'You find any dead trees, you fell them. You fell them and Hef'll drag them out and put them with the others, OK?'

After well over a year on the building site, Geth knew better than to ask questions, and he did as he was told. They were working on first thinnings – young trees, about twenty years old or so and easy to fell. Jimmy had got through about a hundred by the time they finished at half four that afternoon. Geth made just under seventy, and was told with approval that that wasn't half bad for a rookie. At the end of the day, the Englishman sauntered over to the pile of dead trees. Geth was already peeling off his felling gloves.

'Oh, no, you don't, mate, not so fast!' Jimmy gestured at the trees. 'How many of these did you fell today?'

'Two, three.'

'Well. Doesn't your mum want any firewood? You could just about fit a small load in the back of that Fiat.'

Geth swallowed. 'Isn't that stealing?'

Jimmy laughed. 'Gethin, *bach*, everybody takes firewood. Don't you worry about it. You get yourself one of those' – he pointed towards his pickup – 'and you can make yourself a tidy profit selling it.'

The other lads in the woods called him 'the Brigadier'. He was tough, but his swagger was somewhere between a cowboy and Mick Jagger. His vowels were too long. In the morning when he'd pulled up at the gate, Geth had noticed that he had been listening to classical music in his truck.

'Everyone does it, then?'

'Listen, mate, I've got two young kids to feed and bills to pay. Do you know what would happen to these trees if we didn't take them? Fuck all, that's what. The guys up there *managing* everything in their offices? They don't know their arse from their elbow, and you don't even want to know how much they're taking home every month, never mind how much they're probably half-inching on the side. The ones that do know? They turn a blind eye because they know we work bloody hard and we've earned it.'

'Right.'

'Take my advice, kid. You take your wages; buy yourself a few less pints at The Boars at the weekend, or whatever it is you spend your money on. Put a bit aside. You save up for a truck, so you can really start delivering, and it'll be worth it if you're clever.'

'Right,' said Geth again. He paused. 'How much do you charge for a load of firewood then?'

'Forty quid for hardwood around here. Unless you've got some Southern mug, or a tourist. They'll pay anything for firewood. Townies, right?'

Geth pulled his gloves on again. The sweat inside them

had already started to cool. He thought of Taliesin and Olwen's parents.

'Yeah. Townies,' he agreed.

On the way back to town he dropped in at Tŷ Gwydr, where the first of the ash leaves were just starting to rust. From where he lay at the water's edge, he could count several dead trees, not to mention all of the scrub – the hazel, willow and birch – or all of the wind-blown, self-seeded sycamore that could be 'extracted', as Jimmy had put it. He tried to remember if the actual owner of this place had ever even stepped foot on the property in his lifetime.

When he got home later that afternoon, his mother was in the kitchen. She was leaning on the counter, waiting for the kettle to boil. Megan's mother, Jackie, was sitting at the table.

'Y'right, Geth, love?' Jackie cooed as he came in.

'Boots off, Gethin! In fact, can you get all your gear off outside? I don't want you trailing sawdust and dirt around the house, thank you.'

'First day was great, Mam, thanks for asking.'

'Oh, hissht. I was going to ask when you were sat down. *Paned?*' She pointed at the kettle.

'Please.'

'And Jackie brought a cake round, look.'

Geth glanced up at the Victoria sponge on a plate next to the teabags on the counter. 'Thanks, Jackie.'

'*Croeso*, love.'

He left his boots on the little patio and stripped off his felling trousers and his shirt. Jackie wolf-whistled.

'*Gethin*. Go and put some clothes on,' Ffion said in Welsh. Then, in English, 'He's hopeless, Jack, sorry.'

99

'Oh, don't mind me, I'm not complaining. Gareth certainly doesn't look like that any more.'

Geth loped through the kitchen and winked at her.

'*Brysiwch, Gethin!* Clothes!'

When he sat back down at the table, he told his mother and Jackie about his first day, and after a while, he decided to test the water, and delicately manoeuvred the conversation towards the topic of Tŷ Gwydr and the Dalton estate.

'How often do they actually come and visit, Mam? Like when was the last time you saw the old guy?'

'Pfft. *Never.* Well, not for years, anyway. They moved back to London when I was little, and then they used to come in the summer when we were growing up.'

'But he's not been back since?'

'Apparently, he popped up with his kids to show them a couple of years back. The estate got in touch with me afterwards to tell me that Mr Dalton sends his thanks, or whatever. He lives in France, I think. Somewhere abroad.'

'I don't think they've got much interest in coming back to Llanelgan, to be honest,' Jackie drawled, shunting a fag out of her packet of Benson & Hedges. 'Got plenty of money. Houses everywhere.'

'It's a bit weird, though, like . . .' Geth said. 'That they don't even rent it out or do it up as, like, a holiday house or something.'

'Mm. There was some funny business, I think.' Ffion pushed back her chair and began to clear the mugs and plates. 'Your *taid* told me a bit when I started working for them, about how the old man had been mad about the place. He'd really loved it. He built it himself, you know. He was an architect – designed all these modern buildings. He didn't want to leave much, I think. It was more the

American wife who didn't like it here. *To the manor born,* that one, apparently.'

'Well, he's lucky it's not on the Llŷn Peninsula. Would have got burnt down,' Jackie said.

Geth paused a second. Let the information percolate. 'So it's just sitting there?' he said. He reached to take another slice of cake. 'And what about the woods?'

Ffion peered at him. 'What about it?'

'Well. That's just sitting there too. They could make money out of it, couldn't they?'

She pursed her lips. 'They don't need any more money.'

For the first fortnight working with Jimmy and Hefin, Gethin's muscles ached. Youth and strength helped him keep up, but they still had twenty years of muscle memory behind them. For Gethin, their understanding of the woods quickly developed into something to aspire to.

They'd had an Indian summer that year, and every day when he finished at the Capel Curig job, he would drive over to Coed-y-Grug, park at the top of the hill, pick his way through the trees to the lake, take off his clothes and plunge into the freezing water. The aseptic chill of it against his hot, sticky skin, and the total silence around him – the occasional *scree scree* of a buzzard above the canopy of trees – was heaven. He would stay that way until his skin started to prickle with the cold – floating on the surface of the water until his fingertips creased into dried fruit and his toes began to go numb. He didn't earn a lot, but he earned enough to look after himself, and eventually he started to take Jimmy's advice. By the end of his first year of work in the woods, he had a fair few regular customers for firewood. He got most of it the way Jimmy had taught him: gleaned what he could from the jobs he was working.

Just sometimes, though, he'd supplement a load with timber from Tŷ Gwydr. It wasn't like the Daltons were coming back to claim it any time soon. He never exactly saw it as stealing. It was more like taking an old piece of furniture that someone had left to rot on the street. It was hard to feel guilty about taking anything from people so rich that they didn't even know what they owned.

In the evenings, he would go to one of the pubs in town and have a beer with the lads. Most of the boys he'd grown up with on the estate were still there, and were at the age where their lives were starting to take tangible, concrete form. They worked on building sites, or in shops or pubs in town, or for the county council. They were joiners, or plumbers or plasterers or electricians; they'd all left school when they were sixteen and had gone to college to learn something useful. Geth had been behind, and it felt right to be really working now too. It was a good time. He had two girls on the go, both of whom were conveniently oblivious to the other because of their age difference. Catrin was in her last year of school, and he knew that she wouldn't stay in town for much longer. She wanted to go to university in Cardiff or Liverpool, so a hassle-free, painless conclusion was on the cards. Tanya was older than him. She had two kids and their father had 'fucked off back to Birkenhead'. She was in her thirties, and could do things he couldn't have even imagined were possible. Neither of them particularly wanted to become permanent fixtures in each other's lives. Things were straightforward. Geth was happy.

The extra firewood came in handy when Gethin moved into the bungalow on Ffordd yr Orsaf. In the autumn, a fortnight of heavy rain had swollen the river, and when its banks burst, the estate was inundated. They watched clotted brown water seep into the kitchen and lick the skirting boards. They watched sodden copies of the *Mirror* and rogue socks and trainers float across what had once been the living-room carpet, surrealist versions of the water boatmen that glided across the surface of the lake at Coed-y-Grug. It had been a real dog of a year already, with foot-and-mouth. The news had been a montage of abysmal images: columns of smoke, slaughtered animals, farmers crying on national television. When Geth thought of the flood now, the stench of the water was cut through with the disinfectant that he and the other foresters had washed their boots with to stop the spread of the plague.

Ffion went to live with Danny in the village, and Geth's bungalow wasn't too bad. It gave on to a tiny garden where he could put up a shed to keep his gear. His mother often turned up there on Saturday mornings, usually when he was hungover, or still drunk, or trying to get rid of a girl he'd brought home the night before. She would sit at the kitchen table, smoke, and talk about the past. It was living back in Llanelgan, she said that was dredging up all that old stuff: his father, her parents, Iestyn. Gethin let her speak, and the oblique allusions to Iestyn's past reminded him of that night in the pub with Olwen. He remembered being a kid, lying on his stomach by the tiled fireplace in the front room, the scratchy coils of the polyester carpet itching against his belly, the television drone in the background, and at quarter to, the pulse of the Welsh news jingle. *Sympathy within local communities. Four arson attacks on the Llŷn Peninsula. Politicians from the Welsh Office targeted. Llosgi tai haf.* He remembered shrugging in automatic agreement with Danny when he said that it had 'served them right'.

Subversives, 1980

DETECTIVE CLIVE CUMMINGS had been in North Wales for approximately five hours, and was already more rattled than he'd expected to be. He pulled up outside The Griffin Inn – you knew you were in the middle of nowhere when the pubs had car parks. It was just after eleven. Palm Sunday. Bright, but still so cold around here that his windscreen was getting on opaque with the condensation. So much for spring. He turned off the radio. Pocketed his keys. Adjusted his balls. When he got out of the car he made sure to slam the door as an act of small defiance against his bosses. *North fucking Wales.* Before this he'd been doing a real job: undercover with an anti-fascist group back in Moss Side. For three years he'd lived like one of them. Went on the marches. Read all the literature. Ate his own body weight in bloody lentils. Clive saw his job as an art – immersive. Absolute. Consuming. Exhaustive. Requiring natural talent and, above all, meticulous dedication. He'd been doing it *too* well, that was the problem. The guys at HQ were out of touch. They didn't know how it was to be out on the field any more. Before squatting with the lefties and the West Indians, he'd been in the army: Derry – so he'd had his fair share of demented Celts.

Clive had joined the Special Demonstration Squad around the time that he'd married Debbie. They called the SDS lads 'hairies', because of the ones that grew their hair long like the free-love freeloaders that they were infiltrating. Soldier-artists, that's how Clive liked to think of it. He saw himself as the meeting ground between James Bond and a method actor. Six days a week he spent living in that potpourri rathole with Yvonne, and now this. This is how they were showing their appreciation. *North fucking Wales*. When he reached the porch of the pub, he turned and spat into the flowerbed. He knew North Wales well enough. When he was a kid, his nan used to take him on holiday to Rhyl. The stench of that seafront. Scuzzy nowhere – that's what Wales was. That's what made it so funny that all these nationalists were so busy getting their knickers in a twist about it. Over *this* dump? Bunch of farmers playing with petrol, that's what these so-called insurgents amounted to.

It was dark inside. A thick slab of studded, fortress door and those piddly gridded windows that made you think of Elizabethan assassination plots. Dense, ecclesiastical wood fittings. Low, greenish light and garish Turkish carpets. A right headache. He followed the direction of the radio (Kate Bush, shrieking) to where he presumed he'd find life. They'd just opened and he was the first punter, by the looks of it. There was a good-looking, swarthy type propped up behind the bar with his nose in a book. He was foreign of some flavour. Pakistani? Arab? Maybe even a Greek who'd been left out in the sun for too long; either way, a touch too exotic for around here. Clive cleared his throat loudly and the debonair Indian took a drag of his cigarillo. 'Can I help you?' he drawled. Posh sounding. Clive felt faintly wrong-footed. He shuffled a fag out of his packet of L&Ms, lit it, and made a point of diffusing smoke about his person.

'I'm looking for a room. For at least a fortnight.'

The man took a sip of his coffee. 'All right. Very good.' He set his copy of *The Godfather* on the bar and reached for a ledger book underneath.

Clive glared at the abandoned paperback. 'Don't understand all these books adulating gangsters and criminals, personally.'

'There'll be a Bible in your room, there's no need to worry.'

'I'm not some sort of religious freak. I'm just saying. It's not so glamorous in the real world.'

'I'm sure. Name, please?'

'*Detective* Clive Cummings,' he said, making sure to emphasise his title. People tended to be more accommodating that way. 'And I'll take lunch in my room today, please. I've a guest arriving shortly.'

'It's not really the done thing on a Sunday. Our waitresses will be very busy.'

Clive took a step closer to the bar.

'You indigenous to these parts, *sir*?'

The man rolled his eyes. 'For my sins.'

Clive scowled. 'I'm sure you'll understand then that protecting the security of *our* country is a full-time job. I've an important meeting with my colleague, Detective Ian McNaughton, in an hour and we're going to need at least a modicum of privacy.' He felt a flicker of pride at his vocabulary. 'If you could be so kind as to send him directly to my room?'

Without deigning to look up from the ledger book, the landlord passed him a menu. Clive gave it a cursory glance.

'We'll take a chicken Maryland and a Hawaiian steak. Peach melba and an apple crumble for pudding. *Please.*'

The landlord nodded. 'Anything to drink?'

'We'll be working, actually. But then, it is Sunday. Send up two pints of lager too, yeah? Once my colleague arrives?'

'One of the girls'll show you to your room.' He called a Welsh name. Fuck knows. It was all gibberish to Clive.

★

When the food had arrived, he and Ian had pulled up the desk between them to make some sort of makeshift dining table. After all the time he'd done in that Moss Side squat, Clive had standards. Didn't want to eat on his knees like an animal, did he? Ian – obsequious, ferrety, gingerish sideburns – cut his chicken into small segments as soon as it arrived, so that he could shovel it into his mouth with a fork, and take notes with the other hand.

'Well then,' Clive began, 'good news first. Managed to recruit a grass down at the station in the town this morning, so that's a start.'

'You moved fast, sir.'

Clive allowed himself a moment to enjoy the praise. 'He was taken in for fighting and his name was flagged up as someone with nationalist sympathies. One of the local officers informed me that there'd recently been some rumours about a bit of drug dealing, so I used that on him. Didn't have much *political conscience* whatsoever in the end, so he wasn't hard to convince. Iestyn Thomas, he's called. Local lad. From a village called Clan-something-or-other. You'll find it on the file.'

'Very good, and so he'll hopefully be giving us information on . . .?'

'*Eifion Williams.*' Clive enunciated each syllable with the greatest care, as if he were ordering something outside his usual remit of a nice chicken korma at the takeaway down the road. 'This Williams bloke, he's our man. He's a clever bugger. Just finished a degree at Cardiff University and moved home end of last summer. Made himself known to us down there for various political activities. Textbook subversive really: socialist, pacifist, CND . . . Friendly with some of the Caribbean element down in Butetown, apparently. They're never very original, these left types, are they?'

Ian chuckled obediently.

'Had a run-in with the local police up here when he was a teenager for being part of the Welsh Language Society. Small fry, really. Painting out the English on road signs. Sounds like he's always been a bit of a problem kid. Uncle's an activist too. Was arrested a while back now for trying to destroy a Granada Television mast. Had a couple of court appearances about an unpaid licence fee.'

'I see.'

'Anyway he's come up on our radar here in Hicksville now because he's started his own branch of the bloody Welsh Socialist Republican Movement or something. Trying to galvanise the natives.'

Ian sniffed. 'Shouldn't be too hard round here. They're always chomping at the bit to cover themselves in woad, aren't they?'

'Precisely. I'm sure you're aware that there's been a spate of arson attacks on holiday homes recently?'

'Indeed. Thugs.' Ian's moustache quivered.

'Thursday, Friday last week incendiary devices were left at a Cons Club down in Cardiff and one up here in Shotton. The nineteenth, there was a similar device left at Port Madoc railway station in Gwynedd. None of them went off, mind. But the government are getting twitchy. All the targets seem to be prominent Tories . . . The Prime Minister's due to be visiting Swansea in July . . . And things are only getting worse. Here, you gonna finish those chips?' Clive lunged across the table and made a grab for Ian's plate. 'Cheers. Next bit of good news, though. Operation Fire began at around four o'clock this morning in South Wales. Took about fifty suspects into custody.'

'For the arsons?'

Clive rinsed his mouth out with a gulp of lager. Ian

consciously repressed a shudder at the hiss of liquid swilling around his fleshy mouth. 'So we hope. In all honesty we don't have a lot of evidence on them – yet. They're all involved with this so-called Welsh Socialist Republican Movement, though. Down south, they've been aligning themselves with the Steel Workers, the TUC, the Felindre tinplate works . . . They're pretty patently an undesirable element. Trying to make connections with their *comrades in Latin America* . . .' He rolled his eyes and added gravely, 'With the IRA.'

'I see.'

'Yep. That's what we've got to worry about. It's pretty limp stuff going on here right now. But the last thing we need is some kind of copycat IRA. There's an awful lot of bullshit doing the rounds about British Imperialism and the oppression of the Celtic peoples. See my heart bleed.'

'Right,' Ian said, with an effete little chuckle. He rubbed the grease off his sparse moustache with a hooked, pink finger. 'This Welsh Socialist lot, though. Didn't our man in Pontypridd say that this lot were all into *non-violence*, all that flower-power bollocks?'

Clive laid down his cutlery. 'Your point being?'

'Well. I just mean that . . . Well. I mean, we can't really . . . I mean, if they're just printing leaflets?'

Clive ran his tongue along his teeth to enjoy the last vestiges of synthetic pineapple flavouring. 'How long have you been on the job, Ian?'

He blinked. 'This is actually my first posting with Special Branch, sir.'

Clive inwardly thanked God that Ian wasn't much more than his glorified secretary. He imagined him trying to hold his own with Yvonne and her lot – trying to convince them that he gave a shit about Angela Davis or Huey P. Newton.

He imagined him trying to intimidate a thug like Iestyn Thomas.

'Right. I see. Makes sense. Well, let me give you a bit of advice, shall I? These people are never "just printing leaflets", as you put it. You know, there's a reason why we have to tap their phones. There's a reason why we have to send good lads in to live amongst them. There's nothing *excessive* in the British police force, Ian. I'm sure you're aware of that.'

More of the earnest moustache quivering followed. It occurred to Clive that limp blokes with facial hair are always totally fixated on it, as if they've managed to muster up an overt display of masculinity and now they can't stop fiddling with it.

'These people are dangerous subversives, Ian. They want to undermine parliamentary democracy. They want to overthrow our rightfully elected government and our very way of life. They're communists, polygamists, pansies; they decry marriage, family life, the carceral system, meritocracy, O levels, capitalism – all of it. They'd have us all living in gulags and giving our money to African dictators if they had their way. They want to *change* things. You get my drift?'

'I think so. Yeah.'

'Splendid. Now. We're not going to need anyone under-cover up here, I shouldn't think. Nothing that drastic. The natives have closed ranks and aren't much help, but this snitch should be enough to convict someone. My hunch is that this lot are so thick they'll implicate themselves faster than we can say *sosban fach*.'

'Excuse me?'

'Not a rugby fan, are we? It's a song the Welsh sing. It's about a saucepan. That should give you the measure of what we're up against here.'

Ian laughed with forced, wild enthusiasm. As Clive spoke, he couldn't help but feel stirred. He felt the words thicken into something moving and compelling. He felt like Elizabeth I giving the speech to the English Fleet, and for a moment, he forgot that he just wanted to find a culprit – to get someone inside – as quickly as possible so that he could leave this stagnant shithole. Clive Cummings was what he liked to call an old-fashioned, nineteenth-century moralist. Certain rules were immutable and could not be touched; and it was his job to protect them.

When Ian finally left, Clive took a shower, did some press-ups and decided to treat himself to a little rest. He'd been on duty since about three that morning, after all. He drew the curtains, lay on his back on the single bed and let a series of images register one by one – Debbie, Olivia Newton-John – those satin pink trousers she'd worn on the telly, the stage lights refracting off her adorable little cheek-bones – and then, inevitably, Yvonne.

2016

THEY'D STARTED the job in the evening, because it was burning hot that time of the year, but even at gone eight, the heat still throbbed through his body as he heaved the pickaxe high above his head. His shirt was soaked through with sweat.

'*Iesu mawr.*'

He plummeted the blade back down into the hollowed tarmac, transforming chunks of it into dust. Uncreating. Undoing. He wasn't expecting serious results, but hacking away at the potholes on the track that led down to Tŷ Gwydr was cathartic all the same. When he imagined the arseholes that would end up buying the house, he imagined them driving a low-slung sporty number; not the kind of thing they could possibly get down this track, especially now.

'All right, Geth. I'm beat.' Jimmy let his own pickaxe drop next to his feet. 'We've been at it for hours. I'm not young like you; I'm gonna have a bloody heart attack.'

Geth paused, wiped his brow and examined their work. The holes were marginally bigger than they had been when they'd arrived at half past five.

'Yeah. Come on. I left a couple of beers in the water to keep cold. You want a drink?'

They went and sat out on the jetty. Geth took his work boots and his socks off and lay flat on the boards. The last of the evening sun pulsed pink above the trees and refracted off the surface of the lake.

'They sold it yet, then?'

He closed his eyes and concentrated on the patterns of light webbing across his eyelids. He remembered taking mushrooms once with Tal when they were teenagers, and thinking that the light patterns looked like the cosmos, and then seeing that same current of galactic energy repeat itself along the surface of stones, along the glassy water of the Yateses' garden pond.

'No idea, mate. I decided I didn't want to know, so I stopped trying to find out.'

Jimmy swigged a mouthful of beer from the bottle. 'How much are they asking?'

'For this place? Fucking fortune, of course.' He opened his eyes again, and then he repeated what he'd heard Priya, the photographer, say. 'It'll be some second home wanker, won't it?'

It was the end of summer, and by the time they had finished the beer, the blanched white sky of the sunset had dimmed into night. They took a torch to find their way back up to the track, although Geth could have done it with his eyes closed, had he been alone. Sometimes he had the impression that he knew the contours of every ditch and every root in Coed-y-Grug.

He took the S-bends down at Tan-y-Graig at sixty, the dual beams of his headlights slicing milky blades through the conifers. He turned the music up loud and his head felt pleasantly empty. When he came back on to the long, straight stretch that led into town, he fished his phone out of his pocket to send the last girl he'd slept with a text. She was an unspeakably dull but passable HR manager in Hawarden, whose bedroom had been a sedative palette of pastels, with framed covers of *Vogue* on her mantelpiece and scented candles. Even her skin had smelt of vanilla, but she was very good at giving head. By the time he got level with Cae Gorsaf she hadn't replied, so he pulled up by his, left the engine running, and scrolled vacantly through his other numbers instead.

2002

MEG'S FLIGHT landed at six, so he went straight from work to meet her at the airport in Liverpool. He sat waiting on a cold bench next to the Spar. It was the week before Christmas. Jarring cover versions of seasonal songs dribbled out of the speakers. He watched the families in aertex shirts and puffer jackets trawling plastic suitcases and exhausted, hyperactive children in Mickey Mouse ears and tinsel. Finally, among their number, he saw her, a little apart from the others, self-consciously projecting the air of *the seasoned backpacker*.

'Jesus Christ, it's fucking freezing.'

'Welcome home, *cariad*,' Gethin whispered into her hair, holding her very tight, breathing in the smell of Nag Champa and sandalwood.

They ate tea with Ffion, Jackie and Gareth, and afterwards peeled off to the pub, which was bound to be heaving, given the time of year. Slouching up Prior Street to The Boars, the air was cold and clean. It had rained all afternoon and the night felt rinsed and renewed – dead still. Then the push of the heavy door, and bronzed light flooded from behind the bar; bodies pressed together, swaying, dancing, filtered through feathers of smoke. 'Last Christmas' was playing, and a scrawl of atonal, joyful voices serenaded each other. Glasses smashed.

'Oh. It's really Christmas now,' Meg said. The heat of the scrum was instant and phenomenal.

'They don't do Christmas in Spain?'

'Not like this.'

'I thought they loved God in Spain. Disco Virgin Marys all over the place.'

The pub was rammed. Moving so much as an inch was impossible without bumping into someone you knew, who wanted to tell you how *good* it was to see you, and how they were *really drunk* but *really happy to run into you* all the same. Megan had been pounced on by a lad from the year above them in school and so Geth nudged his way through the press of bodies to get a couple of pints. It wasn't until he'd ordered, till he leant against the sticky edge of the bar and scanned the crowd, that he saw her. She was by herself on a high barstool next to the fireplace, smoking – long, skinny legs just grazing the stretchers. She was wearing clothes that wouldn't normally pass in the pub at that time of year. All the other girls were dressed up in tight, short dresses and glittery heels – it was Christmas, after all. Olwen was wearing a baggy polo neck and trainers. He got the feeling that she'd had her eye on him for a while. When the vague, non-committal look that he'd cast about the room landed, accidentally, on her, and became something meaningful despite himself, she opened and closed her hand as some kind of approximation of a greeting. For a moment he considered nodding, or shrugging or something as scathingly dispassionate as that. It had been three years, or thereabouts. He'd always imagined that when he saw her again he'd give off the impression that he didn't give a shit, that their reunion was a nonevent. When Ger Lloyd, who was working the bar, slammed the pair of pints down in front of him, though, he found himself taking them in his hands; found his legs carrying him on automatic pilot through the crowd towards her.

'Pint?'

Olwen gestured towards a gin on the mantelpiece. 'I'm

sorted. Who was that supposed to be for?' She fixed him through her eyelashes.

He felt a momentary pang for Meg. 'I can drink it. Saves queuing again.' His voice came out gruffer than he'd wanted. Her voice in turn was new. Still posh but certain vowels – the 'o' in 'supposed', for example – coming out as if she'd grown up in east London.

'Haven't seen you for a while,' he said finally, looking at the flecking on the carpet. He felt like he was inside a fish tank. His palms were clammy.

'I don't come home that often.'

'Mm.' A few hideous seconds of silence bloomed between them.

'Mum says you're, like, a lumberjack or something these days?'

'Yeah. Something like that.'

'God. You must be fighting off the girls.'

'I don't do too bad.'

She leant forward and pressed her fingertips into his bicep. 'What a hunk,' she said flatly, making it sound like an insult.

'What about you?' He made eye contact with her again. Decided not to be scared of some spoilt little rich girl doing a homecoming tour.

'Oxford. Finals. Same old.'

'Boyfriend?'

'Hundreds.'

'Right.'

Her fingers were still digging into his arm, which meant that she was now so close to him he could smell her. Images associated with her smell involuntarily inundated his brain. He pictured her straddling him under the chestnut tree in her parents' garden after a party, the grass damp under his arse. He saw her dozing next to him by the lake at Tŷ Gwydr, her blonde hair fanning out across his chest. There she was, giving him head in the old Fiat Panda doing seventy-five on the motorway – making him feel like a fucking god. He felt each new image as something physical. It was actually painful to be in her orbit. She increased the pressure of her fingers on his skin and he flinched.

'Jesus. You're jumpy,' she laughed.

He took a swig of his pint. Swallowed. Wiped his mouth with the back of his hand and looked for something else to talk about.

'How's Tal?'

She smirked. She was enjoying this. 'He's here somewhere. He's with someone, actually – home to meet the parents.'

'Oh, yeah? They're good too, yeah?'

'Mum's always asking after you.' Olwen's voice sounded like honey, or like the voice of the classy English bird in a romantic comedy, or a Marks & Spencer's advert. 'Honestly, I think she fancies you. You know when we were kids she always used to talk about making you out of clay? "Turning your lines into abstract form" or some pseudo-art bullshit like that. She'd probably *die* with happiness if I brought you home.' She let the suggestion linger in the air for a second. He shifted his weight between his feet.

'Who's this someone of Tal's, then?'

She jutted her chin towards the bar. Taliesin was leaning right over it to make sure Ger could hear him. He was standing with an improbably handsome man in a tight white T-shirt and faded blue jeans. Shaved head, a big, silver ring on his thumb. Taliesin's hair skimmed his jawline. The tips were bleached the colour of mushy peas. He was in army surplus and a baggy jumper.

'Huh.' Geth nodded. 'He's brave.'

Olwen rolled her eyes. He started to smoke the cigarette he'd been rolling. Squinted at her through the plumes of smoke.

'Don't think just because you went to university you're on some kind of moral high ground. I haven't got anything against anyone, you know. Tal can fuck whoever he wants. I'm just saying. It's town, you know? Brave move.'

She started to swing her legs, like a child. 'That's exactly why I never come home.'

'Well, good for you,' he said. 'I'm glad you've found such a great alternative.'

Another pause – this one less excruciating because it was filled out with resentment.

'Have you missed me, then?'

Geth didn't answer. Tal and the boyfriend were easing their way out of the dense throng around the bar. Geth watched dozens of eyes swivel round. Felt the effort of them both to act like they couldn't feel the intrusive weight of surveillance. Taliesin's face visibly lit up when he caught sight of Gethin. He pulled him into a laddish embrace and for a splinter of a second, Geth felt himself stiffen. Afterwards he told himself that it was because Tal's enthusiasm had seemed insincere after years of almost zero contact. He caught himself and felt ashamed. He shook hands with the boyfriend, who was called Paolo.

'Y'right?'

Paolo smiled. 'Bit overwhelmed.' He had an accent.

'Had a run-in with Ste Edwards outside.' Taliesin grimaced.

Geth could already feel the needles of attention pinning them from right around the bar. The molecular make-up of the atmosphere had perceptibly shifted. It was a sensation that was alien to him. He'd never felt anything other than at home.

'We'll stay for this drink, and then we're out of here, yeah?' Taliesin said.

Geth picked up his second pint. 'How you getting back to Llanelgan?' He imagined the old Land Rover Defender pulling up at the top of town. David or Margot giving them a lift as if they were teenagers again. Margot saying something embarrassing and fucked up about how she'd love to sculpt the 'unusual form of Paolo's head'.

'We'll just get a taxi, I think.'

Geth half-choked on his beer. 'A taxi? With Nazi Nige?'

Paolo shook his head. 'Wow. This town. You have to be fucking kidding me.'

'Nazi Nige?' Tal asked.

'Yeah. He's the only taxi working nights in town at the moment. Phil Jones lost his licence. Nige is that one from Blackpool way. Beard. St George's tattoo that'd probably get him beaten up round here if people didn't need a lift home. He's into Civil War re-enactment, that kind of bullshit. Plays a lot of Black Sabbath or whatever. Thinks he's a Saxon. You get the picture.'

'Fuck's sake,' Tal whistled.

Geth could feel Olwen looking at him with renewed interest now that the boys hadn't dismissed him as a yokel. He felt a pool of heat spread out across his cheekbones from the bridge of his nose. 'I could give you a lift, like, if you want?' he muttered. 'We'd have to get my car mind, but I don't live far.'

'What about Megan?' It was the first time Olwen had spoken since the boys had joined them.

'Megan?'

'I saw you come in with her.'

'Meg's here?' Tal said. 'I should go say hello, introduce her to Paolo.'

Olwen's gaze burnt into Geth. He matched it.

'Meg's a grown-up. She can get herself home all right.'

Someone had put on 'Fairytale of New York'. A choir of grizzly, faux-Irish voices erupted from around the pool table. Everyone arm in arm, swaying euphorically, one of the lads from the rugby team attempting to instigate some kind of sloppy *Riverdance* pastiche.

Olwen said to Paolo, 'You see why I had to leave.'

'You're gonna have to lie down going through town, like. I've got some blankets in the cab – you can hide under them till we get past The Cross Keys, all right?'

'This is so unfair,' Olwen groaned. 'I want to go in the back. Why didn't you tell me you had a pick-up truck before I called shotgun?'

'They're gonna freeze their fucking bollocks off, Ol. Trust me, you're better up front with me.'

Part of him despised them for how excited and horrified they were to ride up to the village in the back of the truck; how this was some kind of tourist attraction and would become part of an anecdote to their friends when they got back to London. Another part of him, however, was enjoying the outlaw cachet, acting as if this was a totally habitual mode of transporting passengers, the kind of thing he did every Friday night. 'Get your foot up on the wheel,' he said to Paolo. 'There we go.'

In the passenger seat, Olwen's face flushed. 'What if we get caught?'

He put the truck into gear, glanced over his shoulder and turned the wheel with one palm, his other arm slung around the back of her seat. 'We won't get caught,' he hummed, 'unless these dickheads decide to start making a show of themselves.'

In the cab of the truck the light was blue and the tension between them so acute that it was less of a physical presence and more some kind of total shift that altered every atom of the air they were breathing, of the grey plastic of the dashboard, of the fabric of the seats.

'It's so dark,' Olwen said as they took the S-bends through the forest. 'You forget how dark it is out here.'

'I won't come in,' he said to the three of them when they arrived at Tawelfan. 'It's late. Don't want to disturb your mum and dad.'

At the front door, Taliesin embraced him again and they both told lies about catching up sooner rather than later, about the sofa bed in Tal's flatshare in Camden, and looking at train tickets. When the boys had both gone in, Olwen lingered at the threshold. She pressed her fingers against the frosted glass of the porch.

'So,' she said.

'So.'

'You still got the keys for Tŷ Gwydr, then?'

Geth hadn't been up to the house for a fortnight or so, and he hadn't been there at night since the end of autumn, when the days started segueing directly into darkness at the end of the afternoon, and it got too cold to sleep there. 'It's pitch-black up in the woods,' he told Olwen. 'We won't be able to see a thing.'

He had a torch in the truck but she had to cling to his arm anyway when they made their way down the last bit of the track and along the veranda. His eyes had adjusted to

122

the night by now, to the lunar glow reflecting off the lake. Inside, she stayed pressed up against him. The feel of her hand through his coat made his skin tingle. He'd imagined the two of them back in this house together again since he was twenty. She breathed in deeply. 'God. I feel like a teenager. This is mad.'

He placed the torch upright on the floor as some kind of makeshift lamp and he watched the spectral light play across her features. He felt the pressure in his throat, across his collarbone. She turned to face him. Stood very close. His senses brimmed as if he was drunk. She smiled shyly and he felt it tenfold. She pressed her fingers into his chest. He got the fish-tank feeling again.

'You know why I really wanted to come here, don't you?'

He smirked. 'I think I can guess.'

'You, too?'

'What do you think? Though it would have been a sight less cold up at yours, wouldn't it?' He pulled her towards him by the lapel of her coat.

She laughed and then just as she closed her eyes, just as she tilted her head up to his, her body tensed. 'Did you hear that?'

'Hear what?'

'There's someone out there. On the veranda.'

'Pfft. There's no one here, Olwen.'

'Look!'

Sure enough, a silhouette flashed just beyond the glass. 'The fuck?' he murmured.

'Oh my God.'

'Stay here, don't move.'

By the time he made it outside, the person was already gone. He stood very still and listened for the direction of footsteps cracking in the undergrowth above the sound of his own breath. They got as far as the lake and then they stopped. He threw the beam of the torchlight in their direction, and when he clocked who it was he almost laughed. He took the staircase in a couple of long strides.

'Iestyn? Fuck are you doing here, you fucking perv?'

His uncle was glaring at him. 'Oh, please. Don't flatter yourself.' He scoffed. 'I was checking for your mam, that's all. I saw headlights going down the turning.'

'You saw headlights all the way from the farm? What, you got bionic vision now or something?'

Iestyn thrust his thumbs into his belt loops. 'I was out. Couldn't sleep.'

'And you just happened to come all the way here?'

'Told you. I saw headlights. I was checking for your mam.'

Geth looked his uncle up and down. There was something tense and unsteady about him. 'You been drinking?'

'Have I fuck? Blydi cheek.' He glanced furtively up towards the track and then back again. Raised his eyebrows. A look of smug triumph appeared on his face. 'Does Ffi know you got her keys?'

When Gethin didn't reply he grinned. 'Huh. Thought as much.' Geth watched his posture visibly loosen. He gave an exaggerated bow, tipped an imaginary hat. 'Suppose neither of us will be mentioning this to anyone then, will we?' As he backed away, up towards the track, he said, 'Don't you worry, Gethin, *bach*, your secret's safe with me.'

He found Olwen standing in the doorway, one foot on the veranda, one foot in the house. She'd put her collar up over her chin against the cold.

'You took forever,' she hissed.

'You'll never guess who it was.' He pulled himself up the steps by the wooden rail.

'So there was someone?'

'Iestyn.'

'What? Your uncle Iestyn? Why was he here? Is he gone?'

'I got rid of him, don't worry.' He wasn't sure that she *was* worried necessarily, or even if he had really actively *got rid of* Iestyn, as such, but he remembered how she responded to that; to the implication that he was looking out for her, and it made him feel good too – satisfied some kind of unpalatable, masculine impulse that he was embarrassed to admit to, given it was probably a pretty backwards way to feel. He put his hands on her hips. 'Come on, you've seen it now,' he said. 'Let's go back to yours. It's Baltic up here.'

Her bedroom at Tawelfan was unchanged; there was still the same poster of Jeff Buckley in a wifebeater with his guitar on his lap. The Sony Hi8 video camera that her parents had bought her for her eighteenth still sat on the dressing table, next to the Bombay Sapphire bottle she'd been using as a candlestick since Lower Sixth. He remembered sitting on the little stool and picking at the clumps of wax with his fingernails on the day that she'd told him about Will. He dismissed the memory before he could feel anything about it. There was the photo of her with the bald one in their school uniform, and another of Margot and David, smoking stylishly at some art school party in the 1960s, with matching Jeff Beck haircuts. There were her copies of *The Go-Between*, *Persuasion*, and *Brideshead Revisited* stacked up by the mirror. She sat on the edge of the bed, watching him take in the strange tableau – strange because it was a splinter of his adolescence, preserved in aspic.

'Do you still read much?'

'No, I had to give it up when I became a manual labourer.'

'Shut up, I didn't mean it like that.'

'Yes you did.' He grinned at her reflection in the mirror. She was still in her coat. Her parents didn't believe in central heating. He turned around to face her and she shrugged it off.

'That's good. And the jumper too,' he said quietly. He made his voice stern, how she liked it and, stepping forward, he knelt down in front of her. He put his palms on her thighs and parted her legs, and he smiled to himself at the intensity of her response, the pin-fine inhale; he'd always loved that, how responsive she was.

'Are you sure you want to do this?' he said, to hear her say yes. She nodded.

He kissed the inside of her thigh, moved his hands up under her skirt to peel off her tights. 'Tell me that you want this.'

'I want this so much.'

He moved over her body, crushing it under the weight of his own. He felt her nails dig into his shoulder blades as he unbuttoned his jeans and he felt drunk with it. He heard himself whisper an expletive as her hands moved up and down the ladder of his spine. Heard her say again, 'I want you so much.' But then, after, when he was inside her, his hands covering hers, pushing them into the duvet, he looked at her face, at the familiar shape of her open mouth, and he felt something shift; he was conscious of the fact that he loved her, and that his wellbeing was contingent on how she decided to move through the world. He felt the heady feeling of power drain from his body. He felt heat along the bridge of his nose and at his temples, and his breath grate against his chest.

'*Fuck.*' He swallowed. She opened her eyes and said his name, and he closed his, and said, 'I want you like this,' and when he'd turned her over, when he had her held down, he tried to detach himself entirely, and pretend that she was anyone. He tried to make his heart blank and think entirely with his body.

2008

GETH FOUND OUT about her first film by chance. He was doing a job out Llyn Elsi way with Jimmy and Hefin, and by the time they stopped work for *paned* at half nine, the gauze of mist in the air had thickened into rain. He was in a bad mood anyway and was more than happy to retreat into the cab of his truck alone. He didn't want to speak to anyone. It was only September but they'd had a stretch of bad weather already. At the end of the working day, the damp seeped through his muscles and skin and clung to his bones. He was sure he was coming down with something. Ffion had been in and out of hospital for a good few months now, and he wasn't sleeping much.

Outside, the rain began to fall more solidly. He turned the dial of the car radio and got his Thermos and the old margarine tub that he used as a lunchbox out on his lap. The windscreen turned opaque with steam, and the voice of the BBC newsreader filled the cab of the truck with words like 'severe downturn', 'Lehman Brothers' and 'government bail-outs'. He turned it off again. He had no desire to hear about the end of the world. Lads were just starting to get laid off. One of the pubs in town had started doing a 'credit-crunch menu' – chicken korma and chips for £1.75. It sounded like something an advertising exec had come up with: *credit crunch*. It was jolly and surmountable – possible to digest in small chunks.

In the footwell of the passenger seat he found a copy of last week's local paper, and he flicked through the first few pages as he ate his cheese and pickle sandwich. It was on the bottom of the fourth page, hardly a paragraph, but his eyes snagged on the tiny photograph of her next to the words. A current of electricity pulsed through his fingers as he held the pages closer to his face, as if he could get more of a sense of them that way. The rain fell harder.

WATCH OUT, SPIELBERG!

LOCAL GIRL HEADS FOR
SILVER SCREEN STARDOM.

A young filmmaker born and raised in Llanel-gan, Olwen Yates, is starting to make a stir in the glamorous milieu of movie-making. Yates, 26, has managed to scoop the top prize for a debut at not just one, but TWO major European film festivals. The success of her short film, *Raw Material*, made as part of a master's degree course in filmmaking, has led to the young director securing funding for a feature-length project, so watch this space! Yates, of course, isn't the first local to make it big in cinema. In 1978, local lad Richard Parry . . .

Geth stopped reading. He was aware of the sound of his breath as he tried not to react to the words on the page. Of course he was happy for her. Obviously he wanted Olwen to do well in life. He wanted her to be happy. He stared at the photo. He did a quick calculation and worked out that it had been around six years since that Christmas. He'd never called her when she'd gone back to university like he'd said he would, and on the odd occasion that he ran into Margot or David he was too proud to so much as say her name aloud. A year or two after that, they'd sold up and left the village anyway. The photo looked professional. It was a headshot. Dead moody. She'd had a fringe cut, which, he noted happily, didn't suit her. Other than that, she still looked dis-hearteningly the same. He was very happy for her. He made himself think the words again, imagined the way the letters were formed on the page, almost said them aloud. He put his sandwich back into his lunchbox. He'd been starving when he'd got into his truck, but now the only feeling he could experience was the shape of the words, 'I'm happy for her', as he consciously thought them over and over again.

He swore loudly when Hefin rapped on the window of the truck. He rolled the window down. 'Jesus fucking Christ, Hef. Give me a fucking heart attack why don't you?'

Hefin grinned at him. 'Come on, sweetheart. Get your stuff together. It's pissing it down. Gonna storm in about an hour. We're out of here.'

There were a lot of things that Geth liked about his job in his twenties. He liked the way it made his body feel, the way that it kept him lean whilst some of the other lads he'd grown up with were just starting to get a little bit doughy. He liked the surprises: a cluster of monkey puzzle trees right there in the middle of a patch he'd been felling; a pair of stoats playing chase in the undergrowth when he'd got to the woods one morning, like some kind of real-life David Attenborough bit. He liked that magical time in spring when the conifers broke bud and you got that fresh, clean, acid-green growth against the dark jade of the old needles. Sometimes, tiny flowers emerged that looked like little red pine cones. He liked it when it had been snowing, and he'd be the first person to get to a patch of virgin forest, the trees laden with unblemished white snow getting down the back of your neck when the branches moved. Above all, he liked being alone. That was the real thing. Geth didn't want some boss at his shoulder, making sure he was being productive. He liked getting to the woods in the morning and being his own agent: having a break when he wanted one, being the master of his own time. Sometimes, if he was completely by himself, he would lie down, close his eyes and listen. Once or twice, he'd experienced total silence – no farm machinery, no cars, no chainsaws. He'd got that vast, cosmic feeling then – like he could have been there any time in a chain link of thousands of years.

He drove directly to Tŷ Gwydr from work. Since his mother had been ill, his visits had gained a veneer of legitimacy, as the Dalton Estate had asked him to take over as caretaker. He'd made jokes about feudal lords having inherited staff, but he'd taken the job without the slightest bit of hesitation. He didn't want anyone else from town getting involved up at the house, which he essentially saw as his own, and the Daltons – who didn't know about the mattress that he kept up there, or the firewood that he'd been harvesting on a regular basis for several years now – saw his employment as convenient.

By the time he arrived, the storm that Hefin had predicted was at its miserable peak. He legged it down the track but was still soaked by the time he made it inside. He boiled a pan of water on the little camping stove and watched the rain turn the enormous windows into something liquid. He made himself a cup of instant coffee, sat down on the grubby single mattress, and focused very hard on not thinking about his mother, about words like 'metastasis', and on not thinking about Olwen, and her glamorous new life and her ugly new fringe. He tried very hard to empty his head entirely, but life had started to overwhelm him somehow recently. Things that had once been manageable were no longer manageable at all.

131

Click, 1980

IT STARTED AROUND the time of the spate of arrests in South Wales. 'Operation Tân' the police called it. When Eifion first heard that he had to laugh. They weren't subtle, were they? *Operation Fire*. Sounded like jackboots and windowless interrogation rooms and violence. It sounded like the kind of thing an eleven-year-old would invent in a game about guns and Nazis, but then, they were policemen, not poets, after all. Most of the arrests took place between four and six in the morning, for extra chilling effect. He heard all sorts of horror stories that first week. One lad was held at the station in Pen-y-Bont for eighty-one hours. Another guy – a middle-aged high school teacher in Llandaff – was arrested by *eleven* men before dawn on Palm Sunday. An entire football team of officers. The neighbours were horrified. It was clear that the police had no actual leads with regards to the arsons, the incendiary devices, or even to the letters sent to the *Echo* or the *Western Mail* that claimed them. They needed to show results, and so they were arresting anyone with any kind of 'suspected political affiliations'.

The arsons – *llosgi tai haf* in Welsh – had begun the previous December. On that first night alone, there were two on the northern side of the peninsula in Nefyn, and another pair down in Pembrokeshire. Within the month, eight empty second homes had been torched by the group calling themselves *Meibion Glyndŵr*. After each one – as the news got around – there was a perceptible shift in the atmosphere, some kind of climactic, conspiratorial excitement.

One morning just before Christmas, Eifion happened to come home first thing, before dawn. It was still dark out. Inside, his father was sitting at the kitchen table, socked feet up on the Rayburn, flicking through the newspaper as he waited for his porridge to set. He started at the sound of the front door.

'What are you doing coming in at this time? It's barely six.'

Eifion registered that he wasn't just laying down some kind of arbitrary, paternal authority, but that he looked genuinely scared.

'I was just at Angharad's, Dad. Don't worry about it.' He slipped out of his boots. His father's eyes tracked him around the room to the sink where he started to fill the kettle. He knew what he was thinking.

'I'm not involved in any of that, Dad. Don't worry – really.'

He heard his father sigh, and then: 'I wouldn't blame you if you were.'

After he had left for work, his sister, Gwenno, had come into the kitchen. She sat in the same chair as she waited for her porridge, and picked up the discarded newspaper. Eifion was just finishing his tea when she started to make all the obvious noises that signalled that she had read something that she disapproved of and was angling to share it with him.

'Did you know, in 1976, there were 8,500 holiday homes in Gwynedd. Now there are close on *14,000* and on Pen Llŷn, *one in four* houses is a holiday cottage.' She gasped. 'And house prices have *quadrupled*! Fat chance for us then, hey?'

There weren't many people who felt sorry for the English that winter.

★

Eifion's old flatmate from university was taken in on Palm Sunday. When he spoke to the guy's boyfriend on the phone later that week, he'd told him that the interrogation had mostly been about breeding fear. They didn't have anything on him, but one of the officers had said that he was 'guilty until proven innocent'; that he didn't have any rights. They asked him if he liked the Tories, if he sympathised with the IRA. If he considered himself an anarchist. If the arsons made him happy. They even asked him about his sex life. Asked him who was the *man* in the relationship — or if his boss, or his parents knew that he was a 'fairy'.

It was around then that Eifion started to notice the man. The first time it happened he'd been sitting in a caff with Angharad in Abersoch. When Eifion first noticed him, the initial glitter of scorn that he felt pass along the surface of his body was at the audacity that this bloke — this little git, with his weasel face and his scant moustache — had the audacity to be giving Angharad the eye so shamelessly, when he was right there. He stared back and the man's greasy gaze slithered back down to the newspaper he had in front of him. Eifion reached his hand across the Formica table and let it rest on Angharad's cheek. They paid and left, and Eifion didn't notice that the man with the sparse moustache followed them out on to the street. In fact, he'd forgotten him entirely until about a week later. He was having a pint with some mates in a pub in Caernarfon after a meeting and he clocked him, sitting by himself at the bar, reading a newspaper again. He had a pen behind his left ear. The next time Eifion went up to get a drink, he made a point of standing next to him. As the barmaid pulled his pint, he turned to face him and nodded at the biro.

'Taking notes or something?' he said, making the threat implicit.

The weaselly man smiled amiably. 'For the crossword.'

'You know that bloke over there, Rob?' Eifion asked one of his friends as he handed him a pint.

Rob squinted in the direction of the bar. 'Don't think so,' he said. 'Might not be from round here. It's April now – maybe he's a keen tourist. Not long till they all pile in and you won't be able to swing a blydi cat in here. Here, *iechyd da!*'

They touched glasses and drank, and Eifion decided to drop it, but over the course of the next few weeks, he found himself increasingly paranoid. Sometimes there was a car, a dirty blue Escort crawling along the street behind him, not even bothering to be discreet. That was the point where he started to wonder how much of it was about surveilling him, and how much of it was more about scaring the shit out of him. After a while, it was only the weaselly man who even bothered to keep on cultivating a façade of invisibility, with his newspaper, his untouched mugs of tea and his full pint glasses. You didn't get used to it: the feeling of being watched only got more and more corrosive the longer it went on.

At the beginning of May – around the time that an incendiary device went off at the Fairwater Conservative Club in Cardiff – a windowsill was scorched – Eifion heard the click on his landline for the first time. He was on the phone to the old flatmate who'd been taken in for questioning in March. He started when he heard it, like a button being pressed, barely there at all.

'Did you hear that?'

Silence on the other end for a second and then, 'It was like a little—'

'Yeah. Like a click, wasn't it?'

Neither he nor Phil spoke for a moment while they digested the implications of what they both thought they had heard. Finally, Phil cleared his throat.

'I, uh, I best be off then. Got a lot of work to do here.'

'Right,' Eifion said slowly, conscious of how altered his voice sounded. 'Of course. Speak soon then, yeah? Send my love to . . . well, to everyone.'

'Yes. Will do.'

He replaced the phone on the cradle and went and sat down on the settee. He could hear the faintest wisp of the radio in the kitchen, but other than that the house was silent. His family were all at work. He was alone. He was suddenly intensely aware of the sound of his own breath, of the way the air felt around him. His skin was very cold.

He didn't leave the house that day. When his parents came home in the evening, he told them what had happened.

'You see,' his mother said to his father. 'I told you I wasn't going mad!'

His dad sighed and shook his head. '*Delyth*.'

Eifion swallowed. 'You knew about this?'

His mother pursed her lips. 'Last week,' she began, already puffed up with indignation, 'I was on the phone to your *nain*, and after I hung up with her, I rang your aunty Bethan, and I *swear to God*, I heard other voices on the line!' She nodded at her husband. 'Then I realised that it was the same chat I'd been having with Nainy just moments earlier – *playing back at me* – as if it had been recorded! And I got so flustered I hung up on Bethan, and then when I told her – and when I told your dad – they both said I was being daft. But I knew I'd heard it!'

136

Eifion shut his eyes. The low evening light slanting in through the net curtains was too bright.

When he turned down off his street, the blue Escort was parked up on the corner. Standing on Angharad's doorstep, he could hear the rumble of an engine. He didn't dare turn to see the car. He stared at the grey pebble-dash, willed someone to come to the door. After a handful of agonising seconds, the impressionist blur of a figure appeared through the frosted glass.

'*S'mae*, mate? You're as white as a sheet.' Angharad's father peered at him from the other side of the threshold. Eifion ran his hands through his hair. 'Yeah. Hiya, Huw. All good thanks, no worries. Yourself?'

Huw scrutinised him benignly. Eifion followed his eyes as they fixed on something beyond the doorstep – on the car with the engine running.

'You want to come in?' Huw said quietly.

The thought occurred to him then that maybe he shouldn't. That he might get Huw into some kind of trouble. He shifted his weight from one foot to the other.

'No, no, I won't bother you now. I was, uh. I was just wondering if Angharad's about.'

The growl of the engine stopped. He flinched. Huw looked from him to the car and back again.

'No, she's not, actually. She's gone off with that Iestyn lad somewhere. He's not from round here, is he? She knows him from years ago, when they were kids – from the Eisteddfod, I think. You know the lad I mean?'

Eifion nodded.

'She did try and ring you, now I think about it – before she left.'

Eifion felt a wave of revulsion. The phone had rung several times that afternoon, tearing through the house each time as if it were shrieking. 'Yeah. There's been a problem with the line, I think.'

'Well,' Huw chuckled, 'no skin off my nose. The number of times I've told that girl not to use the phone before six. You can tell who pays the blydi bills.'

Eifion attempted to smile and wondered if it was judicious to stick around. He wanted to turn back and see if the car was still there.

'Good-looking bloke, that Iestyn character. Seems very keen too, coming all this way.' He raised a suspicious eyebrow.

The idea of Iestyn's face briefly interrupted Eifion's train of thought. 'I suppose he is, yeah.' He hadn't thought of him in that way. Honestly, he'd had the impression that Iestyn was a bit thick. He'd turned up to a couple of meetings when they'd first set up, had made some snide, arrogant comments and then had dropped off the radar entirely until around Eastertime. All of a sudden, he did seem very keen, though. Huw wasn't wrong about that. The thought occurred to him for the first time that maybe he was interested in Angharad.

'I'll tell her you popped over, if you're sure you don't want to come in for a *panad*? Or there's beer in the fridge, if you'd like?'

Instead, Eifion walked home, got his address book, and drove to his uncle's chippie in Porth Madog, where he used his telephone to ring the people that he needed to tell not to call him any more.

2016

IT WAS GONE NINE in the evening and a serene stillness had settled on the aisles of the supermarket. Geth could very clearly hear the sound of his footsteps unfold across the hard vinyl floor. He could hear the low hum of the fridges, and the metallic rattle of a cage being dragged down an aisle. Two teenage workers in stiff polyester polo shirts were giggling and flirting as they scanned plastic bags of salad and threw them in a crate destined for the skip. They snapped upright when they heard Gethin approach, only to slouch back into their actual personalities again when they realised he wasn't their manager. He always came at this time, just before closing. It was peaceful. The cold, white light that bleached the endless rows of products was less caustic after dusk, and on a purely practical level, he was less likely to be bothered by anyone he knew. Still, it was town, and total anonymity was never to be taken for granted. It surprised him, though, when he ran into Iestyn, rifling through the reductions end of the poultry section. His uncle had never been the type to do the shopping.

'Gethin. Y'right?'

'Yeah. Sure. Yeah, I'm not too bad.'

Gethin wondered for a moment when exactly it was that he'd last seen Iestyn. It had been easier to avoid him, since his mother had died. He'd spot him every so often, behind the wheel of his old Defender, on the road between Llanelgan and town, driving too fast usually. The last time he'd spoken to Danny, his brother had told him that Iestyn 'hadn't been doing so well'. Geth clocked two six-packs in the basket and a couple of bottles of own-brand Scotch.

'Yeah,' he said again. 'All good. And yourself?'

Iestyn shrugged. 'I'm alive, aren't I? Oh, I hear they've put your place up for sale. About blydi time.'

'My place?'

'*Duw*, come on, Gethin, *bach*. Don't give me the run around. You know exactly what I'm talking about.'

He bristled. 'Tŷ Gwydr? Barely even work there any more.'

Iestyn smiled. 'Barely even *work* there. Help yourself to enough of their timber, though, don't you? And you know as well as I do that you're up there all the blydi time. Everyone in the village does. Could do with being a little bit more discreet, like.'

Gethin tightened his grip on the handles of his shopping basket. 'I'm managing the woodland,' he said, which is what he always told himself he would say if anyone from the Dalton estate ever actually deigned to take an interest in the land.

Iestyn leant in close enough so that Geth could smell the sweet trace of booze on his breath. 'No skin off my nose. You take everything you can off those *Sais* fuckers, as far as I'm concerned. They're loaded. Their own blydi fault if they're too thick to see that their caretaker's been robbing them blind.' He started to chuckle. He rocked back on his heels and looked his nephew up and down. 'Here, I tell you what, though. I suppose you've heard who's apparently buying the place, haven't you?'

Part Two

THE BLUE HOUR

2016

THE PHOTO OF the house filled the screen of her phone and she gasped. James, who had been in the middle of a sentence, raised his eyebrows at her. He rustled his copy of the *FT* pointedly. 'I'm sorry,' he said, 'was I boring you?'

'Oh my God.' She sat up on the sofa. She swore. She swiped her thumb from left to right through the photographs of the house. The first one was taken from the opposite side of the lake and showed the jetty and one side of the veranda. Then the kitchen, with its empty teak cabinets and terracotta tiles; the living room with the enormous, sliding glass doors, the water gleaming just beyond them. Even the bathroom was exactly the same, right down to the kitsch pink bathtub and the long, rectangular window above it, brilliant with the vivid green of the Douglas firs.

> #forsale Waterside Welsh Wonder: spectacular
> mid-century property giving on to pristine lake in
> woodland setting. North Wales. Magic guaranteed.
> Follow the link in our bio for sales particulars.
>
> #midcentury #wildswimming

'Oh my God.'
James cleared his throat.
'It's Tŷ Gwydr,' Olwen said. 'It's Geth's house.'

They met at the wedding of a university friend when she was twenty-six and he was thirty-five. It was the summer of 2008. The wedding was in Surrey, which Olwen had

143

decided was undoubtedly hell. Every car was a Range Rover and every field was a golf course. It made sense that Miranda would get married here, because she was marrying a banker. She was selling out. James was with the groom, and Miranda had sat them next to each other at the reception, presumably, Olwen thought, because she was a sadist. She was already drunk when the starters arrived on the table, and their interaction began uncomfortably when she asked him how it felt to be personally responsible for the global financial crisis that, at that time, was still a shiny new topic of conversation at the dining tables of the chattering classes. James had laughed at her, and asked if she worked in development. 'I suppose you're with the Red Cross or something earnest like that? Just finished a six-month stint in Darfur?'

'I'm a filmmaker,' she said, hesitating, because it was still a surreal thing to say aloud at that point. *Raw Material* had just won its second festival, and the funding for her feature had just been confirmed. She still had the feeling that she was saying something fraudulent when she said it out loud.

'Let me guess,' James said, 'documentaries? Are you exposing the racist biases of the carceral system? Or the cultural vilification of the working classes under New Labour?'

She rolled her eyes at him.

'The reality of the university experience for bright kids from council estates who ascend?'

She told him that her graduate short had been a twenty-minute meditation on a housewife losing her mind, and contained a single sentence of dialogue.

'Can't be much money in that,' drawled her other neighbour, who, according to the table plan, was called Piers.

'Piers forgot to choose the charm option when he bought his personality,' said James, and Olwen, despite herself, laughed.

James spoke three languages, had grown up all over the world, had studied French and Philosophy at UCL, and had wanted to be a writer until he'd decided he'd rather be rich. His father, who was a labour lawyer – an epithet easy to negotiate because no one had to know that he was working for the bosses, not the labourers – had pulled some strings, and had got him an internship with an old school friend in the City. Three years after that, James had bought an enormous flat in Bethnal Green. He planned on retiring at the age of forty. He told Olwen that he worked in *green finance*, which was apparently where the 'good guys' operated. Olwen wasn't entirely sure that there were any good guys operating in the financial services industry, but by the time the dessert came she didn't care, because she wanted to sleep with him.

The first time they fucked was at four o'clock in the morning on the bonnet of the car he'd rented to drive down to Surrey. The best man had passed out right across the bed that James had been designated in the guest wing of the stately home, and Olwen had lost the friend from college that she'd planned on camping with. She'd also lost her phone and her purse, but she wasn't particularly worried about that, because rich people didn't steal, except on a corporate level. When she told James this he laughed out loud and said, 'Wow, you weren't lying. You really are a hick, aren't you?'

'None of the tax evaders at this party are going to want my Nokia 8310, trust me,' she said.

'You're not seriously telling me you own a Nokia 8310? That's the most egregiously pretentious east London affectation I've heard all night.'

'That really doesn't surprise me with this crowd.'

He laughed and pressed himself against her, and her body in turn against the cool metal of the car. He slid his hands under his dinner jacket, which she'd been wearing since he'd gallantly draped it on her shoulders when they'd first come outside under the pretence of getting some air. He'd called it a 'DJ', as if it was about to start playing records. His fingers tugged at the hook and eye of her dress and her body felt lithe and alert. When he leant forward to kiss her, his teeth were very white and very straight in the pale glow of the moon, and a strand of black hair fell across his eyes.

'God, your skin is so soft,' he whispered. She could feel how hard he was, and she held him tight around his neck as he pressed the seam of her underwear, and slipped his hand between her legs. There was something about the crisp rustle of the breeze through the dead leaves. About the lunar glow. About the cold shock of the car bonnet. It made her think of Gethin.

They started dating when they both got back to London, and within the year, she'd moved into the flat he owned on the canal. Miranda, whose career as an actress in a contemporary theatre troupe owed its sustainability to her husband's salary, said to her, 'Why do you think I put you next to each other at dinner?'

James was standing behind her now, leaning over her shoulder so that he could see the screen of her phone, which she'd upgraded in the eight years since they'd met.

'Jesus. The site of all your adolescent debauchery. Looks like paradise.'

'It wasn't debauchery,' she said. 'It was pure.'

'Go on then, click on the listing.' He took the phone from her hands. 'Phew,' he whistled when the page had loaded. 'It's going for a song. For what it *is*, I mean. Imagine how much that'd set you back in Sussex, or even in bloody

Cornwall. They're not even asking for a million.' He shook his head as he scrolled through the particulars. 'Jesus Christ. Original bathroom suite. My grandma had one that colour.' He dropped the phone back on to the pillows of the sofa and said, in what she assumed was jest, 'It *is* your birthday soon, darling.'

When he returned to his newspaper, she looked at the asking price, which wasn't far off James's apparent benchmark of seven figures, and the thought landed in her head, clear and fully formed, that James could afford to buy Tŷ Gwydr, and that if she asked him he probably would.

2016

OLWEN HAD very little desire to go to Tony's book launch. Tony was a friend from university; a writer of highbrow, experimental novels, which sold to highbrow, experimental indie presses for about as much as her husband made in a week. He lived in a warehouse in Lewisham and supported himself waiting tables, and everyone agreed that he was poor and noble, and tactfully never mentioned his parents, or their enormous house in Highgate (where Tony still had a bedroom). The party was being held at an aggressively trendy bookshop in Deptford, staffed by elegant, fine-boned young white men with studied geezer accents, and a Black girl with a septum piercing and vivid green hair. It was six o'clock and, of course, not one of her friends had arrived yet, because Olwen wasn't even on time, but was suffering the unique humiliation of being early. She wished that she still smoked, so that she could at least go outside for a cigarette. Finally – mercifully – one of the bespecta-cled, floppy-haired sales assistants emerged from behind the counter and began to set up a long, low trestle table with plastic cups and boxes of rancid-looking New World wine. At least she could finally drink.

She made her way over there, put the books that she'd picked up on the table – placed strategically so that he could see the titles and admire her taste – and reached for the tower of plastic cups. The bookseller, Arthur – she recog-nised him now from Tony's Instagram – arranged his face into a polite grimace and said, 'Hey. So just to let you know we're actually closing now. We've got an event tonight. If you do want to buy those, though, the till's just over there.'

She cringed. 'Oh. I mean I do want to buy them – I'll go now, if you're closing the till – but I am actually here for the event.'

Arthur contrived an expression that she perceived to be one of artificial receptivity, but then, she always was convinced that she was being slighted by these kinds of people; perhaps his warmth was indeed sincere. 'Ah! Nice. Cool. Well. Welcome. Vino? You're into Tony Aiyar then?'

Aiyar. The 'Aiyar' part always amused Olwen. At university he'd been Anthony Strickland, but upon graduation he'd affected to take his mother's maiden name as 'an affront to the patriarchy' and also to discreetly signal the fact that his maternal grandfather was not white.

'Actually, I'm an old friend of his. I mean, I'm a fan of his too, obviously!' She picked up the first edition of Tony's latest and simpered. 'I'm Olwen. Nice to meet you.'

'Oh!' said Arthur. 'Olwen. Yes. Of course. I knew I recognised you. I had no idea you and Tony were mates. Olwen Yates, right?'

She smiled thinly. She had been discovered. 'Uh-huh.'

'Ah, cool. I loved your last film. Nice.'

She hesitated. She tried to find the snarkiest hints of sarcasm in his comment, and when she had decided that his praise might even be genuine, she quietly said, 'Oh, thanks.'

'Yeah, yeah. Great. You working on something at the moment?'

Olwen hated this question. She cast her eyes rather desperately around the shelves, and, landing on a poetry anthology apparently about witchcraft, said, 'I am. About folklore.'

Arthur's eyes creased into crow's feet but he didn't smile, and she sensed that this response was insufficient. Just behind his ear, she spotted a hardback upon whose spine were the words, *END OF EMPIRE: RESIST!*, and she found herself illuminated with a brilliant idea. 'I'm actually working on a project about Wales at the moment, where I'm from. It blends Welsh folklore tradition with anti-British, political resistance in the 1980s.'

For the first time in a long time, she thought about Gethin's drunk uncle in the pub that night. The story he'd told about the police.

Arthur's face lit up. 'Wow. *Interesting.*'

Buoyed by her own quick thinking – and honestly, quite impressed and excited herself about the idea – she said, 'Yeah. People in England have basically forgotten about it, but in Wales in the 1980s there was, like, this huge movement against the English. There was this group of political activists who burnt down English-owned second homes in communities where the language and the culture were threatened. Places where locals were being pushed out. It was Thatcher-era. The English were already freaking out about Ireland . . .'

Arthur was nodding so enthusiastically his glasses were beginning to slip down his nose. He pushed them up with his index finger. 'And the folklore element?' he said.

She looked at the books behind him again. 'Folklore has always been a means to resist the structures of power,' she said. He handed her a plastic cup of wine, and she took a long sip. The purple liquid was viscid and acrid, and burnt right through her throat. She grinned.

2016

THEY GOT THE first note on the day that they moved in, although Olwen never saw it, because it was James who picked it up and, not knowing what it meant, he presumed it was junk, stuffed it in his pocket, and consequently forgot about its existence. He'd been wearing a tatty old pair of jeans that day, and when he threw them in the wash, the note was rinsed into pulp and dispersed through the clean laundry like pellets of papier mâché. It had been about the size of a parking ticket and had two words of Welsh written on it. He didn't even consider that it might be for them. He presumed it was something that the estate agent must have dropped. *Cer Adre!* meant nothing whatsoever to him. Before they'd come up to view the house in the summer, he'd been to Wales a total of three times in his life, and the only word he knew was *ARAF*, because they painted it on the surface of roads there, and it amused him.

They stayed for a long weekend that first time. It was October and a blue chill had settled on the woods. Mornings were softened with nacreous mist and the leaves rusted and fell. They spent the weekend playing house with the furniture they'd brought up from London, receiving texts from friends in their group chat that said things like: 'It looks like the house that Eric Lloyd Wright built Anaïs Nin in Silver Lake.' On the first evening they arrived, they bundled up in jumpers and ate fish and chips on the veranda. Dusk was still and iridescent – none of the jaundiced intensity of the streetlights that they were used to – and then, at night, there was an absurd amount of lucid stars, hazing the black sky around them.

Olwen watched James lick chip grease off his fingers and felt tenderness for him rise in her throat. A lot of her friends judged James, and undoubtedly made cynical judgements about their relationship as well. She didn't need to be a fly on the wall to know what they were saying when he bought Tŷ Gwydr. Superficially they had all come around to him – because he had opinions on Adorno, and he listened to NTS, and because he'd spent the first half of the year canvassing for the Remain campaign and was intending, much to the mirth of his colleagues, to spend the next one canvassing for the Labour Party. Taliesin was the only one who still said things like, 'So he likes art. He still likes money more.' Her brother had spent most of his twenties living in a squat in Marseille, and now taught philosophy at a sixth-form college in Brighton. James said he was politically naïve. He was also wrong. Olwen knew that James cared about her more than he did about amassing wealth, even if the latter was something that he was very good at. Mostly, she found it patronising when people who really knew them couldn't see that their relationship was one of mutual acquisition anyway. It suited him to be able to talk about his wife, *the filmmaker.* They were both accruing some sort of capital from their union.

On the Saturday morning when James decided to drive into town to do some shopping, she felt the first spike of unease. She imagined herself pushing a trolley along the aisles of the supermarket where Geth had worked when they were teenagers, and she felt pre-emptively surveilled. She imagined running into someone she'd known from town when she was a kid. She wondered whether they would recognise her, and if they did, what they would talk about – if they would talk at all. The idea of going to the supermarket made her feel like a fraud.

'You gonna come with me?' James said as he rinsed out the coffee pot over the expensive new Belfast sink that the workmen had fitted. His voice was light and yet the words sent some kind of ripple through her. She stood paralysed in the sea of boxes she was unpacking. She made herself shrug.

'I kinda want to finish this before lunch.'

'Suit yourself,' he said. He came up behind her. He slid his hands under the big old jumper of his that she was wearing, barelegged in knickers and socks, hair tousled still from being in bed. 'Maybe I'll run into your first love in town.'

She rolled her eyes. Since they'd first seen the advert for the house, Geth had become some kind of joke between them. A Mellors-ish caricature of everything that James was not. An 'axe-swinging alpha male', which was an epithet that Olwen found a little rich considering she'd once overheard James drunkenly confess to a friend that he got a 'kick' from having some kind of 'influence over global markets'. He held her close to him. He said into her ear, 'I won't be able to take him. And I guess he'll know the terrain. Understand the land.'

'Of the supermarket?'

He scoffed. 'If he comes here, I mean.' His hands were working their way up her body from the smooth curves of her waist. 'And besides, you know what lumberjacks are famously in possession of, don't you?'

'Surprise me.'

'Chainsaws.'

When he'd left she went and sat out on the jetty with another coffee and watched the hazy morning light harden into something solid. She breathed in the damp, green air, and she remembered how it felt to be seventeen, how her head had reeled with the thrill of autonomy when she and Gethin used to camp out here on warm summer nights. The wooden boards of the jetty always a shade darker and damp first thing. They'd make tea on his camping stove and they'd talk about the future, and as she forced herself to smoke the first cigarette of the day – to impress him and to assert the personality she was trying to cultivate – she would imagine herself in flatshares in London, or on rooftops in New York, surrounded by interesting people, romantically hungover and sleep-deprived; a part of something cinematic and adult and picturesque. It felt like the beginning of everything. Another memory appeared, vivid and immediate, from the same summer. The two of them coming back from the beach one evening, driving along the part of the A55 between Colwyn Bay and Pensarn that clung, like something impermanent, to the endless expanse of the Irish Sea. Geth driving with no hands while he rolled a cigarette. The dashboard gritted with sand because she always used to put her feet up. The smell of his car: leather, tobacco, work-sweat and paint. The cosmic sounds of what she sneerily called his 'classic rock radio cassettes' – bands like The Doors, or Led Zeppelin – insinuating themselves in her memory as sonic representations of the way that sun sets on water and tarmac, colours her mind conflated with more exciting places like Los Angeles or the French Riviera. The coastal road became infinite and vast, like something from a movie. The air shimmered. It was the way the horizon fuzzed above the water, and the velocity of all of the gleaming cars moving alongside it. She remembered the feeling of trailing her hand out of the window and watching the last rays of sun glitter on the blue-slate of the sea like light leaks in a photograph.

She looked out at the lake and she wondered how much longer Geth had come here for. For how many years he'd maintained a futile relationship with this house and this land that now belonged to her. When the estate agent had mentioned a caretaker she'd made a conscious decision not to ask any questions. She told herself that it absolutely couldn't be Gethin. He wouldn't have stayed around here. She wondered, uncharitably, if he'd ever managed to make any money. People in her line of work were always talking about how blue-collar types actually earned dizzying amounts. Parents of her friends from Oxford used to say things like, 'We're trying to convince Phoebe to become a plumber, that's where the real money is,' when in fact they probably couldn't imagine anything more horrifying, hence funding their offspring through an endless mill of unpaid internships after graduation. When she tried to imagine what had happened to Geth she pictured him in Australia, or Canada, or New Zealand. She imagined him having a wholesome wife who liked the outdoors and wore a lot of Patagonia, and who was into *environmental causes* in a sort of nebulous, Instagram-friendly way. He probably didn't smoke rollies any more. She wondered if he still read. She couldn't imagine the wife – yoga-panted and anoraked – lending him novels the way that she used to when they were kids.

Gethin had been the second person Olwen had slept with. The first was a boy from her school, and the experience had been unpleasant. It had been at a party, and was the kind of thing that nowadays would probably be considered to have not been entirely consensual, but that in 1997 had been something that she'd seen as a situation that she'd been stupid enough to get herself into. She let some kind of fictionalised version of it float to the surface, and she would reel it out as a self-deprecating, comic anecdote at subsequent parties that summer. She didn't tell Geth about it – it was too humiliating. It was easier to let him believe in the boyfriend that she'd invented instead.

The thing with Geth had begun because he'd given her a lift. It must have happened in September, because Taliesin had just left home for university a week or two before. She hadn't seen Gethin since the summer. If anything, she'd been avoiding him. She was embarrassed at how she'd behaved: like a prick-tease, that's what the boys at school would have said. Before that she hadn't really spent any time alone with him. He was Tal's friend, more of an idea than a person. When she was a kid, she'd had a consuming, ultra-romantic obsession with him, but from the vantage point of adolescence she knew that it had been ridiculous. He was basically a farmer. Categorically not her type. Then that day in the summer – God, it was hot that day; it was the heat, she told herself – she remembered going home and writing a long, tortured diary entry about it. She remembered, very clearly, thinking that she was being erudite by quoting Camus – *à cause du soleil* (she was studying *L'étranger* at school. She thought she understood it). It had been thrilling, to let him go that far. And then she lost her nerve, and she had committed the unforgivable crime of having led him on. She'd presumed she wouldn't see him again after Taliesin left home.

It was a Sunday morning; so early that the sky was still mostly silver, although the first bit of light was just starting to crack out along the seam between the hills and the horizon. She was walking along the side of the road just before the S-bends up by Tan-y-Graig. She still had at least another three miles until home and, although just a couple of hours before, she'd been drunk and loose and elated, now she felt cold and alert and sober. The road was razor-sharp here and locals took it at fifty. She knew how the light would disappear when she got into the woods. She felt very acutely that her dress was too short, and despite herself, her mind started to accumulate a catalogue of horrible things that she knew had happened around there. She thought about the sad dark eyes and the shapeless white face of the man in the local newspaper who used to run the cinema in Holyhead, and who had buried the bodies of four men in the woods.

She heard the engine coming from a good way off, and she thought about scrambling up the bank but decided it was better to hold her nerve. She kept her eyes focused ahead, and when the car slowed down behind her she felt herself go blank with fear, as if panic had created a vacuum within her. The sensation of consciousness flooding back when she realised that the car belonged to Gethin was overwhelming. He crawled alongside her, rolled down the window and leant across the passenger seat.

'I'm pulling in. At the lay-by,' he called over the growl of the engine, and she could have laughed, she felt so delirious with relief. She ran ahead to meet him.

'Fuck are you doing walking here?' he grumbled, when she slid into the passenger seat. The car was warm and very full of his presence. A country music cassette was playing. He was staring at her, frankly, which embarrassed her, especially given what had almost happened between them. When she didn't immediately answer the question he put the car into gear and pulled back out on to the road.

'What are *you* doing here?' she finally said. 'It's, like, seven in the morning. On a Sunday.'

He didn't look at her. He kept looking ahead at the road. 'Mountain biking,' he said, 'going Snowdonia. I like getting there before all the other fuckers.'

157

'Oh.'

He smirked, 'Good night, was it?'

She felt something then, a spark of sexuality, like that day in June. Something about the way his face changed, or about the way his fingers drummed the steering wheel. She said, 'It was good. Until it got boring.'

He nodded. 'You got a bit of a death wish, though, haven't you? Walking home here.'

She pulled at the hem of the skirt. 'What are you trying to imply?'

His eyes grazed her bare thighs briefly before flitting back to the road. 'It is a bit jailbait, isn't it?'

She bristled. 'Jailbait? Really? That's a sexist thing to say.'

He shook his head, bemused. 'All right.'

The music swelled in the silence – a man droning about codeine and prison and dirty roads. 'I can't believe you actually listen to this,' she muttered, to try to regain some kind of upper hand.

'I mostly meant about the road anyway,' he said, 'It's a bit stupid, like. Cars go like shit off a shovel on this bit.'

'Oh. Right.' She felt foolish then, as if he'd just called her naïve, or even arrogant, and so, to try to seem adult and worldly, she said, 'So you don't want to sleep with me then?'

'Jesus. Fucking hell, Olwen. Why would you say that?'

'So you do? It felt like you did this summer.'

Again, the head shake, as if he were trying to swat away an insect. He didn't deny it, though, and he looked ruffled and wrong-footed. She felt the spark again: an electric charge.

When he cut the engine at the top of her driveway, she said, 'I do not want to go home right now.'

He narrowed his eyes. 'You want to go up to Tŷ Gwydr?'

The first time with Geth was different. It was a month or so after he'd given her the lift. He almost seemed more nervous than she was. He said, 'Are you sure about this?' He held her face in his hands, and he said, 'You have to tell me if you don't want to do this,' and he kept looking at her the whole time – he stayed very close to her, and he kept his hand at the nape of her neck, his thumb on her cheekbone, and he said, 'Tell me what you like the most,' until a point came when she wasn't nervous any more, and she dug her fingers into the hollows beneath his shoulder blades and told him that she liked it like that, and that no, he shouldn't stop. He shouldn't ever stop.

It surprised her that she didn't meet someone at university like that; that the boys there talked about Petrarchan sonnets and Hélène Cixous, that they discussed American foreign policy and Molly Bloom's soliloquy, but that they couldn't work out how to communicate with their bodies; or maybe they just weren't that interested in trying to communicate with hers.

'Well. Was town a thrill?' she asked James when he came home.

'Fucking hell. We need to get those potholes sorted out. I'm too old to lug all this shit down that track.'

He collapsed in mock exhaustion on the sofa – heaving, reusable shopping bags sagging under the weight of their own abundance all around him. He blew a single lock of floppy black hair out of his face. James would have been a good silent movie star. His expressions were comically mobile. One of the original rewards of closeness with him had been the discovery of all his goofy humour under the hard carapace of ambition and charm. She bounced over to him and straddled him, plastic supermarket packaging crackling as if it were sentient and responding to her presence.

'I missed you,' she said.

'He didn't turn up to keep you company then?'

'Haha.'

'What did you do? You didn't finish any of the unpacking, woman of leisure.'

'I got distracted by the lake. There was a heron.'

'Damn. The pet was supposed to be a surprise.'

'You took *ages*.'

He grinned. 'That's because I got you a present.'

'From the supermarket?'

'I went exploring. I found a charity shop in town.'

'Oh, how sweet. You got me a Marks & Spencer twinset that Nain died in?'

'Oh, ye of little faith!'

'Unauthorised biography of Gary Lineker?'

'Don't underestimate the quality of this town's charity shops, snob. Close your eyes.' He pressed his fingers softly on her eyelids, and after a second or so of rummaging said, 'Lights, camera, action!'

She opened her eyes. He had his head cocked back, one eye closed, and one hand holding an old Canon MV10 camcorder, which he was pointing at her.

'The camera loves you.'

'Seriously?'

'I thought when you come here to work on the script this summer you could make some little films.'

'On a Canon MV10?'

'Only a poor craftsman blames his tools.'

She took the camera and shook her head. Smirked and kissed his nose. 'Please tell me this was under a tenner?'

'You can't put a price on art, babe.'

*

When James bought the house – because it was James who bought it, after all; Olwen's income was neither stable nor swollen enough to even qualify for a mortgage – he made a joke that he was buying her a place to write. At a dinner party in Peckham he ironically insisted that he wasn't becoming a second-home owner; he was becoming a 'great patron of the arts'. Everyone had laughed except a plus one that nobody had met before, who had spent the night in silence, with a face like a smacked arse. He sneered and said, 'Right. Like a Sackler?'

James had laughed graciously, but on the Overground on the way home he said, 'Tariq's new boyfriend is a dick. And he's full of shit. I overheard him telling Theo that he went to boarding school.'

2017

THE NEXT TIME Olwen came she was alone, and the rho-
dodendron was in bloom. The flowers hung in jagged orbs
at shoulder height, and on the afternoon that she arrived,
their petals were beaded with glassy drops of rain. She'd
taken the long route, along the border, through twee,
Housman territory: picturesque English villages, the kind
that inspired retired people to take up watercolours, and
nationalists to make internet video montages with 'Jeru-
salem' playing in the background. The rain started when
she crossed the border into Wales around Oswestry – hard
pellets of it – a whole percussion section thundering down
on the windscreen, turning the glass opaque. The landscape
had changed. The shift didn't register immediately – she had
been too preoccupied with peering through the sheet metal
rain. It was barely perceptible, but there was something different. She'd come off the dual carriageway and the roads
were suddenly lithe and narrow and hemmed in with green,
hardly the width of two cars. It felt wilder somehow, and
she knew she was home.

They'd been planning on coming at Christmas with
the last of their childless friends, but then James's sister had
managed to produce her third son earlier than expected,
and so they were summoned to the family pile in Suffolk
to pay homage instead. Olwen felt the smallest snag of guilt
that she'd left it for so long to come back up to North
Wales. She'd read reports about refugees stranded in Greece
and in the Balkans. She had a friend in Paris who told her
there were camps of men from Africa and the Middle East

living in tents in her neighbourhood, something that the British press barely even deigned to report on, what with the jostling abundance of alternative horror in the news. She thought about her empty house by the lake, a place of ultimate succour, locked up and languishing. The problem was that Olwen didn't really see herself as a 'second home kind of person'. She was an artist. Her personal income was negligible. James was the one with all the wealth, and it didn't particularly suit her idea of herself that she was a beneficial party. She told herself that she was different from James because she had experienced poverty (genteel poverty, but poverty all the same) when she was a graduate. She had worked in shitty hospitality jobs to try to make the rent on terrible flatshares where one of her walls was a curtain. She had known the crawling revulsion of the flesh, watching silverfish skittle across the greasy lino of a communal kitchen floor. She knew how it felt to wash over the bath with a kettle of hot water because she couldn't afford to top up the gas card. She felt in her bones that she was categorically not like James.

In the intervening months since they'd come up to the house in October, James had had a ton of extra work that he'd vaguely put down to 'Brexit fallout'. He kept telling her she should go up to Tŷ Gwydr by herself and she kept insisting that she also had too much on.

'Isn't that why we bought the place?' he'd say, as he headed out the front door in the morning, decked out in Lycra and cycling cleats with his suit rolled up in his bag, 'so that you could start the new script there?'

Now it was June and she couldn't put it off any longer. The singular miracle of spring had swept across London and was ripening into summer, and she felt how keen James was for her to go to *her* place, and 'create', and how keen she ought to be. In reality, the idea of spending months on end alone in the house – which her mind still kept accidentally referring to as Geth's house – intimidated her. When she was at Tŷ Gwydr with James, she could position herself in relation to him, and feel like less of a fraud. She couldn't be an alien when James, who called the village *Clanelgan,* and who had never been north of Oxford before meeting her, was there. This was one of the reasons that they'd bought somewhere in Llanelgan in the first place. Olwen found it easier to reconcile herself with the idea of owning a second home if it was in a place that she could technically claim as her own. She could blithely tell her friends in London about *hiraeth*, a Welsh word that, she'd learnt long after leaving Wales, approximately meant longing for the homeland. She wasn't buying a second home, she was *going* home. She was giving in to a primeval pull.

Of course, the other problem was the work itself. Going to the house meant facing the proverbial blank page, and around that time, Olwen was in the middle of something of a professional crisis. She was thirty-four years old, and was yet to experience anything tantamount to failure in her short life thus far. Getting the funding at the age of twenty-six had been prodigious, and when the film had come out a week after her thirtieth birthday, it was lauded 'an instant feminist art-house classic'. She'd had a steady stream of work since then, and James had provided her with the opportunity to take the underpaid jobs that brought cachet and esteem, rather than having to sell out. Consequently, her reputation had so far remained unsullied, which was why, what she still referred to as 'the Twitter thing', had been so especially hard for her to digest.

It had happened about a month after her second film had premiered in Berlin, around the time that she'd first seen the advert for Tŷ Gwydr on her Instagram feed. A review had appeared in an achingly cool and consciously cerebral journal, and if the review hadn't been about her (or, ostensibly, about her work), she probably would have enjoyed the sheer exuberance of its hilarious, caustic annihilation. It had been written by the younger sister of a girl she'd known in college, and she first came across it when another mutual friend saw said 'kid sister' tweeting it, and sent it to her as 'a kindly heads-up'. Above the link, the newly anointed critic had written 'bored of being asked to identify with the problems of the bourgeoisie,' which was extra galling, because Olwen knew that the writer herself had grown up in a three-storey house in St John's Wood and that her father was on the board of Tate Modern. No one else on the internet seemed to care about these biographical details, though, and over the next three days Olwen became a figure of elated ridicule online. Gaffs she'd made in old interviews were exhumed. Details of her parents' and even her grandparents' incomes were speculated upon gleefully by total strangers. A meme was made and circulated with delight. Her friends tried to convince her that being the subject of a short-lived internet storm was a badge of honour and credibility. James told her she was being thin-skinned and kept evoking the superlative adjectives gushed forth by the five-star review in the *Guardian*. Meanwhile, she sat at her desk, attempted to plough on with the script she'd been working on for the past year, and thought about the person who'd said, 'vapid af! edgy aesthetics aside, this "auteur" (i die) has about as much depth and integrity as 90210 with none of the lols.'

The worst part of the whole thing was that a perceptible shift had taken place in the way that she was framed in industry discourse. About a month after it all happened, her name was evoked in a list of examples in a newspaper article about the 'stultifying elitism of the British arts establishment'. A week or so after that, another appeared in which she was described as 'probably grandfathered'. At the time, she was halfway through the first draft of a script about an ageing classical pianist living in north London. Now, she couldn't read it without cringing. She emailed James and her mother a final copy, and then she deleted it off her computer for good.

It was true, though, that about a fortnight ago she'd been blessed with the new idea. She'd stayed at Tony's book launch for the smallest amount of time possible after the conversation with Arthur. When she'd got home, she'd gone straight to her desk, had taken a blank new Moleskine from the pile she kept in the bottom drawer, and had written two words on the first page.

FOLKLORE

RESISTANCE

The first part was what excited her the most. When she was a child, she'd been obsessed with Welsh folklore – with the idea that magic pulsed closer to the surface of life here than it did in other places; that the membrane between the supernatural and reality, and between the present and the past, was more porous and mutable here than anywhere else. On rainy weekend afternoons, she'd sit at the little desk in her bedroom and she'd write pages and pages of would-be 'novels' plagiarised from Alan Garner, Susan Cooper and Jenny Nimmo. She wrote about Blodeuwedd and Gwyddno Garanhir. She wrote about faithful hounds called Gelert and wizards ossified for eternity in the trunks of ancient oak trees. When she was eleven, she won a children's writing competition for a short story about a man who spent a night on Cader Idris. She could still remember the opening lines:

'In Wales, it is widely known that a man who sleeps a night atop the ancient mountain of Cader Idris will come down in the morning a mad man or a poet.' And so, her new project had a name; she felt a swell of pride and excitement as she took a felt tip and wrote it on a sticky label on the front of the notebook.

THE MADMAN OF CADER IDRIS

The second part was trickier, but she had a vague idea. The story would take place in the 1980s against the backdrop of the anti-British political unrest of that era. She had just started researching the group that called themselves *Meibion Glyndŵr* and burnt down holiday houses across rural Wales. She had vague memories of it from her own childhood, but the thing that really stuck with her was the run-in she'd had with Gethin's uncle all those years ago in the Glan Llyn. The more research she did into some of the practices of the British police force at that time, the more she started to believe that Iestyn's story might have not just been the far-fetched bragging of an old drunk. She'd written him a polite letter telling him that she'd be 'coming home' for the summer. Naturally, she omitted the fact that this 'home' would be a second one. She made a vague outline of the project and told him that she was planning on undertaking some research. She tried to butter up his ego a little by telling him how struck she'd been by his story all of those years ago – she remembered how much of a raconteur he'd been. She told him that she'd love to hear more.

When she parked her car at the top of the track, she remembered how Geth used to arrive sometimes, and would just smile to himself and audibly exhale. 'It's just dead peaceful here, isn't it?' he used to say. She dragged her luggage down to the clearing where everything came into view. The rain had tapered off and the air smelt of wet stone. She craned her neck to take it all in; the flat disc of water, opaque in the light, and then the aqueous glass façade of Tŷ Gwydr, so elegant and elemental it could have been made of the same stuff as the lake. She took a photo on her phone to send to James. Seeing the vista rendered in low definition and within the parameters of her phone screen made her think of the camcorder he'd bought her last time they were here. Once she'd gone around and checked on everything, she went and found it in the bedside drawer where she'd abandoned it to gather dust in October. Of course, she'd need batteries, and cassettes, and presumably something to convert the tapes into digital files. She took the camera to her desk and began to type an email to Zuzana, her DOP, who would surely know a good place to source that kind of retro equipment. She held the camera in her hand, testing the weight of it, and after that she took out her journal and she began to write.

The equipment arrived a few days later, and when she walked up to the post box at the top of the track, she was surprised to find a whole pile of letters alongside it. She'd spent the first handful of days here living almost incognito, and it was surreal to remember that there was an outside world that might try to reach her at this address. It was mostly envelopes addressed to James: bills or bureaucracy that he'd presumably already received as emails and had dealt with. She didn't take too much notice of it, and it was only as she let the pile drop on to the kitchen table that she noticed the postcard. It was a cheap and glossy reproduction of Westminster Bridge and Big Ben, and her heart softened because it must have been from James. She picked it up and flipped it over, but it wasn't her husband's handwriting on the other side at all. Scrawled next to the address were two words in Welsh, *Cer Adre!* She frowned at them. She'd done three years of the language at school in the 1990s and couldn't remember much beyond the weather and the days of the week. She noticed then that there was no name above the address. Obviously the postcard hadn't been meant for her at all.

A day or two later, she was filming the ripples of light on the water when she remembered what *adre* meant. It was one of those Welsh words that Geth would occasionally use with her as a testament to their closeness. It meant *home*. '*Ti'n mynd adre?*' he used to say sometimes, or even just, 'Shall we *mynd adre* then?' to signal the end of a night. She took that as an omen, and when she went back inside to make lunch she tacked the postcard to the fridge and said the Welsh word aloud into the silence.

101, 1980

'HERE, IESTYN. I got a new one for you. You'll like this. Got a bit of *local colour*.'

Iestyn heard his voice reply but he felt, as he often did when he was with Clive, completely disembodied.

'How do you circumcise a lad from Cerrig?' the policeman asked with glee.

Iestyn shrugged.

'You kick his sister in the back of the head!'

On days when the weather was fine, Clive insisted that they get out the car and walk around the woods for their 'little catch-ups'. He liked to begin their painful rendezvous with vapid sermons about the importance of fresh air and movement, and sometimes, if he was particularly cheerful, he told jokes. It was a Friday afternoon. End of July. Hot and dry. The 101 was dusty and smelt of heat – resinous like dried pine needles and sawdust. Conifers in the summer. Like most of the woodland in North Wales, it was an artificial plantation from the beginning of the century – monoculture, all non-native sitka spruce. Iestyn kicked the gravel as he walked down the forest road. Handed over Angharad's Zippo and a hair tie, fuzzed with a couple of long, red strays, that she'd left in the footwell of his car. The sun was razor sharp on his neck. A single buzzard, shadow black, circled high over the trees that fringed the track. He felt hyper aware of every sound as they walked: the snap of the brittle ground under their feet, the growl of a chainsaw somewhere in the woods, the snarl of a motorbike engine tearing along the main road towards Melin-y-Wig.

In moments of clarity, Iestyn could negotiate with himself about the morals of what he was doing. Sometimes, he'd tell himself, you had to do unpleasant things to get ahead in life. Sometimes you had to stamp on other people's necks. Not only that, but the more he went to their little meetings, the more he got the sense that as much as he hated the English, this lot – with their *comrades in Derry* and their *redistribution of capital* – weren't necessarily the kind of alternative that he wanted to get behind. He'd worked every day of his bloody life. He had a fiancée and a baby on the way. Responsibilities. He thought about them cashing their dole cheques (her 'artist's bursary', that's what Angharad called it) and leeching on the state. Thinking they were so superior. He felt bad because he did like her. But at the end of the day she was a kid. They surely wouldn't be that hard on her. And once they had some dirt, they could try to get Eifion. Wouldn't be so smug after that, would he? She'd told him before that none of them trusted him, so why should he have their backs?

These were the things he told himself. Other days it was less straightforward. Other days he felt so hemmed in with dread, he had the impression his skull was being crushed in cement.

2017

OLWEN KNEW that nostalgia was a cheap thing to trade on but it made her feel something overwhelming whenever she experienced it. She had written the word in stark black capital letters towards the front of her notebook and then, like an artistically inclined teenager, she'd written the etymology underneath.

Nóstos/HOMECOMING
Álgos/ACHE

In the morning she would get up as soon as she felt the first blades of light slice through the film of glass and portion up the floorboards into gold and green. Sometimes she would just film that – the mobile patterns that the sunrise animated across the parquet – but sometimes she would go out on to the veranda and film the water; the gauzy blue mist, the chromatic evolution of the sky through the trees. Birdsong. Stillness. Once, she was lucky enough to get the heron in flight. It swooped down from above the trees and trailed like parachute silk across the surface of the lake before taking off again, enormous wings audibly beating the air. A couple of nights before that, she'd seen a flash of russet in the trees that had surely been a fox, and had become determined to get it on film. She saw it as a deeply auspicious omen. She'd read in *Folklore of Wales* that witches sometimes took the form of foxes – a sure indicator, then, that there was magic in the woods.

She watched the tapes back every evening, and the obsolete format that was so evocative of her adolescence made the feeling of *nóstos/álgos* a thousand times more intense. The tapes were like a direct channel into her past, a means of rendering an intangible feeling material. She wasn't bothered that her peers would laugh at the Ancient Greek, or shudder at how painfully teenage it all was. It felt pure, so she didn't care. She even started listening to the music she'd loved when she was a kid but that she'd later learnt to sneer at. She would lie on the sunken floor in the living room and listen to Jeff Buckley, and Mazzy Star and PJ Harvey. She chose sad songs that took the exact time of smoking a cigarette, because she'd taken that up again too. When she worked in her studio in London, she felt an intense pressure to avoid anything that could be accused of being trite or sentimental. She felt that sentimentality was a gendered affliction, and when someone accused her of it, she felt the same kind of instinctive shame that she felt when she was cycling and she messed up in some way, and she could see drivers or pedestrians thinking *stupid bloody woman*. No one would ever see the tapes anyway. They were mood boards. They were creative mulch. After breakfast, she would go to her desk and write. For the first time in months, writing was something kinetic and satisfying. She was collating material.

She didn't see anyone. In the evening she would mix herself a drink and ring James, or her mother, or Miranda, who had remained her best friend since they'd first met at Fresher's Week in Oxford. She even ordered her shopping online to avoid the problem of having to go into town. There had been some initial teething problems. The deliveryman's sat nav had insisted that the postcode didn't exist and had sent him 'to some bloody farm way out in the arse end of nowhere'. He was called Duncan. He was a garrulous Scouser, and Olwen was thankful that the potholes served as a convenient excuse for her to tell him he could leave the delivery at the top of the track. She didn't particularly want to talk to anyone, and she wouldn't have ever even gone into the village shop if she hadn't been so absorbed by her work that she'd forgotten to pay attention to her menstrual cycle. She considered just ignoring it altogether, but she didn't know anything about wood, she didn't want to stain their expensive Danish furniture, and her menstrual cup was in London, because she was so terrible at organising her life. She was averse to organisation; she thought that being *organised* was deeply suburban.

She felt a different kind of immersion in her past as she approached the shop – a kind of exposure. The woman who served her was about her own age, with tight cork-screw ringlets dyed the same matte black as the mascara that crusted her eyelashes. She was so pregnant she looked as if she might give birth right then and there behind the counter, underneath the stacks of toilet roll and tinned food, and she radiated cheer in a way that doubled Olwen's self-consciousness. She placed the box of tampons on the counter along with a few other items she'd gathered to take the edge off: a pint of milk, a tin of beans, a Twix. The pregnant woman spoke to her in Welsh at first. She grimaced apologetically. The woman carried on beaming benignly and said, in English, 'I know your face somehow. You local?'

Olwen hadn't spoken to anyone in days, and this was the kind of encounter that she found the most excruciating. She passed a hand over her forehead and made herself make eye contact. 'Yeah. Well. Sort of.' She attempted a smile. She made a conscious decision that she would try and sound less RP the next time she opened her mouth. The woman nodded encouragingly, a sharp tiny movement that was more of a twitch. Olwen realised she was expected to elaborate.

'I grew up in the village.'

'Oh, well, we must know each other. We must have gone to school together!'

Olwen had spent the past fifteen years resenting her parents for pulling her out of the local comp and sending her to private school, thus depriving her of the cachet of state education. Her cheeks stung. 'I didn't go to school in town for very long.'

The woman was unfazed. She clicked her tongue against the roof of her mouth as she openly scrutinised her. 'I definitely know you, though. What's your name?'

The part where she felt the most fraudulent was when she had to say *Olwen* out loud. She considered lying and using her middle name, but decided that confessing to Helena would be even worse.

'Olwen.'

The woman gasped, '*No.*' She renewed her bright smile. 'Of course you are! I'm Danny's wife! Nia!'

'Oh,' Olwen said, smiling vacantly, 'of course.'

'Danny Bryn Hendre. Danny Thomas?'

It took Olwen a second to make the connection, and by the time she did, Nia had already said, '*Gethin's* brother.'

She carried on smiling stupidly. 'Danny. Yes.' Her fingers curled into fists and she felt very aware of the air that she breathed as an element separate from herself. The box of chocolate bars on the counter throbbed under the white glare of the strip light. 'Geth's brother,' she repeated.

'You're up at Tŷ Gwydr, aren't you?'

'Uh-huh. For the summer, yeah.'

'*Nice,*' Nia said. 'It's lovely up there, isn't it? Really beautiful spot.'

'Yeah.'

'You been in touch with Geth, since you're back?'

Olwen blinked. 'Is he still in town?'

'Where else would he be?'

She could feel the expression on her face ossify into some kind of picture of polite receptiveness as Nia spoke. 'Oh, you have to give him a text. Here, I'll give you his number. He'd be dying to see you, I'm sure.'

She numbly took her phone out of her pocket and typed the number that Nia read from her own. 'Tell you what, I probably shouldn't tell you this but he was gutted when they put that house on the market.'

Olwen felt as if Nia was pointing a very bright light directly at her. 'Oh, yeah?'

'Oh, yeah, big time.'

All the questions she wanted to ask appeared as fully formed sentences in her head but she was too proud, or maybe just too stunned to articulate them aloud.

'Dan's basically running Bryn Hendre these days,' Nia was saying now.

Olwen wasn't sure how she'd moved back on to Danny again. She was aware that Nia was talking with the enthusiasm of someone who'd been waiting for company for several hours, but she was too dazed to process any of the consequent monologue.

'Iestyn's not too well, bless him. Danny's trying to convince Geth to come and work with him because there's so little for him in the woods these days. But you know what Geth's like. Stubborn, isn't he?'

Iestyn's name drew Olwen out of her numb daze. 'Funny that you should mention Iestyn, actually,' she said, trying to make her voice sound as casual as possible. 'I wrote to him a few months ago and never heard anything back. I was starting to wonder if he'd even got my letter.'

Nia looked at her blankly. She cocked her head to one side. 'To Iestyn? You tried to get in touch with *Iestyn*?'

'Uh-huh. It's for a project I'm working on. Research.'

'Right,' said Nia, the vowel long with suspicion. 'Well. As I said, he's really not too well at the moment so I can't see how much use he could be to you. Geth's the one you should get hold of really. He'd love to hear from you. Just give him a text. He'd be dead chuffed, I'm sure.'

'Sure. Geth.'

'And I'm here every Wednesday,' Nia trilled. 'It's voluntary, the shop – run by the community. You can sign up, if you want. Shall I get the form?'

Olwen wrote down her name and a false mobile number, and when she left the shop, she vowed to never go back again.

She smoked her daily cigarette a good five hours early when she got back to Tŷ Gwydr that afternoon. She put *Grace* on the record player, and she lay on the floorboards and closed her eyes. She tried to remember – really remember, not just tell herself that she was experiencing the memory – how Gethin sounded. How the weight of his body felt. The texture of his skin. How he tasted. How it felt when he was inside her – how they fitted together. It was hard, when you were in a relationship with someone, to remember how it had felt to sleep with other people. Two years ago, when they were filming in Romania, she'd slept with her 1st AD. She remembered how, the first time they kissed, his tongue had so felt different to James's that she'd had to overcome a momentary flicker of revulsion. When she tried to re-experience the moment now – the way he had walked her up against the wall of the en-suite in the hotel, the way the carpet had felt on her skin, the scratch of his stubble grazing her thighs – she could only experience it as an observer. She exhaled a fine plume of smoke and she focused on trying to feel Gethin. But she really didn't know him at all any more.

The cigarette was making her head feel light and her whole body was becoming pleasantly insubstantial. She thought about the afternoon that they drove out to Snowdonia and hiked from Betws to Llyn Parc. It must have been 1998 because the Cher song 'Believe' was number one and always on the radio, and Geth had a soft spot for it. He used to turn it up to full volume and croon along energetically, so that being inside the car felt like she was inside some kind of tin-can speaker, rattling along the country roads. He always used to drive fast, and he used to drive even faster when the music was loud, but she was young enough and stupid enough that it felt thrilling. Sometimes she even used to think that Morrissey was right, and that as ways to die go, this one – by his side – would indeed be pretty heavenly. Death wasn't real then. She didn't know anyone that had died.

The real thing she remembered about that day, though, was the old mine. The mines were deep in the forest, where the light was blue-green and negligible, and the tonic air resonant with the sound of the water tumbling over rocks.

'Look, there's an entrance to the old lead mine,' Geth told her. 'Lead or zinc I think it was up here.' He pointed at a tiny arch carved into the rock face, barred with gridded iron and a rusting old padlock. It couldn't have been more than five foot tall at a push, barely big enough for a man to get through. She shuddered.

'When did they close?' she asked. She hoped that it was a long time ago, when men were smaller, like the tombs she'd seen in St David's Cathedral when she was a child.

Geth shrugged. 'Turn of the century? Twenties? You see them all through the woods round here.'

She felt woozy as they drew closer to the dark hollow. She was repelled, and yet there was something compelling about being on the threshold of an unimaginable recent past. She thought about the R. S. Thomas poem they'd studied at school, about Wales being a country with no future and no present, only past. The temperature plummeted suddenly on approach. The air felt bone dry and smelt metallic and ancient. The water ran rust coloured. The lichen was more vividly green, as if it were incandescent. She could almost hear the footsteps of the miners, making their way into the wet, black insides of the earth.

The last time she'd seen Gethin it was four o'clock in the morning. It was Christmas Eve, the kind of weather where the condensation on the single glazed windows of Tawelfan froze. She was lying on her back on her old single bed on top of the duvet, naked and starting to feel the cold now that he'd got up, now that he was collecting his clothes from the floor, holding them in a pile at his chest.

'What are you doing?' Something had happened between them that she hadn't understood.

'Well, I'm not gonna drive home in the buff, am I?'

She sat up. 'You're not going home now?'

He was looking at the skirting boards; he bent over to pull on his boxers. 'Yeah. Got shit to do tomorrow.'

'On Christmas Eve?'

'Mm.'

'Gethin. Don't be absurd. Come here.'

He stood on one leg to get his right foot into a sock. He frowned. 'No, really. Don't be offended I've just . . . I should get out of here like. I don't want to run into your mam and dad, do I?'

179

She was baffled. 'Why? My mum and dad love you.'

'Yeah, well,' he grabbed his jeans, 'send them my love, then, yeah?'

She stared at him. 'What's happening here? Did I do something?'

For a second, he looked genuinely pained. 'No,' he said quickly. 'No, course not. You didn't do anything.'

'Why won't you look at me then?'

He was fumbling with his button fly. '*Fuck's sake.*' He closed his eyes, and when he opened them again, he looked directly at her. 'There. I'm looking at you, aren't I?'

'Geth.'

'Look. I told my mam I'd go round to hers early. I'm taking her to see Aunty Meinir tomorrow. I'll call you, all right?'

'I'm here till the twenty-ninth,' she said.

'Great.'

He looked at the door and then stepped towards her and kissed her on the forehead. After he'd left, she stared at the ceiling. She reached for the Discman on her bedside table, and she skipped to the seventh track on the album (the same album that she was listening to now, almost fifteen years later), and she let tears roll down her cheeks, the kind that she would later self-deprecatingly describe as 'picturesque and self-indulgent' to her friends at university, where she played the story for laughs. So Gethin had shut down again, and nothing had changed. Nowadays they had names for his particular affliction. Nowadays journalists wrote long, pop-psych essays in the colour supplements about the burden of toxic masculinity, about the legions of emotionally stunted young men who couldn't articulate their feelings, who were always blank and closed, much to the detriment of them-selves and to society at large. So many sad and terrible men.

In the morning, she was the last one to come down for breakfast. Her parents, her brother, and even Paolo all eyed her with oppressive expectation.

'Well,' Margot Yates said, voice camp with innuendo, 'we weren't expecting you to be alone.'

Olwen concentrated on breathing for a couple of beats, on composing herself. She laid her knife down next to her plate. 'It was a one-night stand, OK? We're not picking out curtains, you know. What, you think I'm going to move back here and get married? Get a little pebble-dash house on Maes Hafod? Reproduce immediately? Un-fucking-likely.'

Taliesin scoffed. 'God, Ol. You're such a snob.'

2017

SHE WAS OUT ON the jetty filming when she heard the engine at the top of the track. Over the course of the afternoon, a jaundiced, watery sunlight had picked its way through the grey grit that the rain had left, and she'd wanted to get it, the dirty yellow of it, hanging above the water like something nuclear. At first, she was annoyed that the noise of what she presumed was her grocery delivery would ruin her shot. It took her a moment to realise that she wasn't due one.

'Shit,' she muttered. She stood very still, camera still running, and soon, over the sound of her own breathing, over the birds, the breeze, she heard the noise of footsteps biting into the dirt. By the time the person attached to the noise reached the bottom of the track, she was inside and crouched, fully clothed in the bathtub, where she could see the veranda from the long window but where, if she angled it right, anyone on the other side of the glass would have trouble seeing her. So much for rural solitude, she thought to herself. She heard the fuller, smoother sound of foot-steps unfolding across the wooden boards of the veranda, and then a few seconds after that began, she perceived the familiar silhouette through the visual frame of the window, which she'd already thought several times, when taking a bath, was so much like the frame of a camera. As soon as she saw him she felt something tighten inside her. She knew it from his gait, from the way he held himself, from the shape of his shoulders. He stopped, plunged his hands into his pockets and looked around. He rocked back and forth on his heels. After a few steps in either direction, he called her name, and then he turned to face the house, and she saw Gethin's face for the first time in over a decade. The feeling was acutely physical – almost overwhelmingly so. She held her breath. The concurrence of familiarity and estrangement was disorienting, so much so that it took her a moment to register basic, superficial details – like the fact that he was still beautiful, or that he was going grey at his temples, or that his cheeks were even more hollowed than before. She watched him sigh, and close his eyes for a second, and then, without thinking much about it, she pointed the camera at him and began to film through the bathroom window. He called her name a few more times. He did a couple of laps of the house, and when she dared to stand up and risk being seen so that she could get a more generous view, he walked up and down the jetty. Through the viewfinder, she watched him come back to the house. He disappeared for a moment and the doorbell rang, and for a minute or two she dropped to a squat again and tried to breathe as silently as possible to avoid being detected. The sound of her name in his voice – the precise timbre of it so strikingly right and intimate – resounded a few more times, and then finally, it seemed, he gave up. He came back into view. He sat on the edge of the veranda, overlooking the lake, and after a minute or so, he put his head into his hands. She clocked a tremor in his shoulders so discreet it was almost imperceptible, but then there was a time, she guessed – a long time ago – when she used to feel as attuned to the precise movements of his body as she did to her own. She kept on filming as he watched the lake and appeared to unravel, and she knew that what she was filming was good.

*

James called later that evening. They talked about the London Bridge attack and the election. They talked about her work. He wanted to 'fix the agenda for summer'. She resented it when he talked about life like it was a job. She made the right noises as he discussed coming up for the long weekend at the end of June and reminded her about the week with their friends in Sardinia in August.

'Are you listening to me?' he asked, as she relit her cigarette.

'Uh–huh. Sardinia.'

'Are you *smoking?*'

'God, your hearing's good.'

James made a noise that she knew pertained to her potential fertility and she said, 'Don't be such a girl scout. Give me a break.'

He sighed. 'So. Sardinia.'

'Sardinia?'

'Romy's mum's place. August.'

'Ah. Yes. Sardinia. How many of us are there going to be again?'

She pulled the Welsh tapestry blanket around her shoulders. The lake was the lustrous grey of dusk and the bats were out above the trees. She made the right noises but her head was full of Gethin, sitting and looking out at the water; the way that his shoulders were going like that. The way that eventually he'd stood up, had run his hands through his hair, and how reduced he'd looked as he'd left.

When she finally got rid of James that night, she lay on her back on the living-room floor and she watched the footage of Geth again and again. Even within the tiny confines of the camera's screen you could tell (or she could tell, at least) how robust he'd looked at the start of the film, and how diminished he was at the end. Before she went to bed that night, she wrote a single sentence in her notebook.

'The madman of Cader Idris is called Gethin.'

It was different, when he came again a few days later. It was the end of the afternoon on the first really hot day of the year. A white sun burnt like a bleach stain in an absolutely blue sky, and she was at her desk with the blind down in an attempt to force herself to work. She'd been restless all day, and when she heard the truck, she almost felt like she'd manifested his arrival. She knew it was him – she recognised the specific robustness of the engine. She took her camera and darted to her hiding place in the bathroom. The thrill made her nimble. He was more confident this time. He rang the doorbell immediately and when enough time had lapsed to presume that she was out, he only called her name once before striding out towards the jetty. He must have just finished work. He was in an old army surplus shirt, with orange chaps over his jeans, work boots dusty with baked earth. He took the chaps off first and then the boots. She watched his arms make bows as he unbuttoned his shirt and shrugged it off to reveal his broad shoulders, skin stretched taut across the contours of muscle and bone. She felt her jaw go slack and was so moved by his audacity that she stood up in the bath and opened the window to lean out. If he heard anything he didn't so much as flinch, and when he was down to his boxers, he walked out to the edge of the jetty and hurled himself off into the still water. Through the viewfinder of the camera, she watched him disappear – reduced to a dark head and limbs slicing through the surface of the lake. She stopped filming. She put the camera down in the basin and she leant against the cool tiles of the bath-room wall. She closed her eyes and the image of his body seemed to appear in negative as if she'd been staring at a very bright light. She saw his hands first when he emerged, gripping the edge of the jetty. She watched his sinewy arms flex as he pulled himself up out of the water. His damp skin gleamed in the sun. He used his shirt to dry himself off, and then, half-dressed, he sloped off back in the direction of the track. Just before he disappeared entirely from view, he stopped and, surveying the lake, stretched languidly. She wondered if he wanted to get caught.

She couldn't sleep that night. She felt alert to even the tiniest of noises and her body was insistently mobile as she tried to will stillness on it. When sleep finally came, her dreams were so lucid that she wasn't entirely sure if she wasn't in fact awake. In the dream – if that's what it was – she was convinced that she wasn't alone in the house. She could feel the weight of someone else's presence alter the way that the air circulated through the rooms. Someone was watching her, she was sure of it. Mercifully, the surreal intensity of the nightmare eventually opened her eyes, and for the first second that they were open, she could just make out the bluish outline of a person standing on the veranda. She blinked, adjusted to the darkness, and the silhouette that she'd been so convinced of was gone. When she properly woke up, into the soft certainty of daylight, the conviction had vanished, and she knew that there couldn't have been a man there; that the human shape just beyond the open glass door must have been some kind of spectral straggler from her dreams.

It was still early. She went and made a pot of tea, and when that was brewing, she went out to go and feel the pleasant coldness of the morning air on her face. The wooden boards were still damp underneath her feet. She inhaled and her body felt renewed; but then when she looked around she realised that something had changed. Something was off. Just out of the periphery of her vision, she saw a fleck of synthetic green that hadn't been there before. Very slowly, she made herself turn and focus on it, and the flash of colour became two empty bottles of Stella Artois, sitting on the low table by the deck chair. She felt her skin tighten across her bones. Her breath caught in her throat.

'Have you told James?' Miranda's voice on the other end of the phone was insistent – bordering on shrill.

'Of course I haven't told James, are you serious?'

'I mean honestly, if you're going to tell anyone you should probably tell the police.'

'The police? Don't be so ridiculous. I'm hardly going to call the police on him, am I? It's Gethin. I mean, come on. What would I say, like, my childhood sweetheart has been paying me nocturnal visits and consuming negligible amounts of alcohol outside my window whilst I sleep?' She paused. 'Granted it does sound pretty chilling put like that, doesn't it?'

Miranda didn't say anything, and Olwen said, 'He's really not a creepy guy, though. If you knew him you'd know that.'

'Are you even sure it's him?'

'He always used to drink Stella.'

'Everyone drinks Stella. What are you expecting to find, a bottle of artisanal fucking IPA?'

She sighed. 'They sell craft beer here, Miri.'

'The *embourgeoisement* of your shitty hometown isn't the point here, Ol. Can we pause for one second to actually examine the facts? Your ex-boyfriend, who by all accounts never really got over you, which is already weird, by the way—'

'We don't know for sure if that's true.'

'Hmm, the watching you while you sleep would suggest otherwise.'

'Maybe he'd forgotten something, when he came here in the afternoon.'

'What, like his boxers? Olwen, why did he even come in the afternoon? You don't just walk into someone's garden and *take your clothes off*. He's nuts. He's fucking mental. You haven't seen him for fifteen years; he's probably become one of those sad old white guys in a Metallica T-shirt, writing blog posts about feminist bitches depriving him of his God-given right to sex. God, I bet he voted Brexit. I bet he calls women "females" and's big into the great replacement theory. And *close to the bone* comedy. And reptilians.'

Olwen ignored her. 'I don't think this is about me,' she said. 'I think it's about the house.'

'It's your house! It's private property. He can't just swan in for a swim and some night-time boozing.'

When they were at university, incidentally, Miranda used to wear a gold chain name necklace whose pendant formed the letters M-A-R-X in perfect cursive.

'I can't believe I'm even having to tell you how out of line this is,' she said. 'He undressed right in front of you, totally uninvited, in every sense. It's sexual harassment.'

Olwen closed her eyes and remembered his broad shoulders, the way his torso tapered down to his waist, the spare muscularity of his limbs.

'I didn't exactly object,' she said.

After she'd hung up on Miranda, she opened up the notes application on her phone and she drafted a text to send to the number that Nia had given her.

188

It's me. I know you were here last night. Why didn't you come and say hello?

It's me. I know you were here last night. It's out of line and frankly pretty creepy. If you do it again I'll have to do something about it.

It's me. I know you've been coming here. It's out of line and frankly pretty creepy. Knock next time?

It's me. Nia gave me your number. Maybe we could get a drink sometime? It's been a while.

She copied and pasted the final text into the messaging app and she hit send.

When she'd done that, she went back outside to collect the bottles and put them in the recycling. She vaguely registered that there was a rolled-up scrap of paper in one of them, but it had fallen down to the base of the bottle, and there were also a couple of cigarette butts, so she presumed it was just rubbish, the receipt maybe – it was the right size and shape to be a receipt.

She didn't bother to shunt it out on to her palm and investigate further, but if she had, she would have read the words (fuzzed by dregs of beer and morning dew, but legible all the same): 'CER ADRE!'

2017

HE TOLD HER to meet him for a drink at The Boars on Friday at around half five, when he'd be done with work. He said, 'I can give you a lift into town if you want. I'm doing a job up at the farm at the moment, so you're on my way.'

She replied that she wasn't seventeen any more, that she knew how to drive now, thanks. She didn't tell him that she'd only got her licence on the eve of her thirtieth birthday, and that before James had bought the house, she'd only ever driven as a kind of joke on holidays to prove a point to him, and that even now she didn't really like doing it, especially not up around the village, where the roads were thin and elastic. James made fun of her for the way she sat upright in the seat, and peered over the steering wheel like a mole, but she wasn't going to tell Gethin about that. She also didn't tell him that she didn't particularly want to go to The Boars and that she found the idea of going to any pub in town almost nauseatingly claustrophobic. The most important thing of all was that he didn't think she was a snob.

She got there a little early, just after they'd opened, and she felt relieved that the boy on the bar was just that, a boy, and much too young to remember her. He stared at her openly as she approached, which pleased her. She'd put eye make-up on for the first time in weeks before she'd left the house. It was a hot afternoon and she was wearing a sheer summer dress with thin straps. Her shoulders had tanned, and she'd admired her reflection on the way out of the house, in the rear-view mirror of the car, and even in the gleaming surface of the parking meter on the top of town. She looked good. She had the feeling that her body was somehow more vivid, as if physically she were even more alive than usual.

She ordered a gin and tonic because she didn't much trust the wine or the 'cocktails' here, and she took it outside to the beer garden around the back. She had the impression that the pub hadn't changed at all. So much of town was different: the bookshop had gone, the newsagents was an opticians, the art supply shop was an estate agents. A lot of places were just empty, with fading '*AR OSOD*' signs plastered up inside foggy windows. And yet, all the pubs in town still seemed to be going strong. She often used that as a line, in London in her early twenties. She'd say, 'I come from a place with twelve pubs but you have to drive twenty miles to get to a cinema.' She slid into one of the picnic benches and took the book that she'd brought as a prop out of her tote bag, although her thoughts were too mobile to facilitate the kind of concentration that reading required. She looked at the same meaningless sentence again and again; she ran her fingers through her hair to stop it from going flat, and she took small sips of her drink, aware that she hadn't eaten since breakfast and that she wanted to be lucid when he arrived. She picked the book up and put it down again. She touched the screen of her phone to check the time.

She'd sat facing away from the entrance, because her dress was cut low at the back and flattering, and finally, when she heard the door drag across the concrete with a sigh, she felt her body go hollow with anticipation. She didn't turn around, so the first part of him that she saw was his hand as it landed on her shoulder, the rough skin around his fingertips, the dirt under the bitten nails. The shoulder in question tensed – her whole body did, despite herself.

'Y'right?'

She overcame the impulse to press his fingers with her own. He sat down on the bench opposite her, and it was so surreal to see him, this close again, that she had the impression that she was looking at something horrifying or supernatural – a reanimated corpse or a talking animal.

'Hi,' she said.

'Hi.' He almost smiled.

'This is weird, isn't it?'

'Yeah.'

She picked up her glass. 'Well, cheers?'

He clinked his with hers and said, '*Iechyd da*,' and she thought how she wanted to drink a lot, she wanted to be drunk. 'It's crazy to see you.'

'It is, yeah.' He lifted his glass again and then put it back down, and she realised that he was nervous too and felt a *frisson* of possibility.

'I mean it's crazy to be here again, generally. In town, I mean.'

'Yeah.' He felt in his back pocket for his baccy. 'You seen anyone?'

'Anyone?'

'Yeah. You know. From town. Besides me. And Nia.'

She was embarrassed. 'Oh,' she said. 'Honestly, I've just been working. Working loads.'

He was trying to roll a cigarette – something he could usually do with his eyes closed, in the wind, one-handed, holding a drink – but his thumbs were shaking too much to get a purchase on the Rizla. He swore under his breath. He managed to seal the paper around the tobacco at last, and started to smoke; and as each loaded second dragged on, she felt more and more aware of the banal, steady rhythms of everyone else's conversations, and of the silence bulging between the two of them. She willed him to ask another question, but he just kept on looking at her, and it felt as if the feeling between the two of them was such that even reciprocating his eye contact was significant and dangerous.

'So,' they both said at the same time; smiled and lowered their eyes at the same time. His mouth creased and she felt confident enough to say, 'Go on.'

'No, you go on,' he insisted.

She wished he hadn't, given she hadn't actually considered what she might say.

'What's the work you're doing then?' he asked.

She was relieved. 'I'm working on a new project – about Wales, actually. About a guy who spends a night on Cader Idris.'

'Oh, yeah?'

'Yeah. And I want to set it in the 1980s – bring in all that stuff about *Meibion Glyndŵr* – you know, the holiday-home arsons and stuff.'

He raised his eyebrows. 'You're writing about people burning down second homes in your second home?'

She kept the lie as vague as possible, 'Well. We don't know how much longer it'll be a second home, do we?'

He looked perturbed. An uncomfortable beat of silence followed, and she began to ramble to fill it. 'I'll tell you who I've been trying to get hold of, actually, with no success: your uncle.'

'Iestyn?'

'Yeah. Do you not remember that night in the Glanny – Jesus, years ago – Iestyn was there and he was shitfaced, and he told us this story about how he'd got taken in for selling 'shrooms?'

'All right, keep it down,' he said in a low voice.

'Sorry,' she half-whispered. 'But you remember what he said, right? About the Special Branch guy trying to use it to blackmail him, and to get him to snitch on the arsonists?'

Gethin kept his face blank. 'Yeah. I remember.'

She leant in closer. 'At the time I thought it was bullshit. But I've been doing some research, and you know the police did all sorts: tapping people's phones, paying informers, planting evidence, sending in fake activists – you know, like, double agents . . .'

Geth cocked his head. 'Well. You won't get a peep out of Iestyn. I didn't even know about the drugs until then. And when I asked my mam about it she proper froze up. *Crachach* my family were, not the type to get involved in stuff like that.'

'What's *crachach*?'

He smiled. 'Like the Welsh cultural élite. It's why my *taid* was so pissed off when my mam went and got herself knocked up with a carney, as he used to say.'

'Huh.'

'Anyway. It was more west that all that was happening. Pen Llŷn. Pembrokeshire. Iestyn was probably bullshitting – you know what he's like. How would he have even known those people? Iestyn, political? He used to drink his tea out of a Silver Jubilee mug, for Christ's sake.'

'You believed it at the time.'

'I know. And you didn't, remember? Besides. They wouldn't have had anything on him, the police. 'Shrooms used to be legal, didn't they? You remember me and Tal picking them?'

The evocation of their shared past lingered, altered the empty space between them, made the air feel taut. She made herself speak. 'I was convinced you were gonna get poisoned.'

'See, that was the kind of thing we could only do round yours. If my mam found out she would have gone mental.'

'Yeah. Well. Hippy parents. But you think what he said about the policeman trying to recruit him – that was probably bullshit, right?'

'Yeah. I dunno. Maybe they were banking on him not knowing that and thinking he'd fucked up . . . Either way you're not gonna get anything out of Iestyn. Probably scared him shitless.'

'Maybe you could ask him?'

Geth laughed. 'There's an idea. Me and Ietsyn were never exactly best mates, were we?'

Again, the idea of them sharing a past registered and felt significant. His eyes slid back down the table, fixed on his hands. He opened his mouth to speak, but didn't.

'Anyway,' she said brightly. 'The eighties is just a backdrop. It's about folklore more than anything. The guy on Cader Idris.'

'Yeah, I remember you being dead into that.' He smiled. 'Miss *Mabinogion*.'

'Stop it!' She could feel herself blushing, which was dangerous. She took another drink. 'There's a fox in the woods that I'm taking as a very auspicious sign. I've been trying to film it.'

'Christ alive, you must be the only person around here trying to look after the foxes. Don't let any of the farmers know you've joined the RSPCA.'

'Thank God they're not allowed to hunt them any more.'

'You don't need a pack of dogs to kill a fox. Iestyn even used to shoot the moles out on the top field. Pick them off one by one with his old .410.'

An image flashed through her mind of Iestyn, bent over a pool cue at the Glan Llyn. Squinting as he aimed. She grimaced. 'How do you say "fox" in Welsh?'

'*Llwynog,*' he said. 'So the guy. Does he come down from Cader a madman or a poet?'

'T.B.C.'

He drank. 'All right. Mysterious. It's gonna be a film then?'

'Hopefully it'll eventually turn into a film. Right now it's just a sort of collage of like, fragments. Ideas. A mood board. But the idea would be for it to be a film. Yeah. Not like a linear film, though. You know Kieślowski? Have you seen *The Double Life of Veronica?*'

He shook his head and she cringed, and she wondered why she was talking to him about Kieślowski when he probably didn't even watch films. He used to quote *The Godfather* sometimes when they were kids. She remembered he liked *The Terminator* a lot, but she could hardly see him signing up for Mubi, or driving for two hours to go to the Everyman in Manchester to watch a film with subtitles. She tried to correct her mistake. 'I sound super pretentious, don't I? And I'm rambling.' Her voice faltered. He smiled at her.

'You always did used to do that, when you were nervous.'

She swallowed. 'Tell me about you. About your life. How are you?' Her eyes caught on the new cigarette he was already rolling.

'You want it?'

'Yes. Could I, please?'

He leant over and placed it directly between her lips. He lit it and for a second their eyes met and something fused inside her. She imagined how it would feel if he reached out and touched her throat. She turned away and exhaled a thin plume of smoke, and to kill the moment, she said, 'Being here is making me take up all my bad, teenage habits again.'

He raised his eyebrows at her.

'So,' she said. 'You.'

'Am I a bad teenage habit?' He grinned.

'I meant, how are you?'

'I'm all right.'

She said, 'Tell me about your life, though. Like, I don't know . . . Are you married? Do you have any kids? Are you still a *lumberjack*?' She said the last word as if it was something whimsical.

He frowned. 'I was never exactly a *lumberjack*. I work in a skidder team.'

'Gross?'

'All right then – I'm a *chainsaw operator*.'

'Prosaic.'

'Most jobs are. There's a reason why they pay you.'

'And it's going well then? Chainsaw operating?'

He narrowed his eyes. 'It's been better.'

'But you're working with your brother now or what?'

'Dan's got some work he needs doing up at Bryn Hendre. You know what he's like. Likes to act like I'm the one doing him a favour.'

'And after that?'

'Well. Then we'll have to see. There's not a lot of jobs going. It's getting to the point now where I'm going to have to try and get something else. Best-case scenario, if I'm not too old, I retrain as a tree surgeon. Or, I get something with the Forestry Commission. Desk job, even. Or some work as a groundsman. But that's pretty patchy too.'

'And worst-case?'

He shrugged. 'There's plenty of things I could do. I could be a courier. You know. Those Amazon guys. Mostly I just don't want a boss.'

'An Amazon delivery guy? That sounds like a terrible idea.'

He didn't reply.

'Kids, then?' Married?'

'Nope.'

She tried to keep her face blank and he said, 'What about you? You married?'

She hesitated, and then she said she was, as if the fact was an embarrassing one, as if it would be suffixed with a 'but'. 'He's called James.'

Gethin smirked.

'What?' she said. 'What? What's wrong with James?'

He smiled at her. 'What's he like? From London, I guess?'

'He's from a lot of places. His dad travelled a lot.'

'You make it sound like he was in the circus.'

She snorted. 'Hardly.'

'Is he nice?'

'Nice?'

'Is he a nice bloke? Is he nice to you?'

She thought about James, who was pathologically nice; who, after eight years still acted as if her enduring existence was some kind of God-given miracle, and she said, 'Why would he not be nice?'

'Is he rich at least?'

She pursed her lips and then took a large swig of gin. It was starting to glitter in her blood. 'What do you think?'

He smirked and drained his glass. ''Nother one?'

She still had a good third of hers left, but she drank it quickly to chase the glitter. 'Please.'

By seven she was drunk. She couldn't tell if he was

too; he was always better at hiding it. Olwen was a good drunk. She loved being drunk. She loved how much it got her out of herself. How much more porous other people felt. They were talking about politics. She'd started it. She'd felt she ought to, given the election results. She'd voted in Hackney South and was pleased with herself. She started to ask Gethin questions as if he were a spokesperson for his constituency.

'We used to be Labour here when we were kids, though, didn't we?'

'Yeah. But not for ages now.'

She shook her head. She asked him how people in town felt about the result of the referendum.

'Bored of it,' he said.

'Bored of it? God, we're really fucking doomed, aren't we?'

He shrugged.

'I mean, it's a fucking catastrophe, isn't it?'

He shrugged again.

She lit the third cigarette that he'd rolled her. 'Oh my God. Don't tell me you were a Leave voter?'

'Honestly, I really couldn't give a flying fuck. They're all knobs. Westminster. Brussels. The Senedd. Tories. Labour. I don't really see the fuss.'

'Jesus. Were you one of those *iconoclastic* Leave voters?'

He sneered. 'I'm not some prick who believes in *Great Britain* and knobbly cucumbers . . . I don't think the Polish are taking our jobs and Nigel Farage would be a right lad down the pub or whatever. It's all a load of bollocks.'

'So you did vote Remain?'

'What does it even matter what I voted? They're all liars anyway, aren't they?'

She made a noise of exasperation.

'I don't understand why everyone's getting themselves worked up about this one thing. Sure, it's a shit show. But look at everything else they've done over the past five years. Over the past fifteen years, even. New Labour. That was a load of horseshit as well, wasn't it? I really can't believe that all you lot are surprised by this.'

'All us lot?' She decided not to take offence and to change the subject instead, because she'd been enjoying it before, how he'd started to open up a bit after his fourth pint. How he stopped answering things in opaque monosyllables. She felt that she was getting somewhere.

'Speaking of people who are being fucked over by Brexit – Tal sends his love.'

'Taliesin? How was he fucked over by Brexit?'

'He was hoping to move back to France. He lived there for years. With his partner.'

'Oh, yeah?'

'I mean I guess they could just get married. His partner's French.'

'You like him? The guy? It's a guy?'

She resisted making a sarcastic comment. 'Samir's an angel. They've been together for, like, five years now. He's seeing someone else, though, in Brighton, so they'd have to work that out if they moved back.'

'Seeing someone else? How's that?'

'Well, they're in an open relationship.'

'An open relationship? You having a laugh?'

'What's wrong with an open relationship?'

He raised his eyebrows. 'Is that what you're doing? With *James*?'

'Don't say his name like that.'

'Like what?'

'Like he's called like, "Horatio" or something. There's nothing wrong with "James".'

'You're imagining things, love. I didn't say his name like anything.'

'Sure.'

'So, are you then?'

'Are we what?'

'In an *open relationship*?'

She hesitated. She thought about the producer, and about the novelist that she'd met at the Berlinale the year before last. She thought about the feeling between the two of them that was happening right there, that was making the particles of the air between them pulse. She couldn't work out what was sexier – possibility or prohibition – and because she was drunk, she was giving in to the impulse to heighten the electricity between them, even if her sober self would have told her it was a patently bad idea.

'Not exactly,' she said at last, taking a sip of her drink and looking at him over the rim of her glass in a way that was implicitly suggestive.

He looked at her hard, and was about to say something when his phone began to vibrate on the table. He winced and picked it up.

'Y'right?' he said. 'Shit. Yeah. Yeah, no I totally forgot it was tonight . . . Yes. Yes, I know I'm a daft prick . . . Give it a rest, I'll be there.' He looked up at Olwen. 'I'll bring someone, though, if that's OK?'

'Megan never liked me,' Olwen said as they crossed the top of town to The Vaults. 'Are you sure she's gonna want me there?'

"Course Meg liked you. She likes everyone. Besides, it's not like she owns the pub, is it?'

'She thought I was up myself. Tal told me once when we were having an argument. He said all his friends thought I was stuck up.'

'I didn't think you were stuck up.'

'Yes, you did.'

'You had other qualities.' He winked at her and she felt a lick of heat spread across her cheekbones and down into her chest. She lowered her eyes to the kerb. The decking in front of the pub was crowded with people. It was always busy on open mic nights, but especially at this time of year, when the days were getting longer and blanched at the ends. Since the early nineties, when they were kids, the second Friday of the month had always been an event. The open mic was organised by a grizzled, ageing stoner called Keith, who'd had long gingerish dreadlocks when they were at school and was now almost completely bald. Though no one really knew exactly what Keith's official role was, he was as much a staple of the pub as the hand-painted ashtrays with their janky Celtic lettering, or the insipid sketches of local vistas that hung, nicotine-stained, on the walls. Olwen remembered him with surprising clarity. She remembered that he wore exactly the same clothes every time she saw him, like a cartoon character: scuffed bootcut jeans, Cuban-heeled cowboy boots, and a baggy, tan suede bomber jacket, impregnated with the dank, vegetal perfume of decades of booze and pot. He fancied himself a local impresario and a misunderstood Svengali of the arts. During the brief part of the evening where he was still sober, he ran the open mic with military levels of despotism. After his third or fourth pint, he was happy enough to spend the rest of the night in the beer garden, flagrantly smoking joints and

202

lecturing victims on topics as diverse as the Illuminati, Richey Edwards sightings and the health benefits of LSD.

'Mostly I just can't believe that Megan has a son, and that he's old enough to play in a band at open mic,' Olwen said.

'Yeah, well. She was young when she had him.'

'Is he even allowed in the pub?'

'No one IDs at The Vaults,' Geth scoffed.

'Do you remember her band with Taliesin?'

He smiled as they stepped up on to the decking. '*Iesu mawr.* That's going back, like.' He nodded at a pair of men sitting on a bench and smoking. 'Rob, y'right? Luke,' he said. '*S'mae.*'

Olwen smiled awkwardly at the lads, without showing her teeth, and she wished that they could have stayed in the beer garden around the back of The Boars, where they'd been alone and where she'd felt like she was getting somewhere with him. Then he pushed open the door of the pub, and he put his free hand on the small of her back and steered her towards it, and she felt the heat again. On the other side of the threshold she was hit with a wall of sound – voices, laughter, glasses clinking, the hiss of pints being pulled, the riff of 'Another Girl, Another Planet' fuzzing out from the big speakers up on the makeshift stage, where a white guy in a plaid Topman shirt and Converse was playing a Gibson Les Paul.

'It looks like 2006 in here,' she shouted in Geth's ear. She was standing on her tiptoes. His palm still grazed the thin cotton of her dress.

'Oh, yeah?' he said, bemused. He was looking straight past her, towards the bar, towards the photos of the great Welsh rugby squads of the 1970s, towards the bottles of spirits and the liver-spotted mirror, and the brass trinkets lining the shelves.

'Oh shite,' he muttered, 'Meg's been cornered. Do we go and save her? Or shall we do a runner while we still can?'

She followed his gaze and her eyes landed directly on Megan, who was perched on a barstool and being talked at by the man that Olwen recognised as the older and balder incarnation of Keith. It was too late to run. Meg had clocked Geth, and as she enthusiastically raised her hand to summon him, Olwen watched the recognition register at the exact moment when she went on to clock her, standing at his side. Across the room, she watched Megan's mouth make words that were almost undoubtedly, '*Fuck. Me.*' She felt a barbed knot of nerves at the pit of her stomach, and she thought that if Gethin's hand hadn't been there, still brushing the small of her back, she'd be tempted to slink away quietly and never show her face in town again. As if sensing it, he pressed the hand more firmly to her, and he said in a low voice – she could feel the heat of the words on the crown of her head – 'We're all good, yeah?' as he pushed her towards the bar.

'Hi, Megan!' she managed to croak.

Meg fixed her face into a static smile. 'Hi.'

Olwen felt Keith appraising her. He said to Gethin, 'New friend?' and she wasn't surprised that he didn't remember her, even though, for the year or so that she'd been with Geth, she'd come to open mic night every single month. She introduced herself and pretended in turn that Keith's identity was new information.

'Jac about?' Geth asked Meg, hand still in place.

'He's round the back with his mates, in fact – you mind coming out for a sec? So I can ask you about . . . the thing?'

'Jesus, Meg, one sec, yeah? Let me get a drink first. What are we drinking, girls and boys? You still on the gin, yeah?' he asked Olwen.

'You're on good form, aren't you?' Meg said.

'You can go out if you want. I can get the drinks,' Olwen said, to ingratiate herself with Megan.

'Nah, don't be silly,' Geth said. 'It'll take ages to get served. It's rammed in here.'

'She'll get served a sight quicker than you, I bet,' said Meg drily.

'Maybe I could go ahead outside then?' Olwen suggested. 'Get us a table so we can have a cigarette before Jac's band?'

On the stage, Neil Price had finished with The Only Ones and was plucking out the obligatory opening bars of 'Redemption Song'. Olwen resisted passing comment and hoped that he wouldn't attempt an accent.

'That sounds like a great idea,' Megan said.

Outside, the back patio was packed with teenagers drinking and smoking. She sat in an empty corner and watched them, wondering which one of them might be Megan's son, and remembering how novel everything had been at that age, how abundant. She realised, of course, that she didn't have any cigarettes of her own on her, and so she sat there, doubly awkward, with nothing to do. It was good to be out, though. The air was cooler now, and the evening was just on the turn to blue. When Gethin finally came out, he was on his own. He put their drinks down on the empty table and handed her the cigarette from behind his ear.

'Where's Megan?' she asked.

'Oh.' He thought about it for a second too long. 'She ran into someone inside. From work.'

An hour or so after that, she'd lost count of how many gins she'd had, but she loved Jac's band. She loved Jac. She loved The Vaults. She loved that each drink cost less than a fiver. She loved that Jac and his friends played songs by The Libertines. She loved all the kids singing along to them, just like she had with her friends the first time around. She loved Geth, and even Meg, and now she loved some woman called Ceri that she'd met in the bathroom, and who had told her, reapplying her false eyelashes in the mirror, that she looked the spit of the one who used to go out with Jude Law. In short, she loved town. Town was wonderful. Town was heaven.

The next time that they went out to smoke, after the band had finished, the only free spot in the beer garden was at the end of a long picnic bench where Keith was holding court. She slid into the empty space. Geth took the bench opposite her. Their knees touched underneath the picnic table. Electricity. She beamed.

'They were so good!'

He winked at her. He'd been putting it away too and when he smiled now there was something dangerous about it. He produced two rollies – one from his shirt pocket and one from behind his ear.

'You're like a builder,' she giggled.

She could feel Keith's rheumy blue eyes on them. He cleared his throat as if they ought to have been paying attention and said, 'Geth. Joanna Lumley. Nice of you to join us. I was just telling these two numpties about *Roswelsh*.' He gestured at a couple on the opposite side of the table. Geth appeared to know them. Geth knew everyone. He introduced them as Rhys and Heledd, and then Keith said, 'You know neither of them had ever heard of it, Geth?'

'Not gonna lie, mate. I've got no idea what the fuck you're on about either.'

'Fuckin' hell,' Keith wheezed. His chest rattled like a true smoker. 'You kids don't know anything about where you're from, do you?'

'*Iesu mawr*, here we go.'

'Now listen. Your posh bird'll like this – *Croeso i Cymru* and that. So back in January 1974, we had an *extra-terrestrial* incident not so far from here. Round Llandrillo.'

'An extra-terrestrial incident in Llandrillo?' Geth shook his head.

'Pipe down, Gethin, you weren't even fucking born.'

'And you didn't even fucking live here then, mate.'

'It made the national news. And there were sightings in Lincolnshire on the very same night. Coincidence? Well, that's what the *recently declassified* MOD files would have you believe, but the proof's all there. Here, look, I've got it on my phone,' he peered at the screen and began to read: '"On the night of 23 January, 1974, locals reported to have heard a huge bang followed by a burst of brilliant lights over the Berwyn Mountains in North Wales."'

'Bollocks.'

'"Many at the time claimed that the explosion was caused by an alien spaceship crash that was subsequently covered up by authorities."'

'What the fuck would aliens be doing in Llandrillo, Keith?' Heledd scoffed.

'Decent chippie,' said Geth.

'There *is* a stone circle on Moel Tŷ Uchaf, come to think of it,' Rhys mused.

'*Rhys.*'

'Good point actually, Rhys. I hadn't even considered that,' Keith said.

Gethin groaned. 'What on earth would the aliens want with a bunch of stones?'

Keith balanced the flaccid joint on the edge of the ash-tray and cracked his knuckles. 'Open your eyes, Geth. I mean, I personally think they were going for RAF Valley – who were scrambled up to the mountain, apparently, which says enough in itself, doesn't it? But it could have a Druidic connection, now you've mentioned it, Rhys.' He pinched the end of the rollie back up to his pale lips and sucked up the last drag. 'Anyway, the *official* explanation was that there was an *earthquake* combined with a meteor. An earthquake. Round here? How bloody plausible is that?'

'Un-fucking-likely,' Rhys nodded sagely.

'MOD cover-up. No doubt. Here. Listen to this bit:

> Last year, witness, Geraint Jones of Betws GG, told a Channel Five documentary team how he watched in astonishment as the UFO hovered for ten whole minutes above Cadair Berwyn. 'It was definitely a flying saucer,' Jones recalled. 'It was a shame I didn't have a camera on me because it was up there for ages. Big metal thing. Pulsating lights. We were on the way to play darts when something caught my eye. I wrote it in my diary. It was at quarter to seven on Friday evening. If we'd been coming *back* from the pub it'd be different. People would say we'd had a few. But we were on our way *there*. I know what I saw. I never have forgotten it.'

Under the table, Gethin searched for Olwen's hand and gave it a squeeze.

Yes, town was wonderful. Olwen was happy. She imagined ringing Miranda the next day and regaling her with tales of Keith and his tinfoil hat. It was already forming as an anecdote in her head. She wondered if she could even crowbar it into the script somehow, if she could make Keith a character. She made a note to herself to look for the local newspaper cutting on the internet. The darts bit was too good not to use.

The live music had stopped inside but someone had taken over the jukebox and the kids were dancing. 'Heroes' was playing. She felt as if she were at a wedding.

'This song!' she cried. It was only half ten but it could have been three in the morning. 'Dance?'

'No fucking chance,' Geth laughed.

'Come on, don't be such a square. I seem to remember that you had some moves on you, back in the day. When you'd had a few.'

'I've not had enough,' he said. He was grinning, though. The crow's feet at his eyes did something to her. All the opacity had gone. He looked now how he'd looked when they were much younger. She couldn't believe how alive she felt. She took his hand, and for a second, as she pulled him towards her, she saw Meg, sitting at the bar, watching them. Something about the way she looked at them threatened to splinter the moment. Olwen hesitated, and then she decided to smile at her. It wasn't Meg's business. It wasn't anyone else's business. She hadn't missed that about town.

At some point around then Megan must have left anyway, because the next time the two of them went to the bar she was nowhere to be seen, and Olwen was relieved. She had the impression that what had happened when the pub closed wouldn't have happened if Meg had stuck around. They would have worked something out. She couldn't believe that there weren't any taxis in town, especially on a Friday night. Instead, though, when the bell rang for last orders and Geth suggested that they leave, he said, 'You can't drive home in your state. You're gonna come to mine, right?'

He didn't wait for a response, he just steered her out of the pub, hand on the small of her back, much in the same way that he'd steered her in hours before. Her skin felt very hot, even outside, where it was cold – close to midnight now. The air felt freshly laundered and the searing glut of stars was phenomenal – everything was a little silver with starlight: the low, squat buildings, the parked cars, the sweet little clock tower that, as a child, she'd thought was colossal, but that now looked like something built for dolls. Away from the immediate vicinity of the pub, you could hear a pin drop. They crossed the top of town, towards Clwyd Street, and she thought that it was best not to think about what she was doing but to just walk. She thought that at this point, she still hadn't done anything wrong. She could even tell James about this. He wasn't the jealous type; he was far too evolved. He'd be glad she hadn't driven back to the village however many gins deep. Sometimes she felt like James thought she was a very intense person. He kind of liked it – liked thinking that his 'artistic wife' had an 'artistic temperament'. He'd be glad then, to think that Gethin was looking after her.

They were walking into the part of town that, as a child, she'd thought was rough – an idea that seemed sweetly ludicrous now, as everything here felt so bucolic and benign. She couldn't see town for what it was any more.

'Do you think this is weird?'

'What?' he said. They were walking very close to each other; every now and then her bare arm would brush his.

'Is it weird that I'm staying the night at yours?'

He wasn't looking at her. He said, 'I'll sleep on the settee.'

'Don't be stupid.'

They came on to Cae Gorsaf and he started to root in his pocket for his keys. She stood on the kerb under a slice of milk-white light funnelled from the single illuminated lamppost – she did it consciously, arranging the scene – and when he had the keys in his hand, he stopped, and he looked up, directly at her face, for just a moment too long. If she'd been a better person, she thought, she'd have broken the eye contact, but instead she let her lips part ever so slightly, as if she were about to speak, and she held his gaze as he stepped forward, until their bodies were almost touching, until the space between them was tracing-paper thin. The air they were both breathing was full of friction as he raised his hand to her cheek. She closed her eyes. For the first moment of contact, his mouth felt like something foreign and new, but then, as he gently opened hers, and as he pulled her closer to him with his free arm, and crushed her against his body, some kind of long-buried muscle memory resurfaced and she felt her own body become something soft and pliant.

'I'm going to do things to you that we can't do out here,' he said into her ear, with all the confidence and machismo she'd found so appealing when they were teenagers. He stepped away from her, the keys jangled in his palm. 'Coming?'

They didn't switch on the lights. They didn't even make it out of the front room, they only just managed to kick the front door closed behind them. He undressed her first and she wondered if he remembered how much she used to like that, how much the implied imbalance of power turned her on. He kissed her neck, and her shoulders; he nudged the straps of her dress down with his mouth as he did so, and when it fell in a gauzy pile at her feet, he held her tightly by her hips. When she looked at him, he looked as if he were about to laugh. He shook his head.

'I missed this. Us. I knew this was going to happen. I knew this was going to happen as soon as I touched your shoulder in The Boars.'

'I shouldn't be doing this.'

'You want me to stop?' He framed her face with his hands.

'No.'

He pulled his white T-shirt over his head and smiled at her. He still had his work boots on. He'd acquired more questionable tattoos.

She said to him, 'You're hairier.'

He said, 'You're more beautiful.' His hand was on his belt buckle. He stepped back again. 'Let me look at you.'

'It's dark.'

'I can still see.'

The sun rose punishingly early and woke her up. It wasn't even five o'clock. The air felt damp on her face, and when she opened her eyes, the front room was bathed in dingy, grey light; light that was flat and bald, and gave the walls and the awful, fitted carpet a sickly tint. Drizzle flecked the PVC window, and she remembered this specific kind of weather from her childhood, when all she wanted was to leave. It was a kind of watery drabness that evoked petrol stations in out-of-town shopping centres and flowerbeds in provincial council estates. Breakfast radio DJs. Adverts for bingo halls. The synthetic perfume of various modes of Saturday morning consumption.

They'd fallen asleep around two, after the second time, and had been so exhausted that they'd stayed there, knotted together, on the hideous sofa that she could have sworn had once been part of Geth's mum's three-piece suite. She sat up and looked around the dismal little room, and she wondered if she would end up regretting this, if anything bad could come of it.

2017

IT WAS STILL EARLY when she pulled up on the track. In the parked car, she closed her eyes and rested her head on the steering wheel. She focused on the sound of her breath, and she tried to concentrate on that, rather than on all of the beautiful, filthy images that inundated her mind. It was cold outside – colder even than it had been in town – and she remembered that when she was a kid, her mother had always complained that the village had its own microclimate. The drizzle started up again as she made her way down the track, and she pulled the flannel shirt that Gethin had lent her tighter around her shoulders. When he'd given it to her, after she'd left at six – after the third, inevitable time – she'd cynically thought to herself that he was giving it to her so that they had to see each other again. As the drizzle gained substance and turned into rain, she tried to examine her feelings about what had happened, and assess whether she felt guilty about it. She wondered again if this was an action that would have any consequences.

'You fucked the lumberjack, didn't you? I *knew* this was going to happen.'

A slightly pixelated version of Miranda was sitting in her garden in Stoke Newington. The weather was always better in London – she was in a bikini. She was eating gyoza with a pair of chopsticks and she was swearing more than usual because her husband had taken their toddler to Clissold Park.

Olwen covered her face with her hands. 'I don't know how it happened.'

'I do. There's fuck all else to do out there, is there? And he's hot. I found his Facebook. He's friends with your brother.'

'He's not?'

'He is. Very dodgy tattoos, though. The Celtic cross. The swallows. It's like a journey through basic bloke body art from 1990 onwards. It's like you shagged Robbie Williams. Does he have one for his mum?'

'His mum's dead.'

'Even more likely then.'

Olwen pulled a face and Miranda said, 'So, did he do you in his cabin in the woods?'

'He lives in an ex-council bungalow.'

'Oh. Well, at least the mother's dead so he can't live with her.'

'*Miranda*. I knew her.'

'Oh, come on. You don't care. Anyway, be real with me, was it awful?'

'The sex?'

'The bungalow.'

'Oh.'

'It was awful, wasn't it?'

When Olwen didn't say anything, Miranda said, 'Carpeted?'

She nodded.

'Venetian blinds? Black leather furniture?'

'No black leather.'

'How big was the TV?'

'All TVs look big to us. We're not used to them.'

'So massive? I don't want to sound like a Tory but how do these people always afford these huge TVs?'

'It wasn't massive. Do you think TVs are still expensive nowadays?'

'Was it on a glass console?'

'I have no idea.'

'Were there any books?'

'There were books.'

'Because, like, I know we all have the manual labourer fantasy, but I remember once when we were living in that fucking flatshare in Whitechapel—'

'Oh God, that place.'

'Yeah. You remember that electrician I got with?'

'Jamie.'

'How do you remember his *name*? But, yes, Jamie, if you insist. Or as we called him at the time, Sparky Marky.'

'Yes. I remember it well.'

'So anyway, don't get me wrong he was sweet and, like . . . surprisingly *sensual* . . .' She shivered theatrically. 'But I'll never forget going back to his in Leyton and there was just like . . . Not a single book.'

'You sound like Woody Allen.'

'I lie, there were three books. One was by John Grisham, one was about making money, and the other one was Jamie Oliver.'

'You're making this up. Jamie Oliver didn't even exist then.'

'Of course he did, the Naked Chef! Sparky even looked like him.'

'The Lumberjack has books.'

'What books?'

'Real books. When we were teenagers, we were actually, like, painfully literary together. He liked Denis Johnson. And Hunter S. Thompson.'

'Christ, save me,' Miranda groaned. 'So he was a literary

fuckboy as a teenager in 1997. Everyone was. Ethan Hawke was a heartthrob. Blur sang about Balzac. There was no internet then; people were desperate.'

'I don't see why reading is some kind of litmus test for whether someone is a good person or not.'

'Olwen, you sound like a Christian. I don't care if he's a good person. I'm thinking about other things.'

Olwen said nothing.

'All right, then you're obviously not going to indulge me in this un-PC interior design speculation. It's like you have feelings for this guy or something.'

'I do have feelings for him. He's my first love.'

Miranda wiped a speck of soy sauce off her chin and for the first time in the conversation looked something close to serious. 'What, like, dangerous feelings?'

'No,' Olwen lied. 'Not like dangerous feelings.'

When she was off the phone she ran a hot bath and put on a Bill Evans record. She was glad that the weather was bad so she could indulge her hangover. She undressed slowly, looking at herself in the mirror and, trying to see herself through Gethin's eyes, imagining all the parts of her body that turned him on the most. She admired her reflection and she luxuriated in every compliment he'd given her as he'd fucked her. She touched the shoulders, the collarbone, the curve of the belly and the arse that he'd professed to love so much, and she imagined that the hands were his. In the bath, though, she told herself that she couldn't possibly have 'dangerous feelings' for him, because if she did, she wouldn't be able to go to her desk (as she was planning on doing later that evening), open up her notebook, and make notes on the details of his life.

*

She woke up early the next morning, replenished and healthy, with a kind of half-baked, holy idea about purity in rigour. She wanted to obliterate all thoughts of Gethin. She wanted to make herself a better human being. She put on her trainers and stretched a bit on the veranda. Diaphanous mist rose off the surface of the lake like gusts of spun sugar. She selected a podcast where a pair of American journalists attempted to rehabilitate the public images of women unfairly maligned by the press at the end of the last century. She would not think about Gethin. She would learn. She would improve herself. She performed a final sun salutation and stood for a while in Mountain Pose, enjoying the fragrance of the wet trees as she filled her lungs with air.

She had barely even begun her run when she saw something hanging in the branches of one of the oak trees that fringed the track. It was a large plastic panel, and from where she was, she could make out text and a symbol printed on its surface. She slowed down to a walk and scrambled up the bank. The sign was wet in her hands and splattered with mud and dead leaves turned adhesive in the rain. Framed within the red ring of a circle backslash symbol was a stick figure in a helmet thrusting a black hand forward. A banner on the top edge claimed the sign for the *Comisiwn Coedwigaeth Cymru* – the Welsh Forestry Commission – and underneath the stickman and his insistent, angry palm were the words:

> *Dim mynediad heb ganiatad*
> *y tu hwnt i'r fan yma*
> No unauthorised persons
> allowed beyond this point

Her body relaxed. It was a standard issue health-and-safety sign. It was odd that it should end up here, but not beyond the realms of plausibility. The wind, as her mother used to say, was a law unto itself. She shrugged and let the sign fall back down to the ground, but as it did, she noticed that someone had graffitied a pair of words on the reverse side. The red spray paint had bled a little in the rain but the words were stark and clear: 'COFIWCH DRYWERYN'.

She read them aloud and smiled. *Remember Tryweryn* was a Cymraeg political slogan that she'd been reading up on just the other day. It referred to Capel Celyn, a village in the Tryweryn Valley that was flooded in the 1960s to build a reservoir servicing Liverpool. For it to appear here, in her woods, felt wonderfully providential. She turned the sign around again, to display this divine omen to the world.

From there, she ran up through the woods, into the village, on to the next one after that, and then back, looping through the fields towards Coed-y-Grug. The mist had thickened into an unusually thick fog and it had started to rain. She could barely see further than a few yards ahead of her, but she was making good time all the same. She was getting to that point of transcending tiredness. She no longer cared that her lungs could burst, or that the damp was seeping in through her trainers, she could just run, on and on and on. As she skirted the boundaries of the land that belonged to her, she thought to herself that she'd probably make a personal best. She was just coming on to the track when, from nowhere, from within the gauze of the fog, a man stepped out on to the path in front of her. She screamed.

'Oh my God. Oh my God.' She pulled her earphones out. 'Holy fuck. Oh my God, you scared me.'

He laughed as she doubled over and pressed her hands into her thighs for stability. She tried to catch her breath. The man, in a soaked flat cap and a blue boiler suit, watched her, amused. Much like the graffiti, there was something intensely familiar about his face, and yet no matter how much she stared at him – at his pale eyes, at the ruddy, veined, bulbous nose – the nose of an alcoholic who was probably handsome once – or at the grey hair peeking out beneath the cap, she couldn't quite place him. When she'd finally regulated her breathing, she said, 'You know this is private property here, don't you?'

He thrust his hands into the pockets of his oilskin. 'Blydi stupid, running in this weather.' Something glinted in his eye. 'I'd go home, if I were you.'

Trawling, 1980

AFTER THE POLICE had taken Eifion away to the station, five of them charged into the house like a bunch of feral children who'd watched too many American cop films. His mother, Delyth, didn't recognise any of them. Much later, she'd find out they were lads from the Special Branch unit over on Caergybi. A couple of them, unnervingly, could even speak Welsh.

'What the hell do you think you're doing?' she shouted as the first of them bolted straight past her, through the front room and up the stairs.

'We're sorry for the inconvenience, madam, but we've a warrant to search the property,' said his more phlegmatic colleague.

'A warrant? For what?'

The officer sighed. 'Your son has been arrested for some fairly serious criminal offences, Mrs Williams. It's normal procedure to look for evidence. If you could be so kind to direct us towards his bedroom, please?'

Delyth could hardly breathe. 'Let me ring my husband at work.' She could feel that her cheeks were damp, that she must be crying.

'You can speak to your husband afterwards, Mrs Williams. This is a matter of urgency. Come on.'

Two of the young men in uniform were feverishly pulling out her kitchen drawers. She heard the slam of cabinet doors heave against their own hinges as they yanked them open to empty them of their contents. Boots. She kept thinking about their boots all over her nice clean carpet.

'What on earth are you doing?'

They started to work as a pair. One officer held open a black bin liner and the other filled it with her belongings: batteries, a roll of Sellotape, lighters. The smooth tapered candles she kept for power-cuts and Christmas. A craft knife, a bundle of twine. She wanted to go and stop them, but her legs were rooted to the ground. She gripped the banister. 'What are you—'

'Mrs Williams. The bedroom, please?'

She was vaguely aware that she was no longer standing. That she was sitting on the floor by the stairs. She watched the policeman sweep an OS map into a new bin bag with the flat of his palm.

Afterwards she would feel horrified that she had let them do it. That she had watched as they had torn her house apart. Upstairs she heard the thud of boots, the slash of ripping fabric. She pulled herself up by the banister and raced upstairs. When she saw what they were doing to his bedroom, she couldn't speak.

The state that they left the house in. It looked as if they'd been burgled. When Gwenno got home from work and saw it, her first thought was to ring the police. In Eifion's bedroom, the mattress had been tipped on to the floor and torn right through. His clothes and books were everywhere. They'd turned an ashtray over the bedclothes. Powder and ends of cigarettes were strewn across the floor, and not just Eifion's either; she imagined the policemen flicking them at the carpet as they ransacked her brother's world.

'Fifty-two hours. Fifty-two hours, they held him.' Angharad propped herself up on her elbows. 'They're not allowed to do that. It's a disgrace.'

Iestyn focused on the twin specks of white in the distance. Lots of the English tourists had boats now in Porth Madog. In the winter, a couple of them were torched. He closed his eyes and imagined the sails going up in flames, billowing red-hot gusts. He imagined what it would look like if it had happened way out there in the infinite blue of Cardigan Bay. The flat, fibrous, amethyst of the horizon breached with volcanic tongues of fire. Like something biblical. It'd be spectacular.

'And at the station they just kept telling his dad that they "weren't at liberty" to tell him where he was being held. Can you imagine? His poor mam was going spare.'

Clive hadn't told him that they were going to make an arrest. He'd not mentioned that it had happened when he telephoned the farm last night to make sure that Iestyn was still going through with the plan. He'd been setting Angharad up for over a fortnight now, laying down the foundations, collecting 'evidence'. He wondered, hopefully, whether this might mean that Clive would call the whole plan off.

'You spoken to him?'

'Briefly. Yesterday. He's going down to Penarth tomorrow to see some friends. I don't know them.'

'He's away a lot, isn't he?'

She shrugged and pursed her lips. Glared ahead of her at the horizon and started rooting in her jacket pocket for a cigarette.

'Here you got a lighter?' she asked him, fag balanced on her bottom lip. 'Lost my Zippo, didn't I. Loved that lighter.'

He handed her his own and focused on the white sails again, bobbing on the perimeter of the horizon. It looked like a child's drawing of the sea, and the purity of the image gave him a bad feeling. He leant back on the bonnet of the car. Felt the hot metal warm his back. The sky above him was indecently blue.

The following evening, he was on his way out the house when his mother called him into the kitchen.

'Bloke on the phone for you. Friend of yours, apparently.' She thrust the telephone in his direction. He waited until she'd left the room before speaking into the receiver.

'It's me,' Clive said.

'I thought it might be.' He sighed. 'What do you want?'

'Did no one ever teach you any social niceties?'

He ignored him. He fingered the telephone cord nervously. 'Well?'

'Plan's off with the girl.'

He exhaled. The lightness was immediate. He felt his shoulders float and soften; his jaw unclench for the first time in months. Involuntarily he started to laugh. 'It's *off*?' Opiate relief swam through his limbs. He closed his eyes.

He heard Clive light a cigarette on the other end. Heard the hiss of his first drag. He hadn't seen the policeman smoke before, but it was a Friday night. 'You're of no use to us any more, unfortunately. When we were questioning the suspect, some of the things he said . . . We think he can smell a rat.'

Iestyn sat down on the stool next to the phone. He pinched the bridge of his nose between his forefinger and thumb. The immediate swing to the other extreme of feeling was dizzying. He felt like he might throw up.

On the other end of the line, Clive paused to take another drag. 'So in short, you're off the hook, mate. Congratulations. Job done.'

He gripped the edge of the stool. He felt vertiginous,

as if he might slide right off it. He had the impression that the phone was sweating in his hands. 'Do they know it was me?' he whispered.

'Speak up! Line's bloody terrible.'

He tried to repeat himself but the words came out as a hollow wheeze. His voice was disintegrating.

'Anyway, don't worry about it, I'm sure they don't know it's you. You're in the clear. But just be careful, all the same. And, Mr Thomas, thank you for all your help. If it wasn't for the information you've supplied us with we'd never have closed in on Eifion Williams, and I'm sure we're not far off now, with the girl. So thank you for trying at least.'

'I didn't want to try,' Iestyn said. The line went dead.

THE POET LIVED IN an old stone cottage just outside Beddgelert. Olwen had been up that way before, a long time ago, with Geth, and she once again had the feeling of being almost drugged by the stupefying effects of nostalgia. The beginning of the journey was over the moor where the road glared black under the sun, and you had the impression that you were in closer proximity to the horizon. The land up there was flat and exposed – long feathery grass oxidising under the elements; sun bleached, totemic telegraph poles, and once in a while, the colossal towers of the new wind turbines, looming ominously, their blades loping with a low, science-fiction hum.

She was recently retired but had been a history lecturer at Bangor University before that. She wrote her poetry in both Welsh and English, and Olwen had found her through her work, and had exchanged several emails with her before arranging to meet in person. She was the only political activist who had responded to her attempts to get in touch. She hadn't expected it to be so difficult. She'd always seen the Welsh as enthusiastic raconteurs; practitioners of a story-telling tradition that manifested itself in everyone, from the great bard, to the gleeful town gossip. And yet her emails went unanswered. Even Gethin seemed to shut down by proxy on behalf of his uncle.

There were three other cottages clustered around the little stream – all of them built in the same grey stone, and all of them with the same dark slate roofs. She parked by the water, behind an ancient Defender with a *YesCymru* bumper sticker on the spare wheel. The movement of the stream was audible when she got outside, and it was cooler here than it had been in the Vale of Clwyd when she'd left that morning. She found the cottage, which was called Tyddyn Llan, half-obscured by an enormous hydrangea. She pushed the gate and as she did so, an eruption of canine angst tore through the stillness of the morning. The voice that presumably belonged to the poet shouted, '*Tanwen! Shhht!*' and the dog fell immediately, impressively silent. Framed in the top half of the stable door, she looked much as Olwen had been expecting. Thick grey hair pulled back sensibly, a zip-up fleece, and several tiny silver hoops in each ear, one with an ankh cross and another with a drop of amber.

'Angharad?' Olwen asked.

'*Bore da.*' Her voice was warm and mellifluous. 'You want to go round the back straight into the garden?'

For a second, she wondered if there was some kind of significance in the closed lower half of the door, in the instruction to proceed directly outside. But Angharad had invited her here. It was a nice day. Drinking a cup of tea in the garden was surely an innocuous suggestion, made with the intention of profiting from the sun. There was a little wooden picnic bench around the back, and so Olwen sat down and waited for her to come out with the tea. The garden was also full of the lulling sound of the water moving over the stones, which calmed her nerves a little. Tanwen came first, bouncy and newly affable.

'*Ty'd yma, Tanwen,*' Angharad called, appearing at the back door with a tray of tea. The scrupulously obedient dog leapt across the garden only to trot back directly alongside her owner. Angharad placed the tea and a plate of biscuits on one of the damp, greenish planks that made up the table.

'You have any trouble finding us?' she said.

'No. I used to come here a lot, when I was a kid,' Olwen said, to reiterate – in spite of her accent – her native credentials.

'You're from the Vale of Clwyd then, aren't you?'

'That's right.'

'Oh, well. It's lovely round there. Nice rolling hills. You're down in London now, though, you said?'

'Yeah, for a long time,' Olwen replied, omitting the fact of Tŷ Gwydr.

Angharad reached for a custard cream and began to talk about her youngest daughter, who had apparently just moved into a 'criminally substandard flatshare in Camberwell'. At the end of the story, she sighed. 'Never did I think they were going to get *worse*,' she said, *they*, presumably being landlords, the powers-that-be, the invisible, nebulous forces hellbent on screwing over the young and the poor. Olwen grimaced and delicately removed the teabag from her mug. They carried on with the preliminary small talk for a while, and then finally, after the polite interval had passed, cut to the chase. She even took out a notebook, to look professional.

'So you were very involved in politics then, in the eighties?'

'Not just the eighties. For my whole life, from the cradle. Both my parents were in Plaid and Cymdeithas from the early days. I remember them campaigning against the flooding of Tryweryn when I was little, and then protesting against the investiture of Prince Charles. When we were kids it was very much about getting equal status for the Welsh language, but it wasn't just that – my parents were socialists as well.'

She gave Olwen a rough sketch of her political history. 'I was in my twenties when the arsons were happening. That's what you're really interested in, for the film, isn't it?'

'Yes . . . I mean, tangentially. The film isn't about the arsons, but they are the backdrop. They're going on whilst the protagonist . . .' she paused, '. . . negotiates his own problems, I guess. They're part of the landscape of the film. Or, I don't know . . . a motif?'

Angharad nodded sceptically, and Olwen wished she hadn't reduced what was presumably a huge part of her past to an aesthetic device.

'It's not really *about* anything exactly. It's experimental. But I wanted to be diligent, you know, try and speak to people who were involved.'

Angharad tutted at the perceived indiscretion. 'I wasn't burning down houses, if that's what you're implying.'

Olwen felt herself blush. 'No, no, of course not. Don't worry, I wouldn't assume that – I mean, I wouldn't even ask.'

'I was arrested, though, funnily enough. Later on, when I'd just moved back home from college.'

'Arrested?'

'For writing a poem, if you'd believe it. It was just after a holiday house was burnt down near Llanbedrog. I wrote a poem that wasn't exactly critical of *llosgi tai haf*. They got you in on all sorts, back in the day. They were getting desperate because they weren't getting anywhere catching the actual lads who were doing it. And we all supported them. No one local was helping the police, were they?' She ruffled the fur between Tanwen's ears and said something to her in Welsh.

'The police aren't looking great, in the research I've done so far,' Olwen said.

'Oh, no, they were dreadful. Very underhand. Planted evidence, held people for longer than they were allowed, had people followed . . . My ex-boyfriend was followed for a long time, to intimidate him more than anything. And then they got him in on some completely bogus charges. Absolute disgrace it was. Awful.'

229

'I can imagine.'

'You expected, as an activist, to be arrested. That's what direct action was all about. We used to try and get arrested when we were in Cymdeithas, as a statement. But this was different because it was so invasive, so sly.' She scrunched up her nose. 'Poor Eifion, he never really got over it, you know. Makes you paranoid, being watched like that. I often wonder what happened to him, after he moved away.'

Olwen took a sip of her tea. 'I did have one question, actually, about that. Bad policing, I mean.'

'Is there such a thing as good policing?'

Olwen blushed again. 'A long time ago, when I was a kid, a relative of a friend of mine told us that when he was young, back in the day, the police had tried to recruit him as a snitch.'

Angharad brushed the table with the flat of her palm. 'Wouldn't surprise me in the least.'

'Really?'

'Oh, there were all sorts of informers. It's always like that with politics, isn't it? We had one lad who came to our meetings for a while – we all knew there was something with him. Funny bugger. They used to pay them, the police did. Twenty pound a week, one lad was offered. Then they even had undercover agents,' she laughed. 'That's why no one's talking to you, I imagine. People have long memories.' She whistled for the dog, who had disappeared down the other end of the garden. 'Blydi animal, she'll be rolling in fox shit. *Ych a fi*. Tanwen!'

An hour or so later, just before Olwen left, Angharad disappeared into the house and returned with a framed photograph in her hands.

'Here's one for you, to illustrate my point from before.'

It was black and white, and probably from the late sixties,

given the haircuts and the clothes. Two children were standing in front of a pebble-dashed house, and hanging in the window was a banner that said, 'CARLO CER ADRE'. Olwen read it aloud under her breath. Cer adre. She pictured it, compact and scribbled in black biro. The postcard of Westminster Bridge appeared in her mind.

'What does that mean?' she asked.

Angharad smiled at the photo. 'It was just before Charles Windsor's investiture. It's me and my brother. Carlo's what we all called Prince Charles. Like the Dafydd Iwan song, you know?'

Olwen pretended that she did. 'And cer adre?'

Angharad tutted again, and she could imagine her as an imposing seminar leader, intimidating undergraduates.

'You need to get your Cymraeg back up to scratch, my dear. Cer adre means "Go home" of course. So it's "CHARLES, GO HOME".'

Olwen felt the two flat syllables strike. She swallowed. 'Go home?'

'Ynde, that's right.'

It was late afternoon by the time she got back to the house. She'd spent a long time driving around and thinking; she drove right down to Blaenau, where the landscape had been made alien by the magnificent, asperous scars of the old slate industry, the raw insides of the earth, turned out and made monolithic. She headed west for the coast, and she followed the A497 right out to Llanbedrog, in honour of Angharad's poem. She drove without much purpose other than motion. Cer adre. The beer bottles on the veranda. Gethin emerging from the lake and stretching out as the air cooled the water on his skin. Cer adre. But it couldn't be Gethin. She knew Gethin. She had known Gethin. She drove because she didn't want to go home, because home was something compromised. She drove and drove, and when she looked down at her hands, her knuckles blanched from gripping the steering wheel, each one bony and tense and anxious. *Cer adre.*

By the time she got back to Tŷ Gwydr she'd managed to convince herself it couldn't be anyone at all. Talking aloud to no one, she said, 'No one cares this much about you.' She made herself laugh. 'This is mad. You're mad. Completely fucking mad.' She slammed the car door loudly, much in the same way that she used to shout when she was scared of the dark as a child – to make herself more substantial, less precarious. The sound echoed through the woods, and she forced herself to renew the bright smile, to scale the steps up to the veranda vigorously, with a spring in her step. She started to whistle, to make all of her robust cheer appear, assertively, in the woods as sound. This was her home.

On the low table on the veranda, the ashtray – which she was sure she'd emptied that morning – was full. She stood a good metre away from it, as if it might spontaneously combust. She looked at it through her fingers. *Cer adre, cer adre, cer adre.*

2017

GETH DIDN'T contact her until mid-way through the week; neither had she made any attempts to communicate with him, but, given that she was married, he surely wouldn't have been entirely surprised by her silence. Of course, Gethin had no idea that he was no longer just the embodiment of guilt regarding her marital transgressions; he didn't know that over the handful of days that had lapsed since he'd last seen her – barefoot in the living room, pulling on stale, newly inappropriate clothes – the idea of him had taken on an altogether more sinister aspect. That said, she'd calmed down significantly since the evening she'd come home from Beddgelert, since the frenzied evacuation, destruction, and eventual disposal of the ashtray, an object now irredeemably infected with paranoia. Once that had been dealt with, she'd marched into the kitchen with the intention of meting similar annihilation upon the postcard. It was only as she was standing there with it in her hands, about to tear it in two, that she thought better of it. She closed her eyes, exhaled, and replaced it underneath the jolly little magnet left by the council encouraging residents to *AIL-GYLCHU* or RECYCLE, depending on their language of choice. She opened the fridge door, took out a beer and told herself – aloud again, to reassert her presence in the empty house – to breathe. On the veranda, she smoked a cigarette, and eventually, when she'd calmed down enough, she called Miranda, who'd confirmed that she was indeed going 'full-on demented'.

'Was it a nice ashtray?'

'It was some shell I found on the beach. Who even has ashtrays any more?'

'A shell? How the fuck do you smash a shell?'

'A blunt tool was involved.'

'Not remotely insane.'

'I'm aware.'

Miranda paused. 'Do you think maybe you're a little bit . . . *isolated* out there? All work and no play makes Jack a dull boy?'

'I *am* playing. I played. Look at what happens when I bloody play. Oh my God, Miranda. I feel sick. What if it really is him?'

She said nothing.

'I'm feeling judged here,' Olwen said.

'Look, I just think, if you're not going mad – like, if this is really happening – maybe you just shouldn't be there by yourself right now.'

Miranda's concern – the funereal gravity of her voice – had the adverse effect on Olwen. 'Miranda, at the end of the day, if it is Geth, at least I know he wouldn't actually do anything.'

Miranda made a noise that was entirely unconvinced consonants.

'I know Gethin,' Olwen insisted. 'He's a good guy. This is me being mad. You know what this is: this is guilt about what happened the other day manifesting itself as paranoia so that I can become a victim and absolve myself of all sins.'

'Olwen, I know you're a stubborn bitch, but if this is real, please don't let your stubbornness put you in danger or I will personally call the police on that incel bastard.'

'The police!' Olwen said, thinking of Angharad. 'They're not the good guys here.'

'Oh Jesus Christ. This is really not the moment to be

scrawling ACAB on the toilet-stall door, babe. Please be safe?'

'I'm always safe,' she said. An image flashed into her mind of Gethin's face being shared on the internet, or worse, of the police turning up at his front door – except she was picturing his mother's old front door on the estate, which somehow made the image only more painful.

'And for Christ's sake,' Miranda added, 'tell James! Not about the night of passion, obviously, but about the post-card, the beer bottles, the weird shit. It's his house too, you know.'

Olwen resolved not only to tell Miranda nothing more about any of it, but to make up something – a nice, clean resolution to the story – to throw her off the scent. She double-locked the door and drew the latch that night, but the primal panic had gone.

The text, when it arrived, was a message completely devoid of any kind of adornment, like a telegram.

> *Doing a job for Danny on friday, gonna be sunny apparently. You around*

She took the bait and invited him over.

She was expecting him just after five o'clock, but at quarter to, she went out on to the veranda with a cup of tea and found him sitting, with his back to her, looking out over the lake. Her heart hit her throat. *'Jesus, fuck,'* she breathed, hot liquid spilling over her hands.

He turned slowly. 'Sorry. Did I scare you?'

She held her free hand up to her collarbone as her heartbeat regulated. 'Good God, you're stealthy. Where's your truck?'

'Left it up at the farm. Fancied a walk. Dan and me finished the fencing early and Nia was doing my head in. She's got a right mouth on her, that one.'

She swore again and laughed at herself. 'Sorry. I'm jumpy at the moment.' She attempted to gauge his reaction to this information but he seemed unmoved.

'Must be creepy sometimes, being up here by yourself.'

She carried on studying his face but it remained impassive.

'So,' he said.

'So.'

'You gonna offer me one of those?' He pointed at the cup.

When she came back out with the teapot, they sat in the kind of uncomfortable silence that she would normally have felt obliged to fill. She had told herself that she wouldn't, to try to force him to act rather than react.

'I was hanging on Saturday,' he said at last.

'Yeah. Me, too.'

Now that she was with him, the suspicions that she'd been nurturing over the past few days felt more and more absurd. She watched him, watching the lake, his legs spread wide and his palms flat on his thighs – the sun on his face – and she thought how he'd never had a side to him. Town, like any small town, was always in the grip of some kind of plot or scandal, but Gethin didn't have a conspiratorial bone in his body. She tried to picture him, sitting in the cab of his truck and writing poison-pen letters. It was a stretch.

'What do you think of Prince Charles?' she said.

'Prince Charles?'

'As in, the Queen's son.'

He laughed. 'Yeah. I'm aware of who he is, like.'

'And what do you think of him?'

'Pfft. Not a lot, to be honest.'

'Do you know that Dafydd Iwan song about him, "Carlo"?'

He started to laugh. '*Iesu mawr*, you're really trying to integrate, huh? Listening to Dafydd Iwan. Your sixteen-year-old self wouldn't have liked that.'

'People grow up. Kids are arrogant, aren't they?'

He smiled.

'I met this woman on Monday and she was telling me that when they had his investiture ceremony in the sixties there was loads of protest about it.'

'Yeah. Probably.'

'Do you think he should be the Prince of Wales?'

He gave her a look of total bemusement. 'I couldn't really give a fuck either way, to be honest. Doesn't change anything for me.'

'She showed me these pictures of her and her brother when they were kids with banners saying "GO HOME" . . .' She looked at him sideways. 'How do you say that again? In Welsh?'

He yawned. '*Cer adre.*' He didn't so much as flinch.

'*Cer adre?*' she repeated.

'Uh-huh. *Da iawn, ti.*'

He'd closed his eyes now. Tilted his head back to fully profit from the benign glare of the sun. 'Are you going on about Prince Charles because you don't want to talk about what happened the other night?'

She opened her mouth. Closed it again.

''Cause, fair dos, it's not a bad strategy. He's not exactly a turn-on, is he?' He tipped his chair back until he was almost horizontal. 'God, it's good to be back here,' he sighed, and then, 'You don't have to worry, though, like. I know you're married. We'd had too much to drink, and shit happens, doesn't it? But I don't want you to be worried about it. You know that, don't you?' He shifted up his right hip to access his back pocket. Rizlas, baccy, OCB filters. She stared gormlessly at the latter as he shunted one of them out on to his palm, and she thought of the ashtray again, just before she swept its contents into the bin. Rancid, brick-red ends. She could have laughed at the obviousness of it. Gethin never smoked straights.

He'd sat up now and was looking directly at her. 'All right, though, you don't have to look too relieved. I was never gonna do a Sharon Stone on you, was I?'

'That's the wrong Michael Douglas film. You mean Glenn Close.'

He grinned at her, 'You're still a fucking know-it-all, aren't you?' He licked the Rizla to seal the cigarette. 'Is the lady of the manor gonna let me go for a swim then, or what?'

It was surreal, pretending not to watch him undress and then watching him brace himself – his posture unchanged, everything the same from his knuckles to the tense bands of his Achilles tendons as he rocked back from his heels on to the balls of his feet. To watch his body break the velvet surface of the water, so much like glass shattering with the noise, and the way that the shards of liquid coruscated in the sun. To hear his voice howl at the cold shock of it, to watch him disappear entirely and then re-emerge, elated, hair gleaming like oil, his teeth and eyes very white against his dark face. She had the impression that the years were folding in on themselves. More surreal still was to participate in this exercise in time travel, rather than just watch: to strip down to her own underwear – nothing he hadn't seen before, after all – and to throw herself in after him. She swam out to where he was treading water, to where the grey-blue of the lake and the deep gold of his skin felt ultra-saturated, ultra-aestheticised; Kodachrome colours. The sheer vigour of the afternoon sun gave everything the feeling of being over-exposed, so it felt even more as if she were swimming into a photograph, into a still of the past.

'I love this song.'

It was evening, still light out but cooler. They were a couple of beers in; she was debearding mussels in the kitchen sink.

'I know. I remember.'

He'd been tense when they'd first come in; she'd had to insist. He'd looked agitated as he stepped over the threshold into the kitchen. He'd kept his eyes fixed on the floor, and he had that look about him that very tall men get in very small spaces, as if their mere presence might knock something over. His discomfort was palpable. His eyes were sad.

'Do you want the grand tour then?' she'd said, to defuse things.

'Yeah,' his voice was gruff, 'why not?'

He'd followed her through the rooms, taking it all in. He'd said, 'Yeah, looks dead good. It's really nice. Looks great. Well done.'

They were walking down the corridor towards her bedroom and she said, 'It's nice to finally see it with stuff in it, isn't it?'

He frowned, and she wasn't sure why, but she remembered the first time she'd seen him after the break-up when they were kids. They'd run into each other at a party up in the woods out towards Conwy. He'd hooked up with her best friend and she'd been absolutely mortified, but she remembered the vindication she'd felt when she'd lied and had given them her nonchalant blessing, and how wounded he'd looked before he'd managed to get a hold of himself. Her mother had said the next day, 'Gethin's a vulnerable boy. He doesn't know how to express himself, but he's very sensitive.' Now, once again, he got a hold of himself. He smiled and said, 'Yeah. About time.'

She'd pointed across the corridor to the bathroom. 'The shower's in there. We put a shower in.' She said the second part like an apology.

'Did you get rid of the pink bath?'

'Are you serious? It's like something out of the Barbican – never. There's towels on the shelf. You can go first. Help yourself.'

And now they were both clean, and outside the low sun was hanging bright around the blue silhouettes of the trees, the sky above it gaining dusky transparency, the water pewter smooth. 'Don't Fear the Reaper' was playing and she was preparing the mussels – which he'd never eaten, which he'd looked at suspiciously – and he'd eased up a bit, they both had, and she was telling herself that this was good. This was friendship. He could have been Miranda, or Tony, or Asha. Even the fact that she was attracted to him was negligible. She was often attracted to people. She was a human being.

He dragged his index finger over the trackpad of her laptop. 'What is this, some kind of tailor-made soft rock playlist?'

'Especially for you, babe.'

He narrowed his eyes at the screen. 'Fair dos, some right bangers.' He finished his second Stella.

'There's more in the fridge.'

'Driving.'

'Oh, *and*. Let's cross that bridge when we come to it.'

They ate outside, and by the time she'd finished making the *linguine alle cozze* it was the blue hour, everything was iridescent. The bats were out. They. They were drunk. They were friends. They were good at being friends. They were friends that would sometimes exchange a stray, electric comment; something would be implied, a long, ill-advised look would be shared, and the air between them would crackle and feel delicious and heavy, and her whole body would feel alert, until one of them was sensible enough to look away – and for a good few seconds after that too, the alertness: the imprint of his eyes pressed on to her own – but they were friends. And after dinner, after the bowls had been pushed aside and the big Le Creuset casserole – her grandmother's, she'd never be basic enough to buy a new one – was full of empty shells, tacky in the viscous ends of chilli, garlic, parsley and cloudy wine, Geth rolled himself a cigarette, and she got out her twenty pack of Camels, and they smoked, silent for a moment, enjoying the soft hiss of it and the way that the smoke blushed silver in the moonlight. Then a rustle, something snapping in the woods. Something kinetic made into noise.

'Oh,' said Geth, 'there's Iestyn.'

She sat up straight. 'Iestyn?'

He exhaled a fine plume of lilac and squinted like an actor in a Western. 'You don't remember? Iestyn? That time – at Christmas?'

'Oh,' she said, relieved that he was joking. 'Yeah. *That* time.'

He ground down the end into the cap of his beer. 'What, *that* time?'

'I think it's the fox, you know. Have you ever seen it?'

'I love that you're calling it "the fox", like there's only one. Might be a whole bunch of them. A whole family of fluffy little sadists.'

'I'm so desperate to see it. I want to film it. I was even thinking of getting one of those infra-red cameras like they have on *Countryfile*, but it was just too embarrassing. Also, kind of weird, you know? Feels very CCTV.'

'Well, you'll never see it otherwise. They're not like London foxes. You never see animals in the country any more, do you? Maybe flat on the side of the road. You want me to try and get him for you?'

'Gethin!'

He smiled indulgently. 'I'm obviously taking the piss, *cariad*. You think I'm some kind of savage or something? You can't even eat the fuckers.'

She pulled a face, and after a beat said, 'You always say "London" like it's something risible.'

'What does that mean?'

'Like the way the *Daily Mail* would say "politically correct".'

He shrugged. 'And you think I'd mow down an animal for fun.'

'No. That's not fair.'

'What did you mean *that* time, anyway?'

'You know what I meant, Geth.'

He didn't say anything, and after a minute or so that felt much longer than it actually was, he pushed back his chair and started to clear the table.

In the kitchen, he was scraping mussel shells into the bin. Everything felt surreally bright and sharp in contrast to the moonlit glow of the veranda. The warm, yellow lamplight was exhausting. 'You want me to take these out or something? They're gonna go rank, aren't they?'

'I can do that. You don't have to clear.'

'No, I should help. Done fuck all. It was really nice, by the way, the pasta. Thanks.' He put the casserole down on the hob. He leant back against the stove and passed his hand over his brow. 'I'm really sorry, you know. About that. The last time, I mean.'

'Geth—'

'No, really. It was shitty behaviour. I just . . .' He looked past her, through the open window above the sink. 'I just couldn't, you know?'

'It was years ago. I'd forgotten about it,' she lied.

'I hadn't.'

The playlist had moved on, ignored, while they had been eating outside. A new song began; a mournful synth, a rolling cross stick on the snare drum, and a picked guitar riff that she had always thought sounded like a train, or a freight train specifically, moving forward through a vast American landscape, underneath a vast American sky.

'I used to listen to this song, you know, when I was driving up to the village. I used to think it was about me and you.'

She smiled. 'That's so cheesy.' She didn't say that, clichéd as the song was, it did something to her as well.

'It's a sexy song.'

'It's a very sexy song,' she agreed.

He looked at her directly for the first time since the apology, and she felt her breath sharpen as she inhaled, felt it disseminate right through her body. He detached himself from the stove. He walked her backwards into the kitchen counter, and more dangerous than all of this renewed physical proximity – his left hand on her hip now, moving her to the slow beat of the song, the hard denim seam of his jeans pressing on to her bare skin as he nudged her legs apart

243

with his knee – was more of that eye contact, blunt, fixed, unambiguous. He held her face with his free hand.

'Do you think one more time would make a difference?' He pressed his thumb into her cheek.

She thought how true that was; that the sin had already happened. That this was a morally neutral act.

2017

AFTER THAT, he started to turn up at the end of the afternoon, when he'd finished work at Bryn Hendre. The first time, they barely exchanged more than five or six sentences. She was writing at the little table on the veranda and she heard the engine, with all its singular robustness, at the top of the track. She arranged her face and her posture into something resembling nonchalance, but her whole body went taut with anticipation. She heard him call her name – even his voice got her – and she went over to the steps up from the track, as if his presence were a surprise. He took the stairs in three strides – like a waltz, she thought – and immediately held her shoulders in his hands.

'I can't stop thinking about what happened,' he said, and they both knew straight away that it was going to happen again.

She took to calling James first thing, as soon as she was alone again. He would say things like 'I've got a call with Frankfurt in five – can we chat later on?' but she just wanted to hear his voice. She just wanted to remember that he was still there, that nothing had changed, that she hadn't obliterated her real life, that this was just a surreal and pleasant dream. Temporary.

'Can I film you sometime?'
   'You taking the piss?'

Geth's body was gleaming in the evening sun as he pulled himself up out of the lake on to the jetty. His damp hair was plastered to his head. It was Monday again, so it had been over a week. On Saturday afternoon, he'd taken it upon himself to build a barbecue, and Olwen had watched him from the sun lounger, pretending to read the paper, and allowing herself to indulge in some kind of farcical domestic fantasy. She was grilling trout. The air smelt of smoke, pine needles, garlic and fennel. Gethin wrapped a towel around his waist and loped over to her. 'Why would you want to film me?' He kissed her neck, which was still so much of a novelty that she felt it in her fingernails, in the balls of her feet.

'I told you I'm making a sort of mood board of visual ideas for my new project.'

'What's your new project got to do with me?'

'Nothing,' she lied.

'I thought it was about some bloke going up Cader Idris for a night.'

'It is.'

'And you decided if he comes down a nutter or a poet yet?'

'Top-secret information.'

He held her arm up and kissed along the length of her bicep. 'Well, I'd never do that.'

'Why?'

'Well, for starters, you'd freeze your balls off.' He put his hands on her hips. 'And second, I'm a bit superstitious, like.'

'*You're* superstitious? You used to think all that stuff was bullshit.'

'Yeah. Well. I've not had the best luck recently. Why jinx it if you don't have to?' He grabbed a handful of crisps from the bowl next to the barbecue. 'Hmm. Posh crisps. Why d'you wanna film me, anyway? For this *mood board*.'

She hadn't thought he would ask so many questions. Most people liked to be filmed. 'Just to get your voice. Your turn of phrase. Maybe you could talk a bit, about your life, about town. So I can get the way the guy speaks right.'

'So you think I'm some kind of zoo animal or something?'

Her shoulders tensed. He detached himself from her body and walked over to the table. He sat down and began to roll a cigarette.

'You gonna pay me then?'

'Yeah. Of course. Of course, I would never think of not paying you. Definitely.'

She realised then that he was grinning at her. 'I'm taking the piss.' He fired another handful of the posh crisps into his mouth. 'But just so you know, I'm camera shy.'

James sent her text messages about train times, about how much he missed her. He sent her a link to the song 'My Old Man', and said that the bed was too big, and the frying pan was indeed too wide.

There were several instances when the membrane that divided these two realities was breached. She was showing Geth something on her phone once when it began to shudder in her palm, invaded by a phone call from James. She locked the screen, and Geth said – a hard, alien edge in his voice – 'You can take it if you want. It's not like I've never been with someone married before.' Sometimes he didn't talk, and she would resent him for placing the entire burden of the conversation on her. There were times when he'd shut down inexplicably, and it wasn't like when they were kids. She tried not to think too much about it – she tried not to think too much about anything – but the silences were heavier. Longer. One evening, a clear one, they were out walking and she was in the middle of an anecdote that his unresponsiveness was making arduous. He came to a halt in front of a tree.

'This ash needs felling.'

She hadn't particularly noticed the tree before, but now she felt attached to it. 'This one? Why? It's so big, it must be super old?'

He shrugged. 'Yeah. Riddled with ash dieback disease, though, by the looks of it. You should get rid of it, before it spreads.'

She didn't know what ash dieback disease was, but it sounded alarming. 'It can spread? Is it dangerous?'

'Don't worry, love, you're not gonna catch it.'

'How can you tell?'

'You're the wrong species, for a start.'

'Funny.'

He pointed up to the top branches. 'Look up there. No leaves.' He pulled a lower branch towards her. 'And look at these ones. There's still a lot of leaves down here but they're starting to all go brown. It's a kind of fungus.'

She winced. There was something physically repulsive about the word 'fungus'. She had the impression that he was touching something infectious. The tree, with its balding crown, and all the bare, white sky above it, had shifted from something unremarkable and benign into something stark and ominous, and she wondered how many of the others – velvety, blue silhouettes, vague and unreal now that the sun had set – were infected, how much toxicity had insinuated itself in the root systems, in the soil, in all the dark buried places that she couldn't see.

'Can you do it?'

'Yeah. Course. No problem. I'll do it this weekend.'

The crow's feet at his eyes deepened, and she knew that the idea pleased him.

'We'll pay you, obviously.' She immediately regretted the plural pronoun.

He was still fixed on the fine, supple young branch that he was holding in his right hand. He fingered the dying leaves, rubbed his thumb along the smooth new stem. He nodded. 'OK. Thanks.'

She wasn't good at keeping secrets, and about a week or so after she'd had to lose Miranda as a confidante, she rang Tony and spent forty-five minutes on the phone with him, almost saying something. Tony was a safer bet. Tony wasn't married to James's best friend from primary school. Tony didn't even technically approve of James, and in no way approved of monogamy; *plutôt mourir*, he told her on her wedding day. They talked for a long time about the film. They talked for a while about a friend of a friend who had just got a six-figure book deal for a novel that Tony had read and dismissed as 'working class cosplay'.

'It's because she's Irish,' he said, 'people think she's working class, but she's not, she's just *Irish*.'

Olwen imagined how she would put what was happening in words. 'I'm fucking my first boyfriend again.' 'I'm sleeping with my childhood sweetheart at least five nights a week.' 'I'm falling in love with Gethin.' No, not love. Sex and love were not the same thing.

'She went to private school, I swear to God.'

Tony talked and she realised that she didn't want to tell him, she didn't want to cheapen it, which she realised was

249

not something you thought about someone you were just fucking, so she told herself that she kept quiet in the name of self-preservation instead. She told herself, she told herself, she told herself.

'Take off your dress,' Geth said.

She started to laugh. 'Excuse me?'

'Take off your dress.' His voice was blank too, and there was something unfamiliar about him. Her body began to respond. His words were hot liquid, coating her skin. She undid the buttons, one by one, shouldered it off.

'Go to the bed. Kneel on the floor. Go on. And close your eyes.'

She heard him come up behind her. Heard the sound of him unzipping his jeans. He pressed his body against hers and he put his fingers around her throat.

'We shouldn't be doing this, should we?'

She agreed that they shouldn't.

'But you like it, don't you? You want it?'

'Uh-huh.'

He increased the pressure of his fingertips ever so slightly. 'What's that?'

'I want it.' He moved his hand around to the nape of her neck, grabbed a fistful of hair.

'Am I hurting you?'

'A little,' she breathed.

'Should I stop?'

'Don't stop.'

He put his free hand on her waist, then around and down to her stomach and between her legs. 'Oh God, you're wet,' he exhaled. He let go of her hair and held her face, pushed two of his fingers into her open mouth, and he let out a low moan as she moved her tongue up and down the tip of one, just how she knew he liked when she was blowing him. He jerked his hand away.

'Tell me that you want me more.'

'More?'

'More than him.'

Because it was a game, she told him that she wanted him the most. More than anyone. 'I want you more,' she said.

'It's better than before, isn't it?'

'I hope so,' she said, resting her chin on his chest, 'I'd like to think I've learnt a bit over the years.'

'Oh, you have.'

She slapped him.

'What? I wasn't complaining back then, was I?'

She grinned. It was like her body was made up entirely of endorphins; surely a good thing – proof that this was physical, chemical, controllable.

They went into the kitchen. 'Beer in the fridge,' she called as she went to choose a record. 'Or there's some whisky and some gin in that cupboard up there.' She didn't bother to go through everything else they had, just named the things that she thought he would like. The other night, when she'd poured him a measure of the Douglas fir eau-de-vie that James had picked up on his last trip to Toronto, Gethin had laughed in her face.

She flipped through the stack of albums. She played records, rather than Spotify playlists, when she felt some ceremony was due. She wanted something that would show him how worldly she'd become, how much she'd grown up. Ideally, she wanted something he wouldn't know. 'You like Alice Coltrane?' she said, 'Or how about Caetano Veloso?'

He didn't reply to either so she tried a different tack altogether and put on *The Smiths*, to remind him of when they were young, and of the summer when he'd had a copied tape of it that he'd subjected her to on an endless loop when they used to drive around in the old Fiat. The opening bars of the 'Reel Around the Fountain' still didn't rouse any kind of reaction, and when she looked up he was standing in front of the fridge, apparently absorbed. The door was closed.

'What have you found?' she asked.

She padded over to him and slipped her arms around his waist. He was looking at the postcard of Westminster Bridge.

Outside, the heron was perched on the far bank of the lake. The early evening sky was the same pearled grey as its plumage, radiant with sunset. They sat on the veranda with the bottle of Scotch. The lake was still and opaque, and other than the occasional, crisp stirring of the leaves, the woods were silent. The click of Geth's lighter detonated the calm.

'Have you had any others?'

'Other what? Postcards?'

'Anything,' he said, words creased around the cigarette hanging at his bottom lip. He puffed out a cloud of smoke and then swallowed a mouthful of whisky. 'Has nothing else weird been happening? Since you got here.'

She wondered if she should tell him about the beer bottles, the ashtray, and then she decided that she would, that she wanted to see how he would react, to test him. 'There were a couple of things,' she said, 'but it's nothing.'

'What was it?'

The whisky burnt the back of her throat. She said, 'A few weeks ago, I couldn't really sleep one night, and I was convinced there was someone here.'

'In the house?'

'No. Not exactly. Like just outside; here.'

His mouth went lax.

'But then I figured it must have been a dream. And when I woke up everything was fine and normal.'

'Right. OK?'

'Yeah. Until . . .'

'Until what?'

'Till I went outside in the morning and there were a couple of empty bottles of Stella sitting on that table over there.'

'You what?'

'Yeah, it was weird.'

'And they weren't yours?'

'Of course they weren't mine. I'd remember, wouldn't I?

He closed his eyes. Swore. He leant back in the deck chair. 'And you didn't tell anyone?'

She wondered, for an unexpected, treacherous second, if it was suspicious that he was so concerned about whether she'd told anyone. 'Honestly,' she said, 'I kind of thought it was you.'

His eyes clicked open again. 'Are you having a laugh?'

'No.'

'You serious? You're serious, aren't you? What kind of fucking weirdo do you think I am? You think I'm some kind of creep? Jesus. Fucking hell, Olwen. Cheers.' He finished the last of his whisky and poured himself another two fingers. His hands were shaking.

'I mean. No offence, but who else would it be?'

He downed the two fingers in one. He shook his head again. '*Iesu mawr*,' he hissed, 'thanks a fucking bunch, Olwen. Nice to know you think I'm such a fucking creep.'

'Well, you're the only one here who still knows me.'

He snorted. 'Right. Because that's what this is about. Trust me, love, it's nothing personal. They don't have to know you. This isn't about you. There's plenty of people around here who'd have a problem with someone like you buying this place. And not even really living here.'

'Someone like me?'

'Yeah. Someone like you.'

She felt as if he'd leant forward and slapped her smartly across the face. 'Right. Great. Good to know. Thanks.'

On the other side of the lake, the heron unfurled its wings and took flight. The bridge of Olwen's nose was hot, and she had a horrible feeling that she might start to cry. Geth sighed. After a while he said, 'It's complicated, you know? You go over towards Pen Llŷn, every other house is a holiday home. More, even. Locals can't even afford to live there any more.'

'Locals could never afford this house anyway.'

He raised his eyebrows.

'And besides, we're not on the Llŷn Peninsula. No one comes on holiday round here,' she said flatly.

'Yeah. But I guess this guy obviously just has some issues in general and he's taking them out on you.'

'How do you know it's a guy?'

He slapped the table with the flat of his palm. 'Ohhhh fuck-in' hell, Olwen. I dunno, do I? Just seems more like the kind of thing a guy would do, that's all.'

She rolled her eyes.

'You don't trust me, do you?'

In the silence that followed she could make out the respiratory continuity of the wind in the leaves. 'You wanted to live here, didn't you?' she said.

He stubbed out his cigarette. He smiled. He shook his head. After another eternity of silence, he stood up. 'I think I better go back to mine tonight.'

'Fine.'

He waited there for another handful of seconds whilst the air between them snapped like kindling spitting embers.

'See you round then,' he said as he left.

Over the next twenty-four hours, she checked her phone compulsively. Miranda sent her memes about Theresa May. A group chat that she kept forgetting to mute fine-tuned the details of a housewarming in Walthamstow. Her brother berated her parents for being 'centrist boomers' in another. Sometimes, she would allow herself to open up the conversation thread with Gethin, and she would tell herself that if he was online too, it was a sign, and she would send him an olive branch. It happened several times and each time her thumb hovered over the keyboard, but she never went through with it. On the second morning that she woke up alone, the four messages that she'd received while she was asleep were from James. She felt guilty that his name disappointed her.

I miss you so much

I want to fuck you

Thank God it's this weekend.

I can't wait to see you

Because it was already the end of the month. Because James would arrive on Thursday night. She dropped her phone back on to the bedside table, lay on her back, eyes fixed on the ceiling, and she told herself that Geth's silence was categorically a good thing.

2017

SHE WAS SO RELIEVED and reassured when she saw James that she told him about Gethin. Not all of it, of course. She told him that they'd reconnected as friends. She almost told him that Geth was married before self-preservation kicked in, and she remembered that town was too small a place to maintain that level of untruth. She told him about the ash tree and then regretted it immediately because James was even more disturbed than she had been, and wanted to call Geth to come and sort out the problem as soon as possible.

'My grandparents lost all of their elms to Dutch elm disease at The Rectory,' he said. James was from the kind of family where houses were referred to by their names and anthropomorphised as eccentric cousins. 'These things are really serious. And if this guy's short of work anyway we should get him on board – he'll be grateful.'

It had been over four days since she'd heard anything from Gethin. She kept thinking about the way he'd slapped the table with his palm. The way his voice had fractured when he said goodbye. Now that James was here, she concentrated a lot of her energy on not letting herself think about it. When her mind strayed and began to recreate moments with Geth, she worked hard to obliterate the images with words: I am so lucky, she consciously thought. I love James so, so much.

On the second evening that he was there, they were sitting out on the veranda, and she heard the truck at the top of the track. She sat up in the deck chair.

'Ooh, hello,' James said. 'Visitors?'

Her mind started to move at double speed. 'It sounds like Geth,' she said. 'I'll go up and meet him.'

James yawned. 'You think he'd call first. It's dinner time. Country people.'

She was already standing up. 'He's like that. No communication skills.'

She managed to intercept him just at the bottom of the track. He was wearing a clean white T-shirt and a pair of Levi's. When she got closer to him, she smelt aftershave and the synthetic mint of toothpaste, and the idea that he'd made an effort sent a twinge of pain right through her.

'James is here,' she said quietly.

'I saw the car.'

She looked at the ground. 'I'm sorry.'

He narrowed his eyes as if the light ahead of him was painfully bright. 'It's fine. I shouldn't have come in the first place.'

'Please don't go. He knows it's you. It would be weird if you went.'

He laughed. He pinched the bridge of his nose between his forefinger and thumb. 'Right.'

'Please come up to the house. I'm so sorry.'

'Well, this is fucking great, isn't it?'

James was laying the table outside. He lunged across it and seized Gethin's hand in his own. 'Welcome!' he said. 'Am I laying another place?'

Geth ran his hands through his hair. He focused his eyes on the spot just past James's right ear. His face moved unnaturally. 'I'm good thanks, mate, I've eaten already. Cheers.'

James beamed at them both with his excellent teeth. 'Well, pull up a pew anyway. You want something to drink?'

'Nah, nothing for me. I'm driving. I won't be long, I

just, uh, I was just in the village, at my brother's. Thought I'd drop in.'

'Oh, yeah? You ate with him then?'

'Excuse me?'

'God, James, you don't have to interrogate him.'

James looked bemused. 'Was I interrogating? Anyway, please, Gethin, sit down. I'm going to the kitchen, come on – one little beer?'

Geth agreed with the lower half of his face. When James was inside, he muttered, 'Could fucking use a drink, fair dos.'

Olwen closed her eyes.

'He looks like James Bond.'

She ignored him.

'Do you love him?'

'Gethin.'

'I wouldn't blame you. He looks like a film star. Like the posh cunt in every—'

'Geth.'

'And he is rich, isn't he? You can tell. Proper classy. Looks like a watch advert.'

James reappeared with three bottles of Stella from the six-pack that Olwen had bought a week earlier for Gethin. He opened them with his teeth.

'What are you *doing*?' she said.

'Couldn't find the bottle opener.'

She cringed. She knew for a fact that the bottle opener was on the kitchen counter, next to the hobs where James had been cooking. He handed her a bottle, and then Geth. He grinned. 'Cheers, mate.'

Geth nodded.

James sat back down and began to make charming small talk, and Olwen was grateful for his ability to generate conversation, even if every new word held some kind of potential threat. She wanted to go into the kitchen and plate the food to escape, but to leave the two of them together without her felt even more perilous. Geth answered in monosyllables, and she knew that James would think he was rude. James was performing 'man of the people'; legs splayed wide, everyone was 'mate', including the 'lads' that he played five aside with. Did Geth follow the footy? Who was his team? A Liverpool man? James was City himself, a fact that he always enjoyed advertising and that Olwen found faintly absurd, given that the devotion stemmed from a single, cherished and oft-evoked, self-made, northern grandfather. He talked about the transfer window and penalties with the same dexterity and grace he exhibited when talking about economic models, the shadow cabinet, or a controversial pavilion at the Venice Biennale. It was a skill that impressed Olwen – the ease with which he moved between worlds. She didn't usually find it so unbearably smug.

'So, Ol told me about the ash problem,' he said finally, when he realised he wasn't getting anywhere with the beautiful game.

Geth tilted his chin. 'Huh. Yeah.'

'So you think you could get rid of it, then?'

She wondered if Gethin actually winced, or if she just knew his body so well that she could read his discomfort under the performance of normality. 'I can try,' he said.

James beamed. 'Splendid,' he said. He'd started saying 'splendid' years ago as a joke, as a parody of his own class. Now it just sounded authentic. 'I actually thought that we might sit down and have a chat some time. I've been thinking more about the woodland. I've been thinking that, well, I know fuck all about trees' – that wasn't entirely true. James had a passing knowledge of most things. There was nothing that he knew nothing about – 'and there'll be moments when we can't get up here for a while, so I was thinking – obviously we'd sit down and talk about it properly, I'll get your number, we'll chat – but I was wondering if maybe you'd be interested in managing the woodland for us?'

Olwen watched the tiniest muscle twitch, briefly, in Geth's jaw, and wondered if James saw it too. He kept his eyes very open. He placed his dead bottle on the table and wiped his palms down on his jeans. He made a show of looking at his watch. 'Yeah, let's talk about it some time,' he said. He stood up.

The last thing he said to Olwen was, 'Enjoy tomorrow, yeah?', and she was touched that he'd remembered her birthday.

'He's very proud, isn't he?' James said later, as he sharpened the knives to carve the roast chicken.

On the morning of her thirty-fifth birthday she woke up before half six. The first thing she noticed was that Gethin wasn't there, a fact that her mind quickly corrected to note the primary absence of James instead. She experienced a momentary plunge into horror: he was gone because he'd found out. He'd found a pair of Gethin's boxers, or a forgotten condom wrapper under the bed. Geth himself had sent a cool, rational text, telling him, quite plainly, that he'd spent the past fortnight fucking his wife. James was halfway down the M1, drinking a rancid coffee at some miserable service station in the Midlands, driving very calmly, within the speed limit, but hands gripping the steering wheel as if it were something alive that he wanted to kill.

Of course, he wasn't. He was up early out of habit. She found him on the veranda, laptop open, a pot of coffee next to him on the low table. He was frowning at his computer screen, and when he greeted her, he didn't mention her birthday, and she knew straight away that he was planning something. He was physically incapable of deceit.

'HOLY CUNTING CHRIST!' Miranda crowed as she emerged at the bottom of the track. 'Fuck! This *place*! You should charge entry. How much are the National Trust paying you to keep their seat warm?'

She was wearing an enormous pair of black Doc Marten sandals that her indulgent husband called orthopaedic, and so much jewellery that she was essentially half human, half percussion instrument. She strode across the veranda, crushed Olwen in a hug, and whispered, 'Does he know about the lumberjack?'

'Christ, no.'

They were joined by Miranda's husband, Freddie, and by Asha and Tony, the remaining half of their old university clique. James appeared last, laden down with bulging canvas shopping bags and looking bashfully pleased with himself. Olwen slipped her arms around his neck and pretended to be surprised.

'Very well played,' she lied, and he grinned, softening her heart and reminding her that she had been saved, that this was her life – her beautiful life – and that she would never see Gethin again. The idea was reassuring and she consciously held on to it, imagining it as something tangible like a smooth pebble, warmed by sunlight on the beach, something that she could hold. She showed her friends around the house, assigned them all bedrooms. They were all appropriately impressed. They all wanted to swim, except for Tony, who was a creature entirely of the urban environment and convinced that the lake was full of leeches. 'My black bile is all good, thanks,' he drawled, 'but maybe I'll consider it if my next date gives me syphilis.' Miranda insisted on nudity and floated on the water on her back like a dead Pre-Raphaelite muse. James and Freddie treated the activity as a competitive sport, and Asha, who had never forgiven Miranda for marrying Freddie, and who only just tolerated James said, 'Who'd have known Patrick Bateman was so adept at butterfly.' They pulled themselves up on to the jetty to join Tony, who was lying in the hot sun, smoking.

'I'm trying to protect myself from all this fresh air.'

'Give us a drag,' said Olwen.

'Surely by now you can afford your own?' He gestured around him as he handed her the rollie. His judgemental glare landed on Miranda, and he sighed theatrically. 'I must say I'm most disappointed at the fervour you're all embracing this "wild swimming" business with. Very earnest. Very smug postgrad clutching canvas tote bag and copy of the *LRB*; very using *radical* as an adjective.'

Asha sniggered. 'Radical subversion of hetero-patriarchal understandings of menstruation.'

'Radical recreation of cum stains rendered in watercolours and mixed media.'

'Radical revalorisation of working-class foodstuffs – bourbon biscuits to bring down the bourgeoisie.'

'Radical retail therapy: giving in to capitalism, radically.'

'Isn't that the name of Miranda's last play?'

Tony snorted.

Olwen said, 'You two are as bad as the wankers of Hampstead Ladies' Pond. This isn't *wild swimming*. It's just swimming. I spent my adolescence doing it.'

'Oh Christ, here we go, Ash. She's about to start on

her bumpkin childhood. Did you have electricity in the caravan?'

Olwen slapped him.

Asha said, 'I'm *very* excited to find out the truth about that.'

Olwen frowned at her. 'What's that supposed to mean?'

'From Gareth. When he arrives.'

'Gareth?'

Tony was shaking his head furiously.

'The guest of honour, of course!'

'What the fuck are you talking about?'

'Only the guy you were still completely in love with until you met João in final year.'

'Oh my God, *João*, *stop*!' cried Tony. 'How could I have forgotten *João*, the ultimate literary Latin fuckboy?'

'Do you remember that hat he had?'

'He surely invented the indie fedora.'

'As much as I'm enjoying this trip into my painful heart-breaks of times past, it's my birthday, and I want to know what you're both talking about.'

'I think Gavin was supposed to be a surprise, Ash,' Tony said through gritted teeth.

'Shit,' she muttered. 'Pretend I didn't say anything. I didn't say anything actually. Tony, pass me your phone. Let's try and find out what João's up to these days. Did he ever manage to write anything as long and tedious as *Hopscotch*?'

'Stop trying to divert!'

'All will be revealed soon, darling.' Tony began to tap at the screen of his phone. 'I think João will be too cool for social media, surely?'

'No chance. He was well into curating his own personal brand. What was his surname, Ol?'

'You're talking about Gethin, aren't you? Did James invite Gethin?'

They studiously ignored her. 'Does this look like the right João?' Tony said. He thrust the phone in Asha's face.

James cut a fine front crawl through the taffeta smoothness of the water. He emerged, black hair wet and teeth whiter than ever against his tanned skin. 'Champagne time?'

When they were all out of the water, and when he placed seven glasses on the table and checked his watch, Olwen knew she was right. Five endless minutes after that, she heard the sound of the truck.

He was wearing a hideous buttoned shirt and carrying a bouquet of supermarket chrysanthemums that she saw through the prism of Miranda's reaction to them. James, genetically engineered to make guests feel welcome, was on his feet at the moment that Geth appeared on the steps up to the veranda.

'Geth, mate!' He slapped him chummily on the back and Olwen felt her face twitch into a dazed smile. 'Thanks for coming!'

She crossed over to meet them and Geth, eyes focused on the wooden floorboards, handed her the flowers. They were completely without odour. The Cellophane crackled in her fingers. As she took them, she noticed the leather bracelets on his wrist and could already imagine her friends delighting in ridiculing them. She wondered why on earth he'd ever agreed to come.

'*Penblwydd Hapus*,' he said to the ground. 'Sorry, they're a bit shit, like. The selection wasn't great.'

'They're very *blue*,' Miranda called, in what Olwen realised was a clumsy attempt to be kind. 'I didn't know they grew them in that colour.'

'They don't,' Olwen said. 'They're dyed. They turn the water purple.'

Geth finally made eye contact with her. She was letting him know that she remembered. He used to bring them to her from the supermarket and she used to put them in pint glasses along her bedroom windowsill and watch the water turn violet. 'Thank you,' she said.

'I love them,' Tony said. 'Kitsch as fuck. Very Fassbinder.'

Music carried out from the kitchen. The table heaved. All of the plates and glasses and cutlery looked old and solid. It was like a still from a film about artistic members of the bourgeoisie on holiday, or the *mise-en-scène* of a play. Everything looked arranged. James's shirt billowed open. Tony was wearing round, silver-framed, black sunglasses and was shirtless, head resting on Asha's shoulder – she was rolling a joint. Even the ashtrays looked picturesque, curated and brushed with flattering light. Everyone was visibly unwound, except for Gethin and Olwen, who sat straight-backed in their chairs, as if they were at job interviews, which wasn't entirely untrue for Gethin, considering the interrogation he was enduring.

'So why didn't you want to work on your uncle's farm, with your brother?' Miranda asked, chin ground into the heel of her hand as she leant closer to convey the extent of her interest in Gethin's inner life.

He pulled a face. 'Never been that into farming, to be honest. And you got to be pretty fucking dedicated. Wasn't my thing, like.'

Miranda nodded enthusiastically. 'Really? And you didn't feel, like . . . a pull to the land?'

He raised his eyebrows.

Freddie said, 'I've got a bit of an embarrassing fantasy about packing it all in and starting a farm. I grew up in Somerset. My grandparents had one.'

'Your grandparents were *not* farmers. They just happened to own half of the West Country.'

Freddie ignored his wife. 'Maybe in Wales,' he mused.

Tony snorted. 'I wouldn't pitch up here if I were you, Patrick.'

Freddie had never questioned why Asha and Tony called him Patrick. 'Why?'

'You're English. Everyone hates the English.'

'Yeah, like . . . the Irish. And the Scottish. And everyone we colonised. Fair enough. But Wales?'

'Everybody hates the English,' Olwen confirmed, hoping to avoid detail.

'Do you hate the English, Gethin?'

When the silence had endured for long enough to make everyone alert and uncomfortable, Geth said, 'I don't hate anyone, till I know them.'

Asha ran her tongue along the Rizla and sealed it with her thumbs. She said, 'As much as I'm enjoying everyone ranking former colonies on some kind of worthiness spectrum . . . Who am I kidding? I'm not enjoying it—'

Freddie rolled his eyes and Miranda glared at him.

'—can we please move on to what we all really want to know. Gethin. What was Olwen like when she was a kid? Don't be nice because it's her birthday.'

Geth smirked. 'Well, she had a mouth on her. She was well cocky.'

'*Plus ça change*,' said Tony delightedly. 'What about Margot, did she try it on with you?'

'What, her mum?'

'Tony!' Olwen groaned.

267

'I'll never forget her at your wedding. That woman was *sultry*. The way she *shimmied* when Terence Trent D'Arby came on . . .'

For the first time, Gethin genuinely laughed. 'Now you mention it, she did have a soft spot for me.'

Olwen threw her palms in the air. 'He's not wrong. She did.'

Tony said, 'Oh my God. Is that why you broke her heart? To live out a Mrs Robinson fantasy with our Marg?'

Gethin looked directly at Olwen then, as if they were the only two people at the table. She blushed. If she'd looked at James, she might have seen some kind of recognition flicker on his face. He stood up, pushing his chair back as loudly as he could. 'Are we ready to eat, then?'

By the time he brought out dessert, a kind of languorous and stupefying drunkenness had enveloped the table, and Olwen had let her guard down. Geth was behaving perfectly normally. He wasn't here to destroy her life. His acceptance of James's invitation was odd, but so far, apparently without sinister intent. James himself hadn't noticed a thing. Other than Freddie, no one was making any glaring *faux pas* – and anyway, Gethin had surely clocked by now that Miranda's husband was an idiot, and not representative of the others. Neither, in turn, had Geth said anything un-PC that might antagonise them. Nothing controversial had soured proceedings. Then, when the plates were all cleared, around the time that the gilt edges of the afternoon were silvering into dusk, Tony said, 'Are my sources correct in thinking that you come bearing gak, Patrick?'

Freddie was drunker than everyone else, as he often tended to be. He tapped his nostril theatrically and then said to Gethin, 'Gak means cocaine.'

Geth said, 'Wow. Thanks for that.'

Freddie tipped back on his chair and drew his hands up to the nape of his neck. 'All right then, who's partaking?'

'Me,' said Tony. 'Miranda.'

She shrugged. 'Guilty as charged. I have to celebrate being childless, for once.'

'I'll have the tiniest bump,' said Asha.

James grimaced. 'I'll pass. Thanks.'

Olwen looked at Geth. 'Driving,' he said.

'You can stay here, you know, if you want.'

She wasn't going to have any, she never took drugs any more, but then, the way that he looked at her – hard and sad – changed her mind. She felt a little unsteady again. She could do with a boost.

The sun had set, moonlight flecked the still surface of the lake, and they were on their way into the second gram. Miranda was telling Geth what she did for a 'living'. Her teeth clattered frighteningly as she spoke.

'We focus on participatory practice. Like in this play we're putting on in September, for example, we're going to force the audience to engage in shameful activity in order to realise their full political potential.'

He narrowed his eyes. 'Right. OK.'

'How shameful are we talking?' asked Tony hopefully.

'Are you two scions of the financial services industry planning on going?' Asha asked James and Freddie. As an underpaid, freelance political journalist, Asha was the only one of them who still actually participated in politics in any meaningful way post-university. 'Ready to be engaged?' She grinned across the table.

Miranda laughed. 'Oh, please. Freddie thinks a Molotov cocktail is something you can order at a bar with an olive.'

Freddie dabbed at his septum with the tip of his index finger. 'Fuck's sake. Come on. Bloody hell. Can you all actually hear yourselves? Sitting in the garden of this bloody modernist Barbie dream house talking about your *people's revolution* when you don't even know how to talk to normal people? *Participatory practice?* You really think Gav gives a shit about participatory practice, Miri? No wonder they're all voting Tory. Am I right or am I right?' he said to Gethin.

Geth didn't flinch. He smiled benignly at him and said, 'More of a National Front man myself.'

Freddie, who wasn't sure if he was joking, tittered nervously.

'And go on. Fuck it. I will have a line.'

At that point, had she not been feeling so chemically invincible, Olwen might have sensed the tiniest glimmer of danger.

It was midnight, they were dancing, which was better than talking since Freddie had become such a bore. James had gone to bed. Tony and Asha had dragged the speakers outside. Everyone was the colour of moonlight. Everyone was beautiful. She was exceptionally beautiful. This song was a beautiful song. Geth used to love this song when they were kids. Geth was taking her in his arms. Geth was holding her close. They were dancing. Her whole body was shimmering.

'Jesus, Ol, channelling our Marg right there, you sultry minx,' said Tony as he flitted into their orbit.

She grinned at him and Gethin spun her around clumsily. 'You see,' she said to him, 'I was right, you did have some moves on you.'

He pulled her back close to him and for a fraction of a second she almost forgot herself and kissed him. They were the only people in the world. Her body was full of electric charge, her nipples were hard. He held her gaze for just that little bit too long (pupils black and enormous), and she realised then that everyone was looking at them. Miranda appeared at her elbow and insinuated herself into their pair. Miranda was a good friend. She could be hard work, but the fact remained that she was a very, very good friend. Miranda began to flirt with him even more flagrantly than Olwen had been, pressing her body against his, to make what had just somehow happened seem relatively normal.

Olwen detached herself. She went and sat on the edge of the jetty, and she focused all her energy on inhaling and exhaling the lovely, cool air, and after a minute or two, she became aware that Freddie was watching her. Freddie might have been an idiot, but she knew then that Freddie undoubtedly knew the truth.

In the kitchen at three o'clock in the morning, the electric-yellow lamplight rendered the detail within unbearably lucid. The drugs were wearing off and Olwen felt the first needles of anxiety. Tony and Asha were smoking outside and Gethin had decided it would be a good idea to drive back to town. She hadn't stopped him. Freddie was leaning over the sink, filling pint glasses with water and loudly insisting that they all consume them. She could hear his teeth grinding, and the noise made her nauseous. She watched Miranda put the chrysanthemums in a vase. She fingered the tiny petals of the flowers. 'They are very blue,' she smirked.

When Olwen woke up at eleven or thereabouts, the house was immaculate. Everyone else was presumably asleep,

271

except for James, who she couldn't find anywhere. Miserable, grey light leaked in from outside, and a vaporous chill came in through the open windows. Her head pounded, and every thought she attempted to have was splintered with the image of Freddie, leaning on the table and watching her, leering as their eyes met. She went out on to the veranda and called James's name. The water was black today, and one by one, the first, fat raindrops were beginning to stipple its surface. She found her phone next to the kettle on the kitchen counter. She'd had six messages from Gethin, the last of which he'd sent at four in the morning, so he'd made it home alive, at least. The thumbnail that appeared when you pressed the screen said:

> *thinking about everything im going to do to you*
> *makes me . . .*

The screen went black and she pressed the button again. She pictured James coming in in the morning, while everyone was asleep. She imagined him loading the dishwasher, wiping down the surfaces and opening all the windows to let new air in. She imagined him idly picking up the phone to check the time, pressing the screen as she just had and reading the words:

> *thinking about everything im going to do to you*
> *makes me . . .*

She put the phone down on the counter and gripped the edge of it, and she stayed there – telling herself that maybe he hadn't even seen it – until Tony's voice signalled that she was no longer alone.

'Whose dick do you have to suck to get a coffee in this hotel, then?'

★

She spent the next hour or so like someone awaiting a life sentence, suspended in the hope that it might not happen, every new second feeling more artificial than the one before. One by one, the others drifted into the kitchen. She fried eggs and ground coffee, and they sat around the big table dissecting the details of the evening, tactfully sidestepping the suspicion that had ingrained itself in their collective conscience.

Finally, just after midday, James appeared. He was in his running clothes. His skin gleamed with rain and sweat and his legs were streaked with mud. He was effusive with Labrador buoyancy. Given how averse James was to scenes, she couldn't tell if the buoyancy was real. She studied his face for some kind of molecular shift beneath the semblance of cheer.

'How could you possibly go running this morning?' Miranda groaned.

He grinned. Leant over Olwen's shoulder and grabbed a piece of toast from the table. He took the seat opposite her. 'So,' he said, 'what did I miss last night?'

As she tried to work out if the question were innocuous or loaded, Freddie said, 'Your beloved getting cosy on the dancefloor with the lumberjack for a start.'

James bit down on the slice of toast with a loud crunch. 'You should be careful with him, Ol,' he said. 'I think he's still in love with you.'

2017

THE AFTERNOON that James left was coal dark. The rain was dense, fine and angry. It turned the landscape into something in flux. The sharp arrows of the trees blurred into lichen spots through the glass. The lake became the juddering skin of a drum.

She wasn't dressed appropriately, and in the time it took her to get to Gethin's from the supermarket, where she'd abandoned the car, she was soaked. She didn't register the judgemental looks from the two women smoking under corrugated plastic outside The Parky, or the car that swerved to avoid spraying her as she crossed over the road from the petrol station. The rain rolled down her cheeks and her bare legs and arms, and she hardly even noticed that she was wet. He came to the door immediately.

'Jesus. You're soaking. Don't just stand there, come in.'

The sense of purpose that she'd felt since she'd said goodbye to James began to ebb away as tangibly as dishwater disappearing down a drain.

'Come on, come in the kitchen. I'll put the kettle on.'

He stepped out on to the doormat and pulled her inside with his hand on the small of her back. There was something touching about seeing his bare foot outside, and about the feel of his palm gently making contact with her skin through the wet cotton of her dress. She followed him into the kitchen and she willed herself not to lose her nerve.

'Has he gone then?' he said quietly, as he dropped the teabags into the mugs.

She nodded.

The kettle boiled. 'He seems like a nice guy, you know. Considering.'

She put her head in her hands. 'He is.'

He brought her tea over, but he didn't sit down at the table. He leant against the kitchen counter on his elbows and looked hard at the floor. 'Go on then,' he said finally.

'What?'

'Say what you've come here to say.'

She closed her eyes.

'Say it.' Something in his voice cracked between the two syllables and she felt heat spread along the bridge of her nose and burn at the back of her throat. Seconds, or maybe even minutes, passed and she wanted to live inside each one to delay having to reach a future where action would be taken.

'You know,' he said after a long stretch of silence, voice buckling with the excruciating effort of each syllable, 'we could try.'

She didn't reply.

'Say something.'

'I can't.'

'Tell me why we can't try.' He pressed both of his hands into his forehead. 'I can't believe you're doing this to me again.'

How many more times after that? Because of course, it happened again and again – things like that are never clean and final. It happened that day even, on the grotty lino of his kitchen floor. It happened several times that week, on sordid evenings after endless, elastic days spent waiting and waiting, and thinking that this time would be the last. She'd read enough novels and watched enough films to know that after the giddy euphoria – the transcendence – comes bathos, squalor, banality. She knew that guilt worked like caustic acid on even the most robust of naïve delusions.

But then sublime joy would pierce the cloying film of reality. A day on Anglesey, the sea rippled with silver. Sun lotion glinting lilac and rose quartz on his skin. Sometimes, the guilt would emerge like an extra particle in the air – a sour taste that caught at her throat – but then there was the knot of excitement in her stomach, jagged images of the day that would come back to her later, in flashes, like a camera lens blinking. Gethin's hands on her shoulders, the nape of her neck, and then her collarbone, her breasts; 'let's find somewhere quiet,' he'd said. The dunes. It was a weekday. There weren't that many people around.

'You caught the sun on your face,' he said. They were sitting in his truck at the top of the track. The evening light was low like a bar of gleaming bronze. She knew it was time to go. Her fingertips grazed the door handle. The inside of the truck's cab felt very small. She felt like he was touching her even though his hands were both firmly on the steering wheel. She could smell him. The hairs on her body stood on end, and she was aware of her chest rising and falling as she breathed in and out. She felt the press of his gaze roll along her profile, and out of the corner of her eye, watched him raise his right hand, and then felt the pressure of it on her bare thigh.

'Few minutes never hurt anyone, did they?'

They didn't.

It rained for almost a week, and she took it personally: the universe was punishing her. She tried to absolve herself through work. She finished writing up the treatment, and she let more and more hours pass before replying to messages from Gethin, stretching out the intervals between their bursts of communication. She tried to watch the videos she'd made of him, but to do so felt invasive and fraught with a dubious kind of culpability that she wasn't ready to reckon with. She remembered Miranda, at the beginning of all of this, referring to him as her 'muse', and the flat, heavy, single syllable was freighted with ambient guilt that she was afraid of scrutinising.

The rain fell and fell and fell, and the temperature plummeted. James, whose calls she also ignored – it was too much to hear his voice – started to send her text messages asking if she had plans to come home before the trip to Sardinia. She didn't. She didn't have any plans to do anything. She felt as if she was enduring a prolonged come-down: listless, anxious, exhausted, paranoid.

On one such miserable evening, after a drawn-out, empty afternoon, she was sitting on the veranda in a jumper, the Welsh tapestry blanket pulled tightly around her. A film of precipitation billowed up from the lake, bosky and fresh. The sun's diminishing radiance pulsed under the thick grey clouds, but it already felt dark in the woods. She was staring straight ahead of her, at nothing in particular, and she was so absorbed in her thoughts – she was thinking about Gethin: *I can't believe you're doing this to me again* – that, at first, she didn't notice the fox, standing on the beach at the edge of the water, shoulders hunched, snout slung low, staring right at her. When she finally clocked it, she started. She laughed at herself for being frightened of an animal, but then something about its stillness, about the sheer aliveness of it, and the fact that it was a creature, with eyes and legs and teeth, and its own volition, unnerved her. There was something sinister about its posture, about the angle of its neck. It was unsettling to be confronted with the reality that she shared the space around her with beings that had their own agency; that she wasn't alone. Part of her wanted to go and get her camera, but she knew if she did that the animal would surely disappear again, and anyway, something about the fox was too imposing to film; to do so would be to trespass, to defile. She had the sense that she should play dead. She sat as still as she could and listened to the sound of her own breath. She was aware that her heart was beating unusually fast, that her skin was very cold, and that goosebumps were rising up under the coarse wool of her jumper. It occurred to her that foxes ate geese – not even ate them, that they made art out of annihilating them. As if responding, the fox took a step forward, and then another, and another. She sat up straight in her chair. The fine down on her arms and the back of her neck rose up. The fox kept staring at her and moved forward again, until finally its body was submerged underwater, and only its muscular shoulders and its head (with those unblinking, direct eyes) remained visible above the surface. It swam slowly, in her direction.

She lurched up, sending the deck chair scuttering across the wooden boards of the veranda. She ran inside and pulled the door behind her, leapt back from it as if it were alive. She pressed her chest with her hand. She was tired. She wasn't sleeping. She'd always had an overreactive imagination. Foxes didn't swim.

In the morning, of course, she felt ridiculous. Sitting up in bed she typed 'Can foxes swim' into the toolbar of her internet browser. They could, apparently, but did so rarely, and when she watched a couple of videos, they were surreally cute, not uncanny or ominous. She'd dreamt it. She was tired. And besides, she reminded herself, the fox was her familiar, her friend. It was easy to be rational in the morning, when a fine blue sky clarified the world again.

After a good working day, she decided to go down to the water where she thought she'd seen it. She crouched by the trees, ran her hands over the damp ground. There was no evidence of life to be found, and so she stood up, and decided to walk a little deeper into the woods. She'd been walking for a minute or two when she heard something crack in the undergrowth. Her body tensed immediately, but the daylight reassured her. It was an animal, or a falling branch. Maybe it was even the fox. Another rustle. Her head turned automatically, and that's when she saw the letters carved into the trunk of the beech tree.

CER ADRE

She swallowed, and for a handful of seconds, she remained completely still, transfixed by the words. It was evident that they were done recently: they were vivid and sharp. They were executed skilfully by someone who understood wood and owned a good penknife. She knew it was a beech, because she recognised this specific tree. It was one that she'd known since she was a teenager, that had become exceptional when Gethin had carved their initials into its trunk. She knew that if she walked to the other side she would see the letters, well-formed, but less stark than these ones, given they were almost twenty years old. She ran her fingertips along the grooves in the wood, and she was so engrossed that it took her a second to register the low current of noise coming from the other side of the tree. She stepped back and saw a fly, followed by a second and then a third – each appearing and disappearing behind the trunk – and she realised that the agitated buzz was being made by dozens of them, vociferous in their multiplicity, gathered around something at the roots of the tree. James was always talking about the increasing absence of insects, about the depletion of biodiversity, but she reckoned, from the noise that these ones were making, that there were a lot of them. Grimacing, she rounded the trunk.

The fox's fur was still so thick and glossy that, if hadn't been for the gunshot wound and the vortex of gleaming black flies squirming around it, she could have almost bent down and touched it. She covered her mouth with her hand. A pigeon clattered overhead. She listened for another sound, but other than the flies, there was nothing, there was no one. She was the only person in the woods. She was alone.

2017

IN LONDON, the reality of Wales and the idea of her life at Tŷ Gwydr became something spectral, and she could almost convince herself that she'd fabricated it all. She didn't tell James about it, but the words '*cer adre*' would appear in her head several times a day. She tried to imagine Gethin with his penknife, although she still hoped it wasn't him. 'Don't let any of the farmers know you've joined the RSPCA,' she heard his voice say in her head. She tried to picture him with a gun. Once, when she was watching footage she'd filmed of the woods on her computer, she thought she saw a flash of a silhouette in the trees. She watched it again. It appeared for less than a second, like some kind of Victorian ghost in a sepia-toned photograph. She watched it about five times, and on the sixth, she showed James, who laughed at her and said that it was nothing, that it was just an optical effect. She watched it again, and thought maybe he was right. She thought of the fox, moving through the water.

She didn't reply to Gethin's messages, and eventually he gave up. But she remembered the crow's feet at the corner of his eyes, or the way that he grabbed her hair in his fist as he came, the noise of it. Sometimes, when she slept with James, she would close her eyes and hold on to the idea of sleeping with Gethin. Sometimes, she had an image that she would indulge for a second or two: she'd be buying vegetables on Roman Road, or watching the moorhens glide across the lake in Victoria Park, or going down the escalators on the Central Line, or running along the canal first thing (the water was a hard, metallic blue at that time of year, and half-hidden under all the luminous green duckweed. Everything was incensed with life.) She'd imagine Gethin coming home from work, smelling of sawdust and sweat and tree sap. She'd make a pot of tea, and they'd drink it on the veranda, and they'd tell each other about their days. They'd watch the heron on the far side of the lake. Maybe one summer he'd clear a bit of the woods, and they'd plant a proper garden. Grow vegetables. When she thought about this, chronology would flatten and all of it would happen at once – years of a possible future compressed into a moment.

They went to Sardinia with their friends. Days spent sitting around a table on a terrace, drinking steadily and talking about nothing. Smiling brightly. Rhapsodising over produce, over aperitivo culture, over the picturesque elegance of the locals. The novelist from the Berlinale was there, and one day, when he was driving into town, she asked to go with him. The house was inland, in the mountains, and the road to town hacked a path right through the rock, and felt a thousand miles above the rest of the world. The sun was very hot that afternoon and burnt away any trace of cloud like something corrosive – the car was full of its eviscerating light. They pulled into a lay-by. They didn't even undress. He came, she pretended to, to hasten proceedings, and afterwards, he told her that she should leave her husband, that she should come and live with him on the Calle de la Cabeza in Madrid; could she imagine, both of them working on their art, making love like that, drinking vermouth on his balcony, how perfect it could be? She'd done it to prove she wasn't in love with Geth, and that all she'd ever wanted was to be renewed every now and then by sleeping with other people. It hadn't felt anything like sleeping with Gethin, though. She looked at the novelist, at his fine, smooth fingers, as he dabbed at the cum on his slightly concave chest with a tissue, and she felt physically repulsed.

July 2017

Tape A, Geth Interview 1

The water. Cut.
  —*Let's start with something easy.*
He leans back against the wooden post of the jetty, where he's
  elected to be filmed. He smiles at her, performing confidence
  —*Easy like what?*
  —*I don't know. Tell me your full name.*
Smirks —*Gethin Ryan Thomas.*
  —*Oh God, I'd forgotten about Ryan.*
  —*What's wrong with Ryan? Helena.*
  —*How do you remember that?*
  —*I remember everything.*
One of his intense looks then. He lets it linger for a second and
  tries to defuse it with a laugh.
  —*Tell me about how we met, she says.*
  —*You're joking?*
  —*Well, don't tell me you've forgotten.*
He raises his eyebrows at her —*Yeah. Sure.*
He reaches for the baccy in his pocket, to concentrate his nervous
  energy —*Am I allowed to smoke?*
  —*It's not school.*
Lifts his chin. —*Yeah. All right.*
He separates a Rizla from the packet —*Do you remember?*
  —*Of course I remember.*
  —*What did you think of me?*
  —*You're the one being interviewed here.*
He waits for an answer.

—Fine. I fancied you. Obviously.

—What, when you were that little?

—I was twelve when you and Tal started hanging out.

*Shakes his head, pushes his tongue against his molar —Nuh-uh,
it was before that you and me met. You don't remember, do
you?*

Sweep of the vista. Return to his face. Smoke.

—Tell me a bit about town.

*He's eased into it now. He's enjoying himself. Geth, who was
so good at reading aloud when he was little; who was always
trotted out to do recitations at the school Eisteddfod —What
do you want me to say about town?*

—It's not about what I want you to say.

Eyes gleam.

—Where were you born?

—Llanelwy.

—You weren't born in St Asaph?

He scoffs —Come on, cariad, it's the Welsh name for it. Keep up.

*—Oh. So you were also born in the H. M. Stanley hospital
too? Like me.*

—Uh-huh.

—What do you think of H.M.?

—Not a lot.

*—You know he was like a brutal imperialist? Livingstone,
I presume?*

—Doesn't surprise me.

—So when were you born?

—1979.

She pauses —What song was number one when you were born?

—Oh, come on. Put that thing down—

*The inside of his hand as he leans forward. A squeal of protest
and then a whole load of blank tape, of the floorboards, and*

the sky underneath them. A giggle. Human sounds: tender.
Unmistakable. Yes. Oh God, yes, just like that. Yes.
Afterwards, he takes the camera back in his hands. Films her.
Even though he's off camera, his beatific smile reveals itself
in the timbre of his voice. She's grinning too, like someone in
love.
—'Message in a Bottle' by The Police.

—Tell me about your parents, she says in the next tape.
Breaks eye contact. —Well, you knew my mam, didn't you?
Afterwards, she will wish that she hadn't pushed on the topic,
even if the footage that she gets is so good. When he talks
about his parents, something is dismantled, some remaining
bridge of distance between the two of them. She thinks about
how beautiful the intimacy achieved is without considering
that closeness like that can't be undone.
After that first session he rubs his eyes, which are dry but pink
from the effort of keeping them that way —Fucking hell, he
says, wasn't expecting that. Jesus.
He stands up and sits down again immediately; performs more
laughter.
—Do you want a drink? She feels like a hypnotist.
He put his hands over his face and she listens to the sound of his
breath against his palms. —Yeah. Go on then.
When she comes back out, he's exactly where she left him.
—I'm sorry. That was embarrassing. I don't know where that
all came from.
She sits down next to him. Rests her head on his shoulder. He's
breathing through his mouth and looks dog-tired. He snatches
her hand and presses his thumb into her palm and says —you
know I love you, don't you?
It's like she has stone in the back of her throat. She says,
'I know.'

286

Part Three

A MADMAN OR
A POET

2017

SHE CALLED HIM three times in the space of twenty minutes. When she tried a fourth time, four minutes after that, he felt an unspecific panic, which he identified as concern for her welfare, and so, hating himself, he picked up.

'Olwen,' he said.

It was ten to twelve. He leant out of his bedroom window and felt the cool air on his bare skin. The street was silent and empty, the moon was like a floodlight – everything was lunar blue, once his eyes adjusted to the night.

He said her name again. On the other end of the line, he could hear her breathing; jagged and irregular. He pressed his palms into the window ledge. He asked her if she was all right.

She said his name. She was either crying or trying not to cry. 'I fucked up,' she said. 'I was wrong.'

He closed his eyes. Felt something in his chest contract. He wanted to tell her, after the weeks of silence, that he couldn't do this again.

'I love you,' she said.

He flinched.

'I'm in Italy. I'm with James. I love James, but it's different. I know that now. It's you. I fucked up. I was wrong. I love you.'

He didn't say anything. He couldn't speak.

'Geth.' She tried to regulate her breathing. 'Please tell me that it's not too late. That you still love me too.'

He ground the heel of his fist into his forehead.

'I did something stupid but I think it was good because

289

it made me see I—' She stopped talking and started to properly cry.

He groaned. He said her name.

'Just tell me that it's not too late. Tell me that you love me too.'

He looked at the single streetlight beyond the window and he pictured her standing underneath it at the beginning of all of this.

'It's always been you,' she said. Her voice cracked – she said, 'Please say something.'

He wanted to tell her that he hated her, but already, he could feel the effect of what she was saying work its way through him like a drug. He put a lot of effort into controlling his voice.

'I thought I wasn't going to hear from you again.'

'I know.'

He felt all the distance that he'd tried to put between them over these past few weeks shrink; felt the magnetic drag. 'You have to promise this is real. If you're going to do this.'

'This is real. We fly back the day after tomorrow. It's you. It's always been you.'

He started to laugh.

'I know it's not going to be easy. You know the house isn't mine, don't you?'

He shook his head. 'I couldn't give a fuck about the house any more. Olwen, if we're doing this, we have to do this.'

He was convinced he could hear her smile. 'We're doing it,' she said. 'We're doing this. I love you.'

Now he was really laughing. Now his limbs were weightless. He asked her again if it was real.

'This is real,' she said. 'This is real.'

2017

AT THE FLAT in London, Olwen rarely gave the post more than a cursory glance. James paid the bills, James owned the property, and whereas Olwen enjoyed authentic, physical retail experiences, and shunned internet consumerism, James bought things online, as he tended to be at work when most shops were open. Consequently, when they heaved their suitcases over the threshold, both of them infected with the same, particular genre of irritation that air travel generates, it was James who picked up the pile of letters and packages that had accumulated on the doormat in their absence.

'There's stuff for you here,' he said, dropping some postcards on to the counter. 'Oh, and a parcel!'

She couldn't look at him. For the past forty-eight hours since she'd made her decision, she'd been unable to confront the familiarity of his features; his straight nose, his square mouth, his 'JFK Junior, old Hollywood angles', as Tony liked to put it. In the airport at Cagliari at six o'clock that morning, underneath a wall of adverts, she'd sat on her suitcase and watched him eat an overpriced mortadella panino, and she'd felt like the air she was breathing might choke her; she couldn't even swallow the espresso he'd bought. The problem wasn't ever that she didn't love James.

It was just after ten o'clock in the morning, and almost as soon as he'd deposited his luggage, he packed his suit into his practical rucksack, put on his cycling shorts, and headed to work to 'check in'. She tried to concentrate on that – on the small things that irked her: competitive commuting, corporate-speak. She stared at the front door as it clicked shut behind him and felt vertiginous. In the shower, she let herself weep for the first time. It wasn't as cathartic as she'd anticipated. She texted Gethin, *we have to do this quickly.* She didn't add, *before I lose my nerve.* Her brain was so fried with the effort of trying not to feel anything about the decision that she'd made, that once she'd managed to pick herself up off the floor and dress, she'd walked out of the front door without even looking at the post, which James had left for her on the counter.

'The wines that they've got by the glass are actually *very* decent. Imo and I got a bottle of that Chenin when we were here for her birthday, and *really*' – Tom made a hand gesture universally acknowledged to mean *delicious* – 'actually mad that they've got it on by the glass. One of the waiters must have opened a bottle by mistake.'

Since working on a surreal art house film about the inner-workings of a New York restaurant that *AnOther* had described as '*Kitchen Confidential* through the lens of a Fellini fever dream', Tom, Olwen's new executive producer, had got into the galling habit of acting as if he knew how the hospitality industry functioned.

'That said, we should get a bottle given how excited I am about this.' He beamed. 'The treatment's brilliant. You smashed it.'

Olwen was dazed. She shouldn't have agreed to have lunch on the day she got back to town, but she was aware, when Tom had offered an alternative date, that she wouldn't be around for much longer. 'You think so?'

'Oh, dude, I love it. It's unlike anything I've come across. Seriously. It's so original. I'm not normally big on non-linear narratives but I think this one still manages to be accessible? And, form aside, it's so zeitgeisty. Folk horror's a big deal right now, and the way you're subtly bringing in the class stuff, and the *political* element! *Man.* Is all of that stuff real?'

'Real?'

'Yeah. All these Welsh guys in the eighties burning down holiday homes. Did all that actually happen?'

She cocked her head. 'Yes.'

'Wow. Sick. I honestly had no idea about it. You'd never expect that from the Welsh, they're so . . . unassuming? Like, the Scottish, they're all mad into independence, and they've got this, like, *identity* and everything. And the Irish – well, I mean, we were pretty horrific to the Irish, you can't really blame the poor fuckers.'

The waiter, who was model attractive, and had a line drawing of a spilt wine glass tattooed on his forearm, refilled their glasses of Corsican sparkling water. His neatly pressed, button-down shirt was made of such high-quality cotton that Olwen wanted to reach out and rub the fabric between her forefinger and her thumb. She let Tom order, having barely taken in the meaning of the words on the handwritten menu. After an initial crackle of embarrassment at the possibility of being perceived as a bad feminist, he enthusiastically obliged, asking for the clams with morcilla and manzanilla, followed by Dorset snails in persillade.

'Whereabouts do you guys source the pig?' he said.

'Middle White. From Lincolnshire.'

'Ah, dude. Great stuff. OK, we'll get the pork loin with Scottish girolles and sorrel, then. And the hake? Love marsh samphire. It's so *chunky.*'

The waiter smiled congenially. When he left, Olwen said, 'I mean, I probably wouldn't have used it as context if it hadn't happened.'

'Sorry?'

'The 1980s.'

'Ah. Right, yeah, of course. Well, anyway, it's fascinating. I love the way it kind of just looms in the background ominously rather than being what the film is actually about. I think it's going to be super effective. Plus *very* useful for getting funding, if you know what I mean. We could hit up the Welsh.'

The wine arrived. It tasted like oak and citrus and peaches; she held it on her tongue.

'Maybe this is Wales's big moment,' he mused.

She listened to the sounds just underneath his hot air – other voices rendered meaningless in their plurality, cutlery on earthenware, water splashing into glasses, the waiter's footsteps on the parquet, the tastefully pianissimo traces of a John Coltrane playlist that the speakers were diffusing at a barely perceptible volume. Brassy light refracted off the smooth edges of the bar, someone asked for a wine that was 'skin contact-y, but not *too* skin contact-y'. She tried to imagine Gethin in this context. If he'd be embarrassed or defensive.

'—and I love your idea for the final scene. Of him leading all the men in the village in women's clothes with the painted faces and then them burning the policeman's effigy. It's gonna be chilling. Occult-uncanny. How did you come up with all that?'

She swallowed the wine she'd been running along her tongue. 'From my research. It's based on this old folk custom called *Ceffyl Pren*. It means "wooden horse". It was a kind of mob justice. The men would dress up in women's clothes and blacken their faces, and they'd deliver justice on people who had transgressed – like, for snitching, or adultery, or stealing, or bad treatment of workers . . . Then the sinner would be ritually humiliated by the group in front of the community. Like, the ultimate shame.'

Tom nodded, 'I love it. And the cross-dressing – *so* cool.'

She smiled obsequiously.

'And we'd use green paint for the faces – like Morris dancers do nowadays.'

'Sure.'

'Christ, did I ever tell you about my flirtation with Morris dancing at Oxford?'

The starters arrived and spared her. Tom plucked his napkin from the table and said, 'The audio-visual package that you put together. Pretty unorthodox for a treatment, but we loved it.'

Thinking about the videos, she felt her throat constrict again, and worried that she might not be able to eat. Tom swirled the dregs of wine around in his glass, letting it catch the light. 'Who's the guy you interview?'

She felt her eyes fill, as they were wont to at the moment, and she opened them wider.

'Imo's obsessed with him. Matinée fucking idol. Is he an actor?'

'You showed Imogen the video?'

The waiter returned with a basket of sourdough and asked them how they were doing for wine. Tom ordered two more glasses of 'something in the same vein, but maybe a little funkier?' and Olwen decided to get drunk.

'Where did you find him then? Gen X Richard Burton? He's so compelling. That bit where he starts talking about his mum dying – and you can see the level of control he's exerting over his face. God. How is he not a pro?' He scratched his beard to signal contemplation. 'How would you feel about using more of his personal story in the actual film? You don't go into it much in the treatment, but some of the stuff he says in the interviews on the tape – the stuff about his dad . . .' he mimed plunging a dagger into his heart; 'and when he talks about how his work is vanishing . . . I know the film is generally abstract, but a bit of a sob story never goes amiss, does it?'

Olwen winced. 'I don't know. I'm not so sure about that. It's not really what the film's about.'

Successfully extracting a snail from its shell, Tom said, 'But maybe it should be? I had a meeting with some potential funders and, frankly, everyone's interested in you going into that main character more . . . Like we don't want working-class *misery* but . . . well, maybe a sprinkling of working-class misery, you know? Nicolas Roeg imagery, Ken Loach back story?'

She grimaced. 'I'll think about it.'

Dabbing at his mouth with the napkin, Tom said, 'You really should, you know. I don't want to spill too much before it's in the bag, but these are some exciting opportunities. And we're going to need that funding.'

She was trying not to think about that; about funding.

'Fuck me, man. Snails are so good. And so good for the environment too.'

About money generally. About how they would live.

When she got home, James was sitting at the kitchen table, his laptop open in front of him. She knew something was wrong when he said her name.

'You're home early,' she said solicitously, dropping her keys on to the counter.

He said nothing, and then, when she made herself meet his eyes, 'I think you should sit down.'

The shock was physical – she couldn't bear it. He wasn't

supposed to find out this way, before she left. 'James,' she began. Her voice was thick.

He closed his eyes. 'Look, don't be mad at me, but when I picked up those postcards this morning—'

'Postcards,' she repeated.

'The ones that came for you, while we were away.'

He slid the postcards across the table. 'I noticed when I picked them up that they all said the same thing, and I thought that was kind of weird.'

Numbly, she turned the first of them over.

'And I kind of got the idea that they were little billets-doux from the lumberjack, because they were in Welsh.'

She read the two words to the left-hand side of their address.

'So, don't be angry. I know this sounds mad, and jealous, and just awful but . . . I wrote what they said in a note on my phone, and then I looked it up on my work laptop.'

She turned another one over, and another.

James lowered his voice. 'It means "go home".'

Cer adre. Four times. Next to her London address. She stared mutely at the words. He thought she was processing fear and confusion, and put his hands on hers. 'And look, after that I freaked out a bit, and I came home to double-check that's what they really said. And then I remembered there was the parcel too, so look, don't be angry, but I opened it. I was worried for you, and so . . . I know that's not an excuse . . .'

'What was inside?'

He pushed his chair back. He sighed. 'I mean, I guess it would be funny, if it wasn't so fucking creepy.'

When he came back to the table, he placed a shoe box in front of her. Inside was a plastic doll. It was overtly masculine – something with leading-man bone structure and plastic muscularity, something with icy blue eyes and a slash of brilliant, immobile white teeth. The eyes were bluer and the teeth were whiter because someone had blackened its face. It was wearing a lace bonnet with a matching shawl, a black top hat, and a plaid dress with an apron over the skirt. One of its hairless, brawny arms was raised in greeting. It grinned at her. James handed her a slip of paper. 'And it came with this,' he said.

The words were in Welsh: *Rydyn ni'n dy wylio di.*

He shook his head. His tone was so serious it was as if someone had died. 'It means "We're watching you".'

2016

IT WAS FUNNY that it should all come back to the daughter in the end, because Iestyn had always blamed the Yateses for his involvement with Clive in the first place, given that he was so convinced that it was them who'd turned him in. How was he to have known that in reality there'd been a police raid up at the New Age camp near Bryn S.M., and that one of the crusties – recently descended from the suburban middle classes and still uneasy with the law – had sworn to the officers in charge of the raid that all of the mushrooms had come from some farm lad down in Llanelgan, not to mention the weed. Margot and David had put him on to that too – shown him how easy it was; there's a reason why they call it 'weed', she'd said. The Yateses, for all of their sins, were by no means the type to grass, but Iestyn didn't know that, and so decades later, when he read the letter from Olwen, the first thing he felt was aversion, followed immediately by fear.

'Some funny-looking post for you,' Haf said. She was on her way out. The kitchen was fragrant with the rich, urinous tang of frying pig's kidneys.

'Give the eggs another minute,' she said, 'and it's the nice bacon, from Daf, so don't blydi incinerate it.'

She was talking to the skirting boards and her voice was tired. He took off his cap and pressed down on his forehead with his hand. He'd really tied one on last night. He'd only gone out in the yard to prove something to Danny – Christ knows how he'd even got up. He thought to himself, guiltily, that once she'd left for work, he could get himself a little pick-me-up from the fridge. He usually had a rule about drinking before midday, but hair of the dog and all that. He reached out for her as she brushed past him towards the front door.

'Oh, *ych a fi*, Iestyn, you smell like the blydi pub, don't kiss me. What with you and those pissy kidneys,' she flinched.

He dropped her arm.

'Kettle's just boiled too. Have a cup of tea, for God's sake. I've got to go, I'm late.'

Once their daughters were old enough to look after themselves, Haf had trained as a teacher. She taught Cymraeg at the community college. She organised coffee mornings for Macmillan Cancer Support, and went to Zumba twice a week, and for tea with the girls every Saturday morning at the posh new café in town. She'd joined a choir, and volunteered at Ysgol Llanelgan to get a group of kids together to sing in the Urdd Eisteddfod. Every month or so, she'd go to either Liverpool or Cardiff to visit one of their daughters. She'd stopped trying to drag him along after the incident at the Wales–France match last Six Nations, and, honestly, despite the shame, it was a relief. Women, Iestyn thought, were better at it than men – the ones he knew at least. The front door slammed behind her. 'Tra then,' he said to himself.

He went over to the stove to check on his breakfast, and then to the fridge, where he stood with his palm on the handle for a while, telling himself that he wasn't going to so much as open it – that he was going to walk over to the cupboard where the teabags were instead. He wasn't an alcoholic. He didn't get DTs, or piss himself, or wake up with the shakes – well, not often anyway, with the shakes, but that was just getting old. Everybody was a bloody alcoholic nowadays. Everyone was diagnosed with something, weren't they? No one just had normal problems any more. They had to be something clinical. Some kind of *ism*. He pulled the door open. The bottom left-hand corner where the beers lived was newly empty.

'Fucking cow.'

But that was fine, he didn't need it anyway, he just wanted it, he was fine. He was more than happy with a cup of tea, he just wanted to see.

He scraped the kidneys, bacon and eggs on to a plate, followed by the baked beans that Haf had left alongside them. She'd forgotten his toast, but he didn't have the energy for that now, and the smells of the meat – salty, oily, restorative – were too good to resist. He turned on the radio at the plug but the noise was grating, so he turned it off again immediately. What he needed was to eat. Silence, and to eat, and then a little nap. He could leave everything with Danny. Dan was a good lad. He worried about Danny, about what would happen to him after he'd gone. If Iestyn was fair, Dan would have to buy Haf and the girls out. Once, when they were arguing, she'd said that she couldn't give a shit about Bryn Hendre. That as far as she was concerned, she'd sell up once he croaked, and, she'd added spitefully, if he kept on going the way he was, that'd be sooner rather than later. He spooned a mouthful of beans into the cleft made by the eye of the bacon, and as he raised his head to swallow, he spotted the pile of letters on the edge of the table, the *funny* one that Haf had mentioned on the top. He leant over to get it. It was 'funny', he supposed, because the name and address were handwritten, like a proper, old letter, the kind nobody wrote any more. Probably be some charity, begging, but still.

Mildly moved by curiosity, he wiped his knife on his thigh and then edged it along the closed seam of the envelope. The address in the top right-hand corner was a London one.

'Dear Mr Thomas,' it began, 'I'm sure you don't remember me but we met years ago, when I was much younger and lived in Llanelgan. I think you knew my parents, Margot and David Yates.' He put down his fork. Narrowed his eyes at the sheet of paper to check if it really did say that, if he wasn't going mad. Margot and David Yates. You didn't exactly forget the fuckers who poisoned your life.

He could still remember the first time he saw her. He was just twenty and she was a decade or so older than him. It was the end of September, a Sunday first thing. It must have been early because they'd finished the milking and his dad had gone back to the house to get ready for chapel. Iestyn hadn't gone for years, and after he'd finished his breakfast he had a little time to kill, so he went up to the top field and into the spinney at the edge of their land. It was dead calm there, a nice place to think. He liked the smell of the air on dewy mornings, damp and fungal at that time of year. That particular morning was a fine one once the mist had cleared, leaving a very pure light with a soft, cinematic clarity that blushed gold as it came through the trees. It meant that when he first saw Margot, stooped at the foot of a larch, black hair falling in her face, she was literally illuminated. She straightened herself up and smiled generously at him. Brushed the dirt off her bare knees.

'Good morning,' she said. Her voice was warm and husky. Her accent was posh. Iestyn felt wrong-footed by her lack of shame at getting caught in a place she wasn't supposed to be. He could feel his own face burning, and she was just standing there, beaming, like some kind of Jehovah's Witness on the recruit.

'*Bore da,*' he said to the ground, unnerved by the intensity of her expression.

'Collecting blackberries,' she said. She waved a Sainsbury's bag around in her right hand.

He cleared his throat. 'You know this is private property here, don't you?'

Unfazed, she said, 'Do I know you from somewhere?'

He, of course, knew exactly who she was from her voice. He'd heard that at the beginning of the summer an exotic young English couple had moved into Dr Gwyn's old house on the outskirts of the village. Artists, apparently. Must have had money to be able to afford a place like that: a nice Victorian redbrick thing, the best of three, with a big old-fashioned conservatory. He cleared his throat. He felt nervous speaking English; it had been a while.

'This is my dad's farm. Bryn Hendre. I hope you shut the gates.'

'Yes!' she enthused. 'I met your father at the pub when we first got here. He's a sweetie.'

He frowned at her. 'Sweet' wasn't an adjective he particularly associated with Clwyd Thomas.

'I have to admit we haven't been back, though. Very picturesque down there, but not really our crowd.'

He thought of all the old farmers who propped up the bar at the Glanny. An image appeared in his head of Hywel Bryn Glas chalking up a pool cue – his corduroy trousers held up with baler twine. Margot Yates must have been a vision from another planet.

'We didn't realise there were trendy young people in the village,' she said.

He blushed, despite himself. He couldn't work out if she was teasing him; she said it as if it were a challenge.

'In fact, maybe you could help me out with a little mission I've volunteered myself for.' Her eyes rolled up and down the length of his body, taking him in, removing a layer of skin, exposing him. 'You fancy coming up to our house for a cuppa?'

'A cup of tea?'

She started to laugh, a loud, rich cackle full of cigarette smoke and charisma. 'Don't worry, darling, we're not going to poison you. It is the Sabbath, after all. If you really insist, though, I'm sure I could rustle up something stronger.'

Iestyn craned his neck, looked up at the web of mineral green, lambent with golden light. The air smelt of wet earth and sweet conifer. Everything felt significant.

The first thing that struck him when they went into the kitchen through the back door at Tawelfan – other than the sun coming in low through the kitchen window, glazing the room, catching on pan handles and the elegant curve of the cold tap – was the absolute state of it. The kitchen sink was full of dirty plates. The dining table was covered in paint-splattered newspaper and teeming ashtrays, its spindly, turned legs ruined with cat scratches. The culprit, an enormous ginger thing, was sitting on the kitchen work surface, where *food* was presumably prepared. He imagined his mother surveying the squalor: lips pursed, fingers pressing harder into the little gold clasp of her good handbag. Margot raked a hand through her thick black hair and laughed again, the end of it rattling seductively somewhere in her throat.

'Christ, it is a bit of a tip in here, isn't it? I'm so rubbish at tidying up when Dave's away.' She performed a look of faux-embarrassment as she filled the old stovetop kettle. It was racing green, the same shade as the MGB parked up on the gravel drive outside. She struck a match to light the hob and then bent down to light a cigarette with the newly ignited flame. 'Want one?' she said to Iestyn, shuffling a second out of the packet.

'*Ydw.* Please.'

'So,' she said, pausing to exhale smoke through her nostrils, closing her eyes with the pleasure of it. 'What's there to do round here for fun?'

He shrugged. 'Boars is decent. There's the Seven Club on Fridays and Saturdays.'

The smile she met the suggestion with was implicitly condescending. 'You see, I've been dragged here somewhat against my will,' she said, spooning loose-leaf tea into a pot that looked homemade. 'My husband inherited some dosh from an old lesbian aunt and hatched this mad little plan to come and live the rural dream. He liked the idea of Wales. Thinks he's a bloody druid or something.' She sighed. Iestyn pretended to be unmoved by the idea of a lesbian aunt. 'It's all right for him, of course. He's got residencies, and a gallery in London and lots of excuses to rush back there whenever.'

'Town's not that bad, you know,' he said.

'Hmm. I'm sure.' She overfilled the pot and didn't seem to notice the excess of brownish liquid pooling at its base and dribbling off the edge of the counter. When she'd poured the tea, she cleared some of the mess off the table and set the mugs down in the middle of it.

'So you're a farmer?' she said as she sat opposite him.

'What's wrong with that?'

She chuckled. 'Nothing. It's kind of sexy.'

He felt himself blushing again and forced himself to stare at the cat, which had moved now, and was sunning itself on a pile of clean clothes on top of the Rayburn. He tried not to think about the fact that Margot wasn't wearing a bra, and that the tatty, buttoned dress that she had on – that looked like something his *nain* would have worn in the war, if she'd cut a good third of the skirt away – didn't leave much to the imagination. He felt the pressure of her eye contact, and when he forced himself to meet it, her top lip curled in amusement.

'Are you a virgin?'

'No! Am I fuck? You having a laugh?'

She touched her mouth with her index finger. Her eyes gleamed. 'No. Of course not. I suppose you were probably pressing girls down into hay bales as soon as you could get it up, weren't you?'

He wondered if Margot Yates had ever seen a hay bale before. 'Fucking hell,' he muttered, 'are you always this weird?'

'Yes,' she said, not breaking eye contact with him as she pushed the tip of the finger just between her teeth. 'Are you always this uptight?'

Of course, there were plenty of people who did drugs in town, but Iestyn wasn't one of them. He'd smoked a bit of weed, mind you, he wasn't some kind of old nun, but magic mushrooms – before he met Margot and David, at least – were dangerous. When he thought about hallucinogens, he thought about that one from Pink Floyd who lost it on acid. He thought about hippies in California wearing robes and accidentally roasting their babies, or sacrificing pregnant women, or pulling out all of their own teeth because they thought that they were possessed by the devil. The first time he took Margot a handful of the little brown mushrooms that were two a penny up in the top field around the edge of Coed-y-Grug, she asked him if he 'wanted to indulge', and he told her that he wasn't fucking mental, thank you very much. He'd only gone round there because he'd been hoping for a repeat of his first visit. He wasn't disappointed. Afterwards, lying on the kitchen floor, he said to her – because it sounded like something he ought to say – 'I don't think your husband would like this.'

She was already lighting a cigarette. He sensed that he was about to be dismissed. 'Sweet boy. Have you seen yourself? You look like some kind of sylvan Adonis.' She dragged her fingers through his curly hair. 'David would want to join in.'

He swallowed. The cat was sitting on the dining table, eyeing them intently. Even the animals in this house were bloody perverts. He told himself he wouldn't go back again, and when he got home, he spent so long in the bathroom that at tea, his father said, '*Duw*, your sister's already disgraced herself enough. We could do without a poofter in the family as well.'

He took Haf to the cinema in Rhyl the next evening and he told himself that Haf was a nice girl. Haf had been the best-looking girl in his year at school. Haf was girlfriend material. Haf wouldn't put it in her mouth because she said it was disgusting, but he was pretty sure that that could be worked on. He absolutely didn't need to go back to Tawel-fan, and in a few days' time, once he'd managed to digest the oddness of the experience, he'd be able to repackage what had happened with Margot, and it would become a pub anecdote: the posh bird in the big house, who was an absolute fiend, and needed a good seeing to. He still hadn't done anything wrong.

*

307

'I hear you've been keeping Margot company in my absence?'

Iestyn winced, but when he turned round, David Yates was beaming at him with the same ecclesiastical earnestness that his wife had affected that first morning in the woods.

'Dunno what you're talking about, mate.' He coughed.

It was October. A Friday night, The Feathers was heaving, and that Yvonne Elliman song he had a soft spot for was playing. He had been in a good mood – he'd been feeling lighter than he had in a long time. The last time he'd been up at Tawelfan, Margot had informed him that her husband's residency had finished, and although she'd told him not to be a stranger, he'd not gone back since, and he'd felt cleaner for it.

'Pint?' said the same husband, who was now a reality, jostling for space at the bar next to him. 'On me?'

'No, thank you.' He peered over David's head towards the door. 'I wasn't planning on sticking around.'

'Then why are you at the bar?' David made eye contact with Ray Morgan on the other side and held up two fingers. 'Two pints of Wrexham, please.'

Iestyn flinched. 'I'm here with the lads.'

'That's fine. I won't take long. I just had a little favour to ask you, that's all. Thought you might be interested in making a bit of spare cash.' He placed his elegant hand on Iestyn's shoulder, the two big, turquoise rings clicking against each other as he did so. Iestyn shrank.

'Don't worry, darling, nothing untoward. It's your harvesting skills we're after. We're planning a little party with some friends next weekend – you're invited, of course. You sure I can't convince you to come and have a little chat outside?'

*

His first thought when he'd read Olwen's letter was that he couldn't believe he'd ever been quite so fucking stupid. 'I've never forgotten that evening at the Glan Llyn when you told us about the officer who tried to recruit you as a snitch.' Of course, he had no idea which evening she was talking about. He must have been stewed. He couldn't even remember ever having met this girl, let alone talking to her – let alone talking to her about *that*. He pushed his plate across the table. The smell of it was suddenly nauseating. 'Tried,' he said aloud to himself; *the officer who tried to recruit you as a snitch*. The 'tried' gave him hope. At the very least, his drunken self must have had the nous to have lied about what had really happened with Clive. With Eifion and Angharad. He hated even thinking their names, hated hearing them in his head. Now his hands were really trembling; now he could have bloody killed Haf for hiding that six-pack. Interfering old bitch. He pushed himself back from the table so hard that the cutlery clattered to the floor, trailing greasy tomato sauce in its wake. Before he walked out, he grabbed the letter, crumpling it in his balled fist.

> *I'd love to have the opportunity to talk to you about your experience in some more detail. I'm coming home at the beginning of the summer, in fact, I'm moving back to Llanelgan.*

So Margot Yates's daughter had bought Tŷ Gwydr. She must have been doing all right, then. He thought of Geth. Bloody hell, that would sting, having his ex move in up there. He didn't bother to put his boots back on to go out. He knew there was a bottle of Famous Grouse in the footwell of the Land Rover, and he crossed the yard in his socks. He just wanted a little nip to get a hold of himself, to try and work out what he was going to do about this.

'I've already reached out to a number of people involved in the political struggle as part of my research.'

So she was asking questions. He wondered if she would mention his name to try and ingratiate herself with these 'people involved in the political struggle'. What a bloody mess, he thought to himself, yanking open the car door, ferreting around by the pedals. He was tempted to unscrew the cap right there and then, but he had some dignity, he wasn't some old drunk. By the time he got back into the kitchen he was so worked up, he almost hurled the bottle at the wall when he saw the dog.

'SWTAN!' he roared. She must have got in when he'd gone out, and was up on her hind legs, sprawled across the table, snout buried in his breakfast. She fled immediately, and was out the front door before he could even smack her one. He stared at the table, at the unctuous remains of the kidneys, at the wooden top smeared with oily beans and Swtan's drool, and he thought of Clive. He thought about all the unforgivable things he'd done.

Shame. You don't ever lose the smell of it. Once it enters your blood it stays there, like an infection. The worst thing was the dreams. It was Sali, his youngest, who'd told him about *Ceffyl Pren*. She'd learnt about it in school. He'd never heard of it before that. City types seem to think that people in the countryside live in some state of protracted, picturesque paganism, dancing around maypoles and wandering through meadows, wistfully distinguishing different blossom varieties, but Iestyn had had none of that, growing up in the second half of the twentieth century. He knew more about television presenters and pop stars than he did about birds and wildflowers. It was the cross-dressing that Sali had fixated on. 'Men in dresses!' she'd said, wide-eyed.

He didn't think much of it at the time, but a few nights later, it emerged from his subconscious in his sleep. He dreamt that he was fixing one of the fences down the bottom field. It was evening in the dream, a funny time to be working. He was alone, and both the field and the sky above it felt unnaturally vast. There was something nuclear about the silvery blueness of the landscape, something surreal and perverse. A metallic hum came up off the barbed wire, and the trees were very still. He felt a chill raise the hair on his arms and although he didn't know why exactly, he knew that he ought to move, that something unpleasant was about to happen. Just at the point where his land ended, he made out a figure, moving slowly in his direction. It was freakishly tall and thin, and it moved at such a steady, slow pace, it was more like it was floating than walking. It came closer and closer, and he could see now that, despite its obvious maleness, it was wearing a dress. A long red skirt, a plaid apron, a lace shawl and a tall top hat, the white garland of a bonnet frothing beneath its brim. It was the traditional costume that little girls wore on St David's Day, but he knew now that the unholy thing approaching him was Eifion Wyn, and that Eifion knew what he had done.

He woke up tacky with sweat and gasping for air, as if a terrible weight had been pressing down into his chest. The dreams weren't always the same. Sometimes they were vague and symbolic, and often they were quite literal: a band of men would barge into the house, dressed as women with coal on their faces. They would drag him out on to the yard where a whole audience of people from town would be watching hungrily, waiting for the spectacle of his overdue humiliation.

Neither of them was ever charged, as far as he knew, but it wasn't about the consequences, in the end. It was about him. He felt it whenever he was in the pub and people started talking about the English. He felt it when he watched the rugby and he heard the crowd stirring up to sing *Mae hen wlad fy nhadau*. He felt it every time a holiday house was burnt down back in the day, and his mates would be rejoicing, and he would be too – outwardly – but inside he'd just feel sick, like he wanted to throw up. He felt it every time he watched a show on the telly where someone betrayed someone they loved. That was him, that was. He was a snake. A worm. A worthless piece of shit.

Later, of course, when he was much older, and it was all already decades too late, he realised that Clive hadn't even had anything on him – that he'd been had. He could remember, when they'd first got broadband, the hours he'd spent on the internet after Haf had gone to bed, his hands pale and eerie in the blue glow of the screen, moving slowly across the keyboard, picking out one letter at a time, with his index finger. 'Are magic mushrooms legal' and 'Police blackmail'. But it was different then. He couldn't exactly have googled his rights in 1980, could he? And he certainly wasn't going to ask anyone for help, and risk it all coming out. He'd just wanted it gone. As far as he was concerned, the most important thing of all was that no one would ever find out what he'd done. Sometimes, a long time after it had happened, he'd look at the girls, or at Danny or Geth, and he'd realise how young he'd been. Yeah, he'd been had. He'd been had because he was a stupid fucking prick.

'Research', she said. He didn't need anyone sniffing around the past. He felt himself gripped with a new sense of purpose and it was almost invigorating. He took a step towards the table to clear Swtan's mess, and something warm and slimy oozed beneath his foot. He swore as the remains of a kidney soaked through his sock and squelched between his toes. Then he could feel it, like heat beginning to percolate somewhere at the pit of his stomach. Anger. He was tired of being ashamed.

2017

THERE WAS A certain point on the A487 just north of Aberaeron where you could make out the entire outline of Wales on a clear day. Pembrokeshire sloping into the fuzz of blue horizon to the south, and to the north, the extended arm of Pen Llŷn, reaching out into the Irish Sea. The first time Geth had seen it, when he was a kid, he was astounded. It was like seeing a map made into reality – into rock and sky and water. Like magic. The trunk road from Dolgellau clung to the coast from Aberystwyth, skirting the hollow sweep of Cardigan Bay. It was August.

At eight o'clock in the morning, he'd walked out his front door and climbed into the cab of his truck. In the footwell of the passenger seat, he had five litres of tap water frozen in old tonic bottles – a trick from working in the woods in the summer – you froze them at night, and they'd melt over the course of the day. In the back he had the gear, the tent; he'd liked that touch – camping, like they used to when they were kids. He drove to the Texaco first to fill up his tank. Petrol was cheaper in the big Morrisons, but he didn't care, for once. He didn't care about any of it. He was elated. At half past, his phone started going. It was Danny. Dan had no idea – they hadn't told anyone about their plan. He turned the phone face down on the dashboard, and somewhere around Bala, he lost signal anyway.

Down by Brithdir he got stuck behind some gleaming Mercedes; brand new job, smelt of the car wash, crawled along at twenty and then dithered behind a tractor for a good mile. The tourists couldn't cope up here. They certainly couldn't overtake. He could think of worse places to crawl, though. Sinuous roads slicing through the forest, hemmed in tightly by the low dry-stone walls. Old, dark stone houses with barely any windows and the windowsills painted black. Purple slate, tinged with lurid green moss like spray paint. When they were kids, they used to tear along those old country roads like bullets ricocheting off steel. Didn't half make you hard. That morning, though, he was happy to creep along behind some tosser who didn't know how to drive, if he could smoke, if the light was right, if the breeze through the window carried in the fragrance of the trees. That morning, to be fair, he'd be happy doing twenty all the way.

She wanted to do a road trip in Ireland because she'd somehow managed to get to her mid-thirties without ever having been. 'I want everything to be new,' she'd said to him on the phone; she'd called him every night for a week, from the garden after James had gone to bed. For the sake of novelty, she'd even wanted to leave from Fishguard instead of Holyhead. Made fuck all sense, but he was happy to indulge. They were contagious, all her romantic ideas, and fair dos, this whole thing was pretty fucking romantic, considering. He realised, when he booked the ferry tickets that it would be the first time they would ever go away together, and although he'd tried to repress it, he'd felt a kind of adolescent thrill at the idea that he was going on holiday with Olwen – with his girlfriend. Girlfriend? Maybe 'partner' would be better. He was pushing forty, after all. But 'partner' sounded corporate, sexless, like they were a pair of accountants or something. He was embarrassed when he became conscious of the fact that he was even considering it, like some teenage girl, scrawling the name of her beloved on a textbook.

Something had happened to him, though, since they'd made the plan. Even Meg had noticed it. When they'd met for a pint the night before last she'd said to him, 'What are you up to, Gethin? You're hiding something.'

He'd grinned at her. Meg was going to be the hardest to convince, but she'd come round when she realised how happy they made each other.

'You're giddy,' she'd said. 'I don't trust it.'

It was the lightness that got him. Nothing had changed materially – he was still fucked with work, he still had no idea what he was going to do about anything, he was even gutted that they'd lose the house, although he kept that from her, of course; but when he thought about the future, for the first time, he felt all right. He felt relieved.

Just before Machynlleth, the hulking, square ridge of Cader reared up in the distance. He shook his head, thinking of the expedition he'd taken himself on when things were really bad, when he'd thought that she wasn't ever going to speak to him again. It had been about a week before the phone call, a Wednesday, pissing it down, but he'd not been bothered; he'd been well-equipped for the rain. The rain had come in handy anyway; it was important that he didn't see anyone. He hadn't even known if it was allowed, spending a night on top of the mountain; people were so interfering nowadays, so bothered about how you conducted yourself with regards to your own wellbeing and safety. As he drove past, he remembered the vivid green of the bracken. The soothing rush of the stream. For most of the ascent the cloud had been so thick he'd barely been able to see ten feet in front of him. He'd kept his head down and had ploughed on, the rain drumming steadily on his anorak and his waterproof trousers. He remembered the saffron brightness of the gorse against all of that grey and green.

Bald earth. And he'd been right about the rain – he hadn't run into a single other hiker.

When he'd reached the peak, a miracle had happened. The dense blanket of mist had unspooled, and after an hour or so, the sky had cleared up enough for him to see all of the gold green land sweep right down to the beach at Y Bermo and the sea. Clarity. He'd left a little after sunrise the following morning. He hadn't tried writing any poetry yet, and he put how mad he'd been feeling down to the circumstances.

At Machynlleth he picked up signal again: more texts, a missed call. Dan always freaked out when he didn't reply straight away. Over the past couple of months, his older brother had been handling him as if he was something fragile. Made him feel like some kind of nutter. Danny would be over the moon when he found out about all this. Dan had worried about him constantly since they'd lost their mother – he'd always wanted him to settle down. Just south of Aber he hit the coast road again, and after that came the point of mystical convergence, where the land and sea became pen strokes on a map, where he felt a weird swell of belonging and of *hiraeth*, seeing the contours of his homeland take such tangible shape. Rays of sunlight glazed the breakers. He shifted into third. Overtook the Merc in front of him. Picked up some speed. It was still early, but in Aberaeron he stopped for chips, because he hadn't eaten breakfast. He was starving, and he liked the little town, with its handsome terraced houses lining the harbour, and the streets painted in sunny pastels – lemon, pistachio, dusky pink. He sat on the quay for an hour or so in the mellow sun. Smoked a fag and drank strong tea out of a polysty-rene cup. Watched the gulls squabbling, perched on the masts and the prows of the boats. The air smelt of salt, and

317

he felt calm. He thought, briefly, about the first time he'd seen her again, sitting in the beer garden round the back of The Boars, in that dress that showed off her naked back. Looking edgy, uncomfortable. The angles of her face were different somehow – she was more angular generally – her golden skin drawn tighter over her cheekbones, the blades of her collarbone, her shoulders. Her nose wasn't dappled with freckles any more. Everything was smooth, consistent and glossy. He sat there, thinking about her, and he realised he was grinning. He could hardly believe any of it. He did feel bad on James; James really was all right – a decent bloke. Fair dos, though, it wouldn't take someone like James long to get himself back on his feet.

He knew this was going to be difficult. He knew he shouldn't be this happy.

Her train was due in at Fishguard just before half past twelve. She would have changed at Abertawe. Right mission to get there from London; she would have had to leave at the crack of dawn. He left the truck in the car park to go inside and meet her. He wondered if he should find a supermarket, buy a bunch of flowers, but then decided it was better not to overdo it. Ten minutes early by his watch. He was more than happy to wait. 'Giddy', Meg had said. He sat on one of the plastic blue chairs and he watched the platform.

2017

SHE THOUGHT THAT the underground would be empty that early in the morning, but when she changed for the Hammersmith and City at Liverpool Street, the station was heaving with people. It always surprised her – the sheer volume of men in mass-produced suits, and women in dresses and immaculately clean trainers (smarter shoes stowed in backpacks), moving together like hundreds of cells in one giant organ. She stood on the platform, watching them, and she thought that that would be a good last image to take with her, to reassure her that she was doing the right thing, that there was no shame in leaving, in opting out.

The train arrived and she managed to get a seat. She counted the stops until Paddington and then checked her phone, because you often got signal on this line. Nothing. It would be half seven in Brussels, where James would be waking up. They'd chosen that day because she knew James would be away, and she knew that if she'd had to leave him, asleep in bed, like in some hackneyed country-and-western song, that she might bottle out. It was a work trip; he hadn't wanted to leave. Finding out about the notes had unsettled him. 'He's stalking you,' he'd said – he still thought it was Geth. He'd even been talking about selling the house. She wondered, when he realised that she was gone, if he'd remember how insistent she'd been that he didn't cancel his trip.

At Farringdon, the train stalled. Her line of vision was dominated by a poster for a production of *La Bayadère* at

Sadler's Wells, and she almost took a picture on her phone to remind herself to look into it, before realising that she wouldn't be here anyway. She felt a twinge of something. Dismissed it. The doors of the train slid open again, and the man next to her tutted impatiently.

It was a bright morning and the concourse at Paddington was gleaming; all that glass and steel – sunlight the colour of success. She considered which of several generic coffee shops would be the best, and purchased a long black at the arbitrary victor. She made her way to the enormous departures board, and found the platform for the train bound for Swansea. The coffee was good; she hadn't been wrong. She concentrated on that: the coffee, the commuters, the announcements over the Tannoy; she wanted to empty her head entirely. She watched the next train disappear from the board as it departed, and her own move further up the list. She thought that she probably ought to head to the platform, but the thought didn't result in movement. It was funny, she felt completely removed from her body. It was like she didn't exist. Her phone lit up in her palm. It was James.

July 2017

Tape A, Geth Interview 4

*This time inside. Propped up on his elbows on the sunken floor
of the living room. It's evening. Music playing low in the
background.*
 —Did you know I saw you? When you came here after I'd
first moved in?
He's amused. —It wasn't when you first moved in. You moved in
the October before that.
 —All right then, when I first properly got here. Beginning of
the summer.
 —Well, I wasn't very discreet, like, was I?
 —So you didn't care if you got caught?
Silence.
 —If it hadn't been you it would have been creepy as fuck.
 —I missed it here, *he says suddenly. Swallows the end of the
sentence.*
She pauses —Why didn't you just call first? It would have been
easy to work out how to get hold of me, surely?
He looks at the camera.
 —What, to ask your permission?
 —That's not what I meant.
He narrows his eyes —Felt normal coming here. I've always come
here.
She says —As far as I'm concerned this place is always yours.
After a moment he stands up —All right, give it a rest with the
camera. I feel like you're stealing my soul. *Forces a smile* —
Go on, turn it off.

★

Outside again. Late afternoon. He walks in front of her, around the back of the house.

—And this, he sweeps his arm to the right —this bit, I'd clear, bring down those trees just there, to put up my shed. Need somewhere to keep all my gear, don't I?

—Oh, you do?

Grins. —Uh-huh.

—And when are you thinking of doing that?

—Well, when you get your act together and invite me to move in.

She says nothing, and slowly, in the silence, his facial expression shifts. He walks towards her. The viewfinder of the camera drops to the floor.

—I wish things could have been different, her voice says.

His is muffled against the crown of her hair; off-camera, he's holding her. In a second, she'll remember she's still recording and press STOP.

—I know, he says before she does —so do I.

Epilogue

Tŷ Gwydr, 2017

A handful of days after the shortest one of the year and the cold is solid and opalescent like the milky surface of a pearl. It marbles the moonlight, the haze around the stars, the beam of the torch, and every solid mist of breath he exhales as he makes his way down the track. A clean, blue kind of cold. It's coming up three o'clock and sunrise is still a long way off. 'Bible-black', as Dylan Thomas would have put it. Twice he slips, but only because he's nervous. The ground beneath his boots is solid, cracked, frigid. He wasn't surprised when he saw the sign at the top of the track, '*AR WERTH*'. He'd been expecting it.

Late one night when his head was going, he'd googled her, and in a newspaper interview where she'd talked about the film, she'd said: 'Once we'd realised it wasn't feasible for us to properly relocate to North Wales full time, we knew we had to sell. Having a second home there would just make us part of the problem.'

Part of the problem my arse, he thinks.

All at once the house is in sight – a block of ice – and sweeping beneath it, the black agate water of the lake. He feels dizzy, extra aware of the outline of his body, of his fingertips, of just how cold the air is. He pictures very vividly the grain of the parquet, the way the grey winter dawn seeps in through the glass – slower than the direct impact of the light in summer, when he was last here. He swallows. At that time of year, the woods has its particular smell – sweet, green, mineral. In December the aseptic cold sterilises the fragrance of the air. Winter makes a vacuum. The silence is absolute.

He's aware as he approaches the edge of the lake that his eyes are watering and he tells himself it's because of the cold.

On the jetty he unscrews the plastic cap of the jerry can. Strikes a match and shakes it out. He strikes another. He feels something cold and damp skim the bridge of his nose. The weather forecast predicted snow.

Note

The title of the first part of this book is taken from the Dylan Thomas poem, 'The force that through the green fuse drives the flower', 1934.

> *The force that through the green fuse drives the flower*
> *Drives my green age; that blasts the roots of trees*
> *Is my destroyer.*
> *And I am dumb to tell the crooked rose*
> *My youth is bent by the same wintry fever.*

Acknowledgements

Huge thanks to my agent, Charlotte Seymour, for all of her hard work and faith from the very beginning. Thanks to everyone at Johnson & Alcock, particularly Hélène Butler, Saliann St. Clair and Anna Dawson, and to those at Andrew Nurnberg Associates who have made this possible. Thank you to everyone at Headline; at Tinder Press, I am especially grateful to my brilliant editor, Ellie Freedman, for her wisdom and patience, and to Oliver Martin and Ana Carter, who have worked so hard to get this book into people's hands. Thanks to Kate Truman and Yvonne Holland for proof and copy edits. Thank you to Heike Schüssler for the wonderful cover, and to Caroline Young for art direction. Thanks also due to Amy Perkins for early edits.

My mother, Fiona Reece, has always been my first reader and has been Gethin's biggest fan from the very start, *so diolch iddi hi*. This time around however, equal thanks are due to my father, Richard Reece, to whom, along with the late Dei Hughes, this book is dedicated. His knowledge of forestry, the woods, trees and pick-up trucks especially was invaluable. Some of Gethin's thoughts about his job are lifted almost directly from conversations I had with him, and from the wisdom he imparted. Both of my parents were abundant sources of information, especially regarding life in North Wales in the 1970s and '80s. More generally, I owe my love of reading and writing to them. Endless love and thanks.

Diolch yn fawr i Brennig Davies *a* Gwenllian Ellis, who so kindly read this novel in manuscript form, checked the Cymraeg for me and made sure that everything felt sufficiently authentic. Although *gogledd Cymru* is my home, Welsh is not my mother tongue, and this book could not have been published without their care, feedback and help. Thanks also to Anthony Shapland for invaluable conversations about the novel, *'stafell werdd am byth!* Thank you to all of the 2023 cohort of the Hay Festival Writers at Work programme, and especially to Tiffany Murray, Carys Bradley-Roberts, Arddun Rhiannon and Adrian Lambert. *Ac wrth gwrs, diolch yn fawr i* Gordon Hughes, *fy athro Cymraeg*, who brought me back to the Welsh language after several years of estrangement.

Jessica Saxby and Jose Montiel McCann have been reading versions of this novel for four years now. They're not only two of my best friends, they're also wonderful, insightful readers. I love you both so much, thank you.

Thanks to Melissa Davies, Virginia Brewer, Dave Lewis, and to my sister Eleanor Sadeghian-Tehrani for putting up with many 'research conversations' regarding our shared adolescence in Ruthin in the 2000s. Thanks as well to Sasha and Brendan Lines for doing the same regarding theirs in the 1990s. The staff at Ysgol Stryd-y-Rhos are also due a big thanks, as I know my mother used the staff room as a sounding board throughout the writing of this book. Thanks especially to Eira Ellis, and to Dee Baker. Thank you to Eileen Jones and to Bethan Hughes.

Grazie mille to everyone at Civitella Ranieri; the time that I spent there in the summer of 2022 was instrumental in getting this novel written; thanks also to Desperate Literature and the de Groot foundation for facilitating that stay. *Danke* to Daniel und Felix Giese, and to Julia Nau for their

327

wonderful hospitality in Outeiro that same summer, and *merci* to Clara Bermann for use of her studio in Marseille.

Thank you to Chrissy Ryan, Lucy Dale-Harris, Chandler Bray, Thom Nyhuus, Camilla Chetty and Amy Glover: my wonderful bookshop family. Your support of this novel has been incredible, and I've loved working with all of you. It's been a total joy.

Thanks to Jessica Andrews and Kate Loftus-O'Brien for early feedback. Thanks again to Jess, and to Keiran Goddard, Tom Benn, James Clarke and Gwenllian Ellis for taking the time to read advanced copies of this novel and for giving such kind, perceptive and gorgeous quotes.

I'm almost certain I've forgotten somebody, so huge thanks to all of my friends and family in Paris, London, Rhuthun and Clawddnewydd. Special thanks to my beloved Chris Jowitt; this novel began when I was locked down with you, Jan and Jose at Riquet in the spring of 2020. I still miss living with you every day.

A note on research: several texts published by the Welsh Socialist Republican Movement (*Mudiad Sosialaidd Gwerini- aethol Cymru*) in the early 1980s were key when writing this novel, as were Socialism for the Welsh People by Robert Griffiths and Gareth Miles (1979), and several old issues of *Y Faner Goch*. Above all, I owe a huge debt to *Political Policing in Wales* by Dr John Davies, Lord Gifford QC, and Tony Richards (1984), a document which profoundly informed the novel. Richard King's excellent oral history, *Brittle with Relics*, published by Faber & Faber in 2022 was also a huge help, and I'd like to thank Mike Jenkins, who was kind enough to answer some questions I had when I was undertaking initial research.

Most of all, thank you to Jan Gilles, who is everything and more. *Caru ti.*

First published in Great Britain in 2024 by Tinder Press
An imprint of HEADLINE PUBLISHING GROUP

1

Cataloguing in Publication Data is available from the British Library

Hardback ISBN 978 1 4722 7224 9
Trade paperback ISBN 978 1 4722 7225 6

Typeset by EM&EN
Printed and bound in Great Britain by Clays Ltd, Elcograf S.p.A.

Headline's policy is to use papers that are natural, renewable and recyclable
products and made from wood grown in well-managed forests and other
controlled sources. The logging and manufacturing processes are expected
to conform to the environmental regulations of the country of origin.

HEADLINE PUBLISHING GROUP
An Hachette UK Company
Carmelite House
50 Victoria Embankment
London EC4Y 0DZ

www.tinderpress.co.uk
www.headline.co.uk
www.hachette.co.uk

Francesca Reece

GLASS HOUSES

TINDER
PRESS

Also by Francesca Reece

VOYEUR

GLASS HOUSES